P9-BBM-761

**FROM THE HOUSE OF ROMANCE COLLECTION
OF GREAT LOVE STORIES**

THREE FULL LENGTH NOVELS IN EACH VOLUME

3 Great Romances

THE HOUSE OF ROMANCE

HOUSE OF ROMANCE — TRIO 8
ISBN 0-88767-009-1
Published March 1977

The stories in this volume were originally published as
follows:

WHISPERS OF FEAR
Copyright © Brenda Castle 1972
First Published in U.K. by Robert Hale & Co. 1972

LOVE HAS A DOUBLE
Copyright © Robert Hale & Co. 1973
First Published in U.K. by Robert Hale & Co. 1973

ANGEL IN ABBEY ROAD
Copyright © June Mortimer 1974
First Published in U.K. by Robert Hale & Co. 1974

HOUSE OF ROMANCE is published by 'Round the
World Books Inc., Toronto, Canada

Exclusive Distributor — U.S.A. — Promarketing Inc.,
New York, N.Y.

Whispers of Fear

Love Has a Double

Angel in Abbey Road

Whispers of Fear

⁓

BRENDA CASTLE

Jenefer Henekin's murderer was still free and because Dina said she knew who it was the danger was there. Or was she being too fanciful once more? The murderer could be miles away and the Tregarricks had no more secrets than any other family.

Oh why was she pretending to herself? It was not concern over Dina that was troubling her; it was Adam.

CHAPTER ONE

The flowers were fading already. It had been hours since Bethany had bought them. Hours since she had caught the bus that had borne her from Bodmin across the windswept moors and deposited her, after a seemingly unending journey, at the roadside above St Mollith.

It could hardly be called a village—more a cluster of rough-hewn granite cottages set in a cleft in the hills. She walked down the narrow lane from the road just as the purple cloak of dusk was descending from the high ground all around. In one hand she clutched the flowers and in the other a small suitcase.

Before she reached the village darkness was already enfolding her. She had known before setting off that she was wrong to come back so soon. She had intended never to come back for there was no need. Mrs Arkill would have sent on her other suitcase and the train fare together with the night's board would make great inroads into her already dwindling funds.

Lights were already appearing in the cottage windows. There was no one about but that did not surprise her; she had learned during her last stay that the country folk retired early.

A solitary light flickered through the naked trees on

the hill slope. Bethany couldn't recall there being a cottage so far up but she supposed it was possible. The light went out and the hill was dark once more. The silence, to Bethany whose ears had become deaf to the big city roar, could almost be heard.

She shivered and pulled her coat tighter around her throat. It was such a desolate spot with nothing but silent and bare moors for miles around; a strange place for the city-loving Johnny to lie forever. As she came down the gorse-edged lane her heart felt as though it was filled with lead; so remote, so desolate—it might have been world's end.

She passed along the narrow main street and crossed the stream by the little hump-backed bridge. The church stood at the far end of the village. It was almost completely dark by the time she left her case at the lych-gate and went into the churchyard. She knew she should wait until morning but if she did the flowers would be dead. And the same urgency that had brought her back from London compelled her to the churchyard now.

She picked her way along the weed-strewn paths until she came to the newest grave of all. As the last remnant of day faded from the sky she pushed aside the withered wreath to lay her flowers on top of the grave. She stood there with hands clasped in front of her, gazing down at the freshly dug earth. She had travelled the best part of the day to make this futile gesture.

The crescent moon came out from behind a black cloud lending an odd kind of splendour to the old and crumbling tombstones. Her gaze flickered to the grave next to Johnny's. She moved along, as curious about Johnny's neighbour as she would have been if they'd bought a new house or a larger flat.

The inscription was faint in the poor light but as she moved closer she saw the name boldly engraved— JENEFER HENEKIN born in 1950 died 1968. At least Johnny had enjoyed almost thirty years on earth. Not long but more than a girl named Jenefer Henekin who'd had but eighteen. She was comforted by the thought he would not be alone out here; not entirely.

As she turned to leave a sharp breeze suddenly whipped at her hair and the silence was broken by a shrill cry that made her blood freeze. When she heard the beating of wings she relaxed, almost laughing out loud. The cry came again and this time it was nothing like the sound of a human in torment—just a bird calling to its mate.

All at once she was aware of the isolation; the complete loneliness of a place filled with the dead—or perhaps something still alive. The Cornish were a superstitious race and firmly believed in the spirits that were supposed to roam the moors. Tonight was an ideal night for them to do their evil. Suddenly she knew she was not alone; the looming tombstones were crouching in on her and the spirits voiced their evil song.

She started to run back to where she had left the suitcase. A great granite wheel cross stood just inside the churchyard. It was pitted and worn from almost two thousand years of exposure to the sou'westerly wind, but it was still standing and would be for another two thousand years—and more.

She fled back across the bridge towards the welcoming lights of the inn. As soon as she had crossed the stream she stopped running, knowing that the noise which had disturbed her was nothing more than the strengthening of the wind. She would have to be careful not to become as fanciful as the Cornish themselves who would regard the visiting of a graveyard at night a very silly thing to do.

Since the crash that had crushed the life out of her husband Bethany had tried to feel grief for the death of the man she had loved and she had awaited the aching void that never came. All she was able to feel was sorrow at the brutal and useless end of a life hardly begun, not for the loss of a lover. And underneath it all the dread of the loneliness which would start up in greater intensity beyond the shock that had anaesthetized her feelings for the past few weeks. How could she bear to be cast loose again in an uncaring world?

The inn was warm; the fears that beset her in the deserted churchyard dissolved at the sight of the friendly faces grouped around the bar. Mr and Mrs Arkill gazed at her windswept form as she came through the low doorway.

'You came back to see us, did 'ee?' the landlord said with a broad smile.

'Yes,' she replied, dropping her suitcase on the uneven boards. 'I wanted to put some flowers on the grave.'

It sounded inadequate but it was true and she could

hardly say, 'I feel guilty because the love I felt for my husband was not as deep as it should have been.' But perhaps guilt was too strong a word; regret would be more suitable. Now she would never know if she had really loved Johnny or not.

'Well come in and get warm,' Mr Arkill urged and his wife said, 'And we thought you'd be sending for your things. Come into the parlour girl. You look frozen.'

Bethany gratefully followed her into the parlour and sat down on an old and worn settee in front of the peat fire that filled the room with its own unmistakable tang. A simple room, a comfortable room with only the bare essentials in furnishings but everything spotlessly clean and somehow reassuring.

It seemed a long time since she had eaten in the train earlier in the day and she relished every mouthful of the meal the landlord's wife put in front of her.

'I hope the room is still vacant,' Bethany asked after she had finished, feeling rested and restored.

'We don't get many visitors 'ere, 'specially at this time of the year. Come all the way from London today did 'ee?'

'Yes, I didn't want to spend the night in Bodmin.' She didn't add that she could hardly afford to do so.

Mrs Arkill looked shocked. 'Came down from the road tonight did 'ee?'

'As you know the bus doesn't actually come into the village. It must be at least a mile walk.'

'It's a wonder you weren't pisky laden! You might have been wandering round 'til mornin'.'

Bethany remembered the solitary light she had seen shining through the trees and how cold she had felt, and then she laughed. 'The piskies don't worry me Mrs Arkill. It's a straight road so I doubt if they could have misled me.'

'Don't laugh at the little folk Mrs Ryder. They don't like it. An' there's some things there's no explanation for. I remember one evenin' Granny McArdle saw ravens gathering on the roof of the Henekin cottage and sure 'nough next day they found poor Jenefer up in the woods.'

Bethany did not laugh. 'Yes, I saw the grave in the churchyard. She was only eighteen.'

'Aye an' as pretty as they come. She was treated pretty badly by some all 'cos she was so pretty and 'cos she weren't a good girl. But when she were buried there weren't one of us who weren't sorry for not being kind to 'er. It takes a death to do that, more's the pity.'

Bethany folded her hands around the thick mug containing the good strong tea and said softly, 'Yes, I know what you mean.'

Mr Arkill was alone in the stone-flagged kitchen when Bethany went in the next morning.

'You be an early bird,' he said with a smile.

'I wasn't sure of the time of the bus and I hate to rush.'

'But you only arrived yesterday evenin'.'

Bethany looked around the kitchen with its open fire and iron stove from which Mrs Arkill managed to produce such mouthwatering fare. 'It was an impulse to be quite truthful, and an extravagant one.'

'Martha's gone along to the farm to get fresh eggs; she'll be back soon. Sit 'ee down and 'ave some toast while 'ee waits. The tea's good and strong 'less 'ee be wanting coffee.'

Bethany smiled gratefully. 'Tea will do nicely.'

She poured the dark brown brew into a mug and helped herself to a thick slice of toast, spreading the rich Cornish butter thickly on top of it.

'Seems a long way for 'ee to come just for one night,' Mr Arkill mused.

'I suppose it is, but once I get fixed up with a job it will be a long time before I can come again.'

'Looking' for a job eh?'

'I'm afraid so,' she replied wryly. 'A job and somewhere to live. That's why I want to get back as soon as I can. I can't afford to be unemployed for long.'

'But you an' 'im had a house, didn't 'ee?'

Bethany helped herself to another slice of toast, this time adding a layer of chunky marmalade. 'More accurately it was three rooms in a converted house. It wasn't much but better than a bed-sitter, which is what I shall be looking for now.'

Her heart felt leaden again at the thought of the loneliness of such an existence; Johnny had shielded her against that and now her shield was gone. 'There should be no difficulty in getting a job; I worked in a shop before I was married. I might even get my old job back. And the landlady of the flat was very kind;

she offered to keep my things there until I find some-where else.'

'Looks as if it weren't a very 'appy week,' the landlord said, eyeing her shrewdly. She shook her head and sipped the tea. 'Not left any money 'as 'ee?'

She shook her head again and after a moment's silence looked up and said, 'There was a small insurance policy but then I discovered Johnny had a bank overdraft that I'd known nothing about. When that's paid there is little left.'

Mr Arkill took a deep breath. ''Tis a proper mess and no mistake.'

Bethany rushed to defend Johnny. 'He could hardly have known he was going to die so soon.'

''Tis a great pity,' the landlord agreed gravely, 'but you still be left in a spot, don't 'ee?'

She smiled gratefully at the fatherly concern he was showing. In the time she had spent at the inn after the accident and during the inquest Mr and Mrs Arkill had been kindness itself, far exceeding that necessary for the small amount of board she was paying. Had her own parents been alive she could not have expected more solicitous treatment.

'Not while I can earn my own living,' she replied brightly.

The landlord refilled his own mug and seemed to be deep in thought. 'I know where there's a job to be 'ad,' he said after a moment, 'and one that'll provide accommodation too...' Bethany looked at him with interest. 'The Tregarricks 'ave been lookin' for someone to look after the little girl. She's been ill y'see. They've 'ad a couple o'ladies but they've not stopped longer than a day or two. We're too isolated they say.'

Bethany smiled. 'I'm neither a nurse nor a teacher Mr Arkill. I shouldn't think I'd be a very likely candidate.'

'They'd a nurse when the little girl was ill. She's better now, or so's I've heard. Just needs someone to keep 'er out o'mischief 'til she goes to school in the spring.'

'I still don't think I would be suitable,' Bethany said doubtfully, wondering if a position in a household could be the answer to her problem. 'Do the Tregarricks live in the village?'

'At Tregarrick Manor. It's up-along the trees.'

Bethany could not help but smile to herself. Here was the simple, earthly answer to the light in the trees. The piskies abroad last night were very human ones.

'I saw a light last night,' she said, 'but I don't remember seeing a house up there.'

'Hidden by the trees, but if you look closely you'd see the chimneys above 'em. The Tregarricks like their privacy. Leastways lately they do.'

The outside door flew open and Mrs Arkill hurried in carrying her basket. 'Good mornin' Mrs Ryder,' she said in some surprise. 'You could almost be a country girl being up at this hour.'

She shrugged off her coat and scarf and wasted no time in going over to the iron stove. Within a couple of minutes the bacon began to crackle in the pan and the kitchen was filled with a mouth watering aroma. The landlord's wife cut thick slices of bread which Bethany popped on to the end of a toasting fork and thrust in front of the fire.

'What's this I 'eard about the Tregarricks as I come in?' Mrs Arkill asked at last.

To Bethany's surprise Mr Arkill looked sheepish and she replied, 'Your husband was telling me there might be a job going at Tregarrick Manor.'

Mrs Arkill deftly flipped the eggs on to a plate and piled up the bacon next to it. She shot him a venomous look, 'You take no notice of 'im. That's no place for a decent girl.'

'Now, now Martha,' her husband admonished, 'don't gossip.'

'It ain't gossip Jess and you know it, don't 'ee?'

Bethany looked at them, interest quickening. Then her attention was taken by the plate put before her. 'You'll put pounds on me Mrs Arkill,' she said with a laugh.

'Eat it up. I've seen you fade to a shadow since you came 'ere. Not that there's any wonder with what you've been through.'

Mr Arkill sat himself down by the fire to toast more bread while Bethany finished her breakfast. Eventually she pushed her plate away and drew a sigh of deep satisfaction. Mutely she allowed her cup to be refilled.

'Stay on a day or two an' I'll soon have you fattened up.'

Bethany laughed. 'I only wish I could, but I'm afraid

the matter of finding a job has become rather pressing.'

'The Tregarricks offer both a job and an 'ome,' Mr Arkill put in mildly.

'Be quiet Jess!' his wife snapped.

'Is there any reason why I shouldn't apply?'

Mrs Arkill frowned. 'Plenty reason. You stay away my girl.'

'But why? At least you could tell me.'

'Aye,' Mr Arkill said with a smile, 'she'll tell you all right.'

His wife pointedly turned her back on him. 'Old man Tregarrick was a rare one for the ladies. There's many a soul in these parts with a drop of Tregarrick blood in 'is veins. Rosanna Penarven's been housekeeper neer on thirty years and twasn't for the love of the place. Twas said Esme Tregarrick would have had 'er out when the old man died but young Adam promised his father before 'ee died he wouldn't allow it. *Missus* Penarven indeed!'

'Martha, 'tis all gossip.'

'I've lived 'ereabouts all my life. I recall the old man in 'is day. 'Tis no gossip and there wasn't a maid safe in this village before young Adam went away. Makes no difference that he came back with a wife; just 'as to be quieter about it now. An' then there's young Theo, forever runnin' off to London and heaven only knows what 'ee's up to.'

'Sounds formidable,' Bethany said wryly, 'but I hardly think my virtue is in danger. I'm sure I could cope.'

'Don't scoff,' Mrs Arkill warned. 'Young Jenefer

laughed at everyone, but now she lies in the churchyard. Found 'er in the woods below Tregarrick Manor they did. Having a child too. Adam Tregarrick's if you ask me.'

'There was nothin' to connect the Tregarricks with poor Jenefer,' Mr Arkill muttered. 'B'sides your own niece works up there.'

'Sally is well able to look after 'erself and she needs to be.'

'So am I Mrs Arkill,' Bethany said, knowing the landlord's wife had kindled an interest that would ensure she went to see Tregarrick Manor and its inhabitants for herself. Suddenly she said, 'If this little girl is well now why does she need someone to look after her? Hasn't she got a mother and father?'

'She's got them all right,' Mr Arkill replied, 'but Mr Adam 'as no time for anyone these days and Missus Grace is sick, so they say.'

Mrs Arkill sniffed loudly as she piled up the plates in the sink. 'Sick? We all knows what it is that ails 'er. It's not as if she's a local girl. Met 'er in London 'ee did. A widow an' all. Nevver came near 'til the old man went an' died. Since then it's all changed. They do say the place has been ill-wished, what with the old man dyin' so sudden, then Mr Theo goin' off. Then we've 'ad Miss Dina so ill, not to mention poor Jenefer.

'She 'ad no mum so's I expect that accounts for 'er behaviour.' But she were the apple of 'er dad's eye.

Couldn't stand the place after she'd gone. Locked the cottage and went to 'is sister's in Plymouth. Nevver come back since.

'I said to my sister I did "Don't you be sending your Sal up there." But Sally can look after 'erself I reckon. Things ain't what they were at Tregarrick Manor these days.' She sighed. 'An' I recall what a bonny boy Mr Theo was then.'

'You've had enough 'eartache; best stay away,' Mrs Arkill added grimly.

Bethany got to her feet, the chair scraping on the stone flags. 'All the same I think I will have a wander up there. If the job is as Mr Arkill says it sounds ideal for me. By the time the child is ready for school I will have had a chance to arrange something permanent. I haven't had time to make many plans so far.'

Mrs Arkill said nothing but scrubbed at the plates furiously. 'It will probably come to nothing and if it does I shall have lost nothing, just delayed my departure a few hours.'

Mr Arkill smiled encouragement. 'Best give them a call on the phone first. They don't take kindly to strangers wandering near the house. Best let 'em know.'

Mrs Arkill turned from the sink. 'An' don't say's you weren't warned.'

CHAPTER TWO

The day was crisp and bright when she left the inn for the walk to Tregarrick Manor. The sun shone without warmth from a pale blue sky and there was a whisper of a breeze in the air.

Her appointment with Mrs Tregarrick was not until eleven o'clock and there was plenty of time for a leisurely stroll. She passed the cottages, smiling at women she had come to know during her brief stay in the village. As she neared the stream she noticed one cottage was empty, its windows thick with grime, and she wondered if this was the Henekin cottage; the one where the ravens had gathered the night before Jenefer had been found dead.

On the old stone bridge she paused to gaze down into the stream that ran down to the sea. Through the transparent water she could see the cobbles and pebbles at the bottom and could imagine the sheer bliss of running barefoot in its icy depths on a hot summer day.

She went straight past the church, this time not wishing to go in and followed the narrow lane that would take her to the manor. As she peered above the trees sure enough she could just see four tall chimneys rising from their midst.

It had been an odd telephone call Bethany decided. The woman who had answered seemed incredulous and then surprised as Bethany had explained why she required an interview.

'You'll have to speak to Mrs Tregarrick,' the woman said finally and Bethany was forced to explain it all again to the gentle-voiced woman who came to the telephone.

'And how did you hear about the position?' she asked.

'From Mrs Arkill at the inn. I've been staying with her.'

'Mrs Ryder you say? Isn't that the name of the unfortunate man who was killed near here recently.'

'He was my husband.'

'Well a widow would be very suitable for the position we have here,' Mrs Tregarrick had said, sounding almost pleased. 'I shall be able to see you at eleven o'clock.'

Before Bethany could say more the receiver had been replaced. Now she paused on the path, which was just wide enough to carry a car, as it entered the sprinkling of trees. It wasn't a very attractive wood; trees found it difficult to survive the constant battering of the gales and storms. These trees had managed somehow to survive but they were permanently bowed in the path of the sou'westerly wind and their trunks bore no lichen or moss to show they even supported life. The ground beneath her feet was bare and rocky, strewn with dry twigs that had snapped from the dead branches and now crunched as she walked.

The path followed closely to the course of the stream; somewhere up in the moors would be its source. The climb was a gradual one and no effort for her legs although she was beginning to realize the house was further away from the village than it had appeared to be. As the ground sloped upwards the trees grew closer together, some of them linking their branches across the path making an arbour that must be picturesque in spring and summer when they were clothed in fresh green foliage. But now they were but skeletons stretching their bones across the stony path.

A flock of birds darkened the sky, shrieking more wildly than a jet aeroplane and filling the air with the sound of their wings. Just as quickly they were gone to be followed by a solitary white gull with the reminder that the sea was never far away. Its cry was as she had heard the night before in the churchyard and she marvelled at its ability to frighten her even if it had been for only a moment. No wonder it was in the night the Cornish believed evil spirits were abroad. Nothing is fearsome when the sun is shining.

She paused and turning she realized how far she had come. The cottages below had shrunk and the whole place took on the appearance of a model village with the sun reflecting on the water of the stream. She couldn't quite see the coast but she knew the pounding Atlantic was there just beyond the horizon.

There could be no more lonely spot than this, she thought, and immediately knew there was; there in the heart of the greatest city in the world.

Only then did it occur to her that the Tregarricks might have already arranged for someone to come from one of the agencies—someone with qualifications and references. She found herself fervently hoping they had not. The idea of living and working with a family had not occurred to her before Mr Arkill had mentioned it. Now she was enthusiastic.

Bethany hesitated where the path branched sharply to the left, realizing she was nearing her destination and unaccountably excited. She told herself it was her three years with Johnny visiting countless old houses that caused her eager anticipation of what was around the corner, but she knew on this occasion it was something more.

The job had to be hers, she knew that now. The availability of such a position at this time when she needed both work and shelter was too providential for it to come to nothing. The mere fact she was a widow gave her a substantiality in Mrs Tregarrick's eyes—that was plain even on the telephone—despite her twenty-six years. A few months here would give her time to recover from the desperate shock of Johnny leaving her so utterly alone; by the spring when the child was recovered enough to go to school Bethany was sure she would feel more like returning to the world with which she was familiar.

The path ended and the appearance of the house was so sudden it almost came as a physical blow. About the time the house had been built a clearing in the trees had been made but after completion no attempt had been made to plant a garden. The house just stood in the clearing like something out of a fairy tale. And in the ensuing years the woods had gradually encroached upon the house again, giving the clearing an untidy edge.

Bethany was not sure what she had expected but somehow it was not this. The appearance of the house was forbidding enough but she put that down to its granite walls and stone-mullioned windows which could hide countless watching eyes. The main door was of stout oak studded with brass and set in a turreted porch.

No creeper grew along the walls nor did any moss cling to the ancient granite slabs; no life could be supported in such a desolate spot.

It was not the look of the house that repelled Bethany; she recognized it was similar to many in the district. It was the atmosphere surrounding it; an air of neglect. It was as if no one cared any more that the brass studs in the door needed polishing or the windows, if not grimy, needed an extra wash. A family lived in the house but it looked for all the world as if it were deserted.

Nearby some dogs began to bark and it took a second or two for her to realize the noise was coming nearer. Two large black hounds came bounding from the cover of the trees, barking and snarling at her, their vicious fangs bared. Saliva dripped from their strong jaws revealing razor sharp teeth—teeth that could fasten around and tear a human limb.

She backed away but one of the hounds came behind her whilst the other stood guard in front. They had obviously been well trained. 'Go away,' she said in a shaky voice and was rewarded by a further bout of barking which ended in snarls.

The hounds were drooling and fearfully Bethany found herself wondering if they had been fed lately. It was with profound relief a few moments later she heard the crackle of twigs heralding the arrival of a pair of human feet.

Her eyes travelled from the hounds, at which they had been staring since the animals had appeared, up a pair of trousered legs, a tweed jacket covering a thick fisherman's sweater, to a tanned face trying hard to contain obvious impatience.

'Here Hero! Minerva!'

The hounds abruptly stopped their baying and loped towards the man who had called them. Bethany studied him now she reckoned the danger of being torn to pieces had receded. He was a big man and his slate grey eyes studied her as curiously as she was studying him. He was strong, she decided, and not just a strength derived from his build; there was a strength of will and character there too.

'I was afraid I was to be their dinner,' she said with a shaky smile.

He frowned, making no attempt to smile back. 'I'm sorry if you were frightened, but they're not used to strangers around here. This land is private and the house is not open to the public.' He turned slightly. 'The path will lead you back down to the village.'

He made to move off and Bethany felt a stirring of anger at such an easy dismissal. 'I haven't come sight-seeing,' she said standing her ground, 'but I do have an appointment with Mrs Tregarrick.'

His eyes narrowed. 'Mrs Tregarrick?' He was dis-believing.

'Yes,' she went on firmly, 'I spoke to her this morning on the telephone. It's about a position available at the manor.' Her chin came up proudly. 'But I hardly think she would want me to discuss it with you.'

A flicker of a smile played around his lips. 'So that is why you've come. Well I can tell you before you go in you are not remotely like the person my mother is expecting; it would save your time and hers if you went back to the village.'

His mother! So this must be Adam or Theo. Surely not Theo who had been such a 'bonny boy'. This must be Adam then; the man Mrs Arkill believed was the father of Jenefer Henekin's unborn child. Now she had seen him her curiosity was intensified even further and her embarrassment at having mistaken the father of the child she was hoping to care for as a hired hand fed her resentment.

'I would rather Mrs Tregarrick tells me herself.'

He shrugged slightly and came towards her, not tak-ing his eyes from her until he had passed. Although his voice contained only a vestige of the soft Cornish burr Bethany suddenly realized that with his swarthy com-plexion, dark curly hair and brandishing a cutlass he might have been one of the pirates who infested this part of the country two hundred years before. Perhaps in the dusty recesses of time the Tregarricks had been even less respectable than they were now. The possibility thrilled her.

He reached the house without looking back and the hounds that now padded obediently at his heels looked so harmless that Bethany wondered if she had imagined their ferocity. Hurriedly she followed him as he waited by the open door for her to join him. Without uttering a further word she preceded him through the turreted porch and into a very large hall.

The hounds threw themselves in front of the fire blazing in a stone fireplace high enough for Bethany to stand in. In the centre of the hall stood a polished oak refectory table, pitted and worn from countless years of service, yet still imposing. Around it stood a dozen straight-backed chairs of ornately worked oak.

The man indicated a wooden settle at the side of the fireplace. 'If you'd like to sit down for a few minutes I shall tell Mrs Tregarrick you're here.'

The walls around the hall were punctuated by several doors and it was through one of these the man went, leaving her alone in a hall that had changed very little since the house had been built.

The hounds made no move to follow their master and Bethany eyed them uneasily but it seemed she had been approved and they were satisfied.

She gazed around her with great interest knowing Johnny would have loved it here. He never gave up hoping one day, in a house such as this, he would discover a painting that would prove to be a lost masterpiece. Poor Johnny, she thought, now he would never find it.

At one end of the hall a wooden staircase led to a balcony running around three sides of the hall ending in a minstrels gallery. Everywhere was the same atmosphere—not quite of decay—of neglect. The wainscoting and the slightly uneven floorboards were of oak and like the balustrade and stairs dull and lifeless, in need of a good polish.

Bethany loosened her coat and put her handbag on the settle. A display of weapons hanging on the wall above the fireplace had attracted her attention when she had come in and now she went to examine them more closely. She had often wondered why so many people desired constant reminders of the turbulent past, and their not-so honourable ancestors, represented by evil-looking daggers and lethal pistols such as these. One of the hounds raised its head and perked its ears causing her to pause but then it laid its head back between its paws.

As she looked closely she noticed they were not ordinary weapons; they were all unusually ornate and the hilts of the daggers were all beautifully worked, some in silver or mother of pearl and one particularly beautiful one studded with moonstones.

Unlike the rest of the house they were all brightly polished and well cared for and she found herself wondering into how many hearts the daggers had been plunged and how many victims the pistols had claimed before coming to rest on the wall of Tregarrick Manor.

She turned away jumping at the sight of the figure in the shadows, only to realize almost at once it was a suit of armour. Almost chuckling aloud she sat down on the settle, but her eyes still explored every corner.

There was a slight sound from above and she craned round, her eyes scanning the ornate oak balustrade. There was no one there, yet she could have sworn ...

Turning away again she sat waiting patiently for someone to come to her. Outside she had imagined the man she had encountered as a pirate but now her mind could plainly picture him as the lord of the manor just returned from hunting, with hounds just like these dozing by the fireside. Family and friends would gather around the table to share the day's bag. The men would sup ale and sing bawdy songs whilst the soft sound of the lute and spinet would drift down from the gallery ...

'Mrs Ryder ... ?'

Bethany sprang to her feet to face a small grey-haired woman whose voice she recognized as that on the telephone. 'Mrs Tregarrick.' Bethany extended her hand and as the woman took it in hers she studied Bethany carefully before saying, 'We will be able to talk more comfortably in the sitting-room.'

As she followed her through the hall Bethany, who never had been considered tall, noticed that Esme Tregarrick was several inches smaller than herself. Her floral printed chiffon dress flapped gently around her knees as she walked very straight-backed ahead of Bethany. The dress was utterly feminine as was the wearer and Bethany imagined she had once been very fair and pretty, although time is rarely kind to such appealing looks. Now the frailty had aged leaving her hands bony, her skin parched and her face hollow.

Mrs Tregarrick led her into a small sitting-room which was comfortable as the hall could never be. No one had given much thought to history when it had been furnished with cushioned chairs and printed curtains, although these were fading now.

The older woman seated herself in a chair by the fireside and indicated for Bethany to sit too. She studied her again with a pair of faded blue eyes and Bethany realized at last this woman possessed a strength of character that belied her frail looks.

'Now Mrs Ryder,' she began, 'I find I'm in a most embarrassing position...' she paused and Bethany looked at her expectantly. Mrs Tregarrick glanced down at her interlaced fingers and then back at Bethany. 'You see, when I spoke to you this morning I somehow...' She gave a fluttery laugh. 'I gained the impression you were much older ... a widow.'

Bethany was quietly angry again. The man outside had known this would happen. 'I am a widow Mrs Tregarrick but my husband did not die of old age.'

'You have my sympathy on that my dear but nevertheless I had hoped for a middle-aged lady.'

'I understood the position was for someone to look after a child. Surely someone the younger the better?'

Mrs Tregarrick smiled uncomfortably before getting to her feet. 'I'm sorry you've come all this way for nothing.'

Bethany stayed seated, wondering why it was so important for her to get this job; she only knew it was. Perhaps it was because she wanted to find out why the interview was being conducted by the child's grandmother and not her mother or why the man outside knew she was not going to be accepted.

'Has the position been filled?'

'Not yet.'

'Then surely it is a matter of urgency to find someone and I am perfectly willing.'

Mrs Tregarrick sat down again. 'We are very isolated Mrs Ryder; you will miss the city and your friends.'

Bethany smiled. 'By the time I start to miss them I've no doubt it will be time for your grand-daughter to go back to school and I shall be leaving anyway.'

'Haven't you heard that this house has been ill-wished Mrs Ryder?' Her voice was harsh and Bethany was startled.

'Why ... yes I had heard some such nonsense. But I'm not superstitious. It doesn't worry me.'

Mrs Tregarrick frowned. 'That is because you're a foreigner. No native of Cornwall would be rash enough to make such an utterance. There was a death here two years ago ...'

Bethany was becoming impatient. Not for a second did she imagine this gracious and intelligent lady believed such superstitions; she was simply prevaricating and it made Bethany doubly determined to stay.

'I think we are wandering from the point Mrs Tregarrick. Am I suitable for the post or not?'

The older woman hesitated and then went over to a bell pull. 'You had better meet Dina.'

Bethany sat back in her chair and they waited without speaking during the minute or two it took for the imperious summons to be answered. It was answered by a young woman with an elfin face beneath an unruly mop of dark hair.

'Sally will you send Miss Dina in to us please?'

Sally gave Bethany a curious look and Mrs Tregarrick added, 'Mrs Ryder will be staying on to look after Miss Dina.'

Sally smiled and Bethany said, 'Your aunt did tell me you worked here. I'm pleased to meet you.'

Sally smiled mischievously again and was gone. Mrs Tregarrick turned to Bethany again. She seemed to have forgotten completely her earlier reluctance to employ her. 'What brought you to this district Mrs Ryder? We get few visitors as you must realize.'

'My husband and I were going to attend a sale of antiques and paintings at Melcatho House.' She noticed the slight raising of Mrs Tregarrick's eyebrows and went on to explain, 'My husband's job was travelling around the country attending such sales, buying paintings for the smaller galleries which aren't able to send their own buyers. I always accompanied him after our marriage and on this occasion we decided to have a few days holiday first as neither of us had ever been to this part of the country before.'

'And that is when your accident happened.'

Bethany winced at the memory. 'It was all Johnny's fault I'm afraid. He was driving like a maniac as he often did despite my pleas. He couldn't take a corner and the car plunged off the road. If he'd been wearing his safety belt he would still be alive, but he wasn't and he was flung right out of the car.'

Her mind was back to those few minutes before the crash and she remembered how they had almost quarrelled because she wanted him to slow down. 'You don't know how to live,' he had teased and belatedly she realized he had probably been right.

'And you were unhurt?'

Bethany returned her attention to her new employer. 'Practically, apart from cuts and bruises and shock.'

'It must have been a very interesting life.'

Bethany was glad she didn't offer sympathy. 'Yes,' she replied, hiding her wry smile and resisting the temptation to add, 'if you're a gipsy.'

'It's very unfortunate,' Mrs Tregarrick said thoughtfully, 'that so many of these gracious old houses have to offer their contents for sale. Times have certainly changed since the war although, thank heavens, both my husband and my son have been very good at managing money.

There came a timid knock at the door and as Mrs Tregarrick said, 'Ah here is Dina now,' Sally came in alone.

'I'm sorry ma'am but I can't find 'er anywhere.'

'Have you searched everywhere for her?'

'Yes ma'am.'

Mrs Tregarrick seemed unperturbed. 'No doubt she'll return when she is ready. Is Mrs Grace around?'

Sally seemed to be smiling slyly to herself. 'Mrs Grace is resting ma'am.'

This time a fleeting look of irritation crossed Esme Tregarrick's face before she said, 'Very well Sally, you may go.'

Bethany felt deeply sorry for this woman who, at that moment, looked a very old and tired lady.

She lifted her faded blue eyes to Bethany. 'You see how badly we need someone to look after Dina.' Then more briskly, 'I shall have Arkill fetch your things up for you.'

Bethany hurriedly got to her feet. 'I would rather make arrangements myself Mrs Tregarrick. It won't take long; I shall probably be back before Dina makes an appearance.'

Mrs Tregarrick got up too. 'There is really no need. You must stay for lunch. It can be arranged quite easily...'

Bethany remained firm. 'Mr and Mrs Arkill were very kind to me after my husband died. I think it would be very ungracious if I were just to go without a word. Besides Mrs Tregarrick on a practical note there are things I have to attend to. I have to let my landlady know where to send my things and I want to let one or two friends know my address.'

'Very well, if you insist,' the old lady said, a little

grudgingly. 'I hope by the time you return, Dina will be here to greet you.'

Bethany was shown to the door by Mrs Arkill's niece. 'You be stayin' 'ere?'

'Yes I am Sally.'

'Don't know why I'm sure. Give me a chance to be off to London and I'll be gone.' There was a far away gleam in her eye as Bethany replied gently, 'I've lived there for quite a while and I can assure you country life has much to recommend it.'

She went through the dim porch and once the great oak door was closed behind her she took a deep breath of cold air. Until then she'd hardly realized the old house had a claustrophobic atmosphere. Now she was outside she was glad she had insisted on this break; Mrs Tregarrick was a very strong personality.

As she entered the woods for the downward trek she glanced back at the house; it looked as forlorn as it had done when she had approached and the reason for it puzzled her more than ever. There was ample domestic help and it was inhabited by a young family. Mrs Tregarrick was hardly the type of woman to tolerate the neglect of her home—or was there some reason why she no longer cared?

Plunging down the path through the woods Bethany shrugged off her meditations and gave herself a silent but firm warning not to become involved with the Tregarricks any more than was necessary in her capacity as employee.

She was so deep in thought that she did not see the

figure standing with one hand on a tree trunk staring down into the valley below. She stopped short and was wondering if she should go straight past without speaking when he turned and smiled at her.

'Leaving so soon Mrs Ryder? You can't say I didn't warn you.'

'On the contrary Mr Tregarrick your mother has employed me. I shall only stay in the village long enough to arrange for my belongings to be brought up.'

His smile disappeared and there was a glint of steel in his eyes. 'You surprise me Mrs Ryder, you really do. I strongly advise you to seek employment elsewhere. Staying at Tregarrick Manor can only mean trouble for you, and for us.'

Bethany did not hide her surprise. 'If you are so set against me surely you have some say in who looks after your daughter.' He said nothing. 'Or perhaps you would care to explain that enigmatic statement Mr Tregarrick. I'm willing to listen to your reasons why my coming will cause trouble.'

'I can explain nothing but I repeat, you'll be well advised to stay away.'

With that he turned away, staring down into the valley as he had done when she had come upon him. Her eyes never left his back for a full two minutes and then she started to run down the path.

CHAPTER THREE

The great hall was lit only by the flickering of the fire and the candles in an eight branched candelabrum standing on the middle of the oak table when Bethany went down to dinner.

On her return from the village it had been later than she had anticipated and it was Sally who had led the way up the stairs to the balcony and along a corridor to a room which, inevitably, overlooked the woods surrounding the house. The room was at the back of the house she realized; the land sloped upwards giving her a fine view of the moors spreading beyond the trees.

Sally informed her that dinner was at eight and Bethany was glad there were a few smart dresses in the suitcase that had been left at the inn. The one she chose was dark and simple and, she hoped, suitable for the occasion and the image she wanted to project during her stay.

She paused at the top of the stairs; no one else was down yet. The table was set for six Bethany noticed and she eagerly anticipated meeting the other members of the family, wondering how they would match up to Mrs Arkill's description.

The flickering fire threw eerie shadows into every corner. Bethany knew the house had an electricity supply and wished someone had switched on the lights, but she guessed that the family preferred to keep the atmosphere as it had been for centuries, only grudgingly accepting the comforts of the twentieth century.

There was a switch she noticed at the bottom of the stairs and she wondered whether she dared put on the lights, then decided she dare not.

She came hesitantly into the hall, trying not to make any sound. The noise of the wind was very clear, almost as if it were present in the house, yet there was little draught. She stepped back almost into the fire, stifling a gasp of fear with the back of her hand; the suit of armour had moved. Then scolding herself for being silly she moved towards it very gingerly. It had moved! She sprang back again just as a white clad figure stepped out of the shadows.

'Did I startle you? I'm very sorry.'

'Yes you did,' Bethany answered with relief at finding the ghost was very human and from the expression on her face not slightly sorry for startling her.

'You must be Mrs Ryder. I'm Dina Tregarrick.'

Dina held one slim hand out for her to shake and when she did so Bethany experienced her second shock in as many minutes. Dina Tregarrick was certainly not the small child she had been led to expect. Bethany reckoned she must be thirteen or fourteen . That she was well-developed for her age was obvious despite the childish, white, lacey, ankle length gown she wore tied with a sash around her slim waist.

The girl was studying Bethany intently too. 'You're not what I expected,' she said, echoing Bethany's own thoughts. 'They said you were a widow. I thought you would be as ugly as the other crows they sent here.'

Bethany laughed. 'In that case I'm glad I'm a disappointment to you.'

Dina moved gracefully to a small table stocked with crystal glasses and decanters. 'Would you like a drink?'

'No thank you—I don't.'

'It's just as well. They don't like drinkers here. Are you going to make me do my lessons? They keep sending books and exercises from school.'

'You'll have to spend *some* time at your lessons I expect. How else will you keep up with the work or be able to pass your examinations?'

As the girl walked up and down the hall Bethany was again struck by the elegance and maturity of one so young. She had a poise that took some women years to achieve and Bethany wondered if it had been inherited from her mother.

'It's a waste of time,' Dina said sulkily, 'I don't need to pass exams; I'm going to be an actress.' She swept her hair away from her face. 'Do you think I will be beautiful enough?'

'Certainly,' Bethany replied quite truthfully, 'but nowadays actresses require both brains and beauty.'

Suddenly Dina smiled quite charmingly. 'That's a rumour put around by plain women.' She studied Bethany again. 'You seem very cheerful.'

Bethany sat down on the settle. 'Is that so strange?'

'Yes it is. You should be wearing black—widow's weeds—for a start. Did you love him very passionately?'

Bethany looked away from Dina's probing gaze. 'I loved him,' she answered, wondering why she had bothered to reply to such an impertinent question.

Dina clasped her hands together. 'If I had lost the man I loved I think I would have killed myself rather than live without him.'

Bethany hid her smile. 'That wouldn't have been very realistic and it wouldn't have brought back my husband.'

'Are you going to spend the rest of your life mourning him?'

'That would be a great waste Dina.'

The girl looked shocked. 'Surely you don't intend to betray his memory by marrying again?'

'I doubt if I shall do that,' Bethany replied, smiling kindly.

'Have you met Uncle Theo yet?' Dina asked, satisfied that Bethany would remain faithful to her lover's memory and when Bethany shook her head Dina smiled. 'You'll like him; he's handsome.' She looked pensive for a moment. 'I think I might make him fall in love with me and then I shall marry him and make everyone jealous.'

'You can't marry your own uncle.'

Dina looked scornful. 'He's not my *real* uncle, no more than Adam is my *real* father.'

Bethany looked at her sharply and Dina laughed

delightedly. 'Didn't you know? We're a funny family. None of us are really related. My father is dead. He was a rich, old man when Mummy married him and then just after I was born he died and Mummy married Adam. Isn't it madly romantic? I'd much rather have Adam as my father than my real one.'

The knowledge that Adam Tregarrick was not, after all, Dina's father shocked Bethany profoundly, although she could not for anything fathom why.

'So Grandmother is not my grandmother at all you see,' Dina went on delightedly, 'and she's not Adam's mother either. His mother is dead and Uncle Theo is only his half-brother.' Her eyes misted wistfully, 'Do you know what I would like to do? I don't think I shall marry Uncle Theo after all. I have had a much better idea. I shall marry a rich old man and have lots of lovers instead.'

'Dina!' Bethany said sharply and then with a laugh. 'What nonsense you talk. Your mother was probably terribly unhappy when your father died.'

'She had dozens of lovers to choose from. She was a famous actress; the most beautiful woman in London. She's told me all about it. It's very fitting that I follow in her footsteps.'

'All the same you will have to complete your education first and stop wallowing in the type of book I think you've been reading.'

'When one is ill for such a long time there's nothing to do but read, and listen. It's surprising what one can learn by just listening to conversations.'

'Don't you know it's very wrong to listen to other people's conversations?'

Dina's eyes glistened. 'But it's interesting.' She paused a moment and Bethany studied her closely; the girl's mind was old beyond her years and she disapproved of the romantic nonsense with which her mother must be filling her head. No doubt Mrs Adam Tregarrick was starved of the adulation she was accustomed to and recounted her colourful past for her daughter's amusement.

'Of course,' Dina continued, 'even if I do marry I shall probably die young leaving my husband and lovers heartbroken and forever faithful to my memory.' She looked at Bethany. 'Just like you are faithful to your husband's memory.'

'Where did you read that?' Bethany asked drily.

'Nowhere,' Dina pouted. 'I heard the doctor tell my mother I was prone to illness and infections especially virus infections. That is what was wrong with me—a virus infection. The Lady of the Camellias was very delicate. She died of consumption and left a lover heartbroken, didn't she?'

'So you've been reading Dumas have you?'

Dina smiled impishly. 'We have a library, through there,' she nodded towards one of the many doors leading off the hall. 'There are some very interesting books; much nicer than those they send from school.'

'Nevertheless Dina those are the ones you will be reading from now on.'

Dina's face puckered into a very childish expression.

'I had an idea you might be a martinet. But you're not *too* old and you've suffered, I can tell, so at least there is a bond between us.'

'What kind of a bond?'

The hall was flooded with light from sconces that once bore candles but which now carried more mundane electric bulbs. Both Dina and Bethany turned together to see Adam Tregarrick and his step-mother standing at the bottom of the stairs. A wide grin appeared on Dina's face and she rushed over to kiss her grandmother gently on the cheek and then, that over, she threw herself in Adam's arms.

Mrs Tregarrick tugged at a bell-pull and said reprovingly, 'So you've put in an appearance at last?'

'Yes Grandmother,' Dina replied, her eyes demurely downcast whilst her stepfather kept one arm around her shoulders.

'And where did you go?' Esme asked.

'Walking on the moors. It was such a glorious day and I was all alone!'

'It's a wonder you didn't catch cold.'

Dina's mouth drooped. 'I wore my coat. I *had* to go; I was called.'

Esme fixed Dina with her stare. 'Nonsense. There will be no more running off alone now Mrs Ryder is here.'

Dina dropped her eyes but Bethany had the clear impression that there was nothing meek about the gesture. 'No Grandmother.'

Bethany tried to behave as though she was not aware

that Adam Tregarrick's eyes had been on her since he had come into the hall and throughout the exchange between Dina and her grandmother. But despite her attempt at normality she realized her hands were tensely clasped in her lap.

She almost started at the sound of a door opening, only to relax again when the housekeeper—the Rosanna Penarvon Mrs Arkill had mentioned—came in pushing a trolley laden with food. Bethany stared at the woman who was rumoured to have been Greville Tregarrick's mistress. She was middle-aged now, but still a big, handsome woman, her fair hair untainted by grey. What a remarkable man he must have been, Bethany thought, to have kept a second wife and a mistress under one roof and she wondered if the rumours about Adam were true.

'We had better take our places,' Esme Tregarrick said and as she looked at the proud, genteel lady Bethany wondered what her feelings for her husband had been and if she had been humiliated by his behaviour. She was quite sure it was one thing Mrs Tregarrick would never reveal.

Adam held the chair at the head of the table for his step-mother whilst she sat down and Bethany noticed the smile she gave him was full of affection. Despite the disjointed nature of the family they seemed to be fond enough of each other.

Dina slid on to her chair as her step-father came behind Bethany to hold her chair. This evening he had discarded his country tweeds in favour of evening dress which, surprisingly, became him. Seeing him like this, his craggy features assembled in an almost attractive way Bethany wondered at ever mistaking him for a hired hand. Tonight he looked a fitting partner to a famous actress; the most beautiful woman in London.

'My wife sends her apologies,' he said without a smile, 'she is not very well tonight.'

He said it loud enough for the others to hear but neither Mrs Tregarrick nor Dina remarked on Grace Tregarrick's absence and Bethany replied, 'I'm sorry about that, but I hope to meet her very soon.'

The housekeeper turned off most of the lights and once again the hall was lit mainly by the fire and the candles. With Adam Tregarrick at one end of the great refectory table, his step-mother at the other and Bethany facing Dina across the middle, Mrs Penarvon began to serve the soup from a silver tureen. The light flickered off the tureen and the daggers on the wall over the fireplace. To Bethany, as she sipped her soup in the silence, four people seated at such an impossibly large table was like indulging in some grotesque ritual.

The main course arrived and Dina began to chatter which relieved a certain awkwardness in the atmosphere. 'I'm glad Mrs Ryder has come,' she said, 'there's so many adventures we can share. I can take her up to the moors and show her all my places.'

'Mrs Ryder can keep you out of mischief,' her grandmother replied drily.

'But perhaps she will not want to stay when she realizes life at Tregarrick Manor is too tame,' Adam said, equally drily.

Bethany knew his eyes were on her and unaccountably her fingers tightened around her knife and fork. Only now did she realize how badly her nerves had been affected by Johnny's death and Tregarrick Manor, she suspected would not prove to be the panacea.

Dina chuckled. 'Nonsense Daddy,' and Bethany was amused at the wheedling way in which she spoke to Adam, 'how can life be dull here? There's so much going on.'

Esme laughed indulgently and Bethany turned towards Adam expecting him to laugh too, but his attention was elsewhere.

His eyes were fixed on the top of the stairs and of one accord Bethany and Esme looked in the same direction. Bethany choked back a cry at the sight of the figure in a bottle green velvet gown weaving an unsteady way down the steps. Her bronze hair was tangled over the greater part of her face and cascaded untidily down her back. Esme drew a sharp breath and Adam got to his feet as the woman almost lost her footing and fell, but she steadied herself and brushed her hair away from her cheek to reveal a face as white as paper.

Dina had not exaggerated when she had said her mother was beautiful, or at least she had been at one time for she was no longer young. Bethany estimated she was not far off forty, and probably a few years older than her husband. Although her features must have at one time been as delicate as her daughter's they were now bloated and her brilliantly blue eyes—so striking against the fiery splendour of her hair—were smudged with dark shadows.

'You shouldn't have come down Grace,' her husband said offering his hand to steady her.

Up above Bethany caught sight of Sally hovering uncertainly in the shadows of the balcony.

'I know I shouldn't,' Grace replied in a thick voice, 'but I had this raging curiosity to see the nursemaid your mother employed to look after my little girl.'

She shrugged off Adam's helping hand and staggered around to where Bethany was sitting. One glance at Dina showed the girl was quite unperturbed and probably quite used to the sudden appearance of her mother in this way.

'Are you going to stay?' she demanded harshly.

Bethany, for a moment taken aback at having such a question thrust at her again, replied, 'Yes I think so. Besides I've only been employed until Dina goes back to school.'

Grace Tregarrick threw back her head and laughed and as the light from the fire caught in her hair it looked as if it were ablaze. 'Every day is like a month here and you know it. That's why I want to know why you've come.'

Bethany wondered if the illness that affected Grace Tregarrick was mental. She looked directly at her and said with a calmness she did not feel, 'I am here Mrs Tregarrick because I needed a job rather badly and this one will tide me over until I can fix up something permanent.'

'You're lying.'

Bethany almost recoiled from the mad fury she saw in her eyes and Adam said sharply, 'Grace. Remember where you are!'

Grace continued to stare at Bethany and said contemptuously, 'I know exactly where I am Adam Tregarrick although I try very hard to forget it.'

Dina was staring down at her plate and Bethany gained the impression she was neither shocked nor frightened at her mother's fearsome behaviour, but somehow enjoying it. Esme looked appealingly at her step-son who came around to his wife's side. 'Come along Grace. You can speak to Mrs Ryder in the morning when you're feeling better.'

She rounded on him ferociously. 'I feel fine now!' Then she turned back to Bethany. 'Now, why are you here? Sally tells me you came from London yesterday. Was it his idea?'

Bethany stared helplessly at Adam and then back to his wife. 'I don't know what you mean.'

Grace Tregarrick bent closer, her face almost in Bethany's and suddenly she knew what ailed the woman —the sharp odour of whisky was unmistakable. 'Do you want me to spell it out in front of the child you trollop?'

At that Adam grabbed his wife angrily, swinging her away from Bethany. 'Enough Grace!'

She collapsed against him, gasping. 'You're hurting me!'

'I'm not hurting you as much as I will if you don't

go back upstairs immediately.'

'Let me go!'

He released her suddenly and she fell against Dina's chair, steadying herself by gripping the back. Sally came hurrying down the stairs towards her mistress and rubbing the arm Adam had so cruelly wrenched Grace allowed her to lead her back towards the stairs.

Adam watched her go before saying to Bethany, who was staring down at the remains of her dinner, 'I'm very sorry you had to see her like this. She doesn't realize what she's saying when she's ill.'

Bethany could not reply; she felt quite certain that Grace Tregarrick knew exactly what she was saying.

Without another word Adam went back to his place and Dina piped, 'Where is our sweet? Mrs Penarvon said it would be Meringue Surprise and that's my favourite.'

As if answering her cue the housekeeper returned with the delicious-looking meringues and as Dina tucked into it with relish Bethany could hardly credit the cold-blooded way her fellow diners were eating theirs after a scene that had made her feel physically sick. Only with the greatest effort did she manage to control her heaving stomach.

Esme Tregarrick must have noticed that the meringue remained untouched just as it had been left in front of her. 'Come along Mrs Ryder,' she said cheerfully, 'Mrs Penarvon will be most hurt if you leave your sweet. She's justly proud of her meringues and they're filled with real Cornish cream.'

'I'm sure they're delicious,' Bethany replied without looking up, 'but I've already eaten enough.'

Esme stared at Bethany then, her eyes shrewdly narrowed. 'You don't want to be upset by Grace. She's very highly strung and she'll be quite remorseful in the morning.'

'I've already apologized for Grace, Mother,' Adam snapped. 'Enough has been said on the subject.'

'May I have your meringue then?' Dina broke in eagerly.

'Of course,' Bethany replied quickly.

'You may,' Adam intercepted from his place at the end of the table, 'but all that cream will surely make you fat and pimply.'

Dina's hand in the process of reaching for Bethany's plate drew back sharply and Adam and Esme both laughed, but Bethany was still too shaken to be amused. Perhaps in time she too would become accustomed to the odd behaviour and the scenes staged by the inhabitants of Tregarrick Manor.

When the interminable meal was over at last Bethany was grateful to escape to Dina's room as the girl insisted on being accompanied. As she slipped between the covers she said, 'Don't pay any heed to Mummy; she was only afraid you'd be more beautiful than she is. Now she knows you're not she won't bother you any more.'

Bethany tried hard not to smile and Dina asked, 'Are you going back downstairs to discuss me with Grandmother and Adam?'

Nothing would induce her to face Adam and Esme

Tregarrick again that night and she said, 'I'm rather tired. I think I shall go to bed too.'

'Mummy hates the way we all go to bed early. She says that when she was in London she was only just getting ready to go out at this time.'

'I expect I shall also have to get used to it. Shall I turn out the light as I go?'

'I'd like to read for a while.'

Bethany lifted the book on the bedside table. '*Jane Eyre*,' she murmured, 'I can't really quarrel with that. Good night Dina. Tomorrow you can begin to show me around.'

Dina, as she lay propped up on the pillows with her hair cascading around her shoulders, looked very much as her mother must have done twenty years before and Bethany considered it a great shame that Grace Tregarrick had changed from such a beautiful creature to something resembling a harridan.

Bethany knew quite well the reason why Adam Tregarrick's wife attempted to forget her problems by drowning them out with whisky. As she lay sleepless between the cotton sheets in the unfamiliar bed listening to the wind relentlessly thrashing against the windows she realized Mrs Arkill had hinted quite plainly at the answer that morning; Adam Tregarrick was as faithless as his father had been and Grace, vain and lovely, had not the strength of character to face it with calmness as Esme Tregarrick had done.

It was all gossip—none of it proven—but Bethany acknowledged that rumour was invariably founded on fact and it accounted for Grace's ugly outburst. She obviously believed Adam had installed her in the house as his mistress just as his father had brought in Mrs Penarvon thirty years before. To Bethany it was almost laughable that Grace could imagine her husband might be attracted to her. Even more than ten years older and ravaged by her sickness Grace had a beauty Bethany could not approach.

But since she had met him Bethany was disturbingly aware that she did not want the rumours to be true of Adam Tregarrick.

CHAPTER FOUR

The following days settled themselves into a regular pattern. Before lunch Dina did her lessons, with surprisingly few objections. During this period Bethany usually read or wrote letters to friends in London. Some women might have found such an existence unbearably boring but after three years continual travel around the country it was all Bethany wanted.

In the afternoons when the weather was fair they invariably went out for a walk, usually down to the village and almost always ending at the inn where they sat in Mrs Arkill's comfortable kitchen consuming tea and home made scones piled high with cream. Dina seemed to enjoy this hitherto unknown treat and Bethany was gratified to see how her strength was returning, for she did not doubt the girl had been very seriously ill.

As for Adam Tregarrick, apart from the evenings she saw little of him. By the time she was up in the morning he was out, rarely returning for lunch which seemed to be a more tense meal when he was absent.

She often caught sight of his large figure striding about the moors above the house like some ghostly spirit unable to find peaceful slumber. Often when the wind howled, hurling vicious sheets of rain against the windows and Bethany, Dina and Esme could do nothing but play rummy to relieve the monotony he would don his black oilskin and brave the weather that imprisoned all but the hardy and he would return, his hair plastered to his face and the water cascading like a waterfall from his shiny oilskin.

And when the wind ceased to drive the rain against the unrelenting walls of Tregarrick Manor the mist curled in from the sea soaking the ground as thoroughly as the driving rain had done. It clung to the bare trees as crystal droplets and blanketed the house in a silence broken only by the occasional cry of a curlew in flight.

No one seemed to resent these monotonous days and Bethany suspected it was due to an inbred Cornish tolerance of the weather. No one seemed to mind, except Grace that is.

Bethany had been at Tregarrick Manor three days before she saw Grace Tregarrick for the first time since that horrible evening. It was almost lunchtime and Bethany had returned to her room to parcel Dina's recent exercises that were to be sent to her school when Grace suddenly appeared on the balcony in front of her.

There was no way past and she felt trapped, panicking slightly at the thought of another attack like the last one with no Adam nearby to prevent it.

As on that evening Grace was wearing the long velvet gown; her face had lost the bloated look but now, in the daylight, even the gown could not hide the way her once voluptuous curves had thickened.

'Ah Mrs Ryder; I have been wanting to speak to you.

I must say Dina seems to have taken to you, which is a great relief to her father and myself.'

Bethany, who had flinched at the sound of her voice, relaxed when she realized Dina's mother was over her temporary inebriation and probably could not even remember her outburst.

She smiled. 'I'm glad you're satisfied Mrs Tregarrick. I'm very fond of Dina.' She attempted to move past but it seemed Grace had not finished.

'I only wish I were well enough to look after her myself,' she said wistfully. 'I'm only too aware of how a girl of Dina's age needs her mother and unfortunately she has inherited my delicate constitution. We very nearly lost her this time.'

Uncharitably Bethany's thoughts flew to the Lady of the Camellias and the fact that Grace Tregarrick had once been an actress; perhaps this had been her favourite rôle. She doubted if mother or daughter were in as poor health as they made out.

After that Grace was seen more about the house, although she was always dressed in a long gown which Bethany suspected covered her nightgown, as if the effort of dressing was too much for her. But no one commented. Her beautiful hair was always unkempt and tangled and Bethany knew that if she possessed a mane of fire like Grace's instead of her own mousey locks she would groom it fastidiously.

Adam appeared to be glad to see his wife around the house and they behaved normally towards each other, if a little more reserved than a married couple should.

Bethany studied them with interest unable to reconcile Dina's romantic picture of their marriage with their politeness to each other. Adam Tregarrick was the perfect example of the patriarchal lord of the manor and apart from an outward warmth towards his family she felt he was, for some reason, holding back his real self, subjucating the real man beneath an outward coldness.

On the face of it the Tregarricks were a happy, although somewhat subdued, family. But somehow Bethany could detect something more—something almost intangible. It was only on one mizzling day when even Adam had for once remained indoors that she realized at last what it was.

Adam had spent the morning cleaning the antique pistols and polishing the fearsome daggers adorning the walls, ignoring them all except for Dina who was tackling an old mathematics examination paper for practise; then he would patiently help to solve any problem she came across. Bethany hid her own disappointment at his failure to mellow towards her. She had not forgotten their encounter in the woods on that first day and she still puzzled over his reluctance to have her in the house and although since then he had not tried to persuade her to leave she felt he was only just tolerating her presence.

Bethany and Esme were both writing letters when Grace put in an appearance. She was obviously surprised to see her husband in the house and for the first time Bethany suspected she was avoiding him.

'How about a game of rummy Mrs Tregarrick?' Bethany suggested as Grace stared morosely out of the window at the dripping trees surrounding the house.

'Now that really is the height of excitement here isn't it?' she answered spitefully, moving away from the window. 'I don't know how you can stand it here day after day. If the wind isn't howling like a banshee it's drip, drip, drip. It's driving me mad!'

Adam became alert, no longer indifferent, at the sound of the latent hysteria in his wife's voice.

'You sit here as if life doesn't exist outside these four walls,' she accused, hugging her arms about her body and shivering slightly although the fire ensured it was always warm in the room.

'Everything you need is here inside these four walls,' Bethany said boldly, without thinking of the impertinence, 'Your home and family. What else could any woman want?'

With the exception of Dina the occupants of the room stared at her as Bethany began to flush, but in that second or two of silence she finally realized what was troubling this family—it was fear; pregnant fear.

'No you wouldn't know would you?' Grace spat out contemptuously, rushing over to the door. Her voice broke the momentary tense silence and the feeling of fear Bethany had detected was gone. 'And,' Grace added before slamming out of the room, 'I pray you never will.'

Adam and his step-mother exchanged glances before he followed his wife out of the room. A short while later Bethany went upstairs on the pretext of wanting to freshen up before lunch but mainly because she wanted some time to herself. She did not know what had prompted her to say such a thing; she only knew she had meant it quite sincerely. But on reflection she realized what would appear to be a fulfilled life for someone like herself, who longed for a settled home, would not necessarily satisfy someone like Grace Tregarrick. How different we all are in our needs, she thought sadly.

Unfortunately she had to pass Grace's room—and she assumed Adam's room also—on the way to her own and whilst she was still yards away Grace's voice carried quite clearly to her ears despite the thickness of the walls and the stoutness of the door.

'Leave me to the little comfort I have left,' she cried in the voice used to reaching the far corners of a theatre auditorium.

'I'm not going to let you kill yourself Grace,' Adam replied calmly.

Grace laughed harshly. 'Don't tell me you'd be sorry if I did. I'd be yet another burden off your shoulders.' She laughed again. 'You know all about killing don't you Adam?'

'You're still deluding yourself Grace. Your life has been wasted for a mirage, nothing more than a dream.'

'You damned hypocrite! Don't you dare be sanctimonious with me! I've seen the way you've been looking at that goody-goody nursemaid.'

'You're talking nonsense Grace.'

'You thought I was too drunk to notice,' she said triumphantly, 'but I've known too many men not to know what goes on in their minds and I know you very well. You tell me why she's willing to bury herself out here? You tell me why Adam!' Her voice softened. 'At least it will keep you from my daughter.'

'Mind what you say,' he warned, 'I'll stand only so much even from you.'

'And what will you do? What have you ever been able to do? Is any woman as beautiful as Dina safe in this cursed house? And she is a woman isn't she Adam?'

There was a moment of silence and then a loud slap that sounded like the crack of a pistol shot before Grace started to cry brokenly.

'I'm sorry Adam,' she sobbed. 'Don't take them away. Oh for God's sake don't take them away! I didn't mean what I said about Dina; you've been a marvellous father to her. When you threaten me I panic and say terrible things I don't mean. And when I look at her and see how beautiful she is I'm frightened for her; frightened she'll end up like me. I know what I am Adam, I know...' She began to sob even more convulsively and then her voice rose to a shriek, 'I'll die. Is that what you want?'

'You won't die Grace. You might even live.'

By this time she was sobbing hysterically, moaning, 'How much more punishment do I have to take?'

'I'll send Sally up with one of those sleeping tablets Dr Sanderson prescribed,' Bethany heard him add from somewhere just inside the door and she was guiltily aware of eavesdropping. She began to hurry away but it was too late to avoid him. The door opened and Grace's sobbing became louder. As Adam came out of the room Bethany caught sight of Grace curled up on the bed.

He stopped in his tracks when he saw her flushing uncomfortably. He stared at her for a moment or two before pushing past her and hurrying down the stairs, but not before Bethany had seen the bottles he was holding in his arms.

Bethany went to her room wondering how often there were hysterical scenes like this between Adam and Grace and more important, how frequently Dina had overheard them as easily as she had done.

A few minutes later, on hearing the sound of the front door closing with a loud bang, Bethany went into the corridor and peered out of the window. A figure clad in Adam's oilskin was hurrying across the clearing bent against the rain, but by the way the oilskin hung loosely the person was obviously not Adam. As the figure reached the trees it turned to glance fearfully towards the house and Bethany caught her breath as Grace, half running, plunged into the enveloping mists towards the village.

The 'mizzling' weather lasted another two days, during which Grace did not make an appearance. Then miraculously one morning Bethany drew her bedroom curtains and the sun was shining and the trees were glistening with dew.

Soon after lunch she and her young charge, warmly wrapped, for the sun as yet gave no real warmth, set out for the village.

Since coming to Tregarrick Manor Bethany had often experienced pangs of guilt at the ease in which she was earning her money; Dina was no child who needed constant care and supervision. But after once voicing these doubts to Esme Tregarrick she had been assured that her presence was very necessary.

'I needn't explain that when we're all in the house Dina is safe enough,' Esme had said, 'but when it is fine she needs the fresh air. Unfortunately she tends to wander away and we were terrified she would get lost or become caught in the marshes up on the moors. Besides Dina has certainly settled down to her work since you came.'

So, in a small part, she was mollified. If Mrs Tregarrick was satisfied there was every reason for Bethany herself to be. And despite the conflicts of the family and stemming from it Dina's strange worldliness she was enjoying her stay at the manor. More than that she had to keep reminding herself that Johnny had been dead only a few weeks; already her three years of marriage seemed unreal—almost part of a dream. Life with the Tregarricks and their odd, repressed, air of fearfulness —of waiting for something terrible to happen—was so much more real. Was she such an unnatural woman to be able to put three years shared with a man—a man she believed she had loved—behind her so completely?

Tea was once again the refreshing and comfortable ritual in Mrs Arkill's kitchen and sure enough when Dina had gone into the yard to see the Arkills' new litter of kittens Mrs Arkill said, ''er mother's well, is she?'

'Yes,' Bethany replied warily, 'why do you ask?'

'Mr Botell at the sub-post office had 'er in the other day. Soakin' wet she were and out on a day when even the spriggans wouldn't venture and all to post a letter.'

'It was probably urgent,' Bethany murmured.

As soon as Dina had finished playing with the kittens and after being satisfied by the delicious tea they set off for the trek back up the hill. They were half-way up, the gentle climb having cured the chill feeling caused by the damp still in the atmosphere, when they heard the sound of a car coming up behind them. There was only just time for them to jump to the side of the path as a bright yellow Mini swept past blaring its horn.

Bethany steadied herself indignantly, brushing off the sleeve of her coat that had caught on one of the trees. 'Well!' she cried, 'I thought at least we'd be free of maniac drivers up here.'

Dina was staring after the car, her eyes ablaze with excitement. 'That was Uncle Theo!' She turned to Bethany. 'Come on Mrs Ryder!'

And with that she dashed off in the direction of the house whilst Bethany hurried after her. When she reached the clearing the Mini was parked in front of the house. She stopped short at the sight of the man talking to Dina. Her first impression was that she had never seen such a beautiful man, and beautiful seemed to be the only adequate description. His blond hair almost touched his collar framing facial features that were almost feminine in their delicacy. There was no mistaking that this was Esme Tregarrick's son; the fair hair, finely drawn features and the illusion of fragility were all hers.

So this was Theo whom Mrs Arkill had described as a 'bonny boy'. Bethany could well believe it.

A bunch of soggy twigs crunched beneath her feet and Theo Tregarrick swung around and his blue eyes narrowed with curiosity. She went forward smiling.

'This is Mrs Ryder; she looks after me,' Dina said with a giggle.

Theo appraised her with a thoroughness that was disconcerning. '*Mrs* Ryder?'

'She's a widow,' prompted Dina.

Theo took her hand in his. 'Madam if I had been your husband I would have died happy.'

Bethany withdrew her hand from his slim, soft one. 'My husband died as a result of an accident only a few weeks ago.'

Theo became more serious. 'My apologies Mrs Ryder. I didn't mean to make fun. I'm pleased to meet you. Very pleased. This is one stay I shall really enjoy.'

Once again she was uncomfortable under his scrutiny. She had never minded male admiration, but this was hardly that. She liked it even less than his half-brother's brusqueness.

She put a bright smile on her face. 'I must admit I've heard a lot about Uncle Theo. It's very interesting to meet you at last.'

He threw back his head and laughed. 'I *bet* you've

heard about me.'

'This is a surprise Theo. What brings you to Tregar-rick Manor after all this time? As if I didn't know.'

Bethany had to turn to see Adam striding from the back of the house, the hounds at his heels. They began to bark frenziedly at the sight of the newcomer who said, 'For God's sake Adam call off the hounds.'

As he had done on the day she had arrived he quickly snapped an order to the dogs who retreated to his heels.

'We'd better go in Dina,' Bethany said, knowing Adam was looking at her in a speculative way she could not fathom, nor could she tell whether Adam was pleased to see his half-brother or not. She often sensed Adam was studying her as if trying to divine something incomprehensible.

As they passed into the house she saw Theo grasp Adam's arm and shake his hand heartily. 'The prodigal son returns,' he said lightly. 'I had that old longing to see the homestead again Adam. Now, how is Grace?'

The hall, once again, was lit only by the candelabrum and the fire. Foolishly since that first evening Bethany had tried not to be the first one down; there was something predatory about the very silence and a presence of evil ever there. And although she knew she was being uncharacteristically fanciful she had to repress very forcibly the instinct to explore every corner that seemed to be alive. Alive with someone or something, waiting and watching.

Tonight she was the first to come down; no doubt the excitement of Theo's unexpected arrival had delayed the others.

The inevitable wind had sprung up once more, rustling through the trees and whispering down the chimneys. Whispering low. But the whispering was human. Bethany's fingers tightened around the newel post to stop her hand from trembling. Then came a laugh. Her eyes were drawn to the far end of the hall from where the laugh had come and she stiffened as Sally materialized from the shadows, for Adam followed her into the hall. She had the impulse to retreat up the stairs but at that moment she was seen.

Sally started and then smiled sheepishly, backing towards the kitchen. 'It's to the kitchen I'd better be goin' or Mrs Penarvon'll be after me.'

Adam Tregarrick's smile faded as the girl left the hall and Bethany flushed because he knew she had seen him with Sally, although what she had seen she wasn't quite sure. For once it was fortunate the lights were out so he could not see the unbecoming colour in her cheeks.

They stared at each other across the hall and then he went to stand behind one of the dining chairs saying, a little awkwardly, 'Sally is really here to look after my wife, although Grace must never realize it.'

'You don't have to explain Mr Tregarrick,' she replied coolly, coming into the room. She was unaccountably pleased to find him ruffled for once and her mind was concentrated on trying to forget the involuntary leaping of her pulses when he had looked at her.

She noticed his hands were gripping the back of the chair and it occurred to her that here was a man under a very big strain, bigger than the problem an alcoholic wife represented.

He turned his steady gaze on her and she could not look away, her treacherous heart beating wildly. 'Don't I? Don't I really?'

'My God! The place is like a damned mausoleum!'

Reluctantly, Bethany drew her eyes away from Adam's as the room was flooded with light, rendering the shadowy corners harmless. Theo went back to his mother's side and she linked her arm in his. It only took one glance for Bethany to see how happy and proud she was to have him home.

'You've met my son Mrs Ryder?'

'I'll say,' Theo remarked appreciatively.

'Yes we've met,' Bethany murmured, glancing at Adam again. His hands were still gripping the back of the chair and his knuckles showed white.

'Anyone care for a whisky?' Theo asked going towards the decanters.

'I will,' Dina answered pertly from the stairs.

'In five years time ask again,' Theo told her as he poured himself a generous measure.

'Do you have to, darling?' Esme asked.

'I do Mother,' he replied fondly, 'and it's about time you realized we're in the last half of the twentieth century and not nineteen twenty-one.' He kissed her cheek to take the sting out of his words and she patted his arm indulgently before tugging at the bell rope to inform Mrs Penarvon they were ready for dinner.

'Does this visit mean you're staying indefinitely?' Adam asked, stirring from the depths of his thoughts.

Theo mused for a moment. 'That depends.' His glance flickered for a split second on Bethany who pretended not to notice. 'I shall certainly stay for a while. Town can be pretty hectic, especially on the pocket.' He turned to refill his glass and Dina rushed up to him.

'Oh do say you'll stay Uncle Theo!'

He turned, studying her gravely for a moment before he smiled and put both his arms around her. 'You make me feel old when you call me Uncle. You're getting a big girl now.'

'We'd better sit down,' Adam said abruptly and Theo released her.

After he had seen his mother seated Theo held Bethany's chair for her, managing to brush her arm as he did so. Dina, her arm linked in Adam's, went round to the other side of the table and Bethany was struck by her looks. Even at such a tender age she was extraordinarily beautiful. Already she had the body of a woman; in a year or two she would *be* a woman. Bethany's mind went back to the argument she had overheard between her mother and her step-father and the wild accusations Grace had made—surely the rantings of a befuddled mind? Unwillingly she raised her eyes; Adam was bending over Dina and smiling at something she had said. Surely not, Bethany thought. And yet there was Sally and the dead Jenefer Henekin.

'Surely you wouldn't start without me?' a voice asked coyly from the stairs.

Bethany froze in her chair not daring to look to where Grace would be standing. Theo's chair scraped back and he went towards the stairs, his arms outstretched. 'Grace! They told me you wouldn't be down tonight.'

'On your first night home Theo? I wouldn't miss that for anything.'

Slowly Bethany turned in her chair and gaped unashamedly. Tonight Grace Tregarrick had discarded her long dressing gown for a blue evening gown the exact shade of her eyes and Bethany needed no telling that the gown had cost a great deal of money. Her bronze hair had been brushed and pinned into a shining crown of fire and her face was beautifully made up with no trace of the former bloatedness. Even the dark smudges had practically faded from beneath her eyes.

As Theo led her to the chair next to his Bethany glanced at Adam who was staring at his wife through narrowed eyes. There was no expression in those eyes— no admiration, no desire, no hatred; nothing.

The atmosphere was light as the meal progressed. Theo was without doubt the centre of attention; a position he so obviously enjoyed.

'Duckling a l'orange?' he commented as the meal was served. 'What no fatted calf?' At which everyone laughed and Grace laughed loudest of all. Bethany noticed how often she leaned across to touch his arm as she spoke to him and how she laughed at quips that were not very funny.

Spirits seemed to thrive in Theo's presence. Bethany wished she could be as enthusiastic about him as the others—not that her opinion mattered she knew, but he was too charming by far and too smooth for her particular taste. Sense told her it was Adam she should distrust, and more than that, dislike. He was the one who had gone out of his way to be unpleasant whilst Theo went out of his way to make everyone happy; yet as they chattered amiably around the table it was Adam who constantly drew her gaze.

The insidious fear she had sensed previously seemed to have receded. Looking at the gathering around the table Bethany saw a normal family—a family with problems like any other, but nothing more sinister. And yet ... and yet ...

'Adam must keep Theo busy,' Esme decreed, 'otherwise he will get bored and leave us again.'

'Oh I can find plenty of work for him to do.'

'Oh for heavens sake!' cried Grace. 'Theo has only just arrived. We have so much to talk about before you take him away from me.' She looked at him as she put one hand over his. 'He's my last link with the civilized world.'

Theo laughed a little uncomfortably. 'There is no reason why I shouldn't find time for everything.' Again his eyes rested on Bethany.

Grace did not miss the gesture; her blue eyes seemed to cloud for a moment and then narrow. 'Theo don't you think it remarkable,' she said, 'that Mrs Ryder should be content to stay here when the others refused to stay more than a few days? Of course the others were elderly. Do you think there is a connection?'

In the infinitesimal silence before Esme said kindly, 'We are very happy to have her here and grateful too,' Bethany steadied herself for another of Grace's attacks, but she could not find it in her heart to blame the woman who was only trying to coax her husband out of his maddening indifference towards her.

'The others left because I wanted them to,' Dina announced and everyone turned to look at her. Becoming the centre of attention was all she needed to spur her on. She smiled triumphantly. 'They all wanted to treat me like a child, so I got rid of them.'

Adam sat back in his chair and studied her seriously. 'Now just how did you manage to do that Dina?'

Dina smiled slyly. 'It was easy. I frightened them away.'

'I don't doubt her ability to do it,' her mother remarked, stifling a yawn.

'I told them all about Jenefer Henekin but I didn't tell Mrs Ryder.'

'Well I don't know what you could have told them that was sufficient to frighten them. away,' Esme remarked.

'I've already heard about the death of that girl,' Bethany put in, glancing hesitantly at Adam who was still looking grave, but not the least bit disturbed by the mention of the girl's name.

'But you don't know the truth,' Dina contradicted,

her mouth drooping sulkily at the threat of being done out of her moment of triumph. 'She was murdered.'

Bethany stopped eating and glanced around the table, not knowing whether to laugh at or reprimand Dina who had definitely gone too far this time. But the disclaimers she expected to hear were not forthcoming. Theo was gazing seriously over his wine glass into space, Grace was picking at her food, Esme continued to stare at Dina whilst Adam heedlessly went on eating.

'You didn't know!' Dina said, 'I knew you didn't.'

'I think we've heard enough,' Esme said, returning to her meal, but Bethany could not tear her gaze away from Dina.

'She was stabbed in the woods a few yards from here.'

Bethany was stunned, stunned into silence. 'Poor Jenefer,' Dina continued, 'can't you just imagine her creeping up the hill for the clandestine meeting in the woods under a full moon?' Her voice dropped to a whisper and through the numbness of her horror Bethany realized what a wonderful actress Dina must be to have claimed everyone's attention. Theo she noticed was crumbling his roll absently into tiny crumbs and Grace was slumped in her chair with one hand across her eyes. Esme and Adam were the only ones who seemed unaffected by the tale; even Bethany found her fingers tightening around the arms of her chair.

And it was as though everyone had stopped breathing —the only sound was the whispering of the wind outside.

'She was waiting unsuspecting at the rendezvous,'

Dina went on, her eyes alight, 'when she heard someone coming through the trees. She turned and her smile became a grimace of horror as the murderer struck with the knife, again and again and again ...'

'Can't someone stop the child!' Grace cried, stirring herself just as Theo made an inarticulate sound deep in his throat. Pushing back his chair he rushed from the room dashing his wine glass to pieces on the floor as he went.

'That's enough now!' Esme snapped, which was enough to subdue Dina.

Grace slumped back in her chair moaning softly, holding one hand to her head. Adam went to her and gently helped her to her feet.

'I'd better get her upstairs,' he said to no one in particular.

Only then did Bethany manage to tear her gaze away from Dina to watch Adam half carry, half support, his wife up the stairs.

'Now look what you've done you bad girl,' Esme scolded. 'The mention of that poor woman always upsets your mother and you know Theo has a weak stomach when it comes to violence. I don't know where you got all this nonsense.'

'I keep my ears and eyes open,' Dina replied with impudence. 'It's not a secret. The papers were full of it. They even took a photograph of me.'

'It will just serve you right if Mrs Ryder leaves us now.'

Dina was unrepentant, that much was clear. She

looked at Bethany and in the look was a challenge. 'I don't think Mrs Ryder is the type to frighten easily.'

'Indeed not,' Bethany said briskly, finding her voice at last. 'Besides Jenefer died two years ago. I see no reason to be afraid now.'

Dina turned her blue eyes, wide and innocent, on Bethany. 'But they never caught the murderer.'

CHAPTER FIVE

The weather kept in tune with Theo's return. The sun shone continuously and became warmer with each passing day. Each day Grace put in an early appearance, often dressed in slacks and a silk shirt with her hair tied back with a blue ribbon. Theo gave her a great deal of his attention, frequently driving her away in his Mini in the morning and not returning until the evening. Sometimes Theo would go off with Adam and when this happened invariably Grace would go too. It was good to see her so happy.

Now Bethany could see how beautiful she must have been when young and her pathetic attachment to Theo proved it was loneliness and lack of attention that was causing her discontent. Bethany felt her anger stir for Adam who could find time to dally with Jenefer Henekin and Sally, and probably countless others, but not his own wife. Guiltily she admonished herself for such feelings; how could she possibly put all the blame on Adam? In truth she did not want to.

The trees were beginning to bud and snowdrops were pushing their way through the barren earth during a period, according to the newspapers, the rest of the country was in the grip of an icy spell. Spring came to the west earlier than anywhere else in the country and although it was an extra bonus of good weather that should be welcomed, Bethany saw it as a warning that Dina would soon be going to school and she would have to leave; and she did not want to leave.

The reason eluded her. Bethany had not made Tregarrick Manor her home, or the people in it her friends. Grace was too unpredictable a person with whom to strike up a friendship, Esme by virtue of her age and standing was as impossible whereas Dina, of course, was nothing more than a perplexing child. As for the men, she hated the way Theo looked at her and the way in which Adam did not and when he did it was disconcerting in its probing intensity. With its strange air of waiting and watching Tregarrick Manor was not a comfortable place to be. But still she did not want to leave.

Bethany was pleased the weather remained fine; it enabled Dina to be outside, which kept her active mind occupied with physical exercise. She was quite happy to wander through the woods acting out plays of her own making, where she would be the beautiful maiden in distress and Bethany would be in turn the hero or the wicked witch.

It was on these occasions that Bethany believed her original judgement, as to Dina having too old a mind for her age, to be wrong and quite the opposite to be correct.

One afternoon just as Bethany was refusing to allow Dina to climb a tree which would serve as Rapunzle's castle they paused to listen to a lusty voice singing, ' 'Twas on a Monday morning that I espied my darling...' just as Theo, his hands in his pockets, came into view.

'It's not Monday!' Dina cried on seeing him. 'But you're just in time. I'm going to be Rapunzle and you can rescue me. Mrs Ryder will be the wicked witch.'

Theo looked at Bethany. 'I don't think Mrs Ryder is a good enough actress for that and I haven't got that much imagination I'm afraid.'

'I saw you go off this morning. Where have you been?' Dina asked, falling into step beside him. Bethany wandered on a little way.

'I've been to Bodmin with your mother little one.'

' "Little one",' she echoed in disgust, 'that's not what you said the other evening...'

Her voice faded. Just ahead of them came the snarling and barking of Hero and Minerva, instantly recognizable as it shattered the peace of the woodland—a sound frequently heard around the manor which invariably turned Bethany's blood into ice.

'What on earth is that?' Theo asked.

Dina rushed forward excitedly, passing Bethany in her haste to get there. 'Hero and Minerva must have caught a trespasser! They'll tear him to pieces. Adam has them well trained.'

'Nice of him,' Theo muttered softly and then he smiled mischievously and lifted his shoulders slightly before he and Bethany followed Dina towards the place from where the noise was coming.

They didn't have far to go; a few yards further on Dina was standing, watching with horrified fascination as Hero and Minerva pulled a rabbit to pieces with their razor sharp fangs.

Bethany took one long, appalled look before turning to Theo. 'Pull them off!'

His face paled. 'Not me. They'd pull me to pieces instead. Better let them have their sport.' He turned to smile at her. 'You fool!' he shouted as she dashed forward.

Hurling herself on to the two hounds she pulled at their fur in a useless attempt to pull them away from the little animal.

'Hero! Minerva!' At the sound of Adam's peremptory command the hounds, with one last growl, dropped the rabbit and slunk away with their tails between their legs.

'Why on earth did you let her do it?' he demanded of his brother, but Theo was staring white-faced at the bloody remains of the rabbit.

With one final look of disgust he turned his attention to Bethany who, suddenly weak with the belated realization of what she had done, was sitting on a tree stump.

'That was a damned stupid thing to do.'

As she looked up at him her eyes filled with tears. 'I know,' she said, 'but I couldn't stand by and watch. It was horrible.'

'You were marvellous,' Dina cried, her eyes bright with admiration. 'You must be very fond of animals.'

Bethany looked up at her stifling a silly hysterical giggle that was rising inside her. 'Not particularly.' She looked down and noticed that her coat sleeve had been torn.

'You've been bitten,' Adam said, seeing it at the same time.

She touched it with shaking fingers. 'No, the material was too thick.' Despite her protestation he pushed her sleeve back and only when he was satisfied she was not hurt did he let it slip down again.

'You don't look well Mrs Ryder,' Dina said, hovering anxiously nearby. 'I think it was a magnificent thing to do even if it was only a rabbit.' She turned to stare at the remains again, remarkably unperturbed at such a gruesome sight.

'It's nothing a good strong drink wouldn't cure,' her step-father remarked looking around for Theo who had gone a little way away out of sight of the rabbit and was physically relieving his feelings.

'Come on Theo!' Adam shouted across to him. 'You won't refuse a drink and this is a splendid excuse for one.'

Bethany was profoundly sorry for Theo who was such a handsome man to humiliate himself in this way. Without a word he stumbled past them and went towards the house as if no one else was there.

'Poor Uncle Theo,' Dina murmured, suppressing a giggle. 'Fancy being sick because of that.'

Adam put out his hand to help Bethany to her feet. She allowed him to assist her up and although their contact was only a fleeting one she felt his strength as his hand closed over hers, squeezing it tightly. Weakness enfolded her again; she could not look into his face for fear of what she would see in his eyes.

She looked instead at Hero and Minerva, panting heavily a few yards away as they eyed the carcass of the rabbit.

'I wouldn't advise you to intervene again in such circumstances,' he warned. 'They're trained to attack and what you did was very dangerous.'

Bethany looked at him then. 'Don't worry I wouldn't dream of it. Why do you keep such vicious brutes?'

He stared ahead of him. 'Someone was killed here two years ago and the murderer was never caught. I'm often away from the house and I owe it to the women to give them some protection. We'd better get back.'

He strode off in the same direction as Theo followed by Dina and Bethany. Once out of sight the snarling of the dogs could be heard again; Bethany knew they would be sharing the rabbit and involuntarily she shuddered at the thought.

When they reached the clearing Theo was nonchalantly leaning against his car and drinking straight from a bottle of whisky. Still shaken from her experience Bethany marvelled at his powers of recuperation. On seeing them approach he dived into the car and came out with another bottle, offering it to Bethany.

Adam strode over and snatched it out of his hand, demanding angrily, 'Where did these come from?'

'Brought them from Bodmin.'

'We don't need them in bulk here!' Adam said angrily, thrusting it back at him.

'They're not mine old boy,' Theo replied with a lazy smile. 'I got them for Grace. Couldn't refuse such a pretty plea.'

Bethany watched fearfully as Adam's colour heightened under his permanent tan and Theo added, 'Well you know how it is Adam.'

Without waiting to hear more she took Dina, who was enjoying the exchange and absorbing every word, by the arm and hurried her inside. By the time she closed the door Adam had gone and Theo was taking another swallow from the bottle. There was a strange, mocking smile on his face and Bethany suddenly had the feeling she was seeing an entirely different side of him.

The fair weather continued and it appeared that the quarrel Adam had had with Theo had passed over.

'Oh don't let's go to the village this afternoon,' Dina begged one day.

'Where else would you like to go?'

'My favourite place on the moors. I'll show you.' Bethany looked doubtful and Dina added, 'It's not far.'

There was no path as a guide but Dina seemed to know where she was going. She scrambled along over gorse and bracken, her bronze hair flying in the wind, and a little breathlessly and less sure-footed Bethany followed. As they climbed higher the wind grew stronger, at times almost tearing their breath away as

they spoke. But the view, reaching to the next county,
was magnificent and worth the climb.

If Dina had been in the habit of wandering so far
from home Bethany did not wonder her family had
wanted someone to keep her company.

By the time she caught up with Dina she was standing
by a great mound at the top of the hill, her hair blown
into a fiery halo around her head, her trousered legs
astride and her arms akimbo. Her deep blue eyes were
fixed on the distant horizon. She looked so beautiful
that Bethany was startled and as Dina turned to smile at
her she was sure the girl was fully aware of her own
allure.

'Marvellous view isn't it?'

The moors rolled away to every side of them, a
never-ending jigsaw of purple, green and brown.
Barren and desolate; windswept and storm driven; un-
changing for thousands of years past and for thousands
of years to come.

'I've never seen such a view,' Bethany agreed.

'This is where I was the day you arrived but I dare
not tell Grandmother or she would forbid me to come.
When I'm here it's like being nowhere else on earth. It's
all mine; I'm the Queen and now I'm sharing it with
you.'

Bethany smiled feeling quite moved. Dina walked
over to the mound. 'Do you know what this is?' she
asked, still in her Queen mood.

'Your castle?' Bethany offered.

'Of course not. It's a barrow—a burial mound.'

Bethany, who had thrown herself wearily on the ground, looked at her sharply. 'Really it is. Three thousand years ago the people who lived around here—probably where the manor is now—buried the ashes of their dead in here. Two years ago some archaeologists came to excavate it but they decided it wasn't important enough to warrant the trouble and they left. That was just about the time Jenefer was killed. Some said the spriggans were angry because the archaeologists had disturbed them and that was why she died, and others said that one of the archaeologists had done it.'

.'You don't believe that—about the spriggans?'

Dina laughed delightedly. 'Of course I don't. And the archaeologists had gone by then so that let's them out. Do you know what Adam said?'

Bethany shook her head, looking away for fear that her confusion at the sound of his name would be noticed by the perceptive child.

Dina laughed again. 'He said it must have been a tramp who was passing through the district.'

'That is the most likely explanation,' Bethany said hesitantly, guiltily aware that she shouldn't be encouraging Dina in discussing the murder, but she could not deny her own curiosity.

'He knows it wasn't a tramp, as everyone knows it wasn't a tramp. She wasn't married but she was expecting a child. She had a lover.'

Bethany stared at her, remembering Mrs Arkill's words; Jenefer had been pregnant and she believed Adam was the father.

'Really Dina you must control your imagination,' she said sharply, not wanting to think about the implications but realizing there was another explanation for her presence in the woods that night. An unwanted baby, a threatened scandal...

'It is not imagination,' came the indignant reply, 'I know who did it.'

Bethany looked at her again and Dina said, 'Oh don't worry, I'm not going to tell you. I told the others and that was why they left not because of my story about how Jenefer died. They didn't believe me either, so I'm not going to tell anyone again. I saw them from my window that night. I know *who* did it and *why*. There's bound to be another murder and when that happens I still won't tell!'

Brushing away her angry tears Dina tossed her hair back and plunged down the hill.

'Dina! Come back!' Bethany stumbled to her feet. Her voice was carried away by the wind and after a moment's pause, hoping that Dina would come back, she began to run after her. Realizing Dina's sense of the dramatic might impel her to do something silly Bethany could only hope to overtake her, but it was impossible; Dina knew the moors and was more nimble and sure-footed.

Her breath rasped painfully in her throat and her heart hammered loudly in her chest. Thankfully she neared the bottom of the hill only to land almost on top of a chestnut roan. She jerked to a standstill gasping at the sudden shock of encounter, for sitting astride the roan was Adam and holding the harness quite calmly was Dina.

Feeling more than a little foolish she said, 'So there you are Dina.'

Adam looked from one to the other. 'Have you been running away Dina?' he demanded harshly.

Dina lowered her eyes but said nothing and he looked to Bethany as she feared he might.

'Why did she run from you?' he asked.

Bethany smiled in a way she hoped was nonchalant. 'It was something I said. It was all very silly.' She could hardly tell him of their conversation or her own conclusion.

He looked at Dina again and Bethany noticed the tightening of a muscle at the corner of his mouth. 'If I catch you running off like this again Dina I shall see you don't leave the house for a week. Is that understood?'

Sulkily, Dina pulled a scarf she had used to tie back her hair from her head and pulled it taut between her fingers. Her hair tumbled to her shoulders and she flicked it back with a defiant toss of her head.

She glanced up at him. 'You can't do that. I'm not a child and you're not my father!'

The muscle tightened again and saying, 'Try it again Dina and you'll find out what I can do,' he dug his heels into the roan's side and cantered away.

Dina turned to Bethany who saw she was entirely unsubdued, 'Did I scare you?'

Ignoring her she replied, 'Don't do that again Dina.'

Dina laughed. 'I bet you thought I would do something drastic, didn't you? Did you think they would find my body floating down the stream? And you would have spent the rest of your life regretting you doubted me.'

'I think you talk a great deal too much. If you run off again I shall tell your step-father and he's already told you what he will do.'

Dina laughed again. 'You won't tell him,' she said and her eyes were mocking.

As Bethany looked into their knowing depths she said roughly, 'I certainly will.' And as Dina just went on smiling in that cunning way Bethany had to look away first.

'Come on then, I'll show you another of my favourite places.'

Realizing, ruefully, that the girl was entirely incorrigible Bethany followed her.

'I liked Jenefer you know,' Dina said as they walked through the woods. 'She always treated me as an equal not as a child.'

Bethany stared, incredulous. 'You knew her?'

Dina twisted the scarf in her hands over and over again. 'Yes I knew her well. She was always around the house.'

'Why was that?'

Dina smiled impishly. 'Don't you know? Well I'm not going to tell you.'

Bethany began to walk more briskly, the fresh air heightening her colour. Dina hurried to keep in step.

'She used to give me money to keep quiet. Not that I'd tell on her. I like knowing people's secrets; it gives me a certain power over them and because they just regard me as a child they say things they wouldn't normally say when anyone else is around. And I always listen and learn.'

'You shouldn't listen to conversations,' Bethany pointed out, more disturbed than she would have liked to admit.

'You are stuffy today,' chided Dina, dancing excitedly ahead. 'It must have been that encounter with Adam.'

When Bethany caught up with her she was standing in a glade by the steam.

'Isn't it lovely?' she said.

Bethany looked around her in amazement. She had never visited this part of the woods before. The ground was a solid mass of snowdrops and bluebells on a carpet of green. The stream tumbled its way downwards under a hump-backed bridge. No sky could be seen through the overhanging boughs of the trees that had recently exploded into green. And as she listened the air was completely still and there was silence.

'It's amazing,' Bethany said with a laugh. 'It's so different to the rest of the woods.'

'It is amazing,' Dina agreed, standing on the little bridge and waving her scarf dramatically. 'This is where Jenefer died.'

The silence was suddenly oppressive. Dina peered unconcernedly over the parapet into the stream gurgling below. 'She used to meet him here.'

'I think we should get back,' Bethany said hurriedly.

'She was waiting on the bridge just like this,' Dina went on. Her eyes were wide and staring and Bethany knew there would be no stopping her until she had finished her story.

'Then she heard a twig crack and another as someone approached. She turned smiling to greet her lover. But the smile became a grimace of horror as the murderer struck, plunging the knife into her breast until there was nothing but torn flesh and bloodstained rags.' Her voice dropped. 'The knife never was found.'

Although she was used to Dina's dramatic narratives, in the quiet of the glade as Dina enacted out the murder with her expressive voice, Bethany listened in fascination.

'There was a trail of blood from the bridge to the edge of the stream where Jenefer ran as she tried to escape,' Dina added in a more normal way, her voice devoid of any emotion. 'They say the stream ran red that day.'

Without a word Bethany turned and walked away from that beautiful and terrible place. Now at last she knew why there was that strange atmosphere in the house; it was the presence of a murderer in their midst

CHAPTER SIX

It was imperative to get Dina away from the house, Bethany decided that evening as she changed for dinner. At her most impressionable age Dina was learning that alcoholism, adultery and murder were normal, even desirable, components of family life and that a young man with good looks and a charming manner was to be admired even though he also happened to be feckless and indolent.

The problem as Bethany saw it was whom to approach with the problem; Adam was the obvious choice but for even more obvious reasons she could not tell him why she thought Dina should go back to school. Grace, she reckoned, would not be interested enough to listen; she was quite satisfied that responsibility for Dina was shouldered by others leaving her time to enjoy Theo's company, or drink.

It was during dinner that she decided to speak to Esme Tregarrick as soon as she could. She could hardly steel herself to behave normally towards Adam and was grateful that he rarely gave her occasion to speak to him, although as always she sensed his scrutiny on several occasions. She wondered what he was thinking when he looked at her and the answer gave her both pain and pleasure.

As he gave his amused attention to his step-daughter Bethany was amazed at how at ease Dina was in the company of her family. She was a most remarkable child to believe she knew who had killed Jenefer and yet be able to behave quite normally in his or her presence. Even more remarkable was the fact that the killer was a member of her own family.

Bethany looked at each in turn unable to understand how the one who had wielded the knife could eat, talk and drink like anyone else. Yet looking at Hero and Minerva peacefully sitting at the fireside it was hard to believe they too had been responsible for the merciless destruction of another creature.

Grace drank deeply of the dinner wine and by the end of the meal was quite merry, announcing that she was going to bed early and collapsing into a fit of hysterical laughter. Sally, smiling in that sly way of hers was called to escort her to bed; Adam it seemed had lost interest in her entirely.

He picked up his glass and walked over to the fireplace. Bethany watched him as he went, a far more impressive man than Theo for all his good looks, and she found herself wondering unwillingly what it would be like to be loved by such a man; to be held by those strong hands against that broad chest. Finding out would be so easy she was sure.

Without realizing it she had been staring at him and as if sensing her eyes on him he levelled his gaze to hers and then smiling slowly he raised his glass in salute.

Hurriedly she got up from the table. 'May I speak to you alone when Dina is in bed?' she asked Esme in a low voice.

Esme's eyes narrowed quizzically and then she said, 'Of course my dear; I shall wait in the sitting-room but don't make it too late will you? I'm rather tired.'

Theo, now his verbal sparring partner had gone to bed, was restlessly prowling around the room. 'I think I shall go out for a breath of fresh air before I turn in,' he announced.

No one answered him and Bethany quickly shepherded Dina up the stairs. When they reached the top, unaccountably, she turned. Theo opened the door and a chill draught swept through the hall. Bethany looked down at Adam who at that moment was staring thoughtfully at the daggers displayed on the wall over the fireplace.

'I'm far too old to be taken to bed at this time,' Dina protested.

'We all go to bed early when we're in the country,' Bethany told her, her mind still occupied. What had Dina said about the knife? It had never been found. How easy it would be to wash it free of blood and replace it where it had always belonged. Why else had she felt so chilled when Adam stared at those daggers? She had done it herself on so many occasions.

Dina was at her most difficult refusing to get undressed and Bethany was hardly able to do it for her. Finally she agreed to get into bed as long as she could stay awake and read.

Sighing with relief Bethany closed the door and went along the balcony and down the stairs. The lights had been extinguished and she steeled herself to walk the length of the hall. Now knowing about the murder made her inexplicable dread of the place more real. As she passed the fireplace her eyes were drawn to the display of weapons; had she always sensed the murder weapon was there?

'I've been waiting to see you alone.'

She spun round to see Theo extricate himself from a chair. He had been sitting in that chair all the time; he had been watching her since she came down the stairs.

'You've gone as white as a sheet,' he said with a laugh. 'Don't tell me Dina's rubbish has affected the sensible Mrs Ryder.'

'I wouldn't tell you anything,' she replied hardly able to contain her anger at such a schoolboy prank. 'Just don't try that on someone who may have a weak heart.'

She moved to pass him but he put a hand on her shoulder. 'I really did frighten you didn't I?'

'Yes you really did,' she answered, realizing he couldn't begin to imagine how much.

'I'm sorry; I really am.' He grinned engagingly in the half-light and went across to the switch, illuminating the hall once more. 'I've never really grown up, that's my trouble.' He came back over to her. 'I only did it because I wanted to see you, for once not surrounded by my family.'

'Your mother is in the sitting-room waiting for me. I must go in to her.'

He put a friendly arm around her shoulder. 'I won't keep you a minute,' he said softly, his lips uncomfortably close to her ear. 'I wouldn't want you to neglect your duty.'

She squirmed slightly but was reluctant to push him away for she did not want to cause an unpleasant scene.

'When is your free time?' he asked in a voice as soft as silk as his lips brushed her ear.

'I don't have any; I don't need it.' Her voice came in breathless gasps. What on earth is wrong with me? she thought. Here I am with one of the most attractive men I have ever met and all I want to do is escape him.

'But you're entitled to have days off. How about taking one and we'll go into Bodmin.' He laughed. 'It's not exactly the centre of "La Dolce Vita" but we can have a meal and take our time getting back.'

'No thank you Mr Tregarrick. I don't think you would enjoy my company.'

He squeezed her so tightly she squirmed. 'I'm sure I would enjoy your company very much. You're a most unusual woman and I want to learn more about you.'

She tried to move away again but he kept her close and she could feel his warm breath on her neck. 'Surely you don't find life at Tregarrick Manor so exciting that you'd refuse the chance of an evening out?' he asked, his voice almost a caress. 'You don't find me repulsive do you?'

'Not at all. I think you're a very good-looking man, and a conceited one too.'

He began to laugh. 'You *are* unusual Bethany and I

am going to have my date with you.'

'Perhaps you're not aware that my husband died very recently.'

'I think you've mourned him long enough,' he said smoothly. 'You're too young to wear widow's weeds for ever.' He paused for a moment before adding, 'Besides I rather suspect you haven't mourned him at all.'

'I've been waiting for you for some time Mrs Ryder.'

Theo released her abruptly and, flushing guiltily in case Esme Tregarrick had witnessed the encounter and believed she was encouraging her precious son, Bethany hurried over to her.

Esme was not pleased at seeing them together, this much Bethany knew, but as they went into the sitting-room the old lady was as gracious as ever.

'What is it you wish to say Mrs Ryder?' she asked, lacing her bony fingers together in her lap.

Suddenly Bethany did not know what to say and it was only after Esme had prompted, 'Well Mrs Ryder?' that she blurted, 'I think Dina should go back to school immediately.'

Esme Tregarrick's eyebrows rose slightly. 'Indeed? So you've decided Tregarrick Manor is not to your liking after all. You wish to leave us already?'

'No, it's nothing like that Mrs Tregarrick,' she paused and then said bluntly, 'Do you know why the other women you employed to look after Dina left so suddenly?'

Mrs Tregarrick gave an infinitesimal shrug. 'Probably

because we're too isolated or because Dina is rather ...
difficult at times.'

'Mrs Tregarrick,' Bethany said with some difficulty,
'the reason they left so hurriedly was because Dina
told them not only about the murder but who did it.'

Esme Tregarrick looked startled and then she smiled,
'And who did do it?'

'She didn't tell me.'

Esme sat back in her chair. 'Why hasn't one of these
women sent the police to see us? Surely one of them
would?'

'Dina said they didn't believe her and that was why
she wouldn't tell me.'

'They had more sense than you,' Esme said, not
unkindly, and seeing the dismay on Bethany's face she
explained, 'Dina is at a very awkward age Mrs Ryder.
Her mother, unfortunately, is unable to give her the
attention she is due ... that all adolescents need. She is
also very imaginative and a talented actress, as you've
no doubt realized; we're quite used to her startling us
with dramatic statements. I don't think it's unusual.
Can't you remember the fantasies you had when you
were her age? I can and I'm a good deal older than
you.'

Bethany leaned forward eagerly, clenching her hands
tensely. 'But the way she described the murder Mrs
Tregarrick, I'm convinced she was in the woods that
night and saw it all.'

Esme listened gravely and then said, 'When that poor
child was killed the details were in every newspaper for

weeks and the police reconstructed the crime several times. Dina was not a child and she is very intelligent. The fact the girl was pregnant and the crime was a particularly lurid one has appealed to her imagination. It's as simple as that. My own personal view is that the girl was murdered by a vagrant who happened upon her as she was waiting for her lover and as *he* was probably a married man he feared to come forward when she was killed. The girl had been involved with several men I understand.'

'Why was she waiting so close to Tregarrick Manor?' Bethany asked sharply.

'These woods have always been a meeting place for sweethearts; there is nowhere else in the area. Since the trouble Adam has bought the hounds to discourage people from coming up here.'

Bethany agreed it was all so simple; Dina had found her receptive to her dramatic visions.

'All the same Mrs Tregarrick I still think Dina should be sent to school. There are too many disturbing influences here. She needs the more normal company of other girls and the discipline of school.'

Esme smiled ruefully. 'You're talking about her mother I gather when you speak of disturbing influences.' Bethany looked away in confusion and Esme said quickly, 'I'm inclined to agree with you but I'm afraid Dina cannot go back to school until the summer term at the earliest.' As Bethany began to say something Esme continued, 'Dina, although she appears otherwise, is rather prone to virus infections. Dr. Sanderson insisted that she remains here to recover completely—our climate is mild and the country air is good for her.'

'But she is perfectly well now.'

'The moment she returns to school she is liable to infection and Dr Sanderson feels it would be a serious matter if she were to be taken ill again so soon after the last time. Neither you nor I can argue against qualified medical opinion.'

Bethany nodded, realizing she was defeated. 'Of course not. I didn't realize the full facts.'

'You meant well,' Esme said kindly. 'I appreciate you have Dina's interests at heart. It is most comforting. But if I were to go to Dr Sanderson and give him those reasons for sending Dina back to school before she is really well I'm afraid he would not be very sympathetic.' She got to her feet to signal the end of the discussion and Bethany did likewise. 'And you must remember Mrs Ryder,' she added as they went into the hall, 'Dina has lived here amongst us since she was six years old, so I don't think a few more weeks will harm her, do you?'

When she reached her room the door was slightly ajar and a light shone through. Rather gingerly Bethany pushed it open further and as she did so her hesitancy was replaced by exasperation; Dina was searching through her drawers.

She pushed open the door startling the girl who looked up and said with a laugh, 'What a fright you gave me.'

'It's less than you deserve,' Bethany replied, glancing around the room. 'Have you seen enough?'

'Don't be angry with me Mrs Ryder; I didn't mean to pry. I came in to ask you something and when you weren't here I sat down to wait—only you were gone so long.'

Bethany glared at her. 'So you started to look around? Have you uncovered all my dark secrets?'

Dina had the grace to look ashamed. 'When I looked around the room I realized it was strange that you didn't have a photograph of your husband on view so I looked for it.'

Tight-lipped Bethany strode across to the bed and pulled a suitcase from beneath. Kneeling on the floor she unlocked it, and after delving around inside for a few moments, she brought out a framed photograph and pushed it at Dina. The photograph, the only one of Johnny she possessed, had been taken on their wedding day and both of them were smiling into the camera in a rather self-conscious way.

Still angry she said, 'So now you know I really was married to him, or would you like to see my marriage lines. They're in here somewhere together with the death certificate—or is your dirty little mind satisfied?'

Dina looked at the photograph for a moment or two before passing it back. 'I'm sorry,' she said.

Bethany softened. 'You'd better get back to bed now.'

The girl looked at her. 'I feel awful asking you this Mrs Ryder, especially after what I've done but would you do something for me?'

Bethany put the photograph back in the suitcase and pushed it back under the bed. 'What is it you want?'

'You know that scarf I was wearing today?'

'Yes...' Bethany answered thoughtfully.

'Well I think I've left it in the glade.'

'Oh Dina that is very careless.' She became impatient again. The day had proved to be somewhat tense and her unsuccessful interview with Esme Tregarrick had not helped.

'I know that, but I did. Do you think ... would you get it for me.'

'Now? But that's ridiculous Dina. It's a fine night and if it is there it will come to no harm before morning.'

Dina put her hand on Bethany's arm. '*Please* Mrs Ryder. It's not mine you see. I borrowed it from Mummy's room and if she finds out she'll be furious. I took it without her permission. She hates my borrowing her things. Oh please get it for me. I promise I'll never borrow anything without asking ever again.'

Bethany crossed to the window. 'It's dark out there Dina. I'll never find it.'

Smiling mischievously Dina brought a small electric torch from her dressing gown pocket and on seeing Bethany's suspicious expression she said, 'It's all right; it's mine. We use them at school for reading or talking in the dorm. after lights out. Besides there's a moon tonight.'

Doubtfully Bethany looked out of the window again but this time her attention was riveted on a movement near the trees. A shadow moved swiftly across the clearing towards the house and out of sight. It happened so quickly she had no chance to see if it was a man or a woman, or indeed if it was anyone at all; most likely it was a cloud crossing in front of the moon. But as she glanced upwards she saw a cloudless sky full of shimmering stars.

'You will go won't you Mrs Ryder?'

Bethany still hesitated but then acquiesced. She came across the room and took the torch from the girl. As she brought her coat from the wardrobe she said, 'You wait here until I come back. And,' she added, 'I shall expect you to keep that promise.'

The hounds were still lying in front of the fire and Bethany was relieved they had not been set loose outside, even though they were used to her. As she passed one of them stirred, raised its ears and growled before settling back to sleep.

The moon gave adequate light so she kept the torch in her pocket, pulling her coat tightly around her. It was still cool at night even when the wind ceased to blow, which was not very often. Somewhere an owl hooted and as she entered the woods a breeze whispered softly through the new leaves.

She stopped abruptly feeling eyes upon her. Trying to control the mounting panic she swung around to come face to face with the unblinking stare of the owl she had heard. Smiling to herself she moved on and the owl hooted gently behind her.

She knew she had been silly to give in to Dina's pleas —going into these woods at night was an ordeal she could do without—but the girl had been really distressed.

She brought the torch out of her pocket and played the beam on to the path ahead until it picked out the flash of blue. Triumphantly she snatched it up and extinguished the beam. For a second or two she stood motionless. The woods seemed almost to be alive. She was not afraid but awe-struck at the repose of the night. The sound of the wind through the trees was almost like the whispering of human voices.

She hesitated before turning back and then she heard the sound; a very recognizable one—Sally's lazy laugh. As if riveted to the ground Bethany stood there listening and when she realized what she was hearing her curiosity turned to revulsion—the whisperings were unmistakably the sounds of two people making love.

It took her only seconds to run from the woods to the house and when she had closed the thick oak door behind her she stood against it sobbing into her hands. The knowledge of what was happening out there in the woods affected her far more profoundly than knowing about the murder.

She lost track of time entirely. At last her sobs subsided and taking a deep breath she went back through the hall—for once heedless of its darkness—and up to her room. Dina was waiting anxiously as Bethany pushed the scarf and the torch into her hands.

'Oh thank you!' She kissed her cheek impetuously. 'I thought you'd got lost, you were such a long time. You weren't frightened were you?'

Bethany shook her head and Dina said slyly. 'There's no ghost—more's the pity. Jenefer hasn't come back to haunt us—at least not yet. It would make everything so much more interesting if we had a ghost. One of the girls at school has one in her house. A woman beheaded by the order of the Virgin Queen. Annabel—that's my friend—says the ghost walks headless and lots of people have seen her. Only she hasn't.'

Bethany sank down on to the bed. 'Please Dina! I'm very tired.'

'I'm a selfish beast,' she said going to the door. 'It's just that I need so little sleep. Good night Mrs Ryder.'

The moment Dina had gone Bethany rushed over to the door and turned the key in the lock. She had to get out of this evil and malignant house before she went insane!

Dragging her empty suitcase from the top of the wardrobe she began to throw things in haphazardly and it was not until it was almost full that she realized there was nowhere she could go at such an hour. And if she could she knew she would not leave Dina now. Bethany was convinced Dina did know something about the murder of Jenefer Henekin and if she were rash enough to boast of it to anyone else she would be in danger herself. No, she could not leave now with an easy mind. Like it or not she had become inextricably involved with the Tregarricks—something she had vowed not to do.

Wearily she removed all her clothes from the suitcase and replaced it on top of the wardrobe as the wind

outside increased in strength, whistling angrily around
the eaves and rattling the old windows. It seemed to be
mocking her, echoing Sally's intimate laughter in her
ears. She recalled the way Adam had gripped her hand
the day the hounds had killed the rabbit and she wondered if it were a prelude to an invitation. Was he
tiring of Sally, or did he want them both?

She removed her coat at last and began to undress
slowly. Wearing only her slip she examined her reflection critically in the mirror. She saw nothing that
would attract a man. A figure that was too thin, a face
neither plain nor pretty. Even Johnny had not loved
her as she longed to be loved. In each other they had
found the antidote to a personal loneliness. They were
two people with a similar need—or so she had thought.
Now she knew it was not true. With all his kindness and
companionship Johnny had given her nothing she really
needed; not even the child she had craved, and certainly
not the love.

'Of course we will have children,' he had said so
many times when she had broached the subject, 'but
when we do we'll need a house and I just can't afford
that yet. But I am getting well known in the trade and I
can't afford to let up yet awhile. And it's not fair to
bring a child into the world when you can't offer it
security.' He would put his arm around her and squeeze
her tightly in the way that would leave her icy cold.
'You're young yet Bethany and besides I'm selfish
enough to want my wife with me wherever I go. I'd
hardly see you otherwise.'

As she slipped into bed she could not rid her mind of the sounds she had heard, of Sally's sly smile and ripe body, and of Adam smiling down at her.

It was no use; she could not sleep. She turned her bedside clock to face her; it was only one o'clock. It seemed as though a lifetime had passed since dinner. She slipped out of bed and put on her dressing gown. The house was silent except for the whistling of the wind outside. Without making a sound in her slippered feet she crept downstairs; a warm glass of milk should help.

As she neared the kitchen the sound of raised voices told her she was not the only member of the household still awake. Through the half open door she could see Grace unsteadily in the centre of the kitchen floor and facing her at the other side of the table was Sally wearing a dress that revealed her well-developed curves all too well.

'You keep away from him do you hear?' Grace shouted, her voice more slurred than it had been when she had gone to bed.

'You be unwell Mrs Tregarrick. Let me put you to bed.'

'I'm not going anywhere until you've promised not to see him again. I'm staying right here until you do.'

'I'm sure I don't know what you mean ma'am.'

'You needn't lie. I saw you with my own eyes. You shameless little slut!'

Sally's eyes narrowed. 'I be young ma'am. You be old and he be tired of you.'

'There's nothing you can give him that I can't,' Grace screamed swaying unsteadily. 'A common little country girl with no manners or breeding. Nothing more than a coarse-tongued harlot!'

She paused for breath and Sally preened herself. 'You think so do you?'

'You just leave him alone.'

Sally turned away from her. 'Can't do that ma'am. What if he don't stay away from me?'

Grace's face contorted into a grimace of rage and as she stumbled across the kitchen throwing aside a chair in her haste Bethany pushed open the door and stepped inside. Sally turned, startled to see someone else in the room, and as she did so Grace flung herself on the girl hurling her against the wall with all her drunken strength. Her scarlet nails raked the girl's face whilst she was still stunned into inaction.

'You filthy little animal!' Grace raged, pulling at Sally's hair. 'Slut, wanton!'

Recovering quickly Sally fought her off and Grace was thrown back against the table which she held on to to stop herself from falling.

Sally's eyes flashed with contempt and anger. 'Slut and wanton I may be but I be more of a woman than you Grace Tregarrick! No man wants an alcohol ridden old hag like you. A home is where they'll have to put you before long. Just you wait and see.'

With an agonized snarl Grace launched herself against Sally again and stifling the disgust she felt at seeing two women fighting over a man like a pair of she-cats

Bethany ran forward and pulled Grace away. Expecting to have to fight her off herself Bethany was surprised when Grace collapsed against her weeping bitterly.

'You'll feel better for some sleep Mrs Tregarrick,' she said soothingly, putting her arm around Grace's waist and leading her towards the door.

Suddenly she stirred from her sobbing and shrugged Bethany away. She turned to face Sally again, her deep blue eyes filled with concentrated hate.

'If I see you with him again I shall kill you,' she said quite clearly and almost stumbling over the trailing hem of her dressing gown she rushed from the kitchen.

It was not until she crept back into her own chilly bed that Bethany realized she had not fetched the milk she had gone for but nothing would induce her to go back for it. She pulled the covers around her ears and suddenly stiffening she lay absolutely still as her ears strained to hear a shrill cry followed by an abrupt silence. Without thinking she leapt from her bed and out into the corridor waiting for the others to appear at their doors. But no one did. The lights were out and silence prevailed.

Going back into her room she crept into bed and pulled the covers about her ears once more. Perhaps it had been the cry of a bird, she mused. But what bird made a noise like that? No it had been made by a human being and, she was convinced, inside the house. So someone else must have heard it. Why then did no one come to investigate? As she snuggled down the

bed the chilling realization came to her—Jenefer Henekin must have screamed before she died. No one
investigated then either.

CHAPTER SEVEN

She slept badly when she finally did sleep and was woken by someone banging repeatedly at her door. Finally she roused herself to see Dina's face peering at her.

'I thought you must be dead,' she said. 'You took ages to come round.'

Bethany eased herself up on her elbow. 'Did I oversleep very late? I must have done if you're up and dressed.'

'Oh I've been up ages. I'm going into Bodmin with Grandmother and Theo.' She went over to the window and pulled back the curtains. Immediately Bethany saw the tell-tale splashes on the panes and the incessant pitter-patter of the rain. 'Foul day for a journey isn't it?'

Bethany agreed, getting out of bed and going over to the washbasin. Dina perched on the edge of the bed and watched her.

'You're not coming to Bodmin with us. Adam wants to speak to you. I'm being got out of the way.'

Bethany peered warily at Dina over the towel. 'What does he want with me?'

Dina shrugged. 'Don't ask me. I'm always the last to

be told. But there is something going on. For one thing Sally's left. But don't worry I shall find out. I always do.'

Bethany stared at her, the towel dropped to the floor. 'Sally's gone? But when?'

Dina shrugged again and Bethany turned away, her mind in a maelstrom. She didn't believe for one minute Sally had left. But if she hadn't? What then?

Aware of Dina's innate ability to sense an 'atmosphere' Bethany smiled brightly as she dressed. 'Are you going to do some shopping in Bodmin?'

Dina was by the dressing table examining the brushes carefully. 'I expect so. Grandmother says I need some new shoes and clothes for school. They'll all be mud brown and plain ugly so you'll have to excuse me if I don't get excited.'

Bethany smiled to herself and secretly sympathized with the girl who would soon leave her beautiful clothes behind for a school uniform. 'Your smart clothes will still be here when you come back for the holidays and you'll appreciate wearing them all the more. You'll be having lunch out too,' she added.

'Oh yes a special treat for the child.'

'It sounds a very nice outing just the same.'

Dina picked up Bethany's lipstick and peering into the mirror smoothed it along her already adequately pinked lips. 'We won't have any time for real shopping because Grandmother has an appointment with Dr Sanderson this morning. She has a weak heart. She says I might as well come too as he wants to see me before I go back to school, but I'm not going back to school just yet so it proves it all an excuse to get me out of the house.'

Bethany removed the lipstick from her fingers. 'You're a very suspicious girl Dina. You can't expect to have good relationships with people if you always suspect their motives.'

Dina went over to the door and opened it. 'That's because their motives are all suspect. Except for yours of course but you're not one of us so you don't count. See you when I get back.'

She popped her head back a moment later. 'By the way I returned Mummy's scarf this morning. She'll never know I had it. She was sound asleep when I went in. Honestly it's no wonder Adam sleeps next door with the way she snores.' Her nose wrinkled. 'I hope I don't snore or I'll never get a man.'

After Dina had finally gone Bethany stared at the closed door for a minute, shocked at the revelation that Adam and Grace did not share the same room, yet at the same time unsurprised.

When she went downstairs the hounds were prowling around the hall which indicated that their master was still at home. There was no one at the table. The coffee was still warm so she helped herself to some and to some hard toast rather than ring for Mrs Penarvon who would be very busy now that Sally had gone. She frowned. So far she had put Sally's disappearance to the back of her mind but despite that the problem was worrying her. Absently she handed some scraps to the hounds who were standing expectantly by the chair.

She would have to find out.

A sound behind her caused her to turn sharply; Adam was coming down the stairs, his arms encircling two empty whisky bottles and a third half full. Bethany thought he looked tired but then realized, scornfully, he had reason to be.

He came across the hall followed by the hounds snuffling eagerly at his heels. He put the bottles on the table with a gesture of a very weary man.

'It's amazing,' he said, 'however many bottles I take away they're replaced almost immediately and she always finds new hiding places for them.' He looked at her then and smiled. 'It's no use pretending is it? She's not ill; she doesn't just enjoy a few drinks or getting merry. My wife is a hopeless alcoholic.'

With one flick of his hand he sent the bottles spinning across the table.

Bethany got to her feet. 'Dina tells me you want to speak to me.'

He straightened up and went across to the fireplace. 'Sally has left; I expect you've heard.'

'Yes. I'm surprised. I saw her here quite late last night.'

He looked at her in surprise. 'You saw her?'

Bethany could hardly repress a bitter smile. She imagined herself saying, 'Oh yes, she was fighting with your wife.'

'Over what Mrs Ryder?' he would say.

'Over you Mr Tregarrick.' Oh no. She couldn't.

Instead she straightened the bottles on the table. 'She

said nothing about leaving, yet one would imagine she knew then. It was very late.'

He appeared to be considering this information and then, a moment later, he said, 'The fact remains that she *has* left and I can't say I'm sorry.' Bethany looked at him sharply and he went on, 'I've suspected for some time that she's been supplying Grace with alcohol. But I wasn't sure and it isn't easy getting someone who is willing to help with Grace. As you can imagine it's neither a pleasant nor a satisfying job.'

You hypocrite, Bethany thought, but what an attractive one. 'Not long after I left Sally in the kitchen last night I heard someone scream but no one else has mentioned hearing it,' she said, staring at him boldly.

He looked away from her. 'It was probably Grace,' he said after a pause. 'She was drinking pretty heavily after she went to her room last night. I heard her stumbling around, knocking over the furniture and when I went in she became abusive and then hysterical.' Bethany was staring at him hard trying to detect any sign of insincerity in his face or in the tone of his voice, but there was none.

He held her gaze levelly. 'Even by her standards Grace was very drunk. I had to hit her I'm afraid. I know that shocks you but it was for her own good. It's the only thing that works when she's in that state. No one else was disturbed because they're used to it.'

She looked away from him and began to refold a linen napkin. 'I know your wife is a very sick and a very unhappy woman,' she said, 'but I don't think a discussion between *us* will help her. You must know what is best for your own wife. Personally I should think a nursing home would be the place for her. She needs specialized help.'

She knew his eyes were still on her but perversely she refused to look at him. 'That has been tried—several times. However,' he went on briskly, 'I've been wandering away from my purpose in talking to you. Mrs Penarvon will find it difficult enough until we find a replacement for Sally so I wondered . . . I hate to ask you this . . . could you do something with Grace? She's in a terrible state this morning.'

She smoothed the napkin between her unsteady fingers before replying coolly, 'I shall do all I can.'

'She was still asleep just now but you can go up.'

They went towards the stairs. 'You'll need to change the bed linen and her nightdress. I hope you don't mind.' He stopped suddenly and frowned. 'You don't have to do it: I should never have asked.'

She smiled at him. 'I don't mind, really I don't.'

He stopped again when they reached the top of the stairs. 'I'm very grateful to you, more than you will ever realize.'

He looked at her for a long moment and then, turning on his heel, he went along the balcony in the opposite direction.

Bethany stared after him in amazement and then she smiled again—a smile of pure pleasure—and as she approached Grace Tregarrick's room her feet carried her along lightly.

She opened Grace's door slowly and peered inside. The air was filled with the odour of vomit and stale whisky. She went straight across to the window and flung it open as wide as it would go. The woman was sprawled across the bed face downwards and her green velvet dressing gown lay on the floor where it had been discarded. Bethany picked it up and as she hung it in the wardrobe Grace stirred.

When she moved Bethany saw where she had been sick in the bed and for once her sympathy was with Adam—or perhaps it always had been. How could any man cope with this? How often had he been forced to do this unwholesome chore?

Grace was heavy and cumbersome as Bethany strived to move her from the bed. Her eyes opened momentarily, 'Never trust a man,' she muttered, 'they love you then cast you aside. But by then you've already ruined your life for them.'

Having managed, with some difficulty, to move her into a chair Bethany soon found the clean linen and after changing the bed she changed Grace's nightgown and washed her face with a damp cloth. This revived her slightly.

As Bethany helped her back into the bed she opened her eyes. 'Where is Sally?'

'She's gone Mrs Tregarrick.'

Her eyes opened wider and there was no mistaking the fear that was dulling the brilliance of their blue. 'Gone,' she whispered. Then gripping Bethany's arm she said, 'Who with?'

'On her own as far as I know.'

'Oh my God!' Her voice rose to a scream. 'She's dead, she's dead.'

Bethany eased Grace back on to the pillows as she started to sob just as she had done the night before. 'What makes you think she's dead Mrs Tregarrick?' she asked in an even voice.

She didn't answer. Bethany went on tidying the room until she became aware that Grace was watching her intently and silent tears were streaming down her cheeks.

'Adam should have married someone like you,' Grace said unexpectedly. She sank back and stared at the ceiling. 'I'm no use to him. I'm not even a good mother to Dina and she likes you. I'd be better off dead, better for everyone.'

'You mustn't Mrs Tregarrick...' Bethany protested after a moment's stunned silence, but Grace had turned her face back into the pillow and Bethany was left to nurse her anger at Adam whose heartless behaviour had rendered his wife to this pitiful state.

Immediately after her solitary lunch Bethany set off in the direction of the village. The rain had slowed to a dismal drizzle which reduced visibility to a few yards. Had there been a deluge she would still have gone; she had to find out what had happened to Sally and the best place to start was in the village.

By the time she had reached the village the sodden ground had seeped into her shoes so thoroughly that her feet squelched as she walked and drops of moisture dripped from her headscarf.

She must have presented a pitiful sight when she entered the inn where Mrs Arkill was in the middle of preparing a batch of scones for the oven.

'Look a real soggy mess don't 'ee?' she said as Bethany pulled off her scarf and draped it over the big stove to dry. 'A cup of tea'll soon warm you up.'

'Don't blame you for wantin' to get out of that house a while,' she said as she poured the tea.

Bethany looked up at her. 'Where does Sally live Mrs Arkill?'

'Fourteen Hallas Cottages but she don't be there now.'

'She left Tregarrick Manor this morning; she must be somewhere.'

Mrs Arkill drew herself up self-righteously. 'We've been 'earing all about it. Sal took the eight-thirty bus to Bodmin. She'll be nearly in London by now.'

'You've *seen* her?'

'No. She nevver said good-bye. Nevver 'ad the time I s'pose but 'er mother came to tell us.'

'Has her mother seen her?'

'Took 'er to the bus stop. Why do 'ee ask?'

'No real reason,' Bethany said quickly, relieved to know Sally was safe. There was nothing sinister about Sally's disappearance after all and Adam had satisfactorily explained the scream she had heard. Anything could appear sinister if one was in an imaginative state of mind and the very nature of the manor house was conducive to such thoughts. If only she could be wrong

about the other things. But there was no doubt about
what she had heard in the woods and if it hadn't been
Adam out there with Sally it must have been Theo; and
Theo would be too afraid of the woods at night.

She pushed her cup over for a refill. 'Did she say why
she left so suddenly?'

Mrs Arkill went over to the stove to take out her
scones. 'Wouldn't tell 'er mother but my sister says
there be great marks on 'er face. Grace Tregarrick must
'ave done it in one of 'er stupors and poor Sal couldn't
stand it no more. It's no work for a young girl lookin'
after a drunkard is it?'

The rain continued on and off for three days by the
end of which Grace's temper had become more frayed
but she remained sober due, Bethany was convinced,
to Adam's successful rout of her stock of whisky. Her
sharpness seemed to affect the others too; Dina was more
than usually restless and unco-operative.

'When you go back to London, Theo, I think I shall
come with you,' Grace said one day in a teasing voice
after staring out of the streaming window for a long
time.

Whatever her opinion of Theo Bethany was glad of
his presence which had a calming affect on Grace and
he had endless patience to play and teach novel card
games to Dina; invariably Bethany and Esme joined in
too and the time went very quickly whilst Theo entertained them with his amusing anecdotes.

'My pleasure sister,' he replied, trumping Dina's ace
to her loud groans.

'I think he cheats,' Bethany remarked.

Theo held out his arms. 'Come and search me. You'll find no spare cards but having a beautiful woman search me will more than compensate for the insult.'

Dina laughed and Bethany replied with a smile. 'Beautiful woman? He's a liar too.'

Esme glanced over her spectacles at Grace. 'If you go to London with Theo who will put you into bed when you're incapable of doing it for yourself?'

Bethany braced herself for the tirade that must inevitably come from Grace but she simply smiled over her shoulder saying, 'Theo of course. Who else?'

And Theo's roar of laughter prevented an out and out clash of words so effectively that Bethany found she was actually beginning to like him.

'Just look at my mad husband,' Grace said a few minutes later. 'He really must be insane to tramp around in the rain all day. Unless of course he's avoiding us.'

'He's making sure you have enough money to live the life of luxury you so enjoy,' Esme said without malice. 'You didn't object to the money coming in from the estate when you were spending it so freely in London. My husband did Adam's job then. Someone has to do it now. Farms don't run themselves you know.'

'There was some point in having money then,' Grace retorted. 'We had a house and friends to entertain. Places to go. I haven't needed to spend a penny on myself in months. There's no one to see me here.'

'There is always your husband,' Esme remarked. 'However, you may not realize it but a house like this costs a great deal to run and the property and land that provides it are well spaced out. That is why your mad husband is out there so often and not on his backside in here where it is warm and dry.'

Bethany felt profoundly uncomfortable at this family exchange—hardly an argument—not only in front of herself but Dina too. But Dina was unperturbably dealing the cards and Theo had an amused smile on his lips as he listened to his mother, and no one seemed to mind Bethany's presence.

'You could have a very nice social life if you really wanted it Grace,' Esme went on. 'There are plenty of people around here with whom you could mix. When Greville was alive we entertained frequently.'

Grace laughed scornfully. 'A bunch of rustics.' And she began to laugh so loudly Bethany feared it would turn into hysterics, but she controlled herself at last. 'I'm not having those hayseeds look at me as though I were a freak,' she added slamming the door as she flounced out of the room.

Bethany, herself, had noticed Adam was frequently out of the house but then she noticed everything Adam did. Despite her own mounting panic at the growing dependence on his presence for her own contentment she could not be indifferent towards him. He rarely appeared at times other than dinner and afterwards he usually excused himself immediately using work as the excuse. Since the day he had asked her to help with Grace they had exchanged hardly a word and Bethany had to admit to herself that she longed for him to speak to her in the warm way he had used on that last occasion.

At the end of three days the mizzle cleared leaving only the dripping trees to soak the ground.

'Thank heavens it's stopped,' Dina sighed. 'Now we can go out at last.'

'It's still too damp,' Bethany replied, smiling sympathetically. 'Let's wait until tomorrow.'

'It will probably be raining again tomorrow,' Dina protested, 'and it could be for another week. Dr Sanderson says I'm fit enough to go back to school for the summer term so I must be all right now.'

'I'll tell you what; I shall ask your grandmother's permission and if she says yes we'll go.'

'And for what do you need permission?' Adam asked lightly as he came in through the front door with his arms full of freshly chopped logs. Hero and Minerva bounded in after him shaking themselves thoroughly in the centre of the floor and Theo came in last carrying a smaller pile of logs.

Dina ran up to Adam. 'I can go out can't I Daddy. I'm so fed up of being indoors I could scream. Say I can go darling Daddy please or I *shall* scream!'

Theo went over to the table after depositing the logs at the side of the fire and perched on the edge, eyeing Bethany insolently. Disconcerted she avoided his gaze.

'When you call me Daddy it means you must really want to go,' Adam said wryly, placing his logs on top of Theo's. 'You've been coddled too much. There's very little the matter with you that a little fresh air and sunshine won't cure and there's plenty of that outside.'

He glanced over her head to Bethany who smiled hesitantly to receive one back, equally as hesitant. He patted Dina's arm, removed the oilskin and went upstairs without another word. Theo, still smiling at Bethany, raised his hand in silent salute and followed his half-brother up the stairs.

'Let's follow the stream up to its source,' Dina suggested when they were outside.

Bethany dug her hands into her pockets. 'I was thinking more of a short walk near to the house.' And then on seeing Dina's smile turn into a sulk, 'It's terribly damp underfoot Dina.'

'You heard what Adam said; there's nothing wrong with me! And we're well wrapped up.'

Bethany gave in with grace; the smile she had exchanged with Adam made her very malleable to Dina's demands. But as the ground became steeper her feet sank deeper into the soggy turf and she began to regret acceding to Dina's demands.

She paused to look back down into the valley and saw a white curtain of mist rolling in from the sea.

'I think we've come far enough,' she shouted to Dina who was bounding ahead, but if the girl heard she pretended she had not. The ground became softer, more slippery and Bethany could hardly make any headway at all. She began to panic when Dina ran out of sight and did not reappear, especially as the ground had degenerated almost into marshland.

Bethany cupped her hands around her mouth. 'Dina!

Dina!' Her foot slipped and she let out a scream as she regained her balance.

'I'm over here Mrs Ryder,' came a faint cry.

The mist swiftly encroached on the moors and a gentle drizzle began to fall again. Bethany stumbled around shouting to Dina, almost weeping with frustration.

'Keep on shouting Dina. Sing. Do anything.'

It was agonizing knowing Dina was probably only a few yards away yet not being able to find her.

'I've fallen into a bog Mrs Ryder and everytime I try to get up it draws me down.'

'Stay still Dina, as still as you can.'

Bethany lost track of time as she floundered around on the slippery ground, finally coming upon the shivering girl lying prone, her clothes pathetically covered with black slime and pieces of reed. Bethany estimated she was only a few yards away from where she had lost sight of her. Tentatively she held out her hand, slowly moving closer, but she could not reach Dina without being trapped herself.

Dina began to cry. 'It's no use. I'm going to die out here and they'll never find my body!'

'Don't talk nonsense Dina!' Bethany snapped. 'You're not sinking. I could go to the house had get help and you still wouldn't have moved by the time I get back.'

'Don't leave me Mrs Ryder! Please don't leave me.'

'I won't leave you. Just keep quiet for a moment while I think.'

'Can you hear something?' Dina asked after a minute

or two during which Bethany had tried gingerly to tread her way to firmer ground, but there was none nearer to the girl. Every time she was within reach of her Bethany sank ankle deep into slimy mud.

Bethany paused to listen. 'It's Adam and Theo!' Dina cried. 'They've come to find us!'

Both Bethany and Dina began to shout in unison and Bethany could have wept with relief when she saw them materialize like ghosts out of the mist.

'I can't get any nearer to her,' she explained as the two men took in the scene.

'Don't worry we'll have her out in no time,' Theo said with a comforting smile.

'Although I think she deserves to stay there,' Adam added.

'Oh get me out!' Dina cried in a plaintive voice.

After testing the ground for a moment or two Adam turned to Theo, 'It's too soft to hold either of us.' He looked at Bethany. 'But if I spread this oilskin down it might hold you. One of us could go back for a rope but Dina's chilled enough already. I think we should try to get her out as soon as we can.'

'Just tell me what to do. It's my fault she's in there. If I hadn't...'

'We'll talk about that later,' Adam said impatiently, taking off the oilskin. 'I'm going to spread it over the ground as near to Dina as I can. When you've caught hold of both her hands Theo and I will pull you out.' He paused, looking at her, 'Don't worry, we'll have hold of you all the time and if you start to sink we'll pull you back straight away.'

She watched anxiously as he spread the oilskin on the ground. 'Now take off your coat,' he ordered and she obeyed, shivering in the thin dress she was wearing underneath. With the promise of a quick brisk walk and a return to the fire-warmed house it was all she had considered necessary.

She got down on to the oilskin and its clammy coldness chilled her to the marrow. She imagined the panic she would feel if the bog began to suck her down into its dark suffocating depths.

Dina lifted her blackened face and gave a chuckle. 'You do look funny.'

'Not as funny as you,' Bethany replied, beginning to inch her way along. She had no fear for herself; Adam would make sure she was safe. But if only she could manage to reach Dina.

Mud began to creep over the oilskin and on to her arms and legs; soon it was covering her legs completely.

'Put your hand out and see if you can reach her now,' Adam told her. 'Now you Dina.'

Their fingers touched and Bethany moved closer gripping Dina's hand as tightly as she could.

'Now the other one Dina. Slowly.'

'I can't. If I move I'll sink!'

'You won't sink so quickly.' Adam told her impatiently. 'Come on Dina you've got to make an effort or we'll have to leave you and go back for a rope.'

Given the necessary incentive Dina began to move her arm very slowly and with a sigh of relief Bethany gripped it in hers.

'I've got her!' she shouted and with a jerk they were both pulled unceremoniously back on to firm ground.

'You little idiot,' Adam said roughly as he caught Dina and pulled her to her feet, 'don't you know these moors by now? You've seen us take enough sheep from these marshes to know better than this.'

Bethany lay there panting with relief and trying hard not to give in to the temptation to cry. Dina she knew was crying in Adam's arms transferring the sticky slime on to him. Bethany wiped as much as she could from her face with a very damp handkerchief.

'Put my coat round her,' she said, sitting up.

Theo picked it up from the ground and put it around Dina's still heaving shoulders. The coat was damp but the girl needed extra warmth and it was the best they could do.

Adam turned around then. 'Take yours off,' he ordered a startled Theo who did so and leaving Dina where she was Adam came across to drape it around Bethany's shoulders.

She looked up at him wordlessly as he bent over her. He held her gaze steadily for a moment or two pulling the coat tightly around her and then abruptly he turned and lifted Dina into his arms, leaving Bethany to follow with Theo.

CHAPTER EIGHT

As Bethany had feared by evening Dina had developed a high temperature, despite the precaution of an immediate bath and going straight to bed.

On their return Grace had been waiting in the hall twisting her hands nervously and obviously in a highly volatile state. 'My poor little baby!' she cried on seeing the mud covered Dina and the pathetic sight she made.

She wheeled around on Bethany who wearily let Theo's wet coat drop from her shoulders. 'You must be completely irresponsible to take a sick child out in this weather. It's criminal neglect! And I'll see you suffer for it.'

'You're quite right Mrs Tregarrick,' Bethany answered in a low voice. 'I know it's inadequate to apologize but I do.'

'You have nothing to apologize for,' Adam said quickly. 'I was the one who told you to take Dina out so it was my responsibility. The weather was fine at the time and I have no regrets. If you had your way Grace she'd be turned into a permanent invalid.'

'I'm just protecting my daughter.'

Adam looked at her coldly. 'You're starting out a little late. If you'd thought about that earlier there would be no need to employ someone to look after her now.'

Grace uttered a cry of anger. 'That's right champion anyone but your wife! I shouldn't be surprised if she got lost deliberately just so someone would have to go after her.' She smiled mockingly at Bethany. 'What a bonus to have Theo come too.'

Theo began to make some inarticulate protest and Adam said, 'You have Mrs Ryder to thank for getting Dina out so quickly. I doubt if you would have wanted to get *your* feet wet.'

Bursting into a storm of tears Grace fled up the stairs leaving Bethany feeling more uncomfortable than her soaking clothes warranted.

'She's right,' she said softly. 'I was employed to protect Dina from something like this. There's no excuse.'

'Instead of arguing the pros and cons Mrs Ryder shouldn't you be getting Dina out of those wet clothes and into a bath?' Esme suggested.

Bethany put her arm around Dina's still shaking shoulders, confident that the girl had learned her lesson at last and would never run off again. She began to lead her towards the stairs leaving a trail of mud as they walked.

'Mrs Ryder,' Adam began and they paused, 'Dina is quite capable of bathing herself; you get yourself out of those wet clothes instead.'

She began to protest then thought better of it; nothing

could be worse than being ill and confined to bed in this house.

The doctor did not arrive until late due to the thick mist that had hampered his progress, and gravely proclaimed Dina to be suffering from a severe chill.

'That means I shall have to stay in bed for days,' she complained.

'And a good deal longer if you don't eat your supper,' Bethany declared as she removed Dina's untouched tray along with her own.

The onus of guilt for what had befallen Dina still weighed heavily upon her despite the secret thrill of pleasure she experienced every time she recalled how Adam had defended her and more so when she recalled the momentary feel of his arms when he had put Theo's coat around her shoulders.

But since then she had seen him only once and on that occasion his manner had been as remote as before and the fact that he had asked her to send in Dr Sanderson to see his step-mother when he had finished with Dina did nothing to ease her conscience. On their return all Bethany's concern had been for Dina but Esme had a weak heart and now when she recalled how pale and pinched her face had been, worry about Dina was probably the cause.

'You'd better sleep now,' Bethany told her, 'Dr Sanderson says plenty of rest.'

'And I can rely on you to make sure I do,' Dina replied sourly.

Bethany closed the door, leaning against it as a feeling of incredible weariness came over her. The rain was pattering relentlessly against the windows and for once the great hall had not been used for the evening meal. With Dina, Esme and Grace absent there was no point.

She straightened up, balancing the trays carefully and as she looked up she froze where she stood. In the dim light at the far end of the balcony Theo, with a full bottle of whisky in his hand, was just going into Grace's room.

As was expected Dina was not proving to be the ideal patient; even her school work was welcomed as a break in the monotony. To add to Dina's displeasure the day had dawned bright and sunny. By the time she had finished picking at her lunch Bethany's patience was well-tried and beginning to crack.

'How's the invalid?' Theo asked brightly, peering round the door.

'Bored,' Bethany answered bluntly.

Theo sauntered into the room and pulling a chair up to the bed he sat down. 'Would a game of cards help to relieve it?'

Dina's eyes sparkled. 'It would be marvellous. Poker?'

Theo produced a pack of cards. 'Not poker. I don't think Mrs Ryder would approve,' he added in a loud whisper.

Bethany, from her position behind him, studied him carefully. She hoped he had not noticed the reserve and awkwardness in her attitude towards him; since last evening when he had entered Grace's room she was not sure what to think. She had been aware of his salacious glances in her own direction but she had considered him to be a harmless flirt, jealous of his brother's reputation perhaps, but afraid of actually emulating him. Now she was not so sure.

She was fully aware that the visit could have been completely innocent, but the way he had entered the room so stealthily did not lend itself to that premise. But even so, knowing Grace's addiction to whisky, actually supplying her with it was wicked and irresponsible in the extreme.

Theo twisted round in his chair. 'Care to join us?'

Bethany shook her head and said to Dina, 'I think I'll take a break. I shall come back later.'

She was still thinking about Theo and Grace when she almost bumped into Adam who was coming towards Dina's room. Because Theo's odd behaviour had displaced her previous exclusive thoughts of Adam, coming across him so unexpectedly made her oddly disconcerted.

'How is Dina?' he asked.

'Much better; complaining anyway so that's a healthy sign. And your step-mother? She's not ill I hope.'

He smiled; a relaxed smile. 'She has some heart trouble—nothing serious Dr Sanderson assures us—but before we came out for you yesterday Grace was becoming agitated and it tended to transfer itself to Esme. A day or so of rest will do the trick.'

'I'm glad. I feel badly enough as it is.'

'Don't. There is absolutely no need. You and I know very well Dina was wrong in going up there on such a day. Anyway we've been through all that. It's forgotten. Is Dina resting by the way?'

Bethany laughed. 'I doubt it. Theo is playing cards with her.'

A shadow darkened his eyes for a moment before he said briskly, 'Dr Sanderson doesn't seem to think this is a set-back. Dina can go back to school when the term starts on the eighteenth of May.'

Bethany stared at him hard for a moment; his gaze did not waver from hers. Then she said, in a deceptively careless way, 'Oh, then I had better start to make my arrangements.'

'Yes you had.'

She was still considering his words when she realized he had gone past her. She turned suddenly, 'Will it be all right if I go out for a little while? I need some fresh air.'

'By all means Mrs Ryder,' he answered without troubling to turn around.

The higher she climbed into the moors the more fresh and invigorating the breeze became. It tore into her hair making her catch her breath and stung her eyes. But the sheer primitiveness of the land with not another soul for miles around excited her with its barbaric beauty.

Scattered between the gorse covered hills were isolated farms now belonging to Adam Tregarrick; the farms that had once belonged to his father, and his father before him. And probably the farmers themselves were sons of the earlier farmers. The permanence of it all gave her an odd kind of comfort, making her own problems seem minute in the infinity of time. And wasn't time the great healer?

It was extraordinary that after dreading being alone in a city she had become so attached to this land where being alone was a physical fact. In a few short weeks she would be leaving here forever and she knew she should be writing after jobs and arranging accommodation but something was restraining her. She didn't want to leave. She felt she belonged here.

Although in a few weeks Dina would be safely at school she would soon return home for the holidays. Back to the strange, strained atmosphere of Tregarrick Manor with its secrets and whisperings and conflicting emotions. Jenefer Henekin's murderer was still free and because Dina said she knew who it was the danger was here.

Or was she being too fanciful once more? The murderer could be miles away and the Tregarricks had no more secrets than any other family. What difference did it make if Adam had a dozen mistresses, if Grace consoled herself with drink and flirting with Theo, if Esme Tregarrick still wanted to act the gracious lady of the manor when those days were long over, or if Dina indulged in dramatic fantasies?

It meant a great deal she was forced to admit. She stood on the brow of a hill staring down at the roof of Tregarrick Manor just visible above the trees and the smoke curling from its tall chimneys.

Oh why was she pretending to herself? It was not concern over Dina that was troubling her; it was Adam. Adam. She mouthed his name silently. The thought of never seeing him again filled her with a pain so great she wanted to cry out from the agony of it.

'May I join you?'

She wheeled round; Theo was approaching.

'If you must.'

He ignored her lack of enthusiasm. 'You looked so sad. I suppose you wouldn't be thinking of me would you?'

'You suppose right Mr Tregarrick.'

'Theo to you. And that is a great pity because I think about you a great deal. You fascinate me. Did you know that?'

She began to walk back towards the house and Theo, far from being put off, fell in step beside her. 'You're not like any woman I've ever known before.'

'In that case you must have known some strange women.'

He roared with laughter and then taking a great lungful of breath he said, 'Isn't the air wonderful. I always come back. I have to somehow.'

Bethany looked at him with interest. 'Why did you come back? You don't really like it here. No gay restaurants, no dolly girls to flatter your vanity.'

'There are compensations.' She looked away from his face and the meaningful smile it wore. 'It must be obvious that I come back when the money runs out.'

He saw her questioning look. 'My father left my inheritance tied up in a trust. I only get it every three months and I'm afraid it is usually gone by the end of the first one. Well, I might as well live while I can. I'm just grateful that I was the second son; it's Adam who is stuck here. Poor Grace hates it.'

There was silence for a moment. 'I saw you go into Grace's room last night,' she said quickly, not looking at him.

He stopped, staring down at the house in the trees just as she had done. Then he looked at her and smiled. 'Grace is an unhappy woman *and* persuasive. I suppose if I were hard like Adam I could say no,' his eyes narrowed, 'but I'm not and I can't say I'd like to be.'

She looked at him carefully. 'You envy him don't you?'

His face registered blatant surprise. 'What makes you say that?'

'It was just a thought.' She stirred. 'I should be getting back. I only came out because I thought you would keep Dina occupied.'

'I haven't left her alone. Adam was with her when I left. That gives you some time for me.'

She ignored him and he said slyly, 'The way he fusses over her you'd almost think he was her real father.'

Bethany looked at him sharply. 'What is that supposed to mean?'

He shrugged his shoulders and she went on ahead of him. As they entered the wood he said suddenly, 'Look Bethany you'll be leaving here soon, going back to

London and so shall I. We could have some fun together.'

She stopped and smiled at him. 'Thank you Theo; I'm flattered but your idea of fun and mine is probably quite different. Anyway I'm not at all sure I shall be returning to London. There are other places.'

'I'm not tied there either. Where would you like to go?'

'I don't know. I don't know anything yet.'

'Do you still think about him—your husband?' he asked abruptly.

She looked down at the ground. 'Not really. It's sad isn't it how quickly one is forgotten when one dies?'

'Yes,' he said softly. 'Yes it is.'

Bethany looked up at him again and for that moment she felt as if she was facing an entirely different person —the man beneath the child's exterior. Then she said, 'I really *must* go. I've been out much longer than I intended.'

He caught her arm. 'You don't have to take your duties so seriously you know.'

'Let me go Theo.'

He tightened his grip and pulled her closer. Her face was very near to his wicked grin. She'd been mad to trust him; nothing was straight-forward or innocent when it was done by one of the Tregarricks. They were wholly untrustworthy.

'If you were this cold to your husband he must have died of sheer frustration.'

Her irritation turned to anger as she struggled to free

herself. 'That remark was totally uncalled for!'

'Show me I'm wrong then. Just one kiss and I'm sure I can persuade you to stay awhile.'

'No,' she gasped, struggling even more, but Theo Tregarrick possessed a strength that belied his girlish looks and there was nothing girlish about the way he was pushing her roughly against the trunk of a tree.

'Just one,' he whispered pressing his lips to hers as she continued to struggle. Her attempts to thrust him away and then to scratch his face were so successfully thwarted that Bethany realized he was accustomed to using force to get what he wanted. In the midst of her struggles against his obscene fumblings she couldn't recall hearing whether Jenefer Henekin had been attacked before she was stabbed. Suddenly she began to fight as if her life depended on it, furiously kicking out at him.

He laughed cruelly. 'You certainly add spice,' he gasped. 'And I thought you were so cool.'

She braced herself as he covered her face with his foul kisses. She heard the sound of tearing and realized it was her own clothes and at that moment she decided there was no point in fighting. Theo was too strong for her and her strength was sapped anyway. She closed her eyes so at least she would not have to look into his loathsome face. There seemed no end to the evil perpetrated at Tregarrick Manor.

She opened her eyes again; the boughs of the trees swayed overhead and she found herself going limp in his arms.

'Beth. Bethany.' She opened her eyes again and found she was looking, not into Theo's grinning face, but into Adam's, tense with concern.

She shuddered and he held her close for a moment. She turned her head; Theo was lying on the ground a few yards away. Adam leaned her gently against a tree.

'Will you be all right?'

She nodded and then she watched a little dazedly as he went back to his brother.

Theo looked up fearfully as Adam stood over him, rigid with fury. 'Go near her again and I'll kill you.'

He sat up, rubbing his chin. His face was expressionless as he looked at Bethany and then back to Adam. 'You want her for yourself,' he accused. 'I just wanted to find out what was so special.'

Adam bent down over him and as he did so Theo instinctively covered his face but Adam simply dragged him to his feet by his jacket lapels. 'Don't say I didn't warn you Theo. I really would kill you. You're no better than an animal.'

'And you I suppose,' Theo said maliciously, 'are nothing less than a gentleman.' He brushed off his clothes and with one last glance at Bethany he ran off towards the house.

Adam watched him go before returning to Bethany. She stood with her back pressed against the tree and her palms flat against it for support. When she saw him coming back she turned her face away, unwilling to look at him.

'Your dress is torn,' he said. 'Your clothes always

seem to suffer, don't they?'

She looked down then, noticing the torn bodice for the first time and her dirt streaked cardigan. 'I don't know what came over him,' she said and to her dismay tears began to roll down her cheeks. 'I'd better go inside and get changed before anyone else sees me,' she added, brushing them away hurriedly with her sleeve.

As she started to walk away he put his hand out to stop her. She paused but did not look at him. 'I want you to leave immediately,' he said. She turned then. 'If it's a matter of money I can arrange a loan.'

She shook her head. 'Dina goes back to school in a few weeks; time enough for me to leave then.'

As she picked in a desultory way at her food she wondered why she had not jumped at Adam's offer, although she knew the answer already. When she had experienced the first quickening of love she had considered it to be resulting from the void Johnny's death had made, but she could no longer delude herself; what she felt for him was stronger than anything Johnny had been able to awaken in her heart.

She glanced at him across the table; he was showing about as much enthusiasm for his food as anyone else. No one spoke. Esme sat, as always, at the head of the table; as always the all powerful matriarch. But now the pride was beginning to crumble and tonight it was very apparent. Looking at her now, still formidable in old age, Bethany wondered how Greville Tregarrick had dared to bring his mistress into the house. If he had been like Adam she imagined he would dare to do anything he pleased and perhaps like herself, Esme had loved him too much to care.

She looked back at Adam whose eyes met hers and she smiled but he looked away again and her heart weighed heavily in her breast.

Theo stared morosely into space only stirring himself long enough to refill, then swiftly empty his wineglass. His face was flushed and his eyes bright and whenever she looked at him Bethany could hardly repress a shudder of repugnance at the memory of his embraces.

'You're all a jolly lot,' Grace remarked mildly. Tonight she had chosen to wear a flowing gown of blood red voluminous chiffon, a colour that clashed so garishly with her hair that Bethany thought she must have been drunk when she had bought it.

'We're all suffering from yesterday's after effects,' Esme said in a tired voice.

'Perhaps you should go to bed,' Adam suggested and Bethany warmed to the kindness in his voice.

Esme straightened up determinedly. 'I shall wait and have my coffee first.'

In front of the fire Hero and Minerva growled restlessly; Bethany shivered despite the warmth of the room. The atmosphere of someone watching and waiting was manifest.

Adam picked up his coffee cup and walked over to the fire, staring up at the display of weapons. Bethany with a studied casualness waited a moment or two before wandering over to his side.

'Everytime I pass them I have to stop and admire,' she said.

He did not look round. 'They are rather grand aren't they? They were collected by my grandfather. He had a merchant ship, bringing tea from India. He often made the trip himself and he made a habit of bringing these home with him.'

'Were any of your ancestors pirates?'

He turned to look at her. 'Pirates? I doubt it. Why do you ask?'

She smiled to herself. 'I just wondered that's all.'

She did not say anything for a moment or two, her mind working out how best to formulate her next question; one that had been troubling her for some time.

'When the police were here,' she said in a low voice that only he could hear, 'did they examine these daggers ... for marks or bloodstains.'

She wondered if he had heard her for he kept on staring at the wall above the stone mantel. When he did turn to her his face was twisted by a strange smile. 'The police turned the house inside out searching for the murder weapon. There was nothing found at all and no bloodstains on these daggers. But,' he added, 'that doesn't necessarily mean one of them wasn't the weapon used.'

'I think I will go to bed,' Esme announced from where she was still sitting at the table. Theo had gone to pour out a large measure of brandy for himself and for Grace.

Bethany roused herself and saying quickly, 'And I'd better check on Dina,' she put her coffee cup back on to the table just as the first scuffling began.

Her hand froze around the saucer, Esme stopped half-way out of her chair and Theo put the brandy glass down on the table to stare towards the fireplace as the air seemed to be filled with a frantic thumping. Hero and Minerva jumped up and stood ears and tails cocked. Adam stepped back as amid a cloud of soot a blackened and terrified bird fell into the fire to be consumed almost immediately by the flames in full view of the horrified audience.

' 'Tis a terrible omen,' said Mrs Penarvon in a shrill voice above the hushed silence of shock.

'We're cursed!' cried Grace in a high unnatural voice before she began to laugh hysterically.

When Bethany came back down again with Dina's tray Adam was no longer standing in front of the fire and neither were Hero and Minerva. Theo stood where Adam had been and in his hand was a full glass of brandy and Bethany doubted if it was the same one she had seen him pour before she had gone upstairs.

Sitting in an armchair beside him was Grace and from the way they stopped talking when she appeared she guessed they had been talking about her. Her face flushed when she remembered Theo's accusing voice. 'You want her for yourself.' And there had been no angry denial. She wondered if Theo had told Grace of his suspicions. Even with her scant knowledge of Theo's nature Bethany guessed he would not be able to resist.

'Here comes the merry widow,' Grace said in a dull voice. The recently banked fire played a weird pattern on her already flushed face. It was evident that in the short while she had been absent Grace and Theo had been plying themselves quite liberally with drink.

'Don't mind my sister-in-law,' Theo said with a nasty grin, 'she's just jealous.'

'Why should Mrs Tregarrick be jealous of me?' Bethany asked wishing she could make a retreat without it looking too obvious.

'I've just been telling of your heroic exploits on the moor yesterday. There you were laying down your life for the girl in your tender care and all because Adam asked you to.'

Bethany felt panic engulfing her. 'I *didn't* lay down my life! There was absolutely no danger to me but I *was* concerned about Dina. Isn't that only natural?'

'Everyone's concerned for my daughter,' Grace said in a weary voice, pouring herself another drink. 'It's amazing how concerned everyone is for my daughter. Kids! I wish someone would tell me why we have them. They're nothing but trouble from the day they're born.' Her voice softened. 'Then they grow up and you can see quite plainly what you were once and when you look in the mirror you can see what you are now.' She quickly finished the drink and poured herself another. She looked towards the fire and said quite soberly, 'We'll get no domestic help up here once Rosanna Penarvon gets the word around about that bird.' She shivered slightly. 'It frightens me. There is going to be more trouble.'

'Now what on earth does that mean?' Theo demanded. 'You're letting yourself get morbid.'

'These signs mean a lot to the locals,' Bethany pointed out.

Theo moved closer to her and involuntarily she winced. 'Now what can possibly happen?' he said in a hoarse whisper. 'Perhaps you think the spriggans will come down from the moors in the dead of night and strike you down as you sleep. They'll march through the woods, little men with green heads and big hands and they'll march through the house striking with their little knives at every mortal they come across.'

Bethany pulled away from him as he laughed harshly, hating to be the butt of his warped sense of humour. Grace began to laugh too but her laugh was tinged with hysteria.

'The spriggans didn't kill Jenefer Henekin,' Bethany said wheeling around.

The laughter stopped and a glint of mischief came into Theo's eyes. 'So that's what is bothering you. You've been working out for yourself who did it and you don't like the answer.'

Bethany stared at him for a long minute before Grace started to laugh again. Theo, who had been carefully containing his own amusement burst out laughing too. Going over to his sister-in-law he put his arm around her shoulders, both of them racked with convulsive laughter. The sound of their near hysteria rose echoing around the lofty hall, mocking Bethany and filling her head with its repulsive sound.

'Shut up!' she screamed, covering her ears with her hands. 'Shut up can't you!'

The sound of her agonized voice sent them into further spasms of coarse laughter and still with her hands covering her ears she ran out of the room.

She would never go back. But a few yards from the house she stopped running, her hands dropped to her sides. There was no longer any sound of insane laughter—just blessed peace.

She stood there for a long time listening to the silence. Dina had said Jenefer's ghost did not haunt the woods but Bethany knew it did and always would until the murderer was discovered and punished.

A sound nearby made her stand very still. She stared into the gloom and put her hand up to her mouth to stifle a cry of fear.

Adam stopped in surprise when he saw her and after staring at each other for a long, silent moment unhesitatingly she went into his arms.

CHAPTER NINE

He was kissing her as if he would never stop. She wanted him never to stop. They were cruel kisses, devouring kisses but she wanted no tenderness; here was all she had sought to find with Johnny. His arms around her were like irons, pinning her close to him. Soon they would surely devour one another with their insatiable hunger. Time enough to regret this moment, but now, now...

It hardly mattered that the man she loved so much might have kissed another girl seconds before she died, or the hands that held her so tightly might once have been stained with blood. It hardly mattered that he was another woman's husband. But it did matter that her heart was brimming with love for a man who only regarded women as pawns in his never ending game of love.

She fought against the vortex of passion that was dragging them both down to the point from which there soon would be no going back.

He let her go and held her away from him. 'I vowed I would never let this happen. Now you know why I wanted you to go.'

'I shall go now,' she said in a shaky voice, pulling away

from him completely, but before she could he had pulled her back.'

'I don't blame you for what you're thinking but I happen to love you. That's another thing I vowed not to do. But I can't let you go away believing I don't care.' She raised her eyes to his.

'You don't have to say that. I won't make any demands on you if that is what you're afraid of.'

'I didn't have to say it but it happens to be true. You don't believe me do you?'

'Why shouldn't I believe you? You've had plenty of practice.'

She started to run away from him, desperate that he should not see her cry, but yet again he drew her back. 'What does that mean?' he said, his voice still rough with emotion.

His hands bit into the flesh of her arms but she was not aware of the pain. His eyes searched hers with such burning intensity she could not meet them. 'I want to know what you meant by that remark.'

'You know what I mean.'

He let her go abruptly. 'I tell you I love you yet you would rather believe the gossips than me.' Then regretfully he said, 'It doesn't matter. It's just that for a moment I thought my feelings for you might be returned; it was pure selfishness that made me speak.'

She looked at him uncertainly for a moment. 'Do you mean that all the talk is *not* true?'

There was no mistaking the silent plea in his eyes. 'Not about me anyway. It's a case of the sins of the father ... When I was a child I heard enough arguments between my mother and father because he brought his mistress into the house. It is something I'd like to forget not encourage again.'

'But your step-mother and Mrs Penarvon get on quite well.'

'My father is dead; there is nothing to fight over now.'

Bethany looked away to the house then back to him. 'If it wasn't you, then who?' Her eyes widened. 'Not Theo? But if it was it means he and Jenefer ... but he's not capable of killing anyone.'

He smiled. 'But I am.' She looked away again and he said, 'Don't think I haven't thought about it until my head aches. There's no answer and there never will be now. It was a terrible thing to happen but it's over.'

'No it isn't,' she said with a sudden shudder. 'Hold me Adam. Please hold me.' He put his arms around her once more and she felt the warmth and strength from his body flow into hers. 'I love you so much,' she said.

He pressed his lips to the top of her head. 'It *was* pure selfishness that made me tell you. If I hadn't you would have gone away thinking the worst about me and that would have been by far the best thing.'

She pressed her cheek against his chest. 'No it wouldn't. There will never be any other man for me now. At least this I can be content knowing you love me.'

He held her away. 'You've seen what my marriage is like, but there's nothing I can do. Grace is worse than a child; she's completely dependent. I suppose that is why the gossips are so quick to link me with every woman under sixty—that and my father's reputation which was well deserved. I expect if I'd had an ideal marriage there would have still been talk; lechery is part of the Tregarrick heritage and no one wants to let us forget it. If only Grace was a normal woman...'

'I know; it's tragic for both of you. Yet I know you must have loved her once.'

He put his arm around her waist. 'Let's walk a little. We're too close to the house.' She put her head back against his shoulder. 'I suppose I did,' he said when they were out of sight of the manor, 'but it's hard to remember how I felt when I look at her now. When I met her I was just up from Oxford and she was already widowed—beautiful, worldly and dazzling. I was dazzled anyway. After we were married we bought a small house in Kensington.' He smiled wryly in the darkness. 'She filled it with reproduction furniture—very tasteful. And Grace settled down to entertaining all her friends; something she did very well.

'And because I had lived out here all my life I thought it was wonderful having so many friends and so many places to go. We had a marvellous time for nearly five years and then my father died and we came here. Once I came back I realized I never wanted to leave again. It wasn't a matter of having to stay—I really wanted to. It was a little unfair on Grace—I had had my youthful fling and now all I wanted to do was stay where I had always belonged.'

'But she did stay with you.'

'She had little choice. It was a matter of living either in comfort and security here or making do in London. And as I had legally adopted Dina, Grace knew I would have fought for custody of her. Whatever impression Grace may give she really is devoted to Dina.'

'Couldn't she have gone back to the theatre?'

Adam laughed softly in the darkness. 'So you've heard about the great actress. She couldn't act herself out of a paper bag.' Serious again he said, 'She had a few small parts in plays but that was all.'

'And the rich man she married?'

He laughed again. 'Dina has given you the full treatment I see, not that she's at fault; Grace has filled her head with a lot of romantic nonsense. Now she *will* make an excellent actress given the chance. Her father was an actor as equally as unsuccessful as Grace. He celebrated Dina's birth by getting drunk with a crowd of his out-of-work friends and then he walked under a bus.'

'It's a pity it didn't serve as a warning to Grace.'

'Yes indeed. She always did frighten me with the amount of alcohol she could consume. Since she's been here she has had little else to do but drink.'

'She could try devoting more time to Dina or to running the house. I'm sure Esme would appreciate it.'

He stopped and turned her to face him. 'Enough about the shambles of my life. What about you and John Richard Ryder? I'm not sure whether I really want to know or not, but I must. It's selfish of me, I know, seeing I'm in no position to be jealous.'

'You know his name?'

'I went one day to see his grave and do you know what I thought? I thought it would be better to die with your love than to live without it.'

Her eyes shone brightly in the moonlight. 'I was fond of him Adam, but I realize now I never loved him. It almost drove me crazy thinking about it for a while but not any more. He was happy with me; he wanted nothing more than I was able to give him. And if he hadn't died I would have gone on being happy with him without ever knowing the difference.'

'How do you know you really love me?'

His hands bit into her shoulders. 'Oh Adam,' she sighed, 'how do I know when the sun is shining?'

They gazed at each other for a long minute before he pulled her close again, kissing her savagely just once before he thrust her away. 'I can't bear to let you go but you must leave here. After I came back here to live and whatever I once felt for Grace evaporated, I knew one day I would meet the woman I could love completely. That day you came I must have suspected it could be you; that was why I didn't want you to stay. I've tried so hard to keep away from you. For your own sake Beth darling go away. Go abroad where there is no chance of our meeting. There's no future for you with me.'

'I can't go. Now more than ever Adam, I can't.'

'If you go you have a chance of meeting a man who is free to marry you. You're too young to waste your life on a man who will never be free.'

'Loving you isn't a waste of my life. I settled for something less than the best once before, but never again.'

She wound her arms around him, 'Don't you think I want you to stay?' he said, his voice muffled in her hair. 'The thought of you going is like being plunged into eternal night, but it would be impossible for both of us if you stayed.'

'I know that,' she answered softly. 'When Dina goes back to school I shall go to Bodmin and find a job.' She looked up at him. 'You can come to me whenever you have the chance.'

His arms tightened around her. 'Haven't you heard a word I've said? I love you Beth, more than I've loved any woman before. Do you think I'd let you settle for two hours on Wednesday and Saturday when what I really want to give you is a home and children.'

'We can have children.'

'The locals will find a dirty word for that.' He took her face between her hands, 'And if you think I would let a child of ours become a dirty joke you are quite mistaken. You don't really want that Beth; it's what you think I want.'

'Does it matter what anyone else thinks as long as we're together?' she asked in a choked voice.

'It matters what you think. Eventually it would destroy our love and the love we feel for each other is the only good thing that has happened in this house for a long, long time.'

'What else can we do?'

He rested his head against hers. 'I don't know, but I'll think of something.'

By the time she awoke the next morning she knew he would be well on his way to London. Before she had left him last night he had told her of his intention to go, 'on long overdue business, but it will give me a chance to think things over'.

The knowledge that he loved her as deeply and as desperately as she loved him threatened to burst her heart with the sheer joy and the wonder of it. She knew she should feel guilt, but knowing Adam was imprisoned in an empty marriage salved her conscience; she had taken nothing from Grace.

Three days he would be gone. Three unending days. By lunchtime on the first day she was missing him so much it was incredible to realize she had known him for so short a time. If nothing else it proved how impossible it would be for her to go out of his life completely.

Dina, now her temperature had dropped, complained ceaselessly. Even Theo's frequent appearances failed to placate her for long. It was a relief when, on the afternoon of the third day, Esme Tregarrick came in.

'It's time you had a break Mrs Ryder. I shall sit with Dina until you come back.'

Bethany got up hesitantly. 'If you're sure you are feeling well enough.'

Esme Tregarrick laughed. 'Does one have to be so fit to stand Dina's company for any length of time?'

'I'm afraid so. Dina is fed up of being in bed.'

Esme sat down in the chair Bethany had vacated. 'Perhaps when Dr Sanderson comes tomorrow he will allow you to get up. He's getting old you know,' she explained to Bethany, 'and he tends to be over cautious. But then that's all to the good isn't it?'

'He'd better let me up,' Dina said, a warning in her voice.

'What shall we do?' Esme asked. 'Would you like to play cards?'

Dina's face puckered. 'I always play cards with Uncle Theo. *He* knows some super games.'

'How about a game of Scrabble then? At least it's vaguely educational.'

Bethany left them still in heated discussion. When she went downstairs Hero and Minerva jumped up and two pairs of limpid eyes gazed at her hopefully. She paused as she passed them, 'You two are a pair of softies after all. You miss him too. He'll soon be back.'

When they followed her to the door she added, 'All right you may as well come along too.'

She tripped down the path to the village, her step light and eager at the thought of Adam's imminent return. The hounds bounded in front of her and she had to run to keep up with them.

Suddenly she stopped, momentarily startled by a figure that stepped from behind a tree. When she recognized Theo she started to walk on past him as he leaned indolently against a tree.

'All alone?' he asked. When she did not reply he

drawled, 'I didn't like what happened the other day. There was no cause for him to hit me.'

'I'm sorry about that too, but you did get rather enthusiastic.'

He put his arm around her shoulder and kissed her cheek. 'Show me how sorry you are.'

She averted her face. 'Let me go Theo. There's no point in making trouble.' Her heart began to thump noisily at the thought of a repeat attack.

'I won't make any trouble.'

She pushed him away. 'But I will. I warn you I won't keep quiet about it this time.'

'You won't be the first to tell. It's always been kept quiet before and it will be again. We Tregarricks stick together and we do have a big pull around here. Oh look Bethany, don't let Adam's chivalrous act put stars in your eyes. Can you guess where he is now?' He looked at her for a moment. 'He's gone to see a certain fancy piece who left here in rather a hurry.'

'I don't believe you.'

'Suit yourself, but why don't you ask him?'

'Perhaps I will.'

'But in the meantime he's away and I'm here. Heaven knows why I bother, merry widow, but I have really taken a fancy to you. I'm offering you a great time.'

Bethany stared at him coldly. 'I don't want what you have to offer.'

'As I said before—give it a try and I guarantee to change your mind. And, remember, this time there is no Adam to charge in and spoil things.' He put his arm around her shoulder once again just as Hero and Minerva bounded back up the path in search of their absent companion. On seeing her with Theo they stopped. Both animals were paused for attack, growling deep in their throats. With an oath Theo let her go and without another word went striding back towards the house.

'I believe I could kiss you two,' she said with a laugh of pure relief as they ran beside her down the path barking joyfully.

She tied up the hounds securely with string in the back yard of the inn, inhaling deeply of the savoury smell emanating from the kitchen. In a matter of minutes she had her hands clasped around a mug of aromatic tea.

'I 'ere there's been an accident.'

Bethany looked at her. 'News travels fast around here.'

'Always does,' Mrs Arkill replied complacently. 'An' how is the young lady?'

'Recovering.'

'Bad things'll always happen in that house. Be a good thing when you leave I'll be thinking. An' that won't be long now will it?'

'Two weeks,' she replied bleakly.

And then what? She would have to leave as Adam had said. She knew there was no choice. Adam wanted it that way and she had to admit it would be the best thing for both of them—especially for him.

'Have you lived in St Mollith long?' she asked, eyeing

the landlord's wife questioningly.

'All my life.'

'Then you must remember the first Mrs Tregarrick.'

Mrs Arkill was elbow deep in suds. 'Oh 'er. Yes I do. One of the Moretons of Padstow she were. A nice lady and they were happy I do believe, but after young Adam were born she took ill and died when he were no more than a babe. Tweren't more than a year later he brought the second bride home. A wealthy farmer's daughter they did say. A bit stuck up she were—still is I dare say, but nevver treated the poor lady right, he didn't. Carrying Mr Theo she were when he brought his fancy piece into the house. There she be today.'

'He must have been a terrible man,' Bethany murmured, remembering how Adam recalled the arguments between his father and step-mother.

'I dare say but it be in 'em you see. My old grandma used to tell a marvellous tale of the old days at Tregarrick Manor. They've always been the same. Times change but people don't.'

Mrs Arkill dried her arms on a towel. 'Might be fortunate 'ee did bring Rosanna Penarvon to the house; no one else'll stay there these days. 'Specially since the bird came into the house. 'Tis a bad sign an' no mistake. You be warned to leave there.'

'I'm not superstitious. It must be the easiest thing in the world for a bird to fall down such a wide chimney,' she said doubtfully, recalling her feeling of horror at the sight of the bird being consumed by the flames. She finished off her tea quickly and got to her feet. 'Have you heard from your niece?'

'My sister 'as. Settling down nicely she be. Says London is a big place and she's got a good job. My sister got a letter only this mornin'. Mr Adam's been to see 'er too.'

The wind had risen to a howling intensity during her short visit to the inn. Hero and Minerva bounded on ahead, barking loudly as they chased terrified birds from their path. The joy she had felt at the prospect of Adam's return had gone. Theo had spoken the truth —Adam had gone to see Sally. Worse than that—he had lied to her. Whatever had gone before he had met her— however many women he had known—did not matter to her. She didn't doubt he loved her—he couldn't fake the tenderness she had heard when he spoke to her—but he had lied.

'It be in 'em,' Mrs Arkill had said.

Hero and Minerva were waiting by the door, their tails wagging wildly. Despite the sadness she felt at Adam's dishonesty she was seized by a sudden excitement—he might be home!

The wind pushed against the porch door but finally, as it blew her hair in front of her eyes and her skirt around her knees, it gave way and the hounds flew inside. Bethany followed, slamming one door and opening the other.

Her excitement died abruptly when she saw Grace standing, rather unsteadily, by the fire. There was a leonine smile on Theo's face when he looked round from his chair.

'Just look what the wind has blown in,' he said nastily. He looked at Grace, 'I don't think she's too happy to see us here Grace. I wonder who that smile was for. Not us do you think?'

'For you, who do *you* think?' Grace said, her voice slurred and her eyes bloodshot.

'Oh, I only wish it were.'

Bethany ignored them and staying at the far side of the hall she began to make her way towards the stairs.

'Don't go just yet,' Grace said moving towards her.

Theo stood up and went to Grace's side. 'I think perhaps when Adam comes back he and I will have to decide who is to woo the merry widow. Adam is married needless to say so I think I stand the better chance.'

Grace's face became redder and Bethany said in a voice thick with anger. 'You're abominable Theo Tregarrick! You're playing everyone off against the other as if we're pawns in a diabolical game of your own invention!'

'But it does relieve the monotony.'

Grace, after staring into space for a few moments, lurched towards Bethany but swiftly Theo pulled her back. 'No fighting,' he said in a tone he would use to a naughty child. Unable to reach Bethany she turned on Theo lifting her scarlet nails to his face. The smile left his lips at last and he pushed her away with a vicious thrust before she could scratch him.

She stumbled back towards the fire saving herself from falling by holding on to the mantel. She looked up and snatched down a dagger from the wall holding it menacingly in her fist. She pointed it at Theo whose face had paled to a chalky whiteness. Theo and Bethany stared transfixed at the dagger waiting, almost without breathing, to see what Grace would do, and not noticing her close proximity to the fire.

It only took a second for the hem of her dressing gown to smoulder in the embers before it burst into flames. Grace began to scream, dropping the dagger and beating ineffectually at the gown with her hands.

'Help me someone! Do something.'

Theo continued to stare at her and Bethany, numbed for the moment, reached for a coat hanging on the stand and rushed over to Grace, hurling her to the floor. The flames were extinguished as quickly as they had flared and Bethany got to her feet leaving the woman unhurt but weeping bitterly on the floor.

Theo stared down at his sister-in-law in horror as Bethany levelled her gaze at him. 'She might have been killed and all because you're bored and enjoy baiting people.'

'What *is* going on?' Esme asked as she came down the stairs.

'Grace's dressing gown caught fire,' Theo explained in a frightened voice, dragging his eyes away from Bethany's accusing stare.

Mrs Penarvon came hurrying in and Esme ordered, 'Take my daughter-in-law upstairs Rosanna. She's had a slight accident.'

Silently they watched as Mrs Penarvon helped the

still weeping Grace to her feet. 'Come on me dear, let's go upstairs.'

The difference between this big, strong woman and the dainty Mrs Tregarrick never failed to amaze Bethany, yet they were both lovers of one man. They were both strong in their way; Esme in character and Rosanna in body.

Bethany turned to Esme and said heatedly, 'You must do something about her Mrs Tregarrick. One of these days that will happen when no one is around and she's going to kill herself.'

Esme Tregarrick's eyes followed Grace as she went, supported by the house-keeper. 'It might be a mercy for us all if she did.' Then turning briskly to Bethany, 'I should like a few words with you in private Mrs Ryder. In the sitting-room if you please.'

Esme was already seated in her chair when Bethany went in. 'Please sit down.' She frowned at Bethany. 'I find this all rather distasteful and distressing Mrs Ryder, but I do feel bound to speak.' She paused and Bethany fervently hoped she did not suspect her love for Adam. 'Theo has told me about the ... er ... encounter you had the other day.'

Bethany looked at her increduously. 'He's *told* you?'

Esme gave a tight-lipped smile. 'You seem surprised.'

'I certainly am.'

'I can well appreciate how you feel Mrs Ryder. I commiserate with your unhappy position as a widow. I have been in that unenviable position for some years myself but I don't consider it an excuse for the way you ...

forced yourself upon my son. I regret having to say this but I am very disappointed in you.'

Bethany stared at her in amazement. 'He told you I ... ?'

'I hope you are not going to deny it.'

'But it isn't true!'

'Are you suggesting Theo is *lying*?'

Bethany smiled. 'No Mrs Tregarrick. But I really think you are mistaken.'

'There is no mistake Mrs Ryder and there's no point in further discussion on the subject. All I ask is that it shouldn't happen again. Remember your capacity in this household; you have charge of a fourteen year old girl.'

Bethany got to her feet, determined to remain dignified despite the indignation and anger that was almost choking her. 'I shall leave immediately.'

'Oh really Mrs Ryder! That is most unfair. All I ask is that you be more circumspect. We hardly have enough staff to keep the house running smoothly and now you want to leave us while Dina is still ill, just because I face you with an unpalatable truth.'

'I just thought you would prefer me to leave in the circumstances. If you're sure I'm safe to be in charge of Dina I shall naturally stay until it is time for her to leave for school.'

Esme smiled happily. 'Well I am glad that is settled. We'll say no more about it.'

CHAPTER TEN

Still fuming with anger she ran up the stairs. She had no doubt Theo had prepared his mother for any complaint she might decide to make—and very cleverly too. So clever she was sure he had done it before, and if he had, did Esme really believe he was the innocent party and not the perpetrator?

Her anger was still intense when she bumped into the man to whom it was directed just as he came out of Dina's room. His face was still ashen from the shock of Grace's accident.

'You really are despicable,' she cried when she saw him. 'But don't think it makes any difference because you can fool your own mother! Adam knows what happened between us and if you so much as look at me the wrong way in future I shall shout so loud they'll hear me in Bodmin!'

Later that evening there was still no sign of Adam's return. Bethany's anger at Theo's tale-telling had not abated and rather than have her meal with him and his mother, she opted to have a tray in Dina's room. Her anger was tempered by her disappointment because Adam had not returned, but the pain in her heart told her he had every inducement to stay away.

She lay wakefully in her bed listening to the wailing of the wind outside, knowing she should be planning the future after she left Tregarrick Manor but unable to imagine a future that did not include Adam. Yet she knew she must. He was tied to a woman totally dependent on him for her well-being and he was not a man to shirk his responsibilities, nor would she want him to.

She hated sleepless nights in the house that seemed to have a voice of its own. Perhaps her imagination was playing tricks upon her but she felt that a tension was building up; the fear she had sensed was becoming more tangible, drawing them inexorably into its net of terror.

She sat up sharply in her bed listening. Somewhere near there was the sound of moaning. Surely not just the wind? Her first instinct was to huddle down beneath the sheets, but after a moment she slipped out of the bed and into her dressing gown. The malaise affecting this house was caused by a human being, and if there was to be peace for any of its inhabitants Bethany felt bound to discover who it was.

Slowly, fearfully she edged along the darkened corridor towards Dina's room. She paused outside, listening, but there was no sound from within and Bethany, her breath coming in nervous gasps, slowly walked back past her own room and along the balcony. Downstairs a faint gleam came from where the fire was dying into embers. The hounds stretched in front of it stirred uneasily before settling back.

She listened again. She must have been mistaken.

The wind in high places could play eerie tricks on a receptive mind.

The moaning came again. This time Bethany knew where it came from. She opened the door to Grace's room. Grace lay on the crumpled bed; she still wore the nightgown from earlier in the evening with scorch marks around the hem. A bottle of whisky lay empty on the bedside table with a pool on the floor beneath it.

As she came into the room Grace moaned again. 'Theo? Theo, is that you?'

'No Grace, it's Bethany.'

She leaned over the bed attempting to straighten the covers but Grace grabbed hold of her arm. 'Jenefer? Oh Jenefer I'm sorry.'

Bethany froze. 'Why are you sorry Grace?' she asked in a slow tense whisper.

'It was my fault,' Grace began to toss in her bed. 'It was because of him. I was jealous. Forgive me Jenefer.'

Her voice tailed off into an unrecognizable babble. As Bethany started to straighten up Grace's voice grew into an agonized plea. 'Forgive me Jenefer!'

'I forgive you,' Bethany whispered softly and Grace grunted before slipping into a more restful sleep.

The wind was still howling the next morning when Bethany awoke. As she dressed the question that had been uppermost in her mind since coming back to her room the night before still irked her—had Grace in her drunken stupor admitted to killing Jenefer?

She was up early, still anxious to avoid Theo and his mother. Her interview with Esme still rankled, but the sheer audacity of his cunning now began to appeal to her sense of humour.

All the questions crowding her mind vanished at the sight of Adam sitting at the table in the great hall. 'Adam!' she cried, unable to conceal her joy at seeing him.

He looked up as she raced down the stairs and there was no mistaking the expression in his eyes. His chair scraped back and he rushed to meet her.

Every instinct urged her to throw herself into his arms but she must never in this house and probably never again. 'When did you get back?'

'Very late. I caught a later train than I had intended.' He gripped her hands tightly. 'I've missed you so much,' he said in a voice so low no one could possibly overhear. 'If there was any doubt about the way I feel there is none now.'

She pulled her hands free, searching his face anxiously. 'Have you missed me so much Adam? Have you really?'

His smile faded. 'You know I have Beth.'

'But you have been with Sally haven't you? No, don't bother to deny it.' She turned away. 'Please don't deny it.'

He pulled out a chair for her. 'Sit down Beth. We'd better look as if we're having breakfast if anyone comes.'

'Yes I went to see her,' he said when they had sat down. 'I had to go. Two years ago a girl was murdered within yards of this house. When another girl left suddenly in the middle of the night I had to make sure she really had gone to London.'

She raised her eyes to his. 'I'm so sorry Adam. So sorry.'

His hand reached for hers across the table and touched it fleetingly. 'Don't doubt me again Beth.'

She smiled at him. 'Did Sally tell you why she left so suddenly?'

'She said it was a break she'd wanted to make for a long time.'

'That's all?'

'That's all she said. I may be mistaken but I had the feeling there was something more; she was afraid and ill at ease.'

'You went away to think things out,' she said softly after a moment. 'Did you?'

He sighed. 'I did a great deal of thinking and none of it very clear. The answer would be to ask Grace for a divorce, provide her with a home and someone to look after her. She'd probably welcome it but...'

'But,' Bethany said with a sad smile, 'she would drink herself to death in no time.' She could almost feel his despair across the space that separated them. 'We couldn't be happy with that on our consciences.'

'My conscience is not very easy now. She was happy until we came here. I know I'm not blameless for her condition.'

Bethany looked down at the polished surface of the table that had seen hundreds of years of service, in both sad times and happy. 'If a woman loves a man she is happy to be wherever he is.'

'You would be wouldn't you?'

'It's no use theorizing Adam, we must be realistic.' She looked up at him knowing that the pain in her own eyes was mirrored in his. 'I'm going from here when Dina goes back to school. I'm sorry I tried to persuade you to let me stay. It would be too hard on both of us, particularly on you.'

'Oh Beth . . .'

'Adam you're back!'

He drew his eyes reluctantly away from Bethany and rose to greet his step-mother. He kissed her on the cheek. 'It's amazing how things never seem to go right when you're away,' Esme said as she sat down and then in a restrained voice, 'Good morning Mrs Ryder.'

'Good morning Mrs Tregarrick. I think I shall go and see Dina; she should be awake now.'

As she went up the stairs Bethany heard Esme say, 'You'll have to telephone the Ministry Adam. John Whittaker was in yesterday; he's heard a rumour of foot and mouth disease in Devon and you know how rumour is worse than the actual thing around here. Oh and Dawson was complaining of a renegade dog worrying his sheep . . .'

'I hope Dr Sanderson comes soon,' Dina said in a plaintive voice. 'I want to get up.'

'He has other patients to attend to besides you,' Bethany replied more sharply than she knew she should.

'Anyway you can't go out.'

'Is it still raining?'

'No but there's practically a gale blowing.'

Dina sighed. 'It's so *boring* in bed. I don't know what's going on. At least Adam is back. I hate it here without him.'

Bethany longed to agree with her but said instead, 'Your grandmother and Theo have been in to keep you company. Your mother too.'

Dina's lips twisted into a smile. 'They've been quite entertaining in their way. They were all quite upset yesterday when I told them. I had to do something to ease the boredom; I couldn't resist the impulse.'

Bethany turned to her after staring out of the window at Adam crossing the clearing. 'Told them what?'

Dina smiled impishly. 'You wouldn't believe me Mrs Ryder.'

Dr Sanderson arrived later in the afternoon and as expected pronounced Dina fit enough to get up for which Bethany was grateful; in Dina's almost constant company Adam would have to keep his distance, a thought which gave her little pleasure.

She stood in front of the house with the wind tearing at her hair watching the doctor's car disappear from sight. When it had gone she turned to go back inside but paused on hearing footsteps on the gravel behind her. She turned, fearing to see Theo, but she relaxed and smiled at Adam.

'Is Dina all right?' he asked.

'She can get up thank heavens. I don't know how you coped when she was really ill.'

He drew her around to the side of the house and pulled her roughly into his arms. She did not resist his insistent lips; just this once she told herself. Just this once to last me the rest of my life.

'This is wrong,' she said in a breaking voice when she was able to speak at last.

'I know but it's the last time. Until you leave I shall keep out of your way except when other people are around.'

'As long as no one has seen us already.'

'They're all inside and we can't be seen from the house.'

She pressed her face against the rough wool of his pullover. 'This place frightens me Adam. There always seems to be someone watching. I never feel as though I'm alone, wherever I go in the house.'

He stroked her hair. 'You are never alone my love. Don't you know my heart goes with you wherever you go.'

She sighed. 'You know that isn't what I mean.'

'That is one reason why I shall be glad when you've gone, although I can't imagine life without you now.'

She looked up at him. 'I went into Grace's room last night. She'd been drinking again and she was having a bad dream.' She paused. 'I'm not sure Adam but I think she confessed to killing Jenefer.'

He looked incredulous. 'Grace?' Then a long sigh escaped his lips. 'It's a terrible thought but I almost wish it were true.'

'Because it would mean a chance for us?'

He let her go. 'All I know is you're leaving in two weeks and I'd do anything to prevent that.'

She looked at him for a moment before saying, 'I'd better go back into the house; Dina will be waiting to get up.'

Bethany watched him anxiously at dinner that evening; he hardly spoke to anyone and she was aware he was deliberately avoiding looking at her.

At being allowed up, Dina had regained her usual light spirits as demonstrated by her immature attempts to flirt with Theo. For once the entire family was present but beneath the apparent normality of the scene Bethany could detect that same atmosphere of fear.

Theo was drinking too much she noticed; Grace was drinking too little; Esme's face was pinched and grey giving her an almost wizened look. The wind howled outside, blowing a draught through the lofty hall.

Bethany stiffened at the sound of its unearthly whispering. She looked around and realized for the first time the whispering was caused by a draught blowing through the minstrels gallery. It was one part of the balcony she had never explored. There was no point; it was a dead end. But she realized now if someone wanted to watch without being seen it was an ideal place to stand. Belatedly Bethany understood why she always felt as if she was being watched; it was not from the murky corners of the hall after all. No doubt Dina had used the gallery for her own snooping on many an occasion.

'I think Mrs Ryder,' Esme said as Mrs Penarvon, silent as ever, poured coffee, 'when it is time for Dina to return to school it will be best for you to accompany her there, seeing you will be leaving anyway.'

'As you wish Mrs Tregarrick,' Bethany replied.

'So it's all arranged,' Grace said roughly. 'It would be a good idea if someone consulted me for a change when it comes to matters regarding my daughter.'

'I'd like Mrs Ryder to come with me Mummy.'

'You'll do as you're told,' Grace snapped.

'When you rouse yourself long enough to take an interest in your daughter perhaps we shall consult you,' Adam replied without even looking at her.

Grace's face contorted into an ugly grin made even more frightening to Bethany by the fact she was quite sober. 'I suppose being her mother means nothing. Any woman who comes into the house has more say providing she happens to be in favour.' He did not reply and she said in a sly tone, 'I'm sure you must have heard about Mrs Ryder's new piece of heroism.'

'I've heard you set yourself alight,' he replied sourly without even looking at her, 'and you were too drunk to help yourself. If it hadn't been for Mrs Ryder's presence of mind you would have been burnt very badly.'

Adam levelled a cold glance at his half-brother who quickly looked away.

Theo is like a child, Bethany realized. He loves to make mischief but he is terrified of the results.

'Would you care?' Grace challenged.

'I care very much when you try to destroy yourself.'

A gust of wind battered against the stout granite walls and for that second it seemed they must surely give way. The lights flickered for a moment.

'What is happening?' Grace cried in a shrill voice.

The lights came on again. 'You should be used to the eccentricities of such an old and exposed building,' Esme said mildly.

'I shall never get used to it. I hate it!'

'I tried to make a telephone call before dinner but the line was dead,' Theo mumbled from the depths of his wineglass. He lifted his bloodshot eyes to Adam. 'Did you know?'

'Yes, the lines are down all over the area.'

'We're completely cut off,' Dina said in a breathless voice. 'How exciting.'

Grace's face contorted once again and she shivered. 'It's horrible.'

Esme surveyed her family. 'I find it remarkable that we've survived the winter without it happening before.'

'Normal conversation, Bethany thought, feeling suddenly chill. But beneath it they're watching each other. Behind the masks they wear for faces a murderer is watching.

She pushed back her chair. 'It's time for bed Dina. You've been up quite long enough for the first day.'

Dina began to protest but changed her mind and said

instead in a piteous voice, 'I do feel rather tired.'

Smiling to herself Bethany led her upstairs and as they reached the balcony she heard Adam say, 'I'd better see if the lines have been repaired.'

'Don't leave me just yet,' Dina begged, once they had reached her room.

'Aren't you feeling well?'

'I just don't want to be left alone.'

Bethany went across to the window and drew the curtains against the gale raging outside.

Dina stared morosely at the windows. 'It will last for days.'

'I expect you will be glad to be back at school.'

'No I like it here.'

'You can't mean that Dina. You must admit you get bored here.'

'I know I get bored and when I do I say terrible things just to see what their reaction will be. But I wish I'd never said anything.' She turned a pair of sad eyes on Bethany. 'You don't get bored do you?'

No I don't, Bethany thought. Living here with Adam, bringing up a family in the space and freedom of the moors and watching the never ending wonder of the trees budding each spring, and shedding each autumn whilst the children grow taller and stronger with each season that passes. And to be able to curl up in the arms of the man I love when the wind and rain fought outside.

No I would never be bored.

Briskly bringing her attention back to Dina she

replied, 'But I don't live here Dina. In the time I've been here I just haven't had time to get bored.'

Surprisingly the girl put her arms around Bethany. 'I hate school Mrs Ryder. When I tell them my mother is a famous actress they don't believe me.'

'But you know it's true Dina and that's all that matters. They are too young to remember when she was on the stage.'

'I'm not like the others. They all have aunts and uncles and brothers and sisters who visit them and take them out to tea. When only Adam comes they want to know where my mother is and why I never invite any of them to stay here during the holidays.'

Bethany kissed the top of her head. 'You're old enough to realize that your mother isn't very well.'

'She drinks,' Dina said disgustedly.

'It's an illness Dina just the same, and you must understand she is a very unhappy woman.'

'No one is happy here Mrs Ryder. No one.'

Bethany when she finally did leave Dina, went straight to her room and she lay for a long time in her bed listening to the wind tearing around the house and wondering what Dina had said and to whom to provoke such an attack of conscience.

She was just drifting into sleep when the knock came on the door. She sat up in bed listening and it came again. 'Who is it?'

'Dina,' came the hushed reply.

Bethany gave a little cry of exasperation. 'Come in.'

And as Dina's white face appeared around the door she said sharply, 'Switch on the light Dina.'

'I can't; they won't go on.'

Bethany stumbled her way over to the light switch and flicked it first one way and then the other. 'The cables must be down.'

'I was reading in bed,' Dina said breathlessly, 'and they went out.'

Bethany listened. 'The wind has dropped. They'll soon be repaired. You'd better get back to bed before you catch another chill and then I will be in trouble.'

'I can't sleep in the dark when I'm alone. I always keep the bedside lamp on during the night.'

'Are there any candles in the house?'

'Loads of them in the kitchen.'

Bethany shivered at the thought of having to go to the other side of the house in the darkness, but despite her abhorrence she slipped on her warm dressing gown. 'You'd better get under the covers while I go.'

'I can stay here?'

'Yes, but in bed. In you go.'

She braced herself to go downstairs; the wind had dropped to the terrifying whisper she hated. Hero and Minerva were stretched by the hearth. She paused as she passed them. They did not stir. Impulsively she stooped and touched Hero, listening to his regular and heavy breathing. The beast still did not stir and as her hand drew slowly away from his head she knew the hounds, who were normally alert to every sound, were not in a natural sleep.

A draught blew through the hall and she looked up to the balcony, slowly getting to her feet. 'Who is there?'

There was no reply. 'Who is there?' she repeated, aware that her voice was rising to hysterical proportions. More than ever she was convinced she was being watched.

Disgusted at her own fear she shouted. 'Is that you Dina? Theo? Whoever you are stop being so childish.'

'Go away Bethany Ryder.' The voice came as a ghostly whisper so that it was impossible to tell if it belonged to man or woman. 'Go away ... go away ...' The voice echoed around the hall and Bethany's legs were paralysed with fear. 'Go away ... away,' the voice whispered again and the hall was filled with the sound.

Bethany's head twisted this way and that as the whispering came at her wherever she turned. 'Come out here and let me see you!' she cried.

The draught came again together with audible footsteps on the balcony above. Completely forgetting her fear Bethany bounded up the stairs. She ran into the terrifying darkness of the minstrels gallery but it was deserted.

'Mrs Ryder,' came a hushed voice, 'what is happening?'

Dina's pale face appeared at a crack in the bedroom door. 'Have you been out here Dina?' she snapped.

'No Mrs Ryder.'

'Go back inside and lock the door. Open it to no one but me. Do you understand?'

Dina nodded fearfully and after waiting to hear the

bolt click into place Bethany went along the corridor to Grace's room. She need not have bothered—Grace was not there.

Moving along the corridor she tapped softly on the next door. 'Adam. Adam are you there?'

Again there was no reply. She pushed open the door. The bed had not even been used. She rushed back into the corridor fully aware of how impossible it would be for her to burst in to Theo's room and equally as undesirable, in view of her weak heart, to rouse Mrs Tregarrick.

She stood almost weeping with her own fear and indecision when she heard the sound of footsteps in the hall below. 'Adam—Grace, is that you?'

She rushed to the balcony just as the front door was opened. The wind roared through the hall brushing her hair back from her head, then it slammed shut closing in the silence again.

She raced down the stairs once more and as she passed the fireplace and the deeply slumbering hounds, her eyes were compelled towards the display of weapons above the mantel. Somehow it came as no surprise when she saw the moonstone dagger had gone.

The wind was cool blowing through the folds of her dressing gown. Her mouth was dry with fear.

There was no sign of whoever had come out. Out there in the sighing, whispering woods someone was at liberty with a dagger that Bethany was convinced had killed one woman. Every instinct urged her back into the house. She didn't have to discover who had killed

Jenefer Henekin—in her heart she did not want to know. But she must if Adam was ever to be free of the bitter taint of guilt that affected them all.

She stood for some minutes shivering in the shadows of the porch. The wind was teasing the leaves with a gentle embrace as it whispered amongst the branches. Suddenly Bethany's heart stood still; a piercing scream rose to a crescendo, dying and rising again to finally die away in a hoarse gurgle. Then there was silence again.

Bethany tore herself away from the shelter of the porch and raced across towards the trees. She hardly knew where she was going except that it was in the direction from which the agonized scream had come. With every step she had to force herself on; not to turn and run back to the sanctuary of her room. She reached the glade with its carpet of bluebells by the little stream.

She stopped breathless, choking back a sob. The moon drifted from behind the clouds illuminating the clearing. The stream gurgled gently beneath the bridge as it always would no matter what happened. Bathed in moonlight the glade took on a new heartrending beauty, and there in the midst of such unearthly charm lay Grace Tregarrick and by her side, his hands stained with the red of her blood, kneeled Adam.

Some sound must have escaped her lips for he looked up to see her and the expression of unbelieving horror in her eyes. He jumped to his feet staring at his hands in disbelief and then back to her. 'Beth, surely you can't think . . .'

She did not wait for him to finish. With tears coursing

down her cheeks she turned, running out of the glade. As she ran through the trees loose branches whipped against her cheeks but she pushed them heedlessly aside. Tears blinded her eyes so she could not see. It didn't matter where she went as long as it was away from him.

His voice echoed in her mind. 'All I know is you're leaving in two weeks and I'd do anything to prevent that.'

Somewhere a voice cried, 'Beth please come back!' as she left the trees behind and began to stumble up into the moors. Finally she could hear him no more, and completely exhausted, she threw herself on to the ground and wept until she could weep no more. Finally dry eyed she stared unseeingly ahead. The night was fine and clear; the chimneys of Tregarrick Manor were clearly to be seen rising above the trees. The moors sprawled out before her; a place apart from any other. A place where law and order did not reign; just naked and primitive passion in all its forms.

As long as she lived she would never be able to obliterate the sight of Grace Tregarrick's bloody body from her tortured mind.

Suddenly she stiffened. 'Bethany where are you?'

Getting to her feet she began to run once more, this time back towards the woods. There was no shelter on the moors. She didn't want to meet Adam, yet she did not want to see anyone else either. Whatever happened now she could never admit to what she had seen.

A scream rose in her throat at the sight of a shadow moving towards her. She clamped one hand over her mouth to stifle it as the shadow materialized into Esme Tregarrick who was still wearing her evening dress. It billowed behind her in the breeze enclosing her small body in a grotesque balloon. Seeing her like this in such a setting she looked less than human.

She saw Bethany then and came towards her, glancing fearfully behind her all the while. 'I'm so relieved to see you,' Bethany sighed. 'We have to get back to the house. Grace is dead Mrs Tregarrick; she's been murdered. We have to telephone for the police.'

'The lines are still not working,' Esme replied, eyeing Bethany warily.

Somewhere behind Bethany could still hear Adam searching and calling for her. Her eyes travelled down Esme's dress. The plain grey chiffon now bore a pattern; a pattern of irregular rust-coloured spots. Bethany looked up again and Esme was watching her, a smile of satisfaction on her face.

'You seem surprised Mrs Ryder.'

'I shouldn't be. You're the only one with nerve enough to kill. I suppose you killed Jenefer too.'

'Yes I killed her. I'm not sorry. She was a bad girl; a shameless woman who used her body to corrupt young men. She was expecting Theo's child. The fool wanted to marry her and I couldn't allow that. She seduced him you see and then she wanted to trap him into marriage. I had to send Sally away too for the same reason.'

Bethany silently prayed for Adam to catch up with her now. 'I can understand that Mrs Tregarrick,' she said in a calm voice, 'but why Grace?'

'She was the one who told me about Jenefer the night I killed her. She was jealous you see. She loved him too.' She was amused at the surprise in Bethany's face. 'Oh yes, from the moment she first saw him she loved him. Adam would never have told you. He prefers to bear the blame for Grace's condition but it isn't so. He ceased to exist for Grace when they came back here to live because she met Theo. But he only amused himself with her so she was no danger—until tonight. I heard her begging him to take her away. He refused but he's weak like his father and he'd agree eventually. So I waited until he had gone and I killed her.'

'I hope you realize Adam will take the blame for this.'

Her eyes gleamed. 'I intend him to.'

Bethany stared at her. 'But why Mrs Tregarrick? You're so fond of him.'

'Fond of him!' She laughed harshly. 'I hate him! Everytime I look at Adam I see my husband and I have to remember the humiliations he heaped upon me.'

She stared at Bethany. 'He never loved me. He never loved anyone but Adam's mother and that's another reason why I hate him. He would never have married me if I hadn't been expecting Theo.'

'You can't want Adam to suffer for what his father did.'

But Esme was past listening. Still with the strange gleam in her eyes she went on. 'Everyone thought I was a lady.' She laughed again in a coarse way. 'A barmaid I was. When Greville brought Rosanna Penarvon into the house I couldn't do anything about it. He used to laugh at me saying I was no better and if I didn't accept her he would tell everyone about me. He threatened to make me a laughing stock in front of all our friends. There was no need; they all knew about Greville's woman and they pitied me.'

A tear squeezed down her cheek and Bethany took a step forward. 'Forget about it now Mrs Tregarrick. It won't help you to hurt Adam. He's been hurt enough.'

'Theo will inherit Tregarrick Manor once Adam is out of the way. That is how it must be. Then he will marry someone suitable—a lady. So you can forget your fancy ideas.'

'I have no designs on Theo. I love Adam. You must see how wrong you are.'

'You think you love Adam but you'll soon tire of him just as Grace did and then you'll want Theo. And he's weak like his father.'

The dagger appeared from behind her back. Bethany stared at it in fascination somehow expecting to see it dripping with blood instead of it being spotted quite innocently with a few dark brown stains.

She looked back to Esme with a plea in her eyes. 'If you kill me you can't possibly blame it on Adam. No one will believe he killed me. I would be the one reason for him to kill Grace.'

'Don't you worry about that; they'll try him for Grace's murder first and that will be enough. Everyone knows he has ample motive for that.'

'Mrs Tregarrick don't do this. Don't do this to Adam.

He's fond of you. He looks on you as a mother.' The moonstones glinted in the moonlight. 'Adam! Adam!' she began to cry as Esme Tregarrick came towards her.

As she stumbled backwards her foot caught in a root and she plunged to the ground, helpless before the woman wielding the moonstone dagger. Esme bent over Bethany who closed her eyes waiting for the searing pain to begin as the blade slashed through her flesh. But it did not come.

She opened her eyes again. Esme was still bending over her but she was staring past her. Her lips mouthed one word. 'Theo.'

'Mother! For God's sake what are you doing?' Then the realization came. '*You* killed Jenefer. You killed her! Dina told me but I thought it was one of her wicked lies.'

'I had to kill her Theo. You would have married her.'

His eyes seemed to be bulging out of his head. 'It was you. Oh mother how could you?'

'Theo don't say that,' she cried.

The moonstone dagger dropped to the ground and Bethany closed her eyes again giving in to the wave of relief that swept over her.

'You killed her,' Theo repeated as if he could still hardly believe it.

'Don't look at me like that Theo.' Bethany sat up slowly unable to believe this pathetic, begging old woman was the one who had cold-bloodedly killed two women and almost a third.

Esme took a step towards her son but he moved backwards to avoid any contact. 'Why were you trying to kill Bethany?' he asked. 'Why her?'

'Because she knew Theo, and I was frightened she'd tell. Can't you see with her and Adam out of the way we shall have Tregarrick Manor for ourselves at last?'

'She's killed Grace too Theo.'

He buried his face in his hands moaning softly. 'Oh my God. It's all my fault.' He looked up at his mother, his handsome face twisted in disgust. 'You stupid old woman. I don't want this hateful old mansion. It means less than nothing to me.'

'But it's yours Theo! You're his son!'

'Do you really think I would stay here with you when the blood of two innocent people is staining your hands? I can't bear to look at you any more!'

'Don't say that Theo.' He ignored her outstretched hand and instead went over to Bethany, helping her to her feet. As he bent over her she noticed the tears glistening on his cheeks. What an awful way for a man to grow up, she thought.

'Are you all right?' he asked in a perfunctory way, hardly looking at her.

She nodded, not trusting herself to speak, and as she did so she noticed suddenly Esme was no longer there.

'We'd better find her quickly Theo. She's capable of doing anything.'

They ran through the trees shouting Esme's name and as they emerged into the clearing Theo shouted 'Look!'

And as Bethany followed the direction of his gaze

she saw the door to the house was open and dense black smoke was pouring out. Without a further word both ran across the clearing. Bethany paused at the porch vainly hoping for Adam to appear.

'Mother must be in there,' Theo gasped.

She looked at him sharply. 'Dina too.' As he rushed forward she cried, 'You'll be killed,' but after a moment's hesitation she followed him inside.

The hall was stiflingly hot, filled with billowing smoke and the acrid smell of burning timber. Flames were already creeping up the wainscoting and the oak staircase.

In the centre of the floor lay Esme Tregarrick with her son standing helplessly over her. In a remarkably short time she had set alight every small article of furniture in the room before she had been overcome herself.

Bethany began to cough. 'For goodness sake Theo get her out!'

He stared at Bethany with the blankness of deep shock. From above came the faint cry, 'Help someone! Help me!'

'Dina,' she whispered to herself and then looking at Theo she said in a choking voice, 'Get your mother out of here before she suffocates.'

Her words seemed to reach him at last, and bending down he picked up the frail body as easily as a rag doll and began to make his way towards the door. From upstairs Bethany could hear Dina still shouting.

The smoke was becoming thicker by the minute

with only the flames licking up the stair rail visible in the gloom. Bethany looked at them hesitantly for a moment, and after a spasm of coughing that racked her body, she gathered her dressing gown tightly around her, and holding her breath she rushed forward and up the stairs.

Flames leaped on either side fed by the draught she made as she passed. At the top she paused, coughing until she thought she would never stop. Then horrified she saw the hem of her dressing gown smouldering by her feet. The sparks danced around her hands as she beat at them frenziedly and when she finally extinguished the last spark she had no time to feel relief.

The smoke was like a blanket around her as she groped her way along the corridor. At last she reached her room and pounded on the door. 'Dina it's Bethany. Let me in.'

After a moment's pause which seemed like a lifetime, the door flew open and a white-faced Dina fell into her arms. She had been standing at the open window and behind her Bethany heard the frightening roar of the flames fed by the draught coming through the open door.

'I was so afraid,' Dina whimpered. 'I didn't know what was going on.'

Bethany closed the door, thankful for the relatively fresh air in the room as she took great gulping breaths. She gently released herself from Dina's embrace, knowing that there was no time to spare if they were both to get out of the house alive.

'We're both going to be quite all right if you do as you're told,' Bethany told her as she went across to the chest of drawers and pulled out a wad of handkerchiefs. She soaked them in the sink before squeezing them out.

'Press this over your nose and mouth and for heaven's sake keep them there.'

Dina looked at her wide-eyed. 'I can't Mrs Ryder. I can't go down there.'

Bethany grabbed her arm roughly and pulled her over to the window. 'Do you want to jump instead?' Dina stared down at the ground before backing away. 'We've no time to lose. Put the handkerchief to your face and keep hold of me.'

The smoke in the corridor was thicker than ever as Bethany groped her way along, one hand on the wall and the other holding Dina's shaking hand in a vice-like grip. 'Hold my gown,' she cried, realizing if she did not cover her mouth and nose neither of them was going to get out. As she fumbled with the handkerchief she heard, 'Beth! Dina! Are you up there?'

Her heart almost stopped. Oh don't let Adam come up here, she prayed. The heat from the flames was almost unbearable.

'No I can't!' Dina cried, seeing the flames leaping up the stair rail.

Not having time to argue Bethany seized her around the waist and half carrying her began to negotiate the stairs. With each step she took the stairs creaked ominously. Suddenly they heaved and Bethany stopped, panic freezing her to the spot. The staircase heaved again and she found herself being propelled into the air filled with Dina's and her own screams.

When she felt firm ground beneath her she realized they must have been near the bottom when the staircase had given way. Through the smoke she saw that the stairs had completely gone.

'Dina,' she said and her mouth was filled with soot. 'Dina where are you?' She got to her feet and began to fumble around half-blinded by the smoke. Her foot struck something and when she bent down she knew it was Dina.

Another figure loomed out of the dark. Without a word Adam scooped the girl into his arms. Behind them the balustrade creaked and shuddered and amid a shower of sparks crashed to the floor.

'Keep close,' he urged. Going through the smoke filled hall was like walking blind but Bethany kept close to him.

The journey through the hall was agonizing in its slowness. With every second that passed each breath taken was more painful than the one before. Behind them the old timbers of the house blazed and crashed to the floor sending up clouds of sparks and spreading the fire even further.

At last they reached the door only to find it barred by a fallen beam that had set fire to it. If Bethany could have felt any emotion she would have cried, but all she did feel was the despair of defeat and what is more she no longer cared what happened to her.

'It's no use; we're trapped.' Her voice tailed off in a spasm of convulsive coughing.

'We're not finished yet,' Adam spluttered. 'Here, hold on to Dina and stand back there.'

She watched him through half-closed eyes as he struggled with the burning wood. Somehow he managed to move the beam and open the door a little. Then he lifted Dina into his arms and carried her outside. A moment later he returned, and when she made no move to go to the door which was now blazing, he swept her into his arms too.

All at once the heat was no longer scorching her skin and the smoke no longer choked her lungs. All around was cool night air. She lay on the ground coughing and gasping air into her lungs.

Finally she stopped panting and her heart no longer felt as though it would burst. She raised her head to see Adam standing nearby watching his home burn. Through running eyes she too watched the flames leaping through the roof and the windows crack from the ferocity of the heat and crash to the ground.

He turned his soot-blackened face to hers. 'Let's get back. We're not safe here.'

He helped her to her feet and they ran to where Mrs Penarvon was standing, a coat over her night clothes. She too was watching the end of Tregarrick Manor.

Bethany bent over Dina's inert form just as her eyes flickered open.

'She fainted. She'll be all right,' Adam said from behind her.

'Grandmother killed Jenefer,' Dina said, her voice harsh from the smoke.

Bethany smiled at her, smoothing back her hair. 'Hush, it doesn't matter now.' Then she looked up at Adam. 'Will the fire brigade be in time?'

He shook his head and then as she was about to say something more he drew a deep sigh and said, 'Let it burn.'

'We must call a doctor for Mother,' Theo cried and Bethany raised her still smarting eyes to see him a little way off, kneeling by Esme's body, her frail hands clutched in his.

'She doesn't need one Theo,' Adam said gently, then he looked down at Bethany. 'She was dead when he brought her out. She must have had a heart attack.'

Theo let out a cry and after staring in disbelief at his mother for a moment he threw himself down, sobbing over her body.

Adam watched, his face impassive, but as Bethany watched Adam she saw his own grief etched quite clearly in his eyes. He had loved her as a mother—the only mother he had ever known—and Bethany guessed her betrayal of his love had hurt him far more deeply than Grace's had done. He had lost so much in one night.

As the wind fanned the flames the blaze gained in strength and she saw Adam's face was running; whether it was tears or perspiration she could not tell. Just as the roof caved in he turned and gave one last look at his home before stooping down by Bethany's side.

She touched his hand and when he winced she realized he had been burnt. 'You're hurt,' she gasped.

'We're alive.'

'Yes, we're alive,' she echoed bleakly, remembering the two who weren't. She looked at him anxiously. 'Hero and Minerva! They were drugged. They must still be in there.'

'They're safe,' he said with a ghost of a smile. 'I brought them out before I knew you were in there.' She followed his gaze to where the hounds were trying to stumble to their feet. 'She used to take sleeping pills.' he added. 'She must have given some to them.'

He looked back at her and put one of his raw hands on hers. 'Beth, before very long this place is going to be crawling with people. Everyone will know what has happened here tonight and ... you realize there's going to be a lot of unpleasantness, probably for a long time.'

Her sore eyes brimmed with tears. 'I know Adam. But don't worry about me.'

They both looked to the still dazed Dina. 'She will need you more than I will during the next few weeks...' She looked at him. 'But later, Beth, later...'

She put her hand up to his grimy face and touched it gently, 'Yes Adam, later...'

Love Has a Double

Love
Has a
Double

BETH GORMAN

"You know what it is," he told her. "Maybe you haven't felt it as long as I have, but it goes back to the night we danced. To the first time I saw you. It was as though an invisible thread ran from you to me. I've been in love with you, Ruth, since then."

ONE

TOGETHER AGAIN

HE'D been to war and that hadn't changed him, and he'd been engaged in his maritime business in San Francisco now for three years, and that did not appear to have changed him either, even though her father had warned her that no man who left Old Dominion Virginia for California ever remained a gentleman.

She wasn't sure what, exactly, a gentleman was. She knew what the term was meant to encompass in her father's day, but that was another time, another world. She wasn't even sure she wanted Phillip Harlow to be a gentleman, and as she watched him coming across the sunswept broad mall of San Francisco Airport, tall and handsome and unsmiling—he seldom smiled—her hands on the chair-arm gripped hard as anxiety and excitement worried her heart.

He was a man women looked at twice, with his athletic build, his curly dark hair, the black eyes and the firm mouth. He had been a commanding person the first time she had met him six years ago, shortly before he went away to war, and afterwards, through their correspondence, she had felt him becoming more and more a segment of her life. Then he had come home for six months, then out here to California because he knew of an opportunity.

Actually, she had only known him personally for that six-month interval. But now, preparing to rise and greet him, she saw him come through the glass doors an individual among all the other people and her sensation of solemn sweetness returned; the same solemn sweetness she had felt when he'd come back from the army, and the same feeling she'd had when she'd gone down to the airport back home to see him outward bound for California.

"A very wilful man," her father had told her when she'd showed him the letter proposing marriage. "Energetic and wilful, sweetheart, but you do whatever your heart dictates."

She saw Phil's dark eyes make their sweep, spot her by the chair and stop stone-steady while he looked at her. He crossed over and held out a hand. She smiled, and blushed too for some reason. He picked up her two suitcases and said, "I got a good accommodation for you, Ruth. We'd better go now unless we want to get caught in the traffic." He looked swiftly at her, black gaze quickening with the dull fire she remembered; then he leaned and kissed her swiftly before they started back towards the glass doors.

She was satisfied; three years had changed nothing, not with him, and not between them. Charley Banks, the boy back in Virginia who had loved her through four years of high school, had said, the last time they met, "Don't do it, Ruthie, not to him. If you do that'll be the sorriest day of your life. Don't take my word for it, ask your father. Just remember this: men can only fool women, never other men."

She had asked her father, and that was when he had said, "A very wilful man . . . but do whatever your

8

heart dictates." Her father had a maxim about one person being capable of living only one life.

She knew, of course, that San Francisco was a large city, but when they were in Phil's car driving away from the airport she was amazed at the haste. Everyone, even those ugly little German car owners, raced by. No one, it seemed, wanted to be late for some appointment, and surely not everyone she saw speeding in, or out, of the city, was actually going to such a critical meeting.

In Virginia there was haste, but only in the largest city, and even then there was also the leisurely way right beside it.

Phil looked quickly at her, then back to the road. "It's very different out here. For one thing this is a highly competitive society, not like back in Virginia. For another thing, you can't be too friendly or polite."

She thought about that. The competition probably wouldn't touch her since this was a visit, and as for the rest of it, she knew how to be chilly. She said, "I'll learn," and smiled at his profile.

His expression of energetic motivation was the same. She had always felt that with the kind of drive he had, eventually he would be a success. He was physically hard, the kind of man other men respected. She also knew that other men did not always like Phil Harlow. That had never bothered her because she attributed it to jealousy, or to inferiority. She remembered how impressive he had looked in his captain's uniform; as though nothing could deter him and no cause he believed in could be vanquished. He was, she felt, born to command, whether in uniform or out of it. At eighteen she had been hopelessly in love with him. Now, at twenty-one, she was proud of what he looked like, of what she was confident that he actually was—a man of unyielding force on his way to the top. A handsome, erect, big, powerful man with all the iron in his make-up it took to succeed.

She said, "California must agree with you, Phil. You look very fit."

He accepted the compliment with a glance at her, then a return of his full attention to the raceway where they were speeding towards the city. "I belong to a country club and play tennis once or twice a month, but I could keep in shape without that, just by trotting around the docks when the ships dock." He was silent for a moment, thinking of something, then he spoke again.

"This is a busy season, Ruth. I've got three ships on the Orient run."

She understood that to mean he'd be unable to be with her all the time, and said, "Work always comes before pleasure, Phil. I understand."

He shot her another of those quick, black-eyed looks of appraisal. "Good. But we'll make it just fine, as soon as things let up a little."

She said, "Three ships, Phil?"

He made a slight face. "It's not as good as it sounds. I'm mortgaged to my neck. But at least we're pulling down a decent profit. Nothing spectacular—yet—but good enough so that I won't have to become a stock company. It's Phillip Harlow Shipping and that's exactly how I want it to remain." He shot her another momentary glance. "How is your father?"

"Fine. So is everyone else back home. They ask about you every now and then."

His lips twitched to a slow droop. "I'll bet. How

about Charley Banks, the lad with the hound-dog eyes when he's around you?"

She remembered how close he and Charley had come to violence once, at a country club dance. "Charley too. You never took the time to know him."

Phil bobbed his head up and down as though less in agreement with what she'd said than in agreement with something he was privately thinking. "Out here, they eat his kind for breakfast every morning of the week. You'll see what it's like, and that I'm not exaggerating. When you go back, you'll have something to tell them they won't believe. The green and rolling Virginia country-side." He shook his head without looking at her, his tone turning flinty with sarcasm. "The Old Southern traditions. There's no comparison. That kind would starve out here."

She smoothed her skirt and looked at the purse in her lap. Phil had drifted to Virginia from Newark, New Jersey, and had been working as a salesman when they had met. He had never felt easy nor liked the Virginia way of life; at least not the way of life among the people who had estates and comfortable incomes. She had always known that, and in a way she hadn't liked the Virginia way of life either, because it wasn't productive, wasn't modern.

Now, she got him off the subject by wondering aloud what her chances would be of getting work, if she decided she liked San Francisco enough to stay.

"No problem at all," he answered briskly. "If I can't use you, there are a dozen other outfits in the same building that can. But look San Francisco over first, Ruth. It's nothing you're accustomed to. Take your time. When I can, we'll hit the nightspots, and the places people are supposed to show to out-of-towners, except that I haven't had much time to see them myself."

They got into the city and she was surprised, not at the dirt, or the ugly old cement and stone buildings: she saw from the expressways. She had seen their counterparts in all big cities, but she was surprised by the fact that San Francisco didn't *smell* dirty. Phil said it was because of the ocean, the bay, all the salt water that kept the year-round temperature brisk and pleasant, and that also brought the inland sea breezes.

He sounded as though he were satisfied with San Francisco, not in love with it, but satisfied with it.

As he turned down a wide street heading for a very tall tan building, which was her hotel except that she had no inkling until he slowed out front, he told her that the San Francisco waterfront was like none other in the world, and when he had the time he'd take her down there.

Getting her established at the hotel didn't take ten minutes. Phil had already made the reservation by telephone. Afterwards, he saw her up to her room, kissed her—pecked her, rather—then made his excuses and hastened away.

She entered the room, found that it was in fact a very nice suite with a bedroom, bath, living-room . It was more like a studio because of all the glass along one wall and a studio couch among the furnishings that also made up into a spare bed.

She showered, got into a robe and went to stand in front of the windows. Miles of rooftops at all elevations ran off to her right, which was northward . Ahead, out beyond the city, was the sea, slaty grey today and dull, as though it were sulking, and nearer she saw the wharves and slips where more ships were tied up than she had ever imagined before at one sitting. Phil had been right, she was about to have the adventure of her life. He was also probably correct about her father, Charley, all the people she remembered back home, never being able to adjust to this frantic place. But there was a reason : they wouldn't have to adjust, and they wouldn't, anyway, because the philosophy of life in Virginia's fox-hunting country was unalterably alien to what she saw, and felt, on all sides of her now.

But *she* could make the transition. She smiled with a pair of tough-set lips when she thought of that. She was different; she belonged where the action was. She was part of this—Phil Morrow's—generation.

She decided to unpack, then to put her hair up. The flight hadn't tired her but it had left her feeling a kind of restless need for some kind of activity. Sitting for hours on end was not her idea of anything people ought to do.

She turned on a built-in stereo that had outlets in every room, made certain the front door was locked and on the chain, then went to the bedroom to prepare for the hair-washing ordeal, which amounted almost to a bath, now that she had long hair again. Before, she'd worn her hair boyishly short and curly, and it had been ridiculously easy to maintain, but Phil liked her hair long. It was a shade of red-rusty-auburn, and he had told her once he'd never seen hair like that on a woman before. He wanted her to wear it long so that, someday, she could pile it on top of her head . Then he'd get her a pearl-and-diamond clip to wear in it so that when they went out in the evenings people would turn and stare.

TWO

THE STATURE OF A MAN

PHIL had been right, Baghdad-By-The-Bay was a city as distinctive as Rome, and like Rome it was built on a number of hills. Ruth Severns' second day of sight-seeing convinced her of two things: one, that no matter where one went in San Francisco it was uphill; and two, that aching leg muscles were the sign of a newcomer.

Phil called once during the day and again in the evening. The last call had been to make a dinner-date with her for the ensuing evening. He was very busy, otherwise, because two of his ships had docked the same day. She could imagine what that meant without him telling her, which he didn't do because, and she remembered this about Phil Harlow from years back, he rarely discussed his affairs with other people, not even with her.

It didn't matter, she was having the time of her life making the acquaintance of San Francisco. She was fascinated with Chinatown, the largest enclave of Chinese outside of Mainland China. She also visited Fisherman's Wharf, one of the main landmarks, and tourist traps, of the city. Then there was the slightly grimy but immensely impressive financial district where the largest bank in the world—Bank of America—had its sky-scraping headquarters.

14

She decided that whatever a person wanted, San Francisco had, including a climate that was never, or at least was very rarely, too hot, and which could never be too cold because of the Pacific Ocean that curved around the headlands in a protective embrace.

It was a sophisticated city; its people liked that idea, and even the newspaper columnists worked hard to maintain the idea.

She had seen New York, Washington, Baltimore, Richmond, and San Francisco was unlike any of them. She had also visited Los Angeles, a long day's drive southward—or an hour's flight southward—but Los Angeles and San Francisco were as unalike as though they were in different countries. It amused her to hear San Franciscans speak contemptuously of Los Angeles, the much larger, upstart community down the coast. It was the same way old-family Virginians around Richmond spoke of Washington.

She didn't wait for Phil to show her the docks, although when she got down there she became aware that it wasn't the best place in the world for an unescorted woman. She took refuge with a grizzled cabdriver, a cynical, disillusioned man with battered features and surly eyes, who said he had spotted her for a tourist the moment he saw her, and after putting her in his cab, toured the docks pointing things out. He then took her back in the vicinity of her hotel and as she paid him he said, "Lady, use your head. This ain't back home. There's more crime in San Francisco by the day than they probably get by the year wherever you come from. It may be a colourful place, but stay up here in your own country or you're going to get damned disillusioned."

It was, she realised, sound advice, Baghdad-By-The-

Bay might be a fascinatingly sophisticated city, but it was still a metropolis and that meant, no matter where a city was located or what kind of reputation it might have, that there was more than enough crime, too.

Phil came by for her the following evening and when she related her adventures, including the cab-driver's advice, he agreed, but his concurrence was slightly offhand, as though his mind was elsewhere.

He was attentive, and where he took her to dinner the atmosphere was delightfully old-worldish and the cuisine was perfect, but Phil's mind kept drifting elsewhere. As he told her, trade with the Orient was entering a critical era. While the Vietnam War was going on any shipping company was able to make expenses and a profit. But nowadays, with Japanese shipping taking a big bite out of the American market by operating at about a third of what U.S. vessels required, it wasn't easy to get cargoes.

She was interested, of course, because this was his chosen field, but for the time being all she could do was listen. All she knew about ships was what she had learned once on a ferry ride in New York harbour. Even her knowledge of business in general was limited. She had worked, back home, for an insurance company as a secretary, but only for five months. So, although she was qualified as a typist and even a passable transcriber of shorthand, the fundamentals of commercialism were only very vague in her mind.

It might have helped if her father had been a business man, but he had retired early, having made a comfortable amount of money and having inherited still more. His life was as alien—as artificial, Phil had once said—

in relation to the dog-eat-dog business world, as a man's life could be.

She asked about his ships and he opened up a little over highballs while they awaited the arrival of their dinner. "Former war-vessels," he said. "Surplus ships that I bid on and got at a fair price. They're good ones, very seaworthy, and in fact not very old. It's not the ships, they cost me a minimum in upkeep and operating expenses—it's the crews. U.S. maritime unions have priced American seamen right out of this world. They are paid more than even West German seamen. What one U.S. seaman makes in a month is as much as many Oriental sailors get a year. Do you know how that kind of thing can stand in relationship to the profit-margin left over when we transport a cargo?"

She could imagine but that was all she could do. Their dinner arrived and although Phil ordered another highball she declined his invitation to do likewise, because she was hungry. She had never been able to develop much of a taste for drinking anyway.

Phil loosened a little, as their meal progressed, and in the subdued but elegant atmosphere of the expensive restaurant, she somehow got the impression that all the other lean, well-dressed men in the room, even the greying older ones with their markedly predatory looks, would sympathise. This place seemed to Ruth Severns to belong to Phil Harlow's environment.

She liked it. There was an exclusiveness to the restaurant that required no vast perspicacity to feel. The men and women were expensively although not ostentatiously dressed. They had the look of people who gave orders, who made money and who spent it. It was doubtful that any street-trade was encouraged. But as she ate

17

and listened, she had to decide that Phil's laments were more habitual than actual; he could not conceal the fact that he was making money. Yet he made it sound as though governments, unions, even the people with whom he did business shipping cargoes, were all conspiring to squeeze him out of business.

She remembered a man named Shaeffer back home, who owned two large mills back in Virginia and Alabama, who never neglected an opportunity to make this same kind of lament . She also recalled her father's laughing comment one time, to the effect that no successful business man ever avoided the chance to moan in despair in order to prevent people from suspecting the truth—that he was growing rich. Her father had said, "It goes with the times, sweetheart. In my youth people admired a man who made money. Nowadays he's supposed to pretend he can't make a dime because people seem to resent profiteering."

She might have thought this did not apply with Phil except that his complaints were so similar to those other ones she'd heard back home. But she kept this to herself, listened sympathetically, and enjoyed her dinnner. Also, she could not escape the conclusion that if Phil hadn't had the second highball he might have been less talkative.

He finally abandoned the subject of his difficulties and when a waiter came to enquire if they were ready for dessert, he surprised her by the way his voice slammed at the man for interfering. The waiter retired, woodenfacedly, and Phil growled something about annoyances and resumed his meal.

She attributed this interlude to his long habit of command, first with the army and now as an owner of sea-going ships whose crews and captains he commanded.

But that wasn't an altogether satisfactory excuse, so she put the interlude out of her mind. Ruth Severns was a loyal person; she had never been otherwise.

Later, replete and relaxed, waiting for their plates to be removed and their dessert to be served, she asked if he anticipated any lessening of the pressure . He gazed at her, his black eyes alive with hard brightness, and said, "The thing to be done, providing it can be brought off, is to bank enough surplus to be certain all forthcoming debts can be met on time, then, as the other little lines get into trouble, to pick up their options and contracts."

It sounded cold-blooded, but it also sounded eminently practical. She summed it up with a little smile across the table. "Become a big fish before the others can do it."

He didn't return her smile but he inclined his head in agreement. "Exactly. Eat them before they eat me."

"Can you do it, Phil?"

He glanced around at the closest tables, then back again. "I'm working on it. It means skimping on maintenance and a few other things. It means walking the razor's edge for a while, but hell, that's what it's all about in this world, isn't it? If you don't know when to gamble, you spend all your life being a frustrated little mediocrity, don't you?"

She didn't know about that, but she didn't have to know. She was a woman, and although her interest in her man's affairs was bound to be lively, it was never supposed to be more, because he would never ask her opinions and she would never be allowed to make decisions. She smiled at him, thinking that he looked very handsome this evening, even with slightly more colour in his face than usual.

19

She said, "I suppose so," and picked up a fork when their pie arrived.

As though she hadn't spoken, he said, "I'm concentrating on a man named Ewell. Jack Ewell, who has two ships, one he personally skippers and one that he hires the crew for. I'll tell you something about this business: the day when a man captained his own ship went out with sails. There's no romance left in the shipping business, if there ever was any, actually. Nowadays a man who goes to sea on his own ship is a fool, because back here in the city the real business men are making deals, are sewing up contracts, and aren't out of touch."

"And this Captain Ewell, can't he make it?" she asked.

Phil ignored the dessert and leaned thick arms upon the tabletop. "Barely. He's been getting by for several years. Any real trouble and he'd have to give it up. He's been hauling for the same four or five exporters and importers, and that's another sure way to get bankrupted. Never sew yourself up like that, serve everyone and spread out in all directions, then one failure, or even two of them, can't hurt you too much." He pushed the pie aside. "Ewell has to fail, and that's what I'm counting on. If I can pick up his two ships, I'll be able to also pick up most of his contracts, and that would lift me out of the ranks of the small-timers." His black eyes retained their hard brightness as he said, "I'll get Ewell, it's simply a matter of waiting."

Ruth finished her dessert and said it was excellent. Phil ignored both the pie and the comment, and lit a cigar. She had seen him do that back home, but never very often, and her impression then, as now, was that cigars, like expensive suits and heavy cars, were symbols of status that Phil had to have.

She liked the idea of his being this way; it verified her belief in him as an eventual success. She also liked the way he put a large bill on the salver when their tab came, because he didn't even look as the waiter leaned a little, then retreated. Phil was not a man to heed the details of living. She thought of him as a modern Caesar. Afterwards, when they were leaving the restaurant, she saw the bow and the deference he got from the greying man she thought was the manager. People did not ever forget Phil Harlow.

On the drive back to her apartment he asked if she'd care to go dancing the following evening, and she accepted. He apologised for being unable to escort her around during daylight working-hours, which was the second time he'd done that, but she understood, better now than ever, how busy he was. It was on the tip of her tongue to ask if there was any way she could help him, but as they reached the hotel he made that kind of a question unnecessary with the remark he made as he held the door for her.

"Six months ought to do it," he told her, flinging away the cigar before entering the building. "After that I'll be able to do a lot of things that I don't dare do right now, like expand, hire more office help, take more time off, perhaps go over to Reno for an occasional weekend. After all, in only three years I've got this far, and when I came out here all I knew was that the stern of a ship was the rear and the bow was the front. I had four thousand dollars, Ruth. Did you know that's all I had when I heard about this company going belly-up?"

She hadn't known. All he'd told her was that he knew of an opportunity out in California and if it worked out he would send for her, then she saw him off at the Richmond airport.

"Four thousand established my credit. I borrowed ten more, picked up the company, and give me six months more, that's all I ask."

THREE

A DIFFERENT KIND OF ATMOSPHERE

SHE slept late the following morning, then only had a cup of tea for breakfast because of all she had eaten the night before. Obviously, if she did that very often she was going to have to pay for it each ensuing day by starving herself, otherwise she would get as big as a horse.

She was content to do her sightseeing closer to home this day, more because her legs ached than because of what the cab-driver had told her.

San Francisco, like London, was a city of shops. There were immense stores, of course, vast emporiums where almost anything could be purchased. For every large department-store-complex, some with their own private malls complete with glass roofs and grass, there were hundreds of little shops. For a woman, San Francisco was a shopper's paradise. When she telephoned her father after lunch she told him in a slightly breathless way that she had found clothing in the Bay City she doubted that anyone could duplicate, even in New York or Washington. She also told him that she was falling in love with San Francisco, and his mild but practical rejoinder was more to the point.

"How about Phil?"

"Fine," she said. "He looks wonderful and he's up to

23

his chin in business. But it's different out here, Dad, it's terribly competitive."

Her father made a unique remark. "Anywhere Phil will ever be, sweetheart, it will be terribly competitive. But tell me your plans—are you coming home shortly or are you thinking in terms of settling out there?"

She answered the question, and thus overlooked the other remark. "I don't really know. I had thought about perhaps staying a month or less, then returning, but it's such an adventure, Dad. . . ."

He chuckled. "I can imagine. Well, do you need any money?"

She said "No", and felt the little lump in her throat. He still considered her his child, his inexperienced daughter, and of course she liked that, even though she knew it wasn't realistic for either of them; she could never run to him with her problems again, and he could never make judgements or decisions for her. "No, thank you, I have plenty. Anyway, I've been thinking of looking for a job out here. Phil doesn't have an opening in his office but he's sure there won't be any difficulty in that regard, and you know how Phil is, he knows things."

Her father said, "Yes, of course he does. Give him my regards, sweetheart, and call from time to time. Maybe one of these days I'll fly out for a visit."

She told him she would love that, and they ended the conversation. Afterwards, the little lump in her throat lingered as she got dressed to go out for a snack. Phil would not arrive for hours yet, she had time to kill, and because she felt slightly restless after talking with her father back home, she needed activity.

She had always been a strong walker. San Francisco was the kind of a town where no other kind of a

pedestrian ever got anywhere. It wasn't really necessary
to walk; there were any number of public conveyances,
including the quaint old cable-cars, which she rode up
and down just to be able to feel that she belonged.
She also felt, aside from the need for a walk, the only
way she was going to prove adaptable to this city was
to master its ups and downs without aching muscles
every time she left the hotel.

She returned to the hotel after four o'clock to shower
and make a leisurely transformation from tailored-
walker to night-person. She even piled her wealth of
reddish, dark auburn hair on top of her head the way
Phil liked it, and the dinner dress she selected was one
he had never seen before and that showed the flatness
as well as the roundness of her figure. It was always
possible, given enough time and the proper clothes and
incentive, for a handsome woman to make herself
beautiful. The way Ruth Severns knew she had succeeded was when Phil arrived and stood in the doorway
looking steadily at her for five seconds before entering
the apartment, making a perfunctory remark about
how well she wore clothes.

It would have been better if he'd said nothing. The
look he gave her was far superior to what he eventually
said.

She went to get her wrap. San Francisco evenings,
even in midsummer, were seldom more than crisp and
breezy with a salt-spray-scent to them.

Phil was more expansive this evening. On the way
down in the lift he recalled saying he would one day get
her a clip to wear in her hair, and promised to do it
soon. He nodded when she told him her father sent his
regards, and when she was bracing for something

sarcastic, which she expected, he simply said, "Fine. When he comes out we can show him around. He'll be interested in San Francisco." He stopped short of adding that he thought her father would also be overwhelmed by the city, and she was grateful for that.

It wasn't, she knew, that Phil disliked her father. Actually, despite their total difference, he and her father got along rather well. What Phil ridiculed was the country-gentleman way of life, the fox-hunting-squire environment her father and his friends maintained. She had agreed long ago that it was, indeed, unrealistic.

She differed in her feeling from the way Phil felt in that she knew her father and his friends could afford to live that way, liked to live that way, and by doing it harmed no one at all, as opposed to Phil's outspoken contempt for people who produced nothing and were committed to nothing but leisure and comfort.

They had never actually argued. She was not by nature argumentative. Her disposition was thoughtfully cheerful, and although she laughed less when she was with Phil Harlow, she wasn't really very aware of it because she loved him and was occupied with whatever she thought was important to him.

This night, when they got down to his car, there was a strong overcast and the night was still, with a few prominent stars showing through a wet-looking haze. Back home, she told herself, this kind of a sky meant rain. When she reminded him he said it meant the same thing in San Francisco. Summer rains were not at all unusual.

He took her to a different kind of place this evening. The atmosphere of expensiveness was similar but the nightclub lacked that other thing, the sensation of exclusiveness, that the restaurant had had. She was interested in the people. They were obviously of different stratas. When Phil noticed her interest he pointed out some of the patrons. One was a ship's captain, another was an owner of shrimp-fishing vessels. A third man, gross with fat and definitely of Italian descent, was a cargo trans-shipper, a man who lined up cargoes, then allotted them to whichever shipping companies gave the best rates, which was the difference between what the standard rate was, and how much he netted. It sounded to Ruth like it was slightly dishonest, or at least unethical, but the fat man also looked capable of doing much worse.

The place had an excellent orchestra and a large bar, both in a different room from where Phil and Ruth had a dinner table. But the noise came through an arched, doorless opening along with clouds of rank smoke, so, except for an inability to see who was drinking and perhaps dancing, it all might just as well have been one huge room.

Several men came by the table and nodded or spoke, or perhaps boldly eyed Ruth, while exchanging friendly remarks with Phil. This place was quite different than the restaurant of the evening before, but in its own way, it was also much more likely to be lively. Phil summed it up as two enormous plates of roast beef arrived, along with a chilled bottle of French champagne.

"Here is where the well-to-do shippers and dockers congregate. I think more business is transacted in there, over the bar, than is transacted anywhere else in the city, during the cocktail hour."

A stalwart man with a gently composed, dark-weathered face and sunbleached short hair appeared in the yonder doorless opening looking over the diners. Ruth looked up just as this strikingly handsome man looked down. It was as though an electrical current had passed back and forth between them. Phil, speaking to a burly, cigar-chewing swarthy man, was too occupied to notice, and Ruth looked away swiftly but she knew the stalwart man was moving through the noise and smoke towards her. She desperately willed him to move right on past to some other table, but he didn't.

When Phil shook free of the cigar-chewing swarthy man and glanced up, Ruth saw his expression smooth out, turn gently bland as the stalwart stranger came up.

Phil raised a hand. "Jack," he said. "I heard this morning you were back."

Jack shook, withdrew his hand and looked deliberately across the table. Up close, he was a wide-shouldered, lean-hipped man about Phil's age, perhaps twenty-nine or thirty, but flat and hard as iron where Phil was not so flat.

Phil saw the look and introduced them. "Ruth, this is Captain Jack Ewell. Jack, this is Ruth Severns from Virginia." He did not say she was his fiancée, but for the time being she hardly noticed. This, she told herself, looking up to meet the dead-calm and commanding grey eyes, was the man Phil was waiting to go under. She smiled and nodded and said nothing. Ewell studied her with a slow regard before speaking.

"Virginia? That's where I got my start, on the Norfolk, Virginia, waterfront. By any chance do you know Norfolk?"

She did, but she knew Richmond and Lynchburg better. "I've been there," she told him, holding her expression steady and casual. "My home is inland."

Captain Ewell made a slow, lazy smile. "Sure. The fox-hunting country."

She resented that instantly. "It's cleaner than the waterfronts, Captain."

His smile remained. "Of course it is. Beautiful country, Miss Severns, full of history and leisure. When I was a kid I rode a bicycle up through those rolling hills for a couple of weeks. I slept under the stone bridges so the police wouldn't run me off as a vagrant. They are pretty strict in the fox-hunting country."

Another man, this one perspiring and not walking too steadily, approached the table and ignored Ruth and Jack Ewell as he levelled a finger at Phil Harlow. "Hey," he said, "you undercut me on three contracts, Harlow, and that's too much."

Phil leaned to rise but the half-drunk man put a hand on his shoulder and pushed. "Sit," he said. "You don't have to do nothing but listen while I tell you what I think of you, Harlow."

Ewell leaned. He seemed to know this newcomer because he smilingly said, "There's a lady at the table. Why don't you wait until another time, Floyd?"

The newcomer reared back and rolled his eyes upwards, indignant more than angry. "Why don't you mind your own business, Ewell? Anyway, this damned Harlow's no friend of yours either, if you knew how he operated."

Ewell smiled and took the other man by the arm. "Go get a drink, Floyd. I'll come buy a round in a few minutes. Don't be obnoxious." Ewell pulled the other man by the arm, and Ruth saw how powerful the grip was from the look of pain that crossed the drunk's face.

"For Chriz' sake, Ewell, ease off," said the newcomer,

29

allowing himself to be propelled towards the doorway and forgetting all about Phil Harlow because of the grip on his arm.

Jack Ewell nodded and released the other man. "Sure. Go have a round." He looked ready to propel Floyd through the archway, but he didn't have to, Floyd went, grumbling to himself and massaging his injured upper arm.

Phil looked bleak. "Thanks, Jack, but you didn't have to do it. I saw him coming."

. Ewell's easy smile was accompanied with a faint nod. "I know." He turned and looked again at Ruth. She concentrated on keeping her expression indifferent. "A dance later," he said, "maybe. If Phil doesn't mind."

She thought Phil would speak, but he didn't, so she gave Captain Ewell look for look as she said, "Thank you, but not tonight," then she looked away.

Phil didn't mention Ewell.

"That damned Floyd Henley has drunk up everything he's got, but, like all of them, it's never anything he's done, it's always something someone else has done."

Ruth looked back. "Who is he?"

"The bum who used to own my shipping company. He started up again this spring, and right away drank himself out of three good contracts. Those are the ones I picked up, and now he's accusing me of undercutting him."

Ruth watched colour come into Phil's face. She had a feeling that although he hadn't actually denied under-cutting the drunk, that he would if she pressed the issue, even though she thought that the drunk had probably told the truth.

FOUR

A FLASH OF TEMPER

AFTER the interlude with the drunk Ruth wanted to leave. It wasn't altogether that, though; the mood —one became accustomed to it—seemed to verge on violence. At first she thought that was her imagination, after the episode with Floyd Henley, but by the time they were half through dinner she had seen several near-crises, each one averted by someone connected with the establishment.

She said something about this to Phil and he shrugged. "Well, I told you this was a very competitive business, a dog-eat-dog city. If they couldn't drink here I doubt there'd be trouble."

He made no suggestion that they leave. She concentrated on her meal, gradually developed a kind of sixth-sense about the surroundings, and when the gross Italian pulled up a chair, uninvited, and polluted the area with cigar smoke, she accepted this as part of the atmosphere. Even the fat man leaning and speaking earnestly with Phil and ignoring her completely.

She barely heard what was being said, but once when she raised her eyes, Phil was shaking his head and looking pained. The fat man shifted his cigar from one side of his mouth to the other and started speaking

31

again. He talked very fast and bunched his words all together, slurring them, almost as though he were projecting thoughts, not sentences. The odd part was that Phil understood all of it.

"Care to reconsider?" asked a deep voice at her elbow. She hadn't seen him approaching, but then she had been purposefully avoiding looking in that direction. She started to answer, but Phil cut across it with a casual remark.

"Go ahead, sweetheart. I'll be busy here for a few minutes. I'll take the next dance."

She was nonplussed, but Captain Ewell wasn't. He already had a hand on the chair to assist her in rising. She stared at Phil, but he and the fat man had their scowling faces together and were snapping back and forth again. She rose, turned, looked upwards, and found the gunmetal-grey eyes considering her almost cynically. Jack Ewell leaned and quietly said, "You didn't know there was a place like this on earth, did you?" He took her arm and as they moved towards the archway she knew people were looking at them.

Beyond the long, dimly lit bar was another room with a second doorless archway. That was where people danced. But to get there they had to cross the length of the bar-room and she felt like something on a slave block as she moved through the gloom, the smoke, the heat, and the noise. Men turned very deliberately all along the bar.

Jack Ewell leaned down and said, "Don't feel insulted. Out here, in this dive, that is a compliment. I haven't seen another woman get that much oggling all night."

She breathed more easily once they got past the second archway. There, with more subdued lighting, she

32

made a discovery: what had sounded exactly like a small orchestra to her, turned out to be a high-fidelity stereophonic installation that reproduced music with absolute precision. There were four speakers, one in each wall, high up. There were also three other dancers, which wasn't a very large percentage for the number of couples in the place, but then she was beginning to understand that dancing was not what people came here for. If it wasn't to eat, to transact business, then it was to drink.

She turned without looking up. Jack Ewell slid a thick arm round her and reached for her other hand, but he did not move, so eventually she tipped her face. Then he moved. He was an excellent dancer, smooth and graceful.

"Write a book about it when you get back home," he said. "The sinful old Barbary Coast comes into its own again. How long are you going to stay out here?"

She didn't feel like answering him, but she did. "I don't know. Perhaps permanently." It was on the tip of her tongue to mention her special relationship with Phil Harlow, and that was when it hit her that Phil had not introduced her as his fiancée, but simply as someone he had known elsewhere.

Captain Ewell said, "Why not? You'll make it, Miss Severns," and whirled her out of the way of the same drunk who had been obnoxious at the dinner table, Floyd Henley, who was lurching across the dance floor with a hard-eyed, platinum blonde, without saying anything more.

She was defensive, although Ewell was not especially aggressive. In fact he was almost matter-of-fact with her, except that the arm round her did not loosen and the deep-set calm grey eyes seldom left her face. She said, "Phil likes it out here," as though by mentioning Phil's name she could invoke something protective.

Ewell was momentarily silent, then said, "He's done very well considering that when he came here he knew as little about cargoes and ships as I know about space capsules. Phil can take care of himself."

She assumed this was a compliment and agreed with it. "He's always been capable, Captain."

"Oh? Have you known him that long, then?"

She explained how she and Phil had met, how he had gone to war, how he had come back, and now, how she had come out to be with him in San Francisco.

Afterwards she thought it all sounded terrible, as though she were trying to create some kind of boy-meets-girl love story straight out of a very old movie.

If he thought anything like that it didn't show. The music stopped, she freed herself, and he led her over towards a small table with two chairs, but she resisted. "One dance," she reminded him. "Now I'll go back."

He considered that, and nodded. "Not alone through the bar," he said, and took her hand. As they moved off in a fresh direction he had a suggestion. "Would you like to see what it's like on a seagoing cargo-hauler? I'm going over across the Bay tomorrow."

It was very easy to decline. "No, thank you, Captain. When Phil gets the time I suppose he'll take me aboard one of his ships, but to be perfectly truthful, I'm a terrible sailor." To take the sting out of her refusal she looked up and smiled, then they were passing back through the bar-room, and she felt as though she were running the gauntlet again.

At the far archway she saw, with despair, that now

there were three men besides the fat one at Phil's table and the four of them were in smoky and very earnest, arm-waving conversation. As she faltered she felt the hold on her hand tighten. Behind her the music started up again.

Jack Ewell was softly laughing when he leaned and said, "I think you're stuck with me for a little while. One more dance?"

She did not often get angry, but this time she did. Shaking free of Captain Ewell, she marched across to the table, picked up her coat from where a beefy man was leaning on it, having taken her chair, and when all the men looked up, annoyed, she said, "I'll take a cab back, Phil, don't bother." It was like a knifeblade in the momentary hush. All those other men heard the implication and the fury and were a little nonplussed. Even the gross man, who had known Phil Harlow had brought this woman, looked at Phil. The others who hadn't known Phil Harlow was alone, simply sat and stared.

Behind her at the archway she knew Captain Ewell was watching. He couldn't have heard what was said from that distance, but she had no illusions about him; he would be able to guess word for word, and that annoyed her still more. His damned calmness and his damned knowledgeability.

Phil coloured, swallowed noticeably, then forced up a palpably false expression of amusement. "Carl," he said, "you have Miss Severns' seat." One of the men rose slowly and looked around for another chair. There were none at the other tables so he motioned irritably for Ruth to be seated and walked off searching for a chair.

She didn't sit, she said, "Never mind, Phil. It's time for me to leave anyway," and that sounded so melodramatic she turned red as she clutched her coat and started towards the front of the dining-room. She heard the chair squeak behind her, heard Phil coming, and did not look around.

Ordinarily, when she had one of these flashes of sudden anger, they did not last more than perhaps two or three minutes, but tonight she marched outside—where it was drizzling, forcing her to stop and put on her coat—and allowed Phil to catch up while she was still furious.

He stopped, looked at the damp pavement, looked at the obscure sky, then looked at her. "Listen, Ruth, I explained when I picked you up at the airport I've got to stay close to other things, to my business. . . . I told you last night that if I can manipulate things for another little while, I'll be able to nearly double the size of the company. I'm sorry, I meant to dance with you, that's why we came here, but—"

"That's not why we came here," she turned and hurled at him. "You have business to transact. That place back there is a combination business establishment and a place where men can show off the women they happen to have with them . . . Phil, why didn't you tell Captain Ewell I am your fiancée?"

"My fiancée," he muttered, then his eyes hardened. "Why, did Ewell make a pass at you?"

She smiled sweetly. "No. As a matter of fact the only man in that smelly dive that has even the bare instincts of a gentleman is Captain Ewell. No, he didn't make any pass, I just want to know why you didn't introduce me as your fiancée."

36

Phil Harlow stiffened. He had been slightly embarrassed up to now, slightly off-balance by an event he had not anticipated and had no experience in handling, but that mood only lasted a short time. Now, his eyes narrowed towards her just a little, but he said nothing until she had finished with her coat, and even then Phil did not answer back. He simply turned and said, "Come on, I'll take you home."

In the car, with her anger turned to ashes, Ruth rode stoically almost all the way back to the hotel, then, because she knew how ridiculous it was to allow something like this to feed upon the pride and stubbornness of two people, she finally said, "I'm sorry, Phil, for my part, but being treated as though I were an inconvenience or like someone you just picked up and took to dinner—being handed over to a perfect stranger to dance with. . . ."

He said, "Yeah. Okay, I didn't handle things too well. But that scene back there isn't going to make me look too good. You know that, I suppose."

She had to hold back, hard, to keep from answering him. *He* hadn't looked too well back there; how had he made *her* look!

He wheeled up in front of the hotel, jumped out and when she alighted at the curb he was there, thick shoulders blotting out a lot of dark sky. "Don't worry about Ewell," he told her, as though that had been part of their discussion. "That's what the meeting at the table was about. I swung two of his contracts that are up for renewal. I won't make a dime on either of them for three months, but after that I'll do fine." He took her elbow as they crossed the slick pavement to the hotel's foyer. As he held the door for her he said, "You have to

37

understand something, Ruth, this isn't a high school prom
out here. We weren't dancing at the hunt club."

"We weren't dancing at all," she said, turning to smile
into his face. "Good night, Phil. Call me." She turned
and marched alone to the lift. He hovered near the doorway as though undecided, then he ducked back out into
the stormy night. She caught a glimpse of his back, then
he was gone.

She rode up to her suite feeling colder than anyone
should have, even out in the drizzle, because it wasn't
that cold a night. When she shed her coat in the
living room and switched on a light, the apartment felt
clammy so she went to the thermostat and turned it up.
At once heat was pumped out of high wall vents.

Then she dragged her coat to the bedroom, hung it to
dry, sat down at the dressing-table and looked at herself.
She hadn't been that angry with anyone since high
school, and that had been a long time ago. She let all
her breath out, looked soberly at the reflection in the
mirror, then grimaced and rose to unzip the dress.
Maybe San Francisco wasn't all she'd thought, after all.
One thing seemed certain: Phil Harlow's environment,
the waterfront world at least, was not simply a place
where dog-ate-dog, it was also a place where knifing
people in the back throve.

She let her hair down, went to get ready for bed, and
afterwards, lying in the darkness, struggled with some
thoughts that, for her at least, were very unusual.

FIVE

SOMETHING UNEXPECTED

ETHICS, unlike honesty which was part of life from vocal childhood onwards, were easier to ignore, and perhaps that was why ethics were scarcely even understood by so many people.

Ruth rose late the morning after the scene at the dining-dancing establishment, deciding that what Phil was doing, while not outside the law, was unethical. But she had scarcely arrived at this conclusion when she also thought that this was what Phil's associates out here on the West Coast used in their bargaining. Dishonesty was punishable under the law, but being unethical was perfectly legitimate, subject only to each individual's conscience. It depended upon how far these men would go; that was how their successes and their profits were determined.

She went downstairs to breakfast in the hotel dining-room, and over a cup of coffee before the main meal arrived, tried to delve through it all to her own judgement, not only of Phil, but of herself for being in love with him, and also to try and guess what the future held.

A large silhouette blocked out her frontal view and a smiling, wide-shouldered man in light tan trousers and jacket, wearing a light grey turtleneck sweater under the jacket, pulled out a chair and sat at the table opposite her, eyes smiling. "It's a bad thing," said Jack Ewell, "to brood over something this long. Forget it. This is another day. Look out there through the rear windows. Did you know that rainfall washed away all the smog and dust and the northward hills are as green as new money?"

She resented his being there, but not terribly because she accepted his presence without protesting. More than anything else, she felt guilty, felt slightly unclean because she knew what someone—Phil Harlow—was moving heaven and earth to do to Jack Ewell, and she also knew she could not warn him, which made her as unethical as Phil. Being an inadvertent accessory to someone else's underhandedness was a new experience, and a decidedly unpleasant one.

A waitress came. Captain Ewell ordered a breakfast steak with potatoes, coffee, and a piece of blueberry pie. The waitress smiled at him and departed. He turned back to Ruth, wagging his head.

"Only brooding types allow a little disillusionment to mar them for life, and you're not the brooding type. Anyway, that was part of your education, Miss Severns. The most boring person on earth is one who never changes environment. When you want an interesting person, find one who's had hell knocked out of them in ten different countries." He smiled. "Phil Harlow has a fanatical side, lady, and he's not going to change just because you're here. Incidentally, he went over to Richmond this morning and won't be back until this evening, late, so you'd better take that boat ride with me across the Bay."

Her breakfast arrived but she ignored all except the

coffee. "Does being a sea-captain make men philosophical?" she asked, lifting the cup, "Or do philosophers take to the sea?"

He chuckled. "I can't answer for philosophers, but I can tell you that there is usually plenty of time for thought, especially in the Pacific, where there are fewer storms."

"Phil Harlow," she said flatly, "doesn't have to change because I'm here, but that episode last night in that waterside dive was inexcusable."

"No, not according to the rules of waterside dives, Miss Severns. *You* were the misfit there, not the rest of us."

"Phil shouldn't have taken me there, then."

Ewell shrugged. "All right, agreed, but he *did* take you there, and now, ten or twelve hours later you're still simmering. What good does that do? Look, come across the Bay with me and you'll forget all that other mess. It's not worth one wrinkle in your forehead anyway."

She answered honestly. "I'm afraid of deep water. I didn't grow up on the Norfolk waterfront."

He did not give in. "All right, let me show you a view of San Francisco and the southern slope you've never seen, and we won't go anywhere near the water."

"You have to cross the Bay," she reminded him.

He brushed that aside with an impish grin. "Did I say I had to do that today? I meant tomorrow."

His breakfast arrived and she was impressed with the size of it. If he ate steak for breakfast very often why wasn't he thicker than he was . There were enough deep-fried potatoes to feed several men. Even his coffee cup was larger. She wondered if San Francisco restaurant owners automatically fed seamen more than other people. He saw her expression and winked.

"Two things cause the habit, boredom and bad weather. When I was a kid on the North Atlantic runs the bad weather encouraged my appetite. Now it's mostly boredom."

She wasn't deceived, she'd felt his powerful arm around her the night before; he worked hard and was like steel, whether he would admit it or not. She went to work on her own meal and for a while they were both quiet, but eventually he sent out a probe.

"About that view I mentioned, Miss Severns: no strings attached, no involvements, just a drive on a beautiful day that has to be better than sitting in your hotel room waiting for Phil to come back and telephone you. Nothing you can't mention to him. You met me at breakfast. We live in the same hotel. I took you for a drive. Any harm in that?"

She had thought, being a ship's captain, he would naturally live on a ship. Of all the hotels in San Francisco, why did he have to live in *her* hotel?

"Do you like history? This peninsula is full of it. The army's Presidio was founded by a handful of Spaniards before anyone back on the eastern seaboard knew there was such a place as California. Those green hills above the city that look so pastoral and beautiful are full of underground military tunnels and old-time fortifications." He paused and waited for some comment, but she was listening, not commenting, for the time being. He assumed this to be encouragement and began again.

"Have you heard of the redwood trees up the coast? They are some of the oldest living creatures, and are the largest trees known to man."

42

She was tempted to smile. "The tourist bureau should hire you, Captain."

He had a quick, warm smile. It came up now. "Maybe I'll apply when I leave the sea."

Her conscience stabbed her. "Leave the sea?"

"Hardly anyone stays afloat until they die any more, Miss Severns. Everyone looks forward to a day when they do something different from their profession. Maybe that's some inherent form of our belief in immortality—we live one life until it's mastered, then we start a fresh one. Anyway, that's part of what I want to show you."

She didn't understand. "Show me what?"

"What I intend to do when I leave the sea. It's about a two-hour drive from here. We can be up there before lunch and back again before you get tired of my company." He jutted his chin. "Look at that sunshine out there. The air in San Francisco after a rain smells like old wine."

Curiosity was only half of her interest in this handsome, calm man. The other half of her interest in him rose from a powerful hope that whatever he intended to do when he left the sea would compensate for what she knew he was about to lose. She felt almost as though, being in secret conspiracy against him, she owed him something, but there was more to her aquiescence : her feelings towards Phil were not so much cast in doubt—one little argument couldn't destroy love—as they were made susceptible to a fresh appraisal, not only of Phil but of herself. An argument couldn't shake her feelings towards Phil Harlow, but something else could; her new and uneasy feeling about his ethics. She had grown up despising thieves and liars above all other people. What she had to decide now, before she saw Phil again, was whether his ethics were really questionable, and that wouldn't be easy for a woman in love.

A drive into the countryside would probably clear her mind. She needed something like that. She didn't feel too pleased with herself for using this ship's captain for her private purpose, but on the other hand she would be companionable and that compensated, she thought, for the other thing.

She finished her breakfast and glanced at her wrist. Ewell saw, and said, "Nine-thirty. We can be back by two. Are you ready or do you need a coat or something like that?"

He made her acceptance easy. She rose, saying she'd have to go after purse and gloves and would meet him in the lobby within ten minutes. He rose until she left, then sat back down to finish the last fried potato and down the remnants of his black coffee.

When Ruth got back to her suite she went deliberately to look out the studio-windows. He was right, there was a golden brightness to this day like none other she'd seen since arriving in San Francisco. She could see those green rolling fat hills to the north and wondered if he had been telling the truth about underground tunnels up there. They looked a little like the rolling, green hills of home, except that they were unmarred by fences and mansions, and if there had ever been any trees growing out there, they had disappeared long ago.

She got a coat, purse and gloves, considered a hat, decided against it, and locked the door after herself. She was in the lift, hand hovering over the down-button when the thought arrived making her wonder what Phil's reaction to this would be. She *was* his fiancée. He had told her that in a passionate embrace shortly after returning from overseas and he had reiterated it at the airport when he'd kissed her good-bye before flying to California.

She stabbed the button fiercely. But last night, for some reason, he had managed very well to give the impression that she was his date only.

Maybe she'd had no valid reason for feeling furious and humiliated, but she'd felt that way, and to a much less degree she still felt that way. When the lift door opened on the ground floor she saw Captain Ewell putting a telephone down over at the registration desk. He looked up, caught her gaze, and slowly straightened up, smiling. He gave her that same look Phil had given her last night when she'd opened the door to him, except that with Jack Ewell it was accompanied with that nice smile.

He held one of the heavy outer doors for her, and afterwards, when she hesitated, he turned her by the arm and led the way to his car, which was parked in a lot at the side of the building . A little flurry of low wind struck her ankles, reminding her that, hot as it might be elsewhere this time of year, in San Francisco a coat year round was a good idea whether it was worn or not.

As they eased out into the traffic he seemed to think she would be wondering about that telephone call he'd made, because he explained.

"Sent the ship across the Bay without me. Nothing very momentous, just a little two-bit cargo to be loaded."

She winced. Was that one of the cargoes Phil had usurped? "You shouldn't be riding around with me, Captain," she exclaimed. "As Phil says—business before pleasure."

He smiled easily and often. "Yeah. Well, the rest of that quotation has to do with all work and no play making Jack a dull kid. And I'm not Phil. I've been at this a lot longer. I don't have to put on a tin bill and get out and scratch with the other chickens as hard as he does."

To reach the overhead highway that by-passed most of the city there were several well-marked routes. Jack Ewell seemed to know exactly where he was going. He ignored two of those approaches and took the third one because it offered a better view of the industrial centre of San Francisco. What he pointed out, like a tour guide, Ruth had not seen before, and was not very impressed by. He got a twinkle in his eye at her tart expression.

"Okay, it's not pretty, but every big city has to have its industrial muscle, and this area happens to be San Francisco's. Not like back home, eh?"

That irritated her. "No, it's not like back home, and I'm a little tired of having that said to me."

"My apologies, ma'am," he grinned. "I didn't mean it as some kind of reproof, but only to show that there is little comparison between the pleasant and the unpleasant life."

She thought for a moment that he, too, was going to tell her what a dog-eat-dog place San Francisco was, but he didn't, and the longer she was with him the more she discovered that he did not very often dwell on things like that, except perhaps as corollaries. By nature, he was neither a hedonist nor a cynic, just a calm and pleasant man who seemed to have struck a very good balance between; a thoughtful man who looked, and thought, like a realist.

46

SIX

A DIFFERENT KIND OF MAN

THE countryside above San Francisco was hilly and green. Where the vast motorway network bore unerringly northward she saw signs of farming, and that struck her as being slightly incongruous because the impression one carried with them away from San Francisco was of a tremendously busy seaport backed up by a smoke-belching industrial heart. There just was no place for agriculture for a good many miles, and by the time a person saw those signs they did not seem to belong.

Captain Ewell had an explanation. "The city curves around the Bay, as you saw from the Golden Gate Bridge, and that usually means that a city faces the sea and starts out, at least, making its living with nets and ships. The industry came much later, after the Yankee take-over about a hundred and fifty years ago. As the city grew inland, away from the sea, it turned to face the new direction and to develop a fresh perspective." He looked, saw how she was studying him, and laughed at her. "Just like a school teacher. Well, to tell you the truth I learned that from a high school history text."

"And you remembered this long?"

His smile showed a little surprise. "I'm not as old as you think."

She fidgeted. "I didn't mean that, Captain. I'm not

exactly rickety either, but I don't remember any history texts very well."

"But you," he said, "learned your history a long time ago, and I have been learning mine a little at a time for the past five years. I have a complete set of high school textbooks in my cabin." He paused to point out an enormous low-flying aircraft making its southward approach to the city, then he resumed his topic. "I didn't finish grammar school. My parents sort of drifted away when I was pretty young so I went to work on the waterfront. Education was pretty much of a luxury for me until a few years ago." He looked down, then back to the road again. "Now you know why I sounded like a school teacher."

She blurted out what was uppermost in her mind after all that. "What do you mean, your parents drifted away?"

"Just that. First, my father moved out, and after about eighteen months my mother left one night with a marine salesman she knew. When I awakened the morning after there was one of her handkerchiefs—with her perfume—on the pillow beside my head, with forty-five dollars in it."

Ruth was speechless. Jack Ewell looked at her, his gunmetal eyes darker, and hoisted wide shoulders, then let them drop again.

"So I didn't go back to school," he said, very calmly, as though all the heart-wrenching pain hadn't even existed.

She said, "Jack, how old were you?"

"Twelve. It's actually a pretty good age. Kids of twelve are like chameleons. They can adapt more quickly than adults ever can. I didn't even wait until the forty-five dollars was gone. I hustled the waterfront until I got a job as a dishwasher in a greasy spoon. That gave me room and board, which I had to have to tide me over until I found a ship."

"At twelve," she said, incredulous. "What can a child of twelve do on a seagoing ship?"

"Did you know," he said, "that some kids get ninety per cent of their adult height by the time they're twelve years old? I read that in a book last year, but I also happen to know from my own experience that it's true. I got aboard a German ship by saying I was sixteen years old. The following year I said I was eighteen and got aboard a Canadian coaster. That was when I first saw San Francisco and fell in love with it."

"Jack, did she ever come back?"

"Nope."

"Or your father?"

"Nope. But at least I heard about him one time. He was a ship's engineer. They make good money, when they're working. He didn't get very many ships after he passed fifty, but it wasn't the age; as a matter of fact most good engineers are past fifty. He was drinking himself to death. When I heard of him he was six months away from dying, and the man who told me offered to give me the money to go see him, but he also said he wouldn't know me because he didn't know anyone, any more."

"Did you go?"

Her question, this time, seemed to hamper his will to answer for the first time. "I didn't go. I've thought since that I should have, but the fact is that I didn't. He died a few months later. I heard about that, too."

Ruth fell into a long silence. She hadn't expected

anything like this, and in fact she'd never before heard anything quite like it although she was not naïve enough not to know it happened. She didn't know what to say. She hadn't expected this confidence, hadn't had any idea his boyhood hadn't been as normal as her girlhood. She stole a sidewards glance at his profile. He seemed so completely normal. Her impression of him left over from the night before was of complete self-assurance, complete confidence; the kind that men grow up having when they've felt secure most of their formative years.

Finally, to break the silence, she said, "I don't know what to say."

He smiled at her. "Why should you feel that way? Be thankful it was me and not you."

"But it's so—sad—so unnecessary. How could a mother do that?"

"I don't think it was easy for her, but women operate on a different emotional wavelength than men do. I can't exactly explain how I've justified it for her over the year, and I've wondered—did the salesman stay with her, or did he find another one when she got a little older. I hope she found whatever she was looking for."

Ruth had a lump in her throat but she wasn't sure whether it was for a heartsick boy of twelve sitting in a room looking at a handkerchief with money in it, or whether it was for a woman who could not accept what life had given her, and ran away to try and find something sweeter.

They left the highway where some shaggy old blue-gum trees stood, ducked down to a lower lane, and went due west over rises and falls that seemed to be set at spaced intervals until the road began to climb towards a vague but hulking distant headland. As calmly as though that other thing had not been mentioned between them, he said, "All this at one time belonged to a vast California cattle ranch. It was only opened up a few years ago, when the taxes ate up the agricultural operation."

When he finished speaking they crested the rise and she saw a tree-dotted plateau that stretched for miles in several directions. They passed through a rustic gate and paralleled a hand-made post-and-rider fence for a quarter of a mile to a low, rambling residence with a cedar-shake roof and cedar uprights of peeled log supporting a veranda that ran the full length of the residence's front, as well as down two sides. He drove onward, past the house and stopped where several massive, low oaks of vast age stood overlooking a distant and steely sea. She was capitivated by the view from this lofty plain. He took her by the hand on over to the trees leaving the car behind, and showed her where a sea-lane was, by pointing out the ships out there moving northward, mostly, but with an occasional one heading southward towards Los Angeles' harbour, far below the distant curve of coastland.

She said, "It's breathtaking."

He seemed pleased but he said nothing until she turned, then he walked with her back to the lovely, low and rambling house. She had a suspicion. "Yours?"

He nodded. "I built it."

That surprised her. "You mean, you actually built it with your own hands?"

He was tickled by her incredulity. "Sure. There's nothing impossible about building a house, as long as you remember the sequences. First the trenching, then the foundation, then the roughening-in, wall studs, plates, rafters, strongbacks, fire-blocks, so forth." He took her to the tile-floored patio where she could see inside. The sitting-room was large, there was a fieldstone fireplace of vast dimensions in the east wall, and the furnishings looked very definitely masculine. She turned slowly. "This is what you meant about retiring?"

He nodded, stepped to the front door, unlocked it and motioned her inside. "According to my schedule I'm going to live here unencumbered for five years, then, if I decide it's too boring, I'll find something else. But for five years I'm going to watch the sea get ploughed by other men. I've been at it almost long enough."

She looked around at the green land. "But what can you do for a living up here?"

He laughed, closed the door after her and leaned on it. "Nothing. I don't plan to make a living up here. I won't have to. I've been operating my two ships for a long time. They've made me money. When I sell them it will just about double what I've put aside. According to my calculations, I'll be able to loaf for five years and still have enough left to get into something, if I feel the need, at the end of that time."

She went over by the fireplace, turned and looked out the front window, which took up half the front living-room wall, but was protected from wind and rain and sun by the veranda roof, that framed and shaded it. She said, "I don't understand you. You're too young to want to sit back."

He continued to lean on the door watching her. "I'll tell you something : I've never had a vacation, not since I was fourteen years old. What it amounts to is that

I'm going to lump all that lost time and take a five-year holiday. It's not the same as sitting back."

She swung and looked at him. "You can't do it, Jack, not for five years. You're not the type."

"No? What type am I?"

"Oh, active, resourceful, energetic. . . ." She stepped to a low, long divan that faced the window and sank down. "When are you going to sell out?"

He astonished her with his reply. "I'm in process right now. The reason Phil was tied up today is because he's angling to take me over. That's what all the scowling was about at your dinner-table last night. He's after my contracts."

She did not dare raise her eyes to him, so she listened, sat perfectly still, and felt the blessed warmth coming in from the big front window.

He shoved off the door and strolled over closer and also sat down. "Smart men like Phil Harlow are sometimes just too smart."

She wanted to ask what that meant but she didn't, and he kept on speaking so the opportunity passed unchallenged.

"Phil could have the ships, normally, but this time I want cash, so I've entered into negotiations with a larger company. As for the contracts, he's outsmarted himself. That fat supercargo who was making all the smoke and the arrangements last night is a dollar short and a day late. Yesterday morning I renewed on the basis of a ten per cent reduction. The contracts were signed and sealed." He leaned to catch sight of her face. "There is just one thing that really puzzled me : Ruth, how much of this did you already know?"

She had had a feeling this was coming, from the

53

drawling way he had told her and from the way he kept looking at her. She sighed and said, "Some of it. Why, did you expect me to tell you?"

He said, "No, any more than I'd expect you to tell Phil if the boot had been on the other foot. But tell me what you think of it?"

"I think it's awful," she said truthfully.

His eyes twinkled when she looked at him, scowling. "Strange that we should agree about something," he said.

She let that go past. "I don't see how people can believe things like that are right."

"If you tell yourself a lie long enough, Ruth, you'll believe it. The Chinese didn't invent brain-washing, people have been doing that to themselves since the Year One. In the shipping business probably more than in most businesses, the shark with the sharpest bite comes out on top. It wasn't this way so much until a few years back, when the U.S. merchant marine priced itself right out of competition. Then everyone in this country who owned cargo vessels had to fight like hell for a share of what little export business there is. Your fiancè had the misfortune to get a taste of the good life just about the time it started souring. He ought to sell out and go into something else. But I couldn't convince him of that and I doubt that you could. So, meanwhile, he turns out to be the shark with a healthy bite. Don't blame him, not altogether. He's an ambitious guy with iron up his back. He just might make it—but not off me he won't."

She considered Jack Ewell. Last night he had known those men at her table were planning to cut him to ribbons, and he'd taken her out to the dance floor, smiling every inch of the way. It occurred to her that Jack Ewell wasn't just a handsome sea captain, he was also a terribly shrewd and knowledgeable rough-and-tumble in-fighter. Phil had met his match and didn't even know it. Maybe Phil had met *more* than his match.

SEVEN

A MATTER OF CHEMISTRY

THERE was a faint breeze across the plateau when they left the house to stroll along the empty heights, and the sun was warmer out here than it was in the city. He told her that of all the headlands he'd got to know as landmarks when approaching San Francisco from the distant sea lanes, this one had come to mean the most to him, and when he heard it was to be cut up and sold, he was one of the first prospects to look up the owner and make an offer. Now, he owned a hundred acres, and his house was in the middle. He'd put it like that, he told her, so that no one could get any closer to him than he wished them to. "The sea," he said, "is a pretty empty place at times, and maybe people think men aboard ships feel crowded, but it's just the other way around; men on ships feel pretty lonely and isolated at times. It's the ones on land that are crowded. Anyway, I got to like the solitude. I still like it." He smiled. "I'm no hermit; I like people and occasionally I don't mind crowds, but most of the time I like being an individual in a world for individuals."

She understood. Back home she had been reared in an atmosphere of leisurely, clanny existence. The nearest neighbour had been a half mile distant, and mostly, the families had about all the entertainment they needed right on their own estates, between the stables and the main house.

It occurred to her, as they walked slowly through the wonderful sunshine and salt-scent, that he did not feel any need to ridicule isolation and the leisurely life, probably because, in a different way, he also wanted to live like that.

When Phil ridiculed it he did so out of impatience and perhaps a little hidden envy, although knowing Phil, she wasn't too sure about the latter reason.

She tried to imagine Phil strolling with them on top of the high plateau, joining their leisurely conversation with candour, ease, and a little humour. She failed, but she told herself that was because Jack Ewell's talk made her concentrate upon him to the exclusion of Phil.

"When you go to sea you find something you can't find anywhere else—dependence upon yourself with no one else nearby to give aid. That's particularly true after you move into the master's cabin. Everyone else aboard depends upon what you do and what you decide. After five or ten years you make judgements without consulting anyone else or even thinking of it." He paused and gazed at her. "I've often wondered if that's good or bad."

"Good," she said, without hesitating.

He continued to pace along for a moment, then said, "And if a man gets married?"

She hadn't thought of that. "Well, I suppose he'd have to make adjustments, but then people have to do that anyway, don't they?"

They came to a jutting barranca, a prominence where a number of weather-harassed old oaks, very ancient and gnarled, stood vigil high above the restless sea. He moved her into the shade of one of those trees and they stood together watching a white cruise-ship heading up in the direction of San Francisco.

"The trouble with marriage," he mused, "is that it's unlikely a man and a woman will have the same values or the same background. Chemistry may work for a year or two, but after that what'll hold them together?"

She smiled. "Captain, too much speculation makes too many sceptics, if not outright cynics. As for what holds them together. . . ." She turned back to watching the cruise-ship. "I suppose it's the conviction that what they're doing deserves to be worked hard at." She shot him a quick, quizzical glance. "Let's hear your opinion."

He grinned at her, leaned upon their ancient oak and said, "I'll tell you something. I didn't know anything about this until last night, but there's more than chemistry. I tried to define it after you left last night, and couldn't come up with anything concrete."

She thought she understood what he was talking about, but it was his initiative, his conversation, and she couldn't have defined it anyway. But it occurred to her that they were having a more intimate conversation than they should have been having. She loved another man. Before he could go on, then, she moved out into the sunshine again and turned to stroll farther out along the barranca, until she came to a slightly sunken place.

There she saw some tiny pink flowers growing vigorously in the lee of their protected place and halted, knowing he was coming up behind her.

He must have guessed her mood because when next he spoke that other, intimate thing was no longer between them. Standing at her side looking at the sunken place, he said, "It's a grave."

She was startled. It looked like a small depression with minute wild flowers growing there, nothing more.

"An old man who used to live up here, a Basque shepherd, is buried there."

She looked at the sunken place. "How do you know that?"

"The man I bought my land from told me. You see, I own the land over here and he wanted me to know. He made me promise never to bother the grave. The Basque worked for him for many years; this was where they ran a big herd of sheep."

She didn't ask the obvious question: Why was the shepherd buried upon this lip of tree-shaded headland. The answer was obvious: Because it was a peaceful and lovely spot high above the sea, and in his shepherd's loneliness he had come to feel both at home and at peace there.

Jack Ewell took her arm and turned back, following out the uneven rim. That white cruise-ship was a speck on the steely-dull surface of the sea now, and distantly to their right, inland where a rounded shoulder of mountain dipped down, Ruth saw another house, something she hadn't caught sight of before.

It was where the elderly ranching couple had retired to after cutting up and selling their acreage. It was a new, very modern, rambling-type residence, and it only half-faced the sea, because it also was turned to look out over the land. Jack said they were delightful people, hospitable to a fault, easy to know and full of humour and anecdotes. They were the third generation of the same family to live up here, but having no children, when the time came they sold the land without a qualm. He said that someday he wanted her to meet those people She smiled, thinking to herself that, in his company, it was so easy to feel that they were old friends; it was so simple to speak out, to walk slowly at his side, to guess some of his thoughts and to share a kind of very comfortable comradeship, although she had not known him until last night.

Eventually, they returned to the house. He offered her a choice : they could make luncheon at his house, or he would take her back now, and buy her luncheon on the way. She thought they should be heading back. He was perfectly agreeable, locked the house, took her back to the car and just before they left he put a long, slow look all around. She saw, and understood that he liked this place very much. She didn't blame him at all. It was peaceful and golden and wonderfully pastoral with a sense of enduring serenity that made it seem more than an hour's drive from a smoke-belching, noisy metropolis.

He knew all the best places to eat between his private world and the city. The one he took her to on the drive back had an airpark where flyers could put down. Connected to the expansive and elegant restaurant was a horseshoe-shaped series of individual cottages, landscaped and immaculate. She could imagine how expensive it would be to park an aeroplane here and spend a few days loafing by the pool, or taking an excursion into San Francisco.

On their way again, making the last lap across the Golden Gate Bridge towards the heart of San Francisco, she told him she had seen an altogether different segment of Bay City existence today.

He agreed, and to conclude it he swung down towards the seafront to show her San Francisco's hectically busy docks and wharves. She felt overwhelmed by contrast.

This was Phil's world of haste and salt spray, raucous seagulls, scuttling cargo-handlers on four wheels and painted yellow, and hectic ships that seemed to face away from the hectic bedlam below where they were moored.

He pointed out a grey-white vessel. "The *Santa Maria*." He grinned as he dropped his arm. "The original idea was to have three of them and name each one after one of Columbus' ships. The *Santa Maria*, the *Pinta*, and the *Niña*. Well, that's the *Santa Maria*. The *Pinta* is docked at Honolulu, and I never got the *Niña*, and now it looks as though I never will."

The *Santa Maria*, for some reason, put Ruth in mind of a naval vessel. Perhaps it was the grey exterior paint, or perhaps it was the lean, greyhound-look. She did not mention this. She simply said, "It seems very clean and seaworthy. But I don't know the first thing about ships."

He sat and examined his ship with a critical eye, then passed a judgement. "She's seaworthy. She's also temperamental and facetious."

Ruth looked at him. "A ship?"

He laughed. "You should have crossed the Bay in her this morning, you'd have seen what I mean. That's why seamen call ships 'she'. Because they have female characteristics."

Ruth laughed. "Like a broad beam?"

Jack's eyes twinkled. "That too, but we don't usually tell people that." He reached to start the car, then hesitated, looking at her. "Would you like to go aboard? She's tied up, there's very little motion. It might help you overcome your feelings about deep water and ships."

She declined. "Right now I think I ought to get home, but it's kind of you to make the offer."

61

He started the car. "Another day." He swung around and drove slowly back up where the major traffic was, away from the pedestrian-world of the waterfront. "Sooner or later you'll have to go aboard, if not my ship, then one of Phil's vessels." He looked briefly at her, then concentrated on driving. "If you plan on being associated with the waterfront it's inevitable that you'll sail some time. If you'll give me a chance I'll give you a perfectly safe and orderly lesson one of these days."

She almost accepted. He was the one person in whom she knew she could afford to have complete trust. Phil was a business man connected with shipping, but he was not a seaman . Although she knew he probably had some very excellent ships' captains working for him, they would be strangers and that wouldn't be the same at all.

As they headed directly for her hotel, with the afternoon sun slanting downward in a reddening way, she said, "I suppose you're right. And I realise it's silly of me to be afraid. While we were watching that cruise-ship I thought about the thousands of people who take that ride because they must enjoy it. Maybe that's what I ought to do—go out on an excursion boat."

He accepted her cautious avoidance of his offer. "That might be the answer for you." When he slowed, seeking an opening in the traffic that would enable him to shoot up into the parking site beside the hotel, he showed a trace of humour around his lips without looking at her. "But excursion ships are the difference between going dancing with your father and going dancing with someone else."

He nipped up into the parking area, found a slot and switched the motor off as he reached for the door-handle. She didn't wait for him gallantly to come around and hold the door for her. She met him behind the car and turned him towards the sidewalk. "Dancing with your father is always safe," she told him, and they both laughed as he took her as far as the hotel entrance, and stopped there. He had to get back down to the dock. She held out a hand.

"It's been a delightful day," she told him, and meant it. "You're not the same man I thought I met last night, Jack. Thanks very much."

He squeezed her fingers. "For what, for not being the man you thought I was?" He released her hand. "I'll look for you at breakfast in the morning." His gunmetal eyes darkened towards her. "Thanks, Ruth, for making this day sparkle for me." He winked, turned and walked back towards the parking area. She stood a moment, then slowly entered the hotel, scarcely looked around the lobby and went directly to one of the lifts.

He made her think of an elder brother. She kept that thought all the way up to her floor, but as she was unlocking the door of her suite she reproved herself; there was no way for a single woman to think of Jack Ewell as a brother, even though he was easy to be with, because consciously or unconsciously, there was that sensation—that chemistry—that would always make a woman aware of him as a man.

He didn't have to touch her; he didn't even have to remind her of their difference with looks or innuendoes. She was very aware of his closeness even when they were the least involved as a man and a woman.

She told herself that he was sweet and considerate. That he was handsome, too, and with a depth that had to be rare in men. As a friend she would cherish him.

EIGHT

A LONG DAY'S ENDING

PHIL surprised her by arriving unannounced and unexpected that same evening. She probably should have
expected him, but he'd said nothing the last time they
had parted downstairs in the lobby.

He acted a little uncomfortable at first, probably
because he remembered their cool parting the previous
night; but she had almost forgotten that so it was easy
to make him feel at home in her sitting-room.

He needed a drink, but she had no liquor so they
decided to go downstairs. There was a bar off the
dining-room. He wanted the drink first, then dinner.
She was agreeable although as a matter of fact she
didn't need a drink, and, because she'd had a belated
lunch, she wasn't hungry.

She left Phil alone while she went to the bedroom to
change for the evening. When she returned he was
standing stiffly looking out at the settling night from the
studio windows. He didn't turn to face her until she
said he looked tense, then he swung and shot her one of
those sultry up-and-down looks that could be so compli-
mentary except that this evening the look was more
sulphurous than languorous.

"I lost a beauty today," he exclaimed. "Had it all

figured out and when I moved in, it just didn't materialise."

She had the same bizarre feeling towards Phil tonight she had had towards Jack that morning. It was like knowing the strategy of different gladiators as they moved around one another to try for the kill. She went to the door, her light evening wrap across her shoulders, reached for the knob and waited for him to cross over.

He came, looking a little surly, a little grey.

Instead of opening the door as had been her intention, she suddenly leaned on it and said, "Phil, maybe we hadn't ought to go out this evening. You don't look as though you'd enjoy it."

He reached past and pulled the door open, then he jerked his head to indicate that she must precede him. "All I need is a pick-me-up," he told her, and waited for her to move.

She did, but as she stopped in the corridor, turned and watched him close the door, she still thought he was going to be a very poor escort. Angry or preoccupied men made poor companions any time, but after dark they were particularly disappointing.

He confirmed her opinion by not opening his mouth on the ride to the mezzanine, but after they found a small table in the hotel's exclusive, weakly lit bar, and Phil had put away a manhattan and sat waiting for the second one to arrive, he loosened a little by swearing with a kind of hopelessness that didn't match his hard, glittering eyes.

"That deal I told you about last night. The gawd-damned thing fell apart today as though everything was arranged wrong before I even got going."

His second drink came and this time he took his time.

65

Her own highball was a frothy, green thing that tasted of mint. She knew an answer to his mood but she also knew enough not to give it : there would be other deals, it wasn't the end of the world.

He rolled his eyes around the room, taking in every other patron, and although she watched, his glance never rested any longer on the women than on the men. Phil had never had lady-fever; it was difficult to imagine him like that because his preoccupation was with making money, with manipulating people and things towards an early retirement with riches. Although he was a large, black-eyed, commanding man, good-looking in the same way Caesar may have been, or Napoleon or Bismarck, and she had seen women stare at him, Phil had never been and probably never would be, a woman's man.

"That damned Ewell jumped the gun," he said, tasting the second highball. "He's been manipulating for a month now."

She said, "Manipulating?"

"Negotiating to sell out. The hell of it is, that the company he's been talking with let him re-negotiate a couple of his contracts, let him accept a discount-offer, and they took them over too at the lower figure. Christ, I had that figured to the penny, plus his ships, plus his credit and standing and all the rest of it. I had him sewed up like a dummy in a canvas sack."

She finally decided to say what she was thinking. "Phil, you had a bad day. It's not your fault Captain Ewell has been negotiating to sell out without you knowing it. Drink your highball and let's go eat."

He looked at her, looked at his glass, hoisted it and tossed off the mixed drink as though it were a straight shot. As he leaned to rise, putting the glass aside, he said,

"The hell of it is I still could have nailed him to the cross right up until about ten o'clock this morning. Then the first mate of his ship came in and said Ewell was tied up this morning, and that he had just received orders from him over the telephone to take aboard the first order on the new contracts. As soon as that cargo went over the side and into the hold, it was his and I'd lost out."

Ruth recalled Jeck Ewell finishing a telephone conversation in the lobby that morning. She could guess to whom he had placed that call, and what instructions he'd given. She stood up, gathered her coat into one hand, draped it from her arm and did not look at Phil until he was standing, impatiently waiting. Then she flashed him a swift smile and walked ahead towards the dining-room. Behind her, he dropped a note at the cashier's cage and wordlessly walked after her.

The dining-room was crowded, and as they waited to be taken to a table, she let her glance wander too casually; she did not want to see Jack out there among those diners. It hadn't seemed the wrong thing to do to go driving with him today, when Phil was otherwise tied up, but now, if he had been sitting out there, perhaps looking across the room at her, she would have felt like a conspirator.

But he was not there. When they were escorted to a table she made a final long look, then sat down, and when the menus were passed across she asked Phil whether losing the deal today was really damaging, or whether it was just a blow to his professionalism, his business man's ego.

He tossed down the menu before replying. "I needed his cargoes and his ships. Ego's got nothing to do with

it. I could have demanded more wharf space if I'd got
a couple more cargo vessels. I could also go after some
of the bigger hauls. That's where the big money is. They
have been making millions hauling out to the Orient for
Uncle Sam. But you can't do it on a shoestring. Give
me five ships and, take my word for it, I could romance
my way into the millions-a-year club."

She said, "But those aren't the only two ships, are
they?"

He flashed a glittering, black look around the room
and back to her again, a restless, impatient kind of look.
"What the hell am I telling you this stuff for, you're
a woman. No, they aren't the only two ships, but they
were the only two that already had some damned lucra-
tive contracts riding with them. I don't want ships that
are rusting at anchor because their owners can't scare
up any cargoes. Hell, I could buy a hundred like that.
Listen, in this business the ships are a dime a dozen, it's
the contracts—the mature contracts that have been paying off on the barrelhead—that you have to get, along
with the ships."

She began to get some idea of what his business
entailed. "Aren't there other ships with contracts to go
with them?"

The waitress came, they ordered, then he glared at
her. "Hell, yes, there are other ships with contracts, but
there are also some damned big companies with plenty
of ready money to grab them up the moment they are
for sale. I'm still walking the razor's edge. I can't dump
a fortune on the line, not yet. But I could have within
a year, if I'd got Ewell today."

Ruth sat back and watched the other diners. Generally
they were older people. They looked established, solid,

the kind of people that were the backbone of a city's business-industrial segment. She had already decided that in San Francisco a great many of the people who resided in hotels were not transients, but were regular residents. It wouldn't have appealed to her at all, but it was easy to understand how people in their late fifties and older preferred not to have to bother maintaining a home, when their business interests were in the commercial or industrial section of San Francisco.

Phil pulled her attention back to him by saying, "Well, that lousy Ewell second-guessed me."

That annoyed Ruth. "It doesn't sound to me as though he second-guessed you, Phil. It sounds to me as though he were negotiating a long time before you ever decided to enlarge. After all, he's been at this a lot longer than you have."

Their meal arrived, and by now they were both hungry. For a while neither of them said anything. Somewhere, perhaps in the bar-room, someone had started a tape of Latin music playing. It was muted and pleasant. Otherwise, there was the constant noise of a large restaurant, a popular dining-room where people ate and departed and more people came to take the vacant tables.

Phil seemed unable or unwilling to abandon his train of thought, and that annoyed Ruth. When he made another remark about his misfortune that morning she raised a cool pair of eyes to his face.

"Phil, it's water under the bridge. How long are you going to dwell on it?"

He didn't respond in anger, but there was a hint of gruffness when he said, "Listen, Ruth, we're talking about a future as well as a current loss. I'm not going to

69

take on any new responsibilities until I'm sure I can support them."

She stared. "Are you talking about a wife, or about a ship?"

He had no chance to answer. A waitress carrying a telephone came to their table, put the telephone close to Phil and leaned to plug the line into the floor-jack. Phil lifted the instrument and gruffly said his name. Ruth watched his face. His mouth was already sucked flat and it did not change, but the dark brilliance of his eyes flashed around restlessly as he listened. When the speaker at the other end of the line stopped talking, Ruth saw Phil's lips loosen a little, and curl. He said, "Are you absolutely certain about this, Gino? All right, all right, I'm not questioning your word, just your sources. Okay, I'll take care of it, and don't worry. If you're right the deal is on again. I'll keep in touch." As Phil put the telephone down, very gently, he saw Ruth's expression, and immediately his own underwent a change. He said, "I made a mistake. I gave up too soon this morning. The deal's on again."

She was puzzled. "The Ewell deal?"

He nodded, and settled back in a more relaxed manner to eat his dinner. He had no more to say about whatever the telephone-caller had told him. Ruth was curious, but she also knew Phil Harlow. No one ever got a word out of him unless he volunteered it. As a matter of fact he had told her more about his business since she'd been with him in San Francisco than he had ever told her before. Ordinarily, he was very tight-mouthed.

When they finished eating he took out a cigar. It smelled good when he lit up. When Ruth com-

mented he held the thing up and looked narrow-eyed at
it. "Cuban. They're not supposed to get into the States,
but I know the skipper who picks them up trans-shipped
to Morocco from Germany, and delivers them in New
York." His black eyes lingered on the cigar, then drifted
to her face and stayed there. "There is more chance to
make a million in shipping today than any time since
the last war. There's also a better chance to go belly up.
But the difference is where I operate, where we all
operate who are in the business today. You can make
it big any day. It's a gamble, but for bigger odds and
better jackpots than they handle over in Reno." He
lowered the cigar, waited until his coffee cup had been
refilled, then leaned upon the table and said, "Ruth,
when I take you up to Las Vegas to marry me, we're
going to leave a trail of hundred-dollar notes all the way
up and back."

She sat watching his face. He had always been so
strong, so forceful. It had thrilled her back home in
Virginia. She finished her coffee and looked round for
her evening wrap. This had been a long day, and for
some reason or other she had not ended up enjoying it.
She said she was tired, and rose. Phil came up smoothly,
dropped some bills on the table — and without a world
escorted her out of the dining-room to the lobby, and
walked her directly across to the elevators. She could
tell from his preoccupied look that he was doing all this
mechanically. So she told him goodnight. He did not
even press to ride up with her. The last view she had
of him was striding purposefully towards the street
doors, lost in cigar – smoke and private thought.

71

NINE

INTO THE PAST TOGETHER

HE WAS there the next morning, waiting for her at the same table. He rose and smiled when she walked over, then he held her chair. It was so normal and natural she felt only quiet pleasure. Some women at a nearby table looked at him lingeringly Ruth noticed, as the waitress arrived. She ordered orange juice and two slices of toast and that was all. Jack was eating another of those breakfast steaks with all the trimmings. She made a face and wagged her head, amused. He chuckled.

"You get in the habit on the Atlantic runs, and the habit continues."

"I should imagine fruit would be better for you," she said, smoothing out a napkin in her lap. "Fruit and vegetables." Then she raised her eyes to his face. "Are you going to sea again soon?"

He gazed at her thoughtfully. "Whatever gave you that idea?"

"Yesterday you had your ship go across the Bay for a cargo. Don't ships usually deliver their cargoes somewhere?"

He kept looking at her. "Yeah, they deliver them, but

72

if it's nothing perishable and if your holds are still two-thirds empty, you don't put out until you're loaded. I'm interested in why you want to know when I'll be putting to sea."

"Just curious," she said, and smiled as a waitress served her breakfast then withdrew.

He resumed eating and for a while they were both silent. She had fallen asleep the night before troubled and restless. That telephone call Phil had got from someone named Gino—probably, she thought, that fat man who chewed his cigars she'd seen at the restaurant the night before last—had had something to do with Jack Ewell, and it was not her opinion that it had anything *good* to do with him. She knew Phil Harlow. What had bothered her for an hour after she had gone to bed was the question whether she should warn Jack or whether she should go right on being neutral, the way she had been up until now.

In the morning as she was dressing she had decided that, rather than strict neutrality, she would try by adroit inquiry to find out what might be going on, then, if it seemed as unethical as she had a feeling it could be, she might—*might*—warn Jack Ewell.

He suddenly made her start by saying, "Hey, lady, you look like you saw a ghost last night."

She recovered and relaxed again. "Maybe I did, but it wasn't your ghost. We had dinner in here last night and you weren't around."

He reached for the coffee cup. "On board with my first officer looking at the cargo manifests he got yesterday. I have supper on board quite often. In fact, if there's no reason, I don't come back here to the hotel at all, some nights." He looked at her. "We? You and

Phil Harlow had dinner here last night?"

"Yes. He was disappointed about a deal falling through."

Ewell nodded. "He would be. He's too quick and too eager. It's nothing against him, but I knew just what he was up to as soon as I saw who he was having that conference with night before last. The way these things work, you have to protect yourself at all times. It's not just Harlow, there are dozens as bad as he is, and a few more who are even worse."

She said, "But you are protected?"

He nodded and put the cup aside, and that seemed to end this conversation as far as he was concerned. He made his infectious smile then said, "Today I'm going to take you up the coast and show you some country and some views."

She was all set to decline, but she still hadn't figured out what it was he hadn't done right, and that Gino had discovered and had passed along to Phil. She knew from her fiancé's actions last night, that whatever it was, had to be very serious.

He was speaking as though nothing but this day mattered to him, and gradually she became aware of his words. "There are vineyards up here that are actually operated by monks. No joking. They make some of the best California wine. When you see those little villages, those old stone vineyard buildings, the hills and valleys, you'll think of France up near the Pyrenees, or Italy down the boot."

She laughed at him. "I doubt it. I've never seen France near the Pyreneees, or the boot of Italy. How about the bluegrass country of Virginia?"

He smiled at her. "No comparison. I'll wait in the

lobby while you get your coat." He hesitated, and that was when she could have declined.

She didn't but on the ride up in the elevator later she scolded herself, but only half-heartedly; her excuse for going with him today was that she had to discover what Phil knew that could hurt him. She would never wring it out of Phil, and she couldn't just come right out and warn Jack without looking in her own eyes like some variety of female Benedict Arnold.

After she got the coat and was riding back down, she remembered this same thing happening the day before, remembered that when she stepped out of the elevator he had just been putting down the telephone. This time when the elevator door opened, he was idly looking at a newspaper over near the streetside doors.

He didn't turn until she came up beside him, then, when he looked at her, he had an odd expression on his face, as though whatever it was that he had seen in the newspaper had meant something.

The look passed, he was bland again as he held the door for her, and on the stroll to the parking area where his car stood, he talked of the weather. There was a brisk little breeze blowing, which was, he told her, common in San Francisco, if she hadn't already guessed as much. "Great in the days of sailing ships," he exclaimed. "I've read where the old-time merchantmen came scudding up through the straits and into the bay all canvas full, a sight to see."

They left the parking area as they had done before, by heading southward towards the elevated highway, but this time he kept to a straight northward course until a wide divergency appeared, then he took the inland road and booted the car out at high speed. The country was

not much different from what it had been over on the
headland until, an hour and a half later, they breasted
a forested pass and down below she saw the first of those
inland, fairyland valleys that filled Northern California
at irregular intervals all the way up to the Oregon
boundary line, and even beyond.

She thought the first valley resembled something as
orderly and perfect-in-detail as a landscape artist might
paint it. Even the distant hills were blue-hazed with
morning warmth, and closer, where tiers of grape vines
climbed every well-drained slope, the earth showed
tawny-bare like a windswept peak top.

He started down the pass. "Close your eyes, then pop
them open and imagine you are in California a hundred
and fifty years ago. Mission padres supervised Indians
in these valleys; the wine was trod by barefoot girls and
the priests blessed the casks."

She laughed at him. "Did you read another book?"

"No joke," he replied. "California history in two
volumes." He eased around a long curve and she saw
the tiled roof, the massively thick mud walls, and the
crumbling old adobe enclosure that had at one time
kept animals in and probably animal-thieves out. But
when she thought it might be one of the famous old
California missions he shook his head.

"Winery. Before, it was a settlement, but it was never
a mission, except that there is a small chapel down there.
I'll show you." He winked. "They welcome visitors.
They will offer you a sample of their wine and you must
not refuse."

She studied the sprawling old adobe buildings as the
road led steadily down into the valley, and she was
certain that many a non-drinker had refused wine and

no one's feelings had been injured. But she wouldn't have said anything like that, it would have spoilt part of Jack's fun.

It was hot down in that valley, much hotter than it was over closer to the coast, and the air was as still as air could be. Not a breath stirred. They left the car parked beneath a huge tree and smiled into the dark eyes of a child who watched them with solemn interest as they avoided the winery and strolled towards a more distant building, built upon the first tier of a sidehill.

The residences of this place seemed to Ruth to have managed somehow to reach the twentieth century without having been modernised. At least on the outside they looked as though no one had touched the adobe walls execpt to whitewash them, in centuries. Then Jack spoilt it for her by stopping to lift an arm, and direct her attention to a higher slope where a glistening, rather large television aerial stood, with cable running back down towards the scattering of residences.

The little building he took her to, on its gentle slope and surrounded by tall trees long-gone people had planted to provide the blessed shade, had walls four feet thick and a lofty ceiling that had been whitewashed many years before in order to provide a sky-like background for the angels and saints long-forgotten hands had painted up there. The building was a small chapel. There was a wooden, life-size carving of the Crucifixion behind the altar, and after so many generations, the scent of incense was as much a part of the atmosphere inside the cool, shadowy chapel as was the fresh air that came through tall, narrow windows someone had left open.

Ruth was fascinated. "It's very old," she whispered, and turned to look up along the altar where that one

77

large carving was flanked by smaller ones. "Are you sure it's all right for us to be in here?"

He thought so, but since it seemed to bother her, he led the way back outside, and down through the golden dust in the direction of the old winery, and there, probably as a result of the small child having carried word that newcomers were in the village, a burly man with a full beard and a mass of reddish auburn hair that clung in ringlets all over his head, came up to meet them. He had a wonderful smile. His name, he said, was Father John, and he would be honoured if they would go to the winery with him and see how the produce of this valley was made. He asked no personal questions, and although his brown eyes missed nothing, he seemed perfectly willing to accept Ruth and her escort as friends.

At first, she was uncomfortable. Father John was not the first celibate churchman she had ever seen, but he was certainly the first one she had ever conversed with at any length, and the first one she had been around that she thought was a monk. Being a Protestant, as much as she was anything, monks, particularly wine-making monks, were a novelty to her.

It had never occurred to her to wonder if Jack Ewell had a religion, although if she'd dwelt upon it she would have realised that he did have because he was far too intelligent, and philosophical, a man not to have. Now, she wondered if he, by any chance, was a Catholic.

Where Father John took them it was blessedly cool. The room was large and bare except for a long trestle-table and several dolorous religious carvings, old and age-darkened. The floor was dull tile, the ceiling was low and heavily supported by ancient oaken rafters, and there was light coming through from one recessed window, and where Father John had left the door open. In this place it was entirely possible for Ruth to feel alienated from everything she knew; this was an ageless, hushed, peaceful world having no recognisable relationship to that world over the mountain and down by the bay.

Father John left, and returned with two glasses of a ruby-red tepid wine. He beamed as he handed Ruth a glass, then handed the other glass to Jack. "Our produce," he said. "If you are teetotallers, why then consider it a tonic for the blood, which it is." He winked, and Ruth smiled back in spite of herself.

The wine was smooth and pleasant. They told Father John as much and he seemed, in fact, to expect to be told nothing less. His interest, Ruth finally saw, was not as much in their reaction to his wine, as it was in his lively interest in them. Evidently Father John was an outgoing man, a person whose oath of service had a very practical application as its core.

They escaped from him, but not without having to employ a lot of tact, and afterwards, with their visit concluded and the sun moving away from the valley as they headed back up through the brushy pass, Jack said, "Well, what do you think of passing through the wall of time to another era?"

Ruth moved closer to him on the seat of the car, rested her head on his shoulder and said, "There are so many different sides to you I wonder if anyone ever gets really to understand you?"

He slid an arm around her supple middle and steered the car one-handed, saying nothing. She closed her eyes, after a while, perfectly relaxed and content.

TEN

TOWARDS SUNDOWN

THEY stopped by mutual consent on top of the pass, and out over the far-away ocean there hung a grey pall. Below it, of course not visible between the intervening heights and where they got out of his car and walked to tree-shade, was the Bay City. She said, "I'm reluctant to return to the twentieth century," and turned to smile. "I can visualise Father John playing Santa Claus at Christmas time, and I can visualise you and he sitting in the shade having theological discussions."

He snorted. "Any kind but that."

She made a slow twist from the waist to look back where they had been. Shadows were tumbling into Father John's valley, the glare was leaving each tiered sidehill, and those glazed tile roofs were turning rusty-red and dull. Elsewhere, as she completed her circuit, there was contrasting afternoon sunglow, and pre-dusk shadow. Roads ran like dark veins in and out of the hills and swales, and while she could not see the express highway , it was also out there, a considerable distance southward.

She raised both hands to rest them upon an old tree, and said, "Jack, what did you see in the newspaper this morning that upset you?" She did not turn from a grave contemplation of the distant rolling countryside as she asked this, although when he did not answer immediately she moved as though she might turn. Then he spoke.

"You know, aside from being very observant, you are also Phil Harlow's girl. Fiancée, I guess. It's one thing for me to like your company very much, and something else for me to confide in you."

That brought her around, blue eyes wide. "Thanks for the vote of trust."

He made a little half-deprecatory, half-apologetic gesture. "Ruth, there was a paragraph on the shipping page of the *Chronicle* this morning saying that the Ewell Shipping Company's vessel *Pinta* was damaged yesterday in a collision in Honolulu harbour."

She listened, heard this, and nodded. It obviously had significance for him, but to her it simply meant that he or his insurance carrier might have to spend some money repairing his ship. Then he continued to speak, probably because of her expression of interest but unconcern, and she acquired some additional education.

"Most contracts have penalty clauses for delay, for loss, for anything than can happen to a cargo that isn't supposed to happen to it. My ship in Honolulu is carrying perishables on a tight delivery schedule."

She leaned on the tree looking at him. She was beginning to guess the rest of the story.

"There is a forfeiture clause for failure to meet the delivery schedule, and a fine imposed by the insurance carrier providing the delay is in any way the fault of Ewell Shipping."

"And . . .?"

"And—whenever two ships collide in a harbour you

can bet your boots the blame will be divided equally. So—there goes all the profit for the *Pinta*'s Orient run, and maybe a little more."

It occurred to her that she had been monopolising him when she shouldn't have been; when he should have been perhaps flying out to Hawaii. But she didn't mention this. Instead, she asked a plain question.

"If you are fined some way, or if the shipper is upset, how bad can this be for you?"

He considered her shaded face for a moment before replying. "You have a reason for asking that, haven't you? Well, the shipper will be upset all right. You can't blame him for that. Even granting that he collects from the insurance carrier, that will be one hell of a lot less than he expected to make in profit."

"Can he cancel the contract?"

Jack nodded. "This particular contract has that kind of a penalty stipulation."

She asked one more question. "Was it possible for someone here in San Francisco to know about the collision last night?"

He smiled. "Sure. After all, it happened yesterday, and the communication facilities between Hawaii and here still operate." His smile lingered but his eyes narrowed. "Let me guess why you asked: Phil knew about it."

She had, in fact, thought that, but she had no proof. All she knew was that someone named Gino had called Phil and reported something that would be harmful to Jack Ewell. Instead of answering, she said, "If Phil could hear about the collision so soon, why didn't your people in Honolulu telephone you?"

He evidently had wondered about that himself, because when he replied his words were crisp and short. "Just for the hell of it, let's suppose someone somehow managed it so that I wouldn't know until today."

"But why would they do that?"

"So that they could contact the exporter, who now has the right to cancel his contract with me, and pick it up themselves."

"But that wouldn't be legal, would it?"

He shrugged. "I don't know that they did any such thing, and neither does anyone else, so—what can be proved?"

"Could they have bribed the chief officer of the *Pinta*?"

His answer this time was very emphatic. "Not a chance in this lousy world. If I had to make a guess as to how that might have been done, I'd say that somewhere along the line either someone impersonated me and took the call in my name, or they intercepted the radiogram." He shrugged.

She straightened up off the tree and stepped over closer to him where she could see the dusky valley beyond, and below, where they were. "Who do you know named Gino that could have discovered all the details of the collision yesterday?"

He didn't even hesitate. "Gino Bruno."

"Was he the fat man chewing the cigar that night we met and danced?"

Ewell nodded. "The same. Supercargo. He's an arranger; in a case like we've been discussing it would be Gino's job to get the shipper interested in going over to Phil from me. Gino would get either a straight ten per cent of the entire contract, or, if it were a five-year deal, he would get a monthly amount based upon the ten per cent figure. . . . Let me guess: Gino telephoned Phil. You said you and Phil had dinner at the hotel last night. Gino called Phil at dinner and you heard."

She admitted nothing although she might as well have. "Jack, wouldn't you have lost that contract anyway?"

He thought so. "When I read the newspaper this morning that's what crossed my mind." He reached to lift a coil of hair from her forehead and push it back. "But that's not what would annoy me; how about someone keeping me from knowing what happened until Mister Someone had had plenty of time to contact the shipper—and Phil Harlow."

She understood his point perfectly. She was also satisfied that between them they had guessed exactly what had happened. But it still bothered her conscience to volunteer anything, so she took him by the arm and turned him to go back to the car, without saying any more.

He progressed almost to the outer perimeter of oak-shade, then pivoted very easily and lay both hands upon her waist, drawing her to him gently. She did not resist although she had plenty of time to do so. She raised up, placed both hands flat upon his chest, and allowed the kiss to come. It was gentle, and she returned it the same way. There was no flash of passion, no twisting or grinding of bodies and mouths, and afterwards when she was smiling upwards she really did not feel that she had betrayed her true love; she liked Jack Ewell, she had kissed him because of that amiable fondness. It had nothing to do with any deeper feeling.

She said, "I couldn't say more even if I knew more, could I?"

He released her, except for one hand which he held

tightly, and went on with her back towards the car. "Nope. But you don't have to. And my thoughts aren't soggy with sadness anyway. I'd have lost the contract, in all probability. If Phil hadn't gone for the jugular vein someone else would have. It's an old, established custom : the minute someone is likely to lose a contract, all the other sharks start manoeuvring." He stopped beside the car and gazed down into her tilted face. "How would you like to be in a business, that after every conference you felt like you had to go take a bath and scrub hard to get clean again?" He opened the door, waited until she was seated, then closed it and leaned on it. "Gino is a slug, a fat, pale slug, but I don't hate him." He paused as though expecting comment. She obliged him.

"But you certainly can't like or respect a man like that."

He continued to lean and regard her for a long moment of silence, then he said, "Ruth, what's the difference between *his* kind—and your friends' kind?" Then he straightened up and went around to the far side of the car and slid in, punched the starter and drove halfway down the south side of the pass before he looked over.

She had initially felt an urge to defend Phil, and through him to defend herself for believing in him, but by the time they were halfway down the pass that impulse had been replaced by a more calm and rational one, so she said, "He told me life out here was different than any kind I'd ever known, and he certainly was correct."

There was a rebuttal to that, but Jack drove and said nothing more. Even when they were heading back over the highway in the thickening gloom of late afternoon towards the Golden Gate Bridge, and beyond that, the major part of San Francisco, he was silent.

She had learned a number of things about him lately and one of them was that when he had something serious to consider, he closed his mind to outside interference. It wasn't actually a novel thing, her father did it too, and she had known other men, including Phil Harlow, who closed out the world when they wanted to think.

She looked frankly at Jack's profile, though, as they drove through the ending day, and decided that his expression of calm, reassured acceptance, meant that he was not being at all bleak or grim. She thought he was actually a very tolerant man; she also thought she knew why that was: she had never known a grown man who did not feel at the very least, kindness towards some woman who had failed him, and for Jack Ewell that kind of a mood had become habit after so many years. If he could not judge the mother who had abandoned a young boy, then he probably would not be able, or at least very willing, to judge anyone else, including Gino Bruno and Phil Harlow.

They turned up the street towards the hotel and he looked, saw her watching him, and winked at her. "Any regrets?"

At first she did not understand. Then she did; he was talking about what they had done together on top of the pass. "None," she replied. "You?"

"I am not engaged," he told her.

"It was friend to friend."

He considered that statement a moment, then slackened speed when they came abreast of the turn-off into the hotel parking area, and swung in when there was a break in the traffic. As the car came to rest in a parking slot he switched it off and twisted towards her. "There's just no way for me to be your friend. No way under the sun." He leaned far over, wrenched the door open on her side, then drew back and for a breathless second their faces were inches apart, then he jack-knifed out of the car on his side and said nothing until she came round where he waited. Then he held out a palm and closed it when she lay her fingers across it. "The sun seems to shine a little brighter every day, lately. Have you noticed?"

She understood that this had to be the ending of something. It hadn't started out to be difficult but now it was. He was being honest though. She knew that he would never be any other way with her, and he could have gone on, day after day, playing their little game and prolonging their pleasure, but there was no deceit in him. He had just declared his feelings and, regretfully, that ended it.

She withdrew her hand. "It was truly delightful, Jack. I'll remember it always."

He kept looking steadily at her. "Tomorrow?"

She returned his stare and shook her head. "No. But I don't expect to enjoy myself so much again, as long as I'm out here." She smiled, then turned and started out of the parking area. He leaned on the car watching. When she turned, on the sidewalk out front, it was possible to catch a sidelong view of him back there. He had not moved.

ELEVEN

AN END TO SOMETHING

THE greeting came when she was inserting the key to open her door. She had not seen anyone down the corridor towards the rear wall, but that was where he had been standing—overlooking the parking area from a corridor window.

"I thought you told me he hadn't made a pass."

Her heart fluttered with guilt as she straightened up and saw him coming towards her in the softly lit corridor, black eyes fiercely accusing. She had to wait a moment for the breathlessness to pass, and during that interval he got close, and stopped beside her, leaned and with a furious push opened the door of her suite.

"In," he snarled, and gave her a slight push. Afterwards, he closed the door and leaned upon it, watching her go across to light a table-lamp. "You didn't have much to tell him though, did you?"

She was recovering, finally. Colour flooded her cheeks. "What should I have told him, Phil?"

"Anything you could get out of me."

"I'd have been ashamed," she shot back. "The things I've learned lately were too sordid to repeat. You said it was different out here, and you certainly were correct, except that I think you had to find this level to be happy, Phil."

Having her flare back at him seemed to mitigate a little of his indignation. "This level? You gawddamned Virginia aristocrat, what do you know about life? If you couldn't inherit it where would you ever get it? By marrying it. By marrying me because you know damned well I'll have it."

She could hardly believe this. "Phil, until just now I wasn't sure, but I can tell you now: I wouldn't marry you under any circumstances."

He sneered. "The gallant sea-captain's embraces are hotter, is that it? You've been seeing him every day. Where do the pair of you go—all day long? Marry me? Why didn't I introduce you as my fiancée? Well, what do you think *now*? I wouldn't touch you with a ten-foot pole."

She said, "Leave, Phil."

He did not seem to have heard. "When I'm finished all you'll get is the bones." He made a ghastly smile. "He's such a gallant skipper. Around the city they say he's the only clean one left. Clean? So clean he sneaks around when my back is turned."

She felt the trembling in her legs and wanted to sit down. She had never been through anything like this with a man before. What made it worse was that deep down she did not really want to defend herself. She felt guilty, and all she had done was kiss him without really meaning it, but the sensation of shame was there as though she had done everything she knew Phil was silently accusing her of.

"How would it sound to your father," he said. "How about loyal and upright Charley Banks, the simple bastard back home that would never believe his lost love could do anything cheap? How would it sound to him?"

She did not believe Phil was serious, but when she saw his expression she was less sure. She knew he could be a man with a long, unforgiving memory, because in the past he had brought up things she had forgotten. There was a kind of inner broodingness to him.

She went to a chair and sank down, and with an effort compelled her voice to be soft and calm when next she spoke. "Phil, it wasn't going to work, so isn't it better for us to know it now than later?"

He sneered again. "Wasn't it? Then why did you come out here? Why did you say all those things to me in the letters when I was overseas? Why did you tell your father and everyone else—including that fool Charley Banks—that you loved me? It *was* going to work—right up until you started meeting Ewell. And since you both live in the same hotel. . . ." He stopped speaking and stood by the door with the look of a man who was listening to secret thoughts. "Right here in this hotel," he repeated, letting each word fall like a steel ball upon glass.

She watched him and told herself it would do no good at all to deny what he was trying to convince himself had been happening. She saw him, over there, exactly as she would have inevitably have seen him some later time, after their marriage, when it would have been too late, when she would have felt sicker than she felt right then.

He called her a name, very softly, and let its echo die in the hush that afterwards settled between them, then he reached behind his back and gripped the latch. She thought he would open the door and step back, but he simply stood there gripping something with a white-knuckled fist, his black eyes shiny with fury and some-

thing she had never seen in them before, but she thought
was hatred.

"Think whatever you wish, Phil, but the thing you
just called me isn't even close, and I didn't tell him anything. Even if I'd known anything, I wouldn't have told
him, and it wasn't because there was something
between us. I wasn't raised to believe in carrying tales
or in betraying confidences."

"You weren't raised for that," he said, sneeringly.
"You weren't raised to betray confidences. There's
nothing lower than your kind of people; parasites,
leeches, gawddamned rich scum that takes everything
and gives nothing. Your father—"

"That's all," she snapped. "You've said it all before,
Phil, I don't want to hear it again."

"You haven't heard it *all*!"

She got up out of the chair, still trembly, but past her
guilt and breathlessness, and ready now to fight.
"Leave," she said again. "Phil, you'd better leave now,
because if you don't I'll telephone for the police."

He must have seen the resolution in her white-set face
because he kept quiet through a long moment of glaring.
"You think you have some rights left," he said. "You
think you can order me out of here? I ought to break
your damned lousy neck!"

She flew at him. "For what? I'm not your fiancée.
I haven't been in months, and you knew it but
wouldn't say it. What have I done that you have any
right to judge me for? Nothing! I'm the girl you took
to a dive and pawned off on another man to dance
with, and that's *all* I am to you. Now leave, or I'll call
the police!"

He went silent again. This confrontation had been in

progress for a quarter of an hour. Phil Harlow was a vindictive, scheming man, but his real temper was one of those white-hot, swiftly burning ones that fed upon itself quickly, and turned to ashes.

He called her that name again, let it drop harshly between them, then he twisted the knob at his back, eased the door open and stepped backwards, all without taking his eyes off her. He closed the door with one swift push.

She stood alone, still braced, still trembly, and could not loosen for a full five minutes after she was alone.

Everything he had said, had called her, was branded inside her mind as though she had been born with it there. Now, with her defences crumbling, she reached to support herself, and wanted to cry but the tears were too far down; she had been angry too long.

She went to stand by the windows and look out over the lighted city. There were a million people who were laughing, who were smiling at each other, and there were also, indubitably, a small number who felt as she felt this evening.

She had never cared much for liquor, but right at that moment she was tempted to call down and have something strong and cold sent up. The reason she didn't was because, as she sat down, finally the tears came.

She cried, but for whatever reason she could not have said. Maybe it was partly because she had lost something that had been treasured for a number of years, and maybe it was partly because she still had a little of that guilty feeling, and she had never before had to feel that way. More than any other single reason, though, her tears rose from a sense of female failure. There could never be anything as damaging to an ego as failure, but to a beautiful woman it had to be even worse.

She had just that one lamp burning so the apartment wasn't warmly lighted, but this suited her mood as she rose to go wash her face, and afterwards to go pick up the telephone directory and search for the number of San Francisco Airport.

There was nothing to stay for, but there was one very excellent reason *not* to stay. It only took ten minutes to get the airline and reserve a seat on the first aeroplane out in the morning. She'd have taken one out this very evening if she had been that sure of being packed in time.

Later, she bathed, got into a dressing-gown and went to watch television. It was the bath that made her feel so much better that when the telephone rang she actually sounded normal to herself when she picked it up and spoke.

The voice that came back was masculine and pleasant. "This is Jack. You didn't come down to dinner tonight."

She told him the truth. "I wasn't hungry."

"I sat there until they began to look at me as though I were a permanent fixture," he said. "I saw Phil on his way out though. He was moving like a bomb going somewhere to explode."

She drew in a big breath to start the explanation, then she eased it all back out again and changed her mind. "He was here."

Jack wasn't surprised. "I talked to my first officer on the *Santa Maria* a little while ago. The ship out in Honolulu did try to make shoreside contact with me yesterday right after the collision, but the message was only to be delivered to be personally, so that is the answer to all those uncharitable things we were thinking about Phil, this afternoon. Maybe that was it; maybe his ears were burning and that's why he stormed out of here a little while ago."

She said, "We had an argument. He called me some names and I wasn't very ladylike in return."

Jack paused. She could almost feel his intuition working. It was almost uncanny the way he'd see through to the real substance of things. Finally he said, "Okay, what was it—us?"

She told him the truth. "Yes. He was up here looking out a window. I guess he saw you holding my hand down in the parking lot, saw us talking down there after we got back."

"That's damned awful, a man holding a woman's hand."

She didn't want to talk about it because then she would have to re-live it, so she changed the subject. "I suppose I ought to tell you good-bye now, because I'll be leaving early in the morning."

"Leaving—San Francisco?"

"Yes."

". . . Must have been some fight," he muttered, then his voice got stronger again. "Listen, Ruth, don't do it. Not for a few more days."

She said, "Tomorrow morning without fail," and meant it.

He probably understood the firmness in her tone to preclude additional argument, because just before ringing off he said, "All right. Just let me drive you to the airport. What time is your flight?"

"Seven in the morning."

He whistled. "That's before breakfast. Okay, I'll be

in the lobby. When they tote your bags down tell them
to put the bags in my car, it'll be out front."

She thanked him, then rang off, and afterwards
wondered if she had let him talk her into that, wondered
if it wouldn't have been much better if she'd simply
taken a cab to the airport and not had this good-bye to
say.

It wouldn't be the easiest one she'd ever said, because
although San Francisco fascinated her, the only person
out of all those hundreds of thousands who inhabited
this hilly metropolis she would really regret leaving
behind was Jack.

She decided it was done, that she wouldn't try to call
him back and cancel out. She also decided that it was
her fate, perhaps, to be just as unhappy leaving San
Francisco as she had been during her last day and
night.

A ship bellowed out in the harbour, and several little
tugs answered with sharp, gutsy snorts, otherwise the
night had only one sound, a kind of throaty rumble as
though a very long way off someone was rolling great
round stones down an echoing corridor. It was the same
night sound she had heard in New York, and even to a
lesser degree, Richmond had it too.

It was the throb of a large city, the pulse of a place
where the heartbeat slowed after dusk but never stopped.
She would remember that San Francisco had it, when
she was back again in the fox-hunting country.

TWELVE

A WOMAN'S PREROGATIVE

FOR some reason she awakened the following morning feeling good. As she showered and dressed she wondered . how that could be; last night she hadn't only lost her love, but she had been branded, even partially in her own eyes, as a woman who did not deserve a man's respect.

When she was ready, finally, she crossed to the studio-windows and stood a moment looking out over the drowsing city where slaty paleness meant that some-where on the far side of her building the sun was up, but was not yet very bright.

She could see the distant ocean and, nearer, some of the docks and wharves. She could also see the different coloured rooftops of varying heights that marched down towards the waterfront, and smiled because she had liked San Francisco and felt a little like someone losing a friend when she thought of leaving it. Then she turned resolutely, took her coat and gloves and purse, crossed to the door and arrived there simultaneously with the smiling coloured man who had arrived to take her luggage downstairs.

She rode alone to the ground floor, and when the door opened it was as though she had been through

this before, because Jack was over there at the registration desk talking on the telephone. He saw her, grinned,
waved, then finished his conversation without haste, and
put the telephone aside only when she had crossed the
room.

She had dressed in a travelling suit of dark blue with
austere white trim, and because she was not addicted to
jewellery, the only piece she wore now was a wristwatch.
He told her she looked very sophisticated, very worldly,
then took her across the empty lobby and into the dining-
room where no other diners had as yet shown up.
Beyond the swinging doors leading, presumably, to the
kitchen, several loud voices were raised in a sing-song,
jocular way, and the aroma of food being prepared
reminded her that she'd had no supper the night before.
As she sat, and put her coat and purse upon an empty
chair, she smiled over at Jack.

He was wearing a white turtleneck sweater under a
jacket that very nearly matched her travelling suit. He
looked shiny from shaving and scrubbing, and he also
looked wide awake.

She knew exactly what he was thinking, or rather
what he was wondering, and she felt a compulsion to
confide in him, so she said, "I suppose, if I'd given it
any thought, I'd have known that Phil was bound to
be angry. But it didn't really seem that terrible."

"He's a jealous man," said Jack. "That's his
chemistry."

She nodded, accepting this for a fact but because she
had never before given Phil any encouragement to be
that way, she hadn't known how truly and savagely
jealous he was.

"It's over," she said, and smiled slightly.

Jack was unconvinced. "He'll be back. It's not that hard to forgive if you're in love."

She knew better, not entirely because of the irretrievable things that had been said last night, but also because, when she had awakened this morning feeling so relieved, it had been because she had somehow, subconsciously, resolved a lot of things; evidently had got a big load off her shoulders. She shook her head and said, "It's over," then their waitress came and they were busy for a moment. Ruth noticed that Jack did not order the breakfast steak this time, and after the waitress had departed she teased him gently.

"No appetite, Captain? How can you keep your strength up on orange juice and toast?"

He met her teasing smile with a droll look. "No appetite because I don't want you to leave. If it's true that Phil won't be back, why penalise all San Francisco by leaving?"

She laughed at him. "I'm sure that all San Francisco couldn't possibly care whether I stayed or left."

"Sure all San Francisco would care – if all San Francisco knew you," he said, and pressed onward. "Look, wait a few days. Don't be rash."

She wasn't being rash. "Jack, what's the point in my staying? The reason I came here—is no more."

"Well, hell's bells," he protested, "you can't stop living because a little corner of heaven fell, can you? There is a lot more to San Francisco than Phil Harlow or people like him." He leaned back when his breakfast arrived and although he was silent throughout, he did not take his eyes off Ruth, and the moment the waitress withdrew he went right on as though there had never been a waitress. "Do I look like I'm going to throw in the sponge, or as though I'm going to drag a bruised soul into a monastery?"

"You are a man," she said defensively, "and anyway it isn't the same for you."

He picked up the orange-juice glass, considered the liquid, then tossed it off as though it had been rye whisky. He made a face, too, and she laughed until he explained that he detested orange juice, and as though that were the most natural thing in the world, he didn't give it a second thought, but adhered to his argumentative effort to dissuade her.

"Look, Phil got Gino to go to all my contract-people last night and paint them a very graphic word-picture of what happened out at Hawaii. His idea, of course, was to make them shaky about shipping with me."

Ruth, holding toast, sat like stone.

"He also contacted the union secretary and hinted that I was nearing bankruptcy, and if the union were smart it would refuse to allow seamen to sign on with me unless I'd put up all wages in advance."

Jack paused, considered his empty orange-juice glass, then signalled for a waitress and asked for black coffee. When he was finished Ruth had a question. "When did Phil do those things?"

"After he went storming out of here," Jack answered. "You're thinking he did them to strike back at me over you. All right, I'll buy that. But my point is, Ruth, every time someone kicks your tail you don't tuck it and run."

She put the piece of toast down and wiped her hand on a napkin. She watched the girl bring Jack his coffee, and she absently-mindedly saw how the girl looked at him, and smiled. She had seen that happen before with Jack Ewell.

"It's just simply unbelievable," she told him, "that Phil could turn out like this."

Jack tasted the coffee, then said, "Why, what's so unbelievable? Your ego is injured because you thought he was true-blue. No one likes to have their personal judgement of other people proved wrong. Me—I never for one moment trusted your ex-boyfriend, and I still don't trust him. He's not through striking back."

She hadn't expected anything like this. As far as she was concerned, breakfast was to be followed by a drive to the airport, then a soaring flight southward. She had put Phil into a separate mental compartment, and there he was supposed to stay for ever after.

"He said he was going to own your company," she confessed. "He said he knew how to get your contracts. His objective is to own your ships so he'll have a respectably large company. I should have told you before."

Jack finished the coffee and ate a piece of toast. His attitude changed gradually until he was smiling at her. "I guessed all that, and I guessed a little more, too—that if someone could make you just hold off a little while and not rush into marrying Phil Harlow, you would eventually wake up and have a second look at him. I don't know how he acted before he came out here, but I *do* know that this is his mud-puddle. He was made for it."

She could have agreed with the generalisations, but she was more interested in something else, something more immediately relevant. "Can he really hurt you, Jack?"

He shook his head when the waitress came to re-fill

his coffee cup, and without taking his eyes off Ruth he answered. "Probably; not with the people I've been doing business with for many years, but with the outfit that's dickering to buy me out. Even if they know what kind of a man Phil Harlow is, they're still bound to feel shaky over what he's trying to do. They won't want to inherit a feud."

She bit her heavy underlip in exasperation. "My fault," she murmured, and he vehemently shook his head.

"Nope. Sooner or later he was going to tangle with me. He said he was after my company long before he knew you and I were friends."

"But that made it worse, Jack."

"Okay, it made it worse, but only in the way that forced Phil out into the open, and maybe that's a good thing. Look, don't worry." He looked at his wrist, rose and dropped some silver on the table, then reached for her coat and hooked it over his arm as he said, "We'd better move out or you're going to miss that aeroplane."

They left the hotel by crossing a lobby that was finally beginning to come to life. Outside, there was sunlight and noise, and a hint of soft sea-breeze. It was going to be a beautiful day. For some reason, as she got into his car, she wondered if it would be as hot today as it had been yesterday, over in that serene valley where Father John minded his vineyards.

The traffic was always bad in the morning. If there was any mitigation, in their case, it had to be in the fact that they were going out of the city, heading towards the shoreline environ where the airport sat, while two-thirds of the traffic was streaming like motorised serpentines into the city.

She did not particularly notice the traffic, nor even the promising, golden softness of a perfect day. It troubled her that she was doing something unheroic : she was leaving two men at dagger points because of her, and was blithely winging out of both their lives without even making any effort at all to create some kind of amends.

When Jack looked quickly over, then back to the traffic again, and said, "Smile, lady," she moved slightly on the seat, until they touched.

"I never would have guessed anything this bad could have come out of my visiting here," she said. "Jack . . .?"

He reached and patted her hand. "Forget it. Like I said, it would have happened anyway. He was going to try pirating me before you ever showed up."

"But my leaving like this—that's running away."

He cheerfully agreed. "Okay, have it your way. You are running away."

They reached the wide turn-off that led into the airport area and here the pace was even quicker. Aside from the shriek of jets and turbo-jets lifting off and arriving with a steady constancy, there were thousands of parked cars, cabs, moving buses, and every variety of wheeled vehicle.

People streamed in and out of a series of massive glass doors on to a raised ramp out front, where cars, mostly cabs, raced in, hesitated, then sped away again with new passengers.

Jack, heading towards that point of disembarkation with Ruth's bags, caught the attention of a greying coloured man, held out a closed fist, and as soon as the coloured man's hand rose to meet the fist, and something crumpled passed between them, the coloured man reached past for the luggage without even glancing at Ruth.

All this took only minutes. Jack could not park there, could not even hesitate more than a minute because other cars and cabs were queuing up behind him to do the identical thing.

He wheeled away, winked at Ruth's harassed look, and drove down where it was possible, by making that fisted gesture one more time, to get someone to take over his car and park it.

As they alighted, Ruth was conscious, finally, of what a beautiful day this was going to be. She picked up her purse, gloves and coat, waited until the car was whisked away, then moved over beside Jack and started the uphill walk back towards the front of the terminal building.

He slid an arm under her arm. They touched at hip and elbow and shoulder as they walked. She was struggling very hard with a decision and did not look up until he said, "You don't have much time left."

She understood what that meant, and leaned closer as she inclined her head. "I don't have, do I?"

He leaned close and said, "Don't go, Ruth. Don't run."

She felt a sting of tears and kept her face averted while she squeezed his arm against her side. "Will you take me back to the hotel?" she asked, and kept her face turned away.

He disengaged his arm. "Wait right here while I find your luggage and have it brought down to the car." His voice sounded almost boyish.

THIRTEEN

VOLTE-FACE

HE DID more than hunt up her luggage and have it taken down to his car, he also telephoned the hotel and got her suite back, in her name. If the registration clerk was surprised, he did not let Jack know it. He promised that Miss Severns would pick up the key at the registration desk some time later in the day, then he went back out front to escort Ruth down to the car. She was just putting away a handkerchief when he came back to her. She smiled up at him from misty eyes.

"Nothing worse than weepy women," she said. Then, in a more matter-of-fact way, she said, "Will you explain to me why I'm doing this? What is the point of it?"

When they reached his car the same greying coloured man had just finished stowing her luggage. He looked up with a smile and said, "Don't feel bad, lady, I'm scairt of flying in them big ones, too."

Jack made that fisted gesture, and the coloured man departed putting another crumpled bill in his pocket. He whistled as he pushed his rubber-tyred hand-car back up towards the front of the busy terminal building.

Jack took Ruth's coat and tossed it upon the back seat, then he held the car door for her, and afterwards

104

leaned down looking cheerful. "I want you to do something for me today," he said, holding her eyes with his gaze. "I want you to come aboard the ship with me."

She flinched, then said, "I'm not dressed for it."

He did not accept that. "You are dressed perfectly for it. You'll impart some beauty and poise to the deck." He stepped away as though that were settled, marched to his side of the car, and as they were picking their way back out of the airport parking area through a hastening flurry of incoming cars, he offered his reason.

"I want you to see my ship before it's no longer mine. It'll be pretty frustrating in the years ahead if I want to talk about the *Santa Maria* and you just sit there looking blank."

She could have picked any part of that to pieces, including the part that had to do with them talking about his ship, or anything else for the matter of that, in 'the years ahead'.

She probably would have, too, except that she was trying to come to grips with her fear so that she could go aboard his ship, and not spoil things for him.

She did not really offer it as an excuse not to accompany him, but she said she had to find a place to stay before going anywhere. He told her what he had done at the airport, so even if her remark had been an excuse, this thoughtfulness of his would have burst it like a toy balloon.

She decided that she was going on board his ship, and she said, rather grimly, "If I faint and humiliate you before your sailors, it's your own fault."

He was driving back into the city by this time, and being one of the incoming drivers, finally, he was compelled several times to slow to a crawl until some snarl up ahead could be unravelled by the police. He grinned at her remark.

"You couldn't humiliate me before my sailors. Primarily, I think, because today is everyone's day off. My first officer will be there, but that's about all. And you aren't going to faint, so stop telling yourself that you are."

Oddly, he was right. Her heart sank when they left the car and walked down the pier to where his ship was berthed, and she had to tilt her head to look up at it. But once she had preceded him up the gangplank on to the deck and could see water off on her right and rooftops on her left, she didn't really feel the panic she had been so certain would overwhelm her.

Jack gave her plenty of time. He stood with her just off the gangplank, and when the deck gently pitched, he distracted her by pointing to an incoming ship with a golden crescent painted upon its superstructure. "Excursion vessel like the one we watched from on top of the headland. Fair-sized ship, isn't it?"

She knew what he was doing and was glad that he'd done it, because the moment the deck moved underfoot she reached for the railing and clung to it, while looking over where that crescent-emblazoned ship was making a very slow and careful way up the estuary. "Very large," she agreed, and forced her voice to be natural. Underfoot, the deck settled and when she was satisfied it would not move again, she released the railing. Jack took her by the arm and passed along towards the front of the vessel. There a slight tilt of the deck which was visible to her made it hard for her to decide whether that made the deck seem uneasy underfoot, or whether it was slightly rolling again. Before she could make up her mind, and while she was clinging hard to Jack, he led her past a great round, mushroom-looking iron object that had the largest rope she had ever seen in her whole life partially wrapped round it. The other part of that leg-thick hawser ran over the side through a metal guard and disappeared towards the dock below.

Jack took her to the railing and showed her San Francisco from this unique vantage point—and the deck pitched again, gently, rolling half-up, half-back again, like the ship was a whale lying uneasily beside the dock. This time the diversion was not good enough. She dug fingernails into Jack's arm and clung to the railing with her other hand.

When the ship settled again, he took her across to the far side and let her see the ocean, the estuary leading down to it from where they were moored, and all the other ships made fast to the docks southward of the *Santa Maria.* This was something she had to become accustomed to. Here, there were no rooftops and no paved streets, only water, gulls wheeling and diving, other ships, and the soiled sea that filled this backwash.

Jack leaned beside her. "It looks about the same in every port, and when you're out at sea, this is the kind of a view you get. No rolling hills, no sunburnt vineyards, no high plateau with an old shepherd's grave. Just water and a lot more water." He grinned. "In its own way the sea is every bit as beautiful as the land." He looked up when a dirty little squatty vessel whose gunwhales dipped right to the water let loose a pair of snorting blasts on a horn, then he smiled and waved. A man on the tug waved from a glassless pilot-house window.

"Now the gossip begins," said Jack. "He saw you up here."

For Ruth, the prospect of being talked about for being aboard Jack Ewell's ship was nowhere nearly as upsetting as the sudden thought she had about why he'd wanted her to come aboard : because he was going to suggest she accompany him when he put out to sea the next time.

She turned her back on the sea and the waddling old tug, breathed more easily with the rooftops and streets on the land side filling her vision, and said, "I thought only idle people gossiped."

Jack jerked a thumb over his shoulder. "He isn't ever too busy to talk. His name's Ed Barnes. He's a topnotch cribbage player. During World War Two he played it for two years in Jap prison camps. He is never too busy to whisper something very devilish in your ear."

He stood watching. Evidently when he thought she was up to it, he took her by the arm again, and this time went back down towards the gangplank, but on the last lap he veered off and took her down the other side of his ship under a partially covered stretch of deck.

When he opened the bulkhead door for her to enter first, she had to step up six or eight inches to avoid bumping, the way the doorway had been built. When she looked down Jack said, "It's to keep the water out when there's a sea running. If the doors were all flush with the deck they'd let water under, and every cabin would have a wet floor." He followed her in and left the door open so that more light would enter.

They were in an immaculate, rather large cabin, where a curly-headed youngish man was working over a fold-away wall-desk. When the curly-headed man looked up, and his eyes met Ruth's gaze, he looked startled. But he recovered almost immediately and stood up. His name was Albert Newman, he was Jack's first officer, and he would have excused himself and departed if Jack hadn't asked a question, then made a statement, both of which interested Al Newman.

"What's new from Honolulu?"

Newman's smile deepened. "The damage has been appraised. She'll be dry-docked for five days, no more. Arrangements have been made to refrigerate the hold from dockside generators. The cargo will come through all right."

Jack winked at Ruth. "There is always hope," he told her, then made his casual statement to the first officer. "I got word this morning that Bruno has been gnawing away at the Hubbard-Orient contract, and that the buyers aren't going to perform if Bruno can get Hubbard-Orient away from us."

Newman's nice smile shrivelled. "Who is it—Harlow behind Bruno?"

Jack nodded. "Yeah. Harlow's been pretty busy the past twenty-four hours."

Al Newman's smile returned, but with a candid wolfishness. "Of course, that can be taken care of," he said, looking steadily into Jack Ewell's eyes. Even Ruth wasn't so naïve she couldn't get what this remark implied. Jack laughed it off and took her back out of the cabin without answering Newman.

Wheeling gulls screamed and cocked bright eyes at the man and woman as they went towards the stern of the *Santa Maria* on the port side. Ruth looked up just once, and that was when they passed from beneath the covered walkway to the sun-smashed stern deck where a lower, grilled railing ended at the fantail near a flag-staff that had a limp U.S. banner at the top, and below

109

that, a second limp flag, a green design of some kind upon a white field.

There were chairs back here, as though this was where crewmen and probably ship's officers gathered in the pleasant evenings to smoke and talk, and perhaps have a bottle of beer from the galley.

Jack led her to a chair, then sat beside her facing the estuary, and now, when the deck rose under her, and gently settled back again, she had two metal chair-arms to grip.

The gulls wheeled overhead, dipped low, and when the pair of seated people ignored them, they finally gave it up and went down among the other slips where ships were tied.

Jack eyed her sideways, then said, "It's not so terrible, is it?"

She looked out at the water, where a fair-sized, sleek yacht was making its way out towards the sea before answering. "No, it's not terrible at all. But I'm still frightened."

He laughed easily. "Lunch . . .?"

She shook her head. "No thanks," and this time she made a rueful smile. "I would fade away to a shadow if I had to eat on board a ship."

He did not dispute that although he certainly could have.

She watched his pleasant profile. He was sprawled there as though he didn't have a worry in the world. He was a deceptive man, at times. Remembering that veiled threat his first officer had made, she asked if there was really any chance of violence.

He continued to gaze at the greasy estuary when he answered. "Probably not. That went out of style

110

some years ago. At least neither I nor Al Newman is going to take a belaying pin and brass-knuckles and go ashore looking for Phil. . . . Of course, if he were to come here being disagreeable. . . ." Jack let it trail off, and turned to look at her without finishing it.

She looked back and saw that the yacht was well along on its rendezvous with the running sea beyond the yonder breakwater. Now, there was another ship beating up the inland waterway from the blue-green ocean. It looked like most of the other ships she had seen tied up at the docks. When it was passing Jack drawled a quiet comment.

"That's one of Phil's cargo-carriers, Ruth. It's been on a run up to Seattle and Vancouver. Up until now he's concentrated mostly on West Coast runs, but he's beginning to reach farther out now, too."

Phil's ship looked trim and well-maintained. It also rode low in the water, as though its holds were full. She watched it bore on past, heading farther up the estuary to its own berth, and she said nothing. Jack watched the ship too, and farther along the port-side deck, leaning over the railing smoking a cigarette, First Officer Al Newman impassively watched also.

There was a delightful breeze blowing on the after-deck. Ruth relaxed without being fully aware of it. When the deck rose gently, and settled, she rose and settled with it. Jack noticed the loosening grip of her hands on the chair-arms and smiled to himself, but he said nothing.

FOURTEEN

A VERY BUSY TELEPHONE

At two o'clock he took her back to the hotel, and there, finally, she had a belated luncheon, although she was not actually very hungry. Jack had to leave. All he would say was that it had to do with some of the contracts. He promised to be back later, perhaps in time to take her to dinner.

When she was upstairs, unpacking in her studio-apartment for the second time, she decided that whatever it might have been that had instilled a terror of ships and water in her, probably in early childhood, could not still be dominating her. The afternoon on his ship had been very pleasant. Even that pitching deck, once a person got accustomed to it, was not unpleasant.

Later, after she had bathed and had put up her hair, the telephone rang. It was Jack. He had an excuse about dinner.

"I can't wriggle out of a conference with one of my contract's people this evening, and I know this bird, he never hurries at anything, so if I can't make it in time for dinner . . .?"

"Then you can't make it," she said, "and that's all there is to it. Tell me frankly, has Phil managed to hurt you very much since last night?"

He chuckled. "Wait until breakfast. I'll be better able to tell you after this meeting tonight. Maybe he's hurt me a little."

"Jack, are the people who were going to buy your company backing out?"

He hadn't spoken to those people since the day before, and all they'd told him then, so he related to her, was that if he lost any of his better contracts, they would have to re-negotiate. "And also, as I think I told you today," he concluded over the telephone, "they don't like the idea of being in the middle of a fight. They aren't afraid of Phil, but they don't want to buy a battle, either, for which we can't blame them, can we?"

She said, "No, we can't blame them. Are you going down to the *Santa Maria* in the morning by any chance?"

He hesitated as though trying to guess her reason for asking, then he answered non-committally. "I could. What's on your mind?"

"Well, it *is* your livelihood, Jack."

He yielded. "Okay. I hadn't planned on going down there until day after tomorrow, when we have to get ready to sail."

Her heart sank. "You'll be leaving San Francisco?"

"I'll explain in the morning," he said. "How would you like to ride up to the headland tomorrow?"

She would like that. She would even have gone down to the ship if he'd suggested that, although if she'd had a choice she'd have preferred the headland. "I'd love it, but that's what's bothering me : I'm monopolising too much of a busy business man's time."

He had a quick answer for that. "Don't try to antici-

113

pate this busy business man. Let *me* say when you're monopolising too much of my time. Goodnight, beautiful lady, see you for orange juice—ugh!—in the morning."

She laughed and rang off, and went over to switch on the television feeling better than she had felt in the full preceding twenty-four hours. But she didn't get to switch the television set on because her telephone rang again. This time it was her father, and after making certain he had the correct number, he said, with some indignation, "After this when you go away, leave your telephone number with me. There must be five thousand people named Severns in San Francisco. At least leave me the name of your hotel."

She promised to do better the next time, and wondered why he had called her, why he had made such an effort to locate her. "Is something wrong at home?" she asked.

He said, "I don't know. I've been gone all day, so when Phil called I wasn't here. He called twice, is what upset me, and he insisted on speaking to me and would leave no message. He didn't leave a number for me to call back, either."

While her father spoke, Ruth's heartbeat slowed noticeably and her cheerfulness vanished as though it had never existed. She made up her mind on a course of action before her father finished, then she told him, without going into a lot of embarrassing detail, what had happened between her and Phil.

Her father's reaction was not surprising. He said, "Come home, sweetheart. Forget all about Phil Harlow and come on home. I'm very thankful this thing came out into the open now instead of a year from now."

She took a big breath. "I can't come home right now, Dad. Phil is trying to ruin a very handsome, and a very likeable man named Jack Ewell. *Captain* Jack Ewell, a ship-owner out here. It's partly my fault, so I can't just run away and leave Jack in this fight alone."

Her father sighed audibly. "Of what possible use can you be to a ship's captain, sweetheart? My knowledge of those men is limited, but what little I do know makes me believe your ship's captain can very probably take care of himself in any kind of company."

That was not her point. "But, Dad, it's partly my fault that Jack is in this mess. You wouldn't expect me to turn my back on him would you?"

This time her father's reply came slow, as though perhaps he had begun to wonder about something. "This handsome ship's captain, Ruthie . . . by any chance is he some kind of double for Phil. Some kind of a substitute?"

She was startled. "A substitute? Do you mean, do I —well—*feel* anything for Jack?"

"Something like that," assented her father dryly.

"He's a friend, Dad. You'd think he's wonderful."

"Is that so? It seems to be that I haven't as yet felt any of your young men, excepting poor Charley, are actually very satisfactory, let alone wonderful."

"You would this one, Dad. He's tall, and he grew up on the Norfolk waterfront, and he owns his own ships, has a wonderful smile and—"

"Growing up on a waterfront, Ruthie, has nothing to do with possessing a wonderful smile. . . . I'll tell you what I think : you're somehow or other being overwhelmed out there. You know perfectly well what kind of a reputation California has."

115

She almost laughed. "A whole *State* can't have a bad reputation, Dad. You're thinking of Los Angeles, of Hollywood. Up here in San Francisco it's as different as night is from day."

"If it's all that different, sweetheart, then tell me just how you got involved in anything as wild as that affair with Phil you just described. Ruth, I really think you ought to come home."

She said, "Shortly, Dad," and made the sound of a kiss over the telephone. "Whatever Phil wants to tell you is a lie. You can help us both by not taking any calls from him. All he'll do, Dad, is try to agitate you with lies. As I told you a little while ago, he threatened to carry his stories to you and to Charley. Dad, what kind of a man would do a thing like that?"

Her father said, "His kind. I could have told you a couple of years ago, Ruth. All right, I won't accept his call, but you give some serious thought to coming right home. Hear?"

She smiled at the wall. "Good-bye, Dad, and I love you."

Afterwards, she sniffled, and went over to stand looking out into the moonless gloom over the rooftops of San Francisco. The hardest part about growing up was resisting the temptation to be smothered by parent-love.

She turned slowly and looked back where the telephone sat. Phil had actually tried to call her father, had actually tried to make good his threat to lie about her to those who would be badly disturbed by his lies. She stood a long while wondering how she ever could have loved Phil, how she ever could have believed in him, trusted him, thought he was so many wonderful things.

For the last time, she finally went over to switch on

the television set. In San Francisco there was one station that broadcast nothing but news, and that was the channel her set was tuned to. It probably wouldn't have mattered if she'd switched on a half-hour earlier or a half-hour later, the news was depressing, and also demoralising. She moved to change channels, and her telephone rang again. She straightened up, flicked the set off with one hand, and came round slowly looking at the telephone. She did not know anyone in San Francisco. With a little shrug she went to lift the receiver and speak her name. Within five seconds she knew who this final caller was even though he did not mention his name right off. Phil.

"You were on his ship this afternoon, weren't you, and I'm surprised that you're not out with him right now or, better yet, down at his apartment."

She started to lower the receiver and remembered what her father had said. "Phil, how can you be so depraved? What were you going to tell Dad today?"

"The truth. I warned you that I would."

"It's not the truth and he knows it's not. You ought to know it's not, but you're not really altogether balanced on this subject, are you?"

"You have turned out to be a pretty damned good liar," he said bleakly. "You make it sound so trite and truthful when you deny what you've been to Ewell. And don't worry, I'll get through to your father just like I got through to Charley Banks, the stupid hick who thought you were the sweetest thing to come down the pike. And that's only for starters. Just give me a few more days. I'll have you spelled out for everyone in San Francisco, too. You and Jack Ewell."

He put down the telephone. She waited, listening to

117

the dial-tone, then realised what he had done and slowly replaced her own receiver.

He hadn't been threatening her. She'd thought that before, but not after hearing from her father. And when he'd said he'd got through to Charley Banks, that had been the truth.

She went to a chair and sank down. What had he meant about spelling out what she was to everyone in San Francisco? That frightened her, not because she had any sensation of guilt, but because now she knew Phil would actually do something drastic.

He obviously was going to destroy her as well as Jack Ewell. The fact that Jack had not seemed particularly disturbed did not mitigate anything for her, because she was not that strong. She was *afraid*. Lies or not, she knew what Phil's kind of filth could do to a reputation, to *anyone's* reputation, and it didn't have to be truthful at all.

She lifted her gaze to the telephone, wondering whether she hadn't ought to call Jack when he got back to the hotel. She decided not to because Phil's threats this time had been aimed at *her*. Whatever he had undertaken against Jack was something else; Jack would handle that, and she hoped with all her heart that he would handle it successfully. She wouldn't put any more on his shoulders.

She rose and went off to bed, forgetting all about television. Forgetting all about how cheerful she had felt only a short while before Phil had called.

FIFTEEN

THE PRICE OF FAILURE

THE solution was in her mind when she awakened the next morning, and without waiting she moved to implement it. The hardest part was locating the correct telephone number for Phil Harlow, and she was about to give up when a gruff-voiced man at the offices of Harlow Shipping told her to try a marine number, and gave it to her. Phil was aboard one of his ships, the one she had seen enter the estuary the day before.

She got him, said what she had to say, and when Phil agreed, she rang off and with shaking hands began getting dressed for the street. It was also in her mind to call Jack and make an excuse about breakfast, but she left him a note downstairs at the registration desk instead, because she knew he'd dig out of her what she was up to. She also knew he would object.

If she'd known San Francisco better she would have made her rendezvous to meet Phil at some handy restaurant, but when she got into the cab out front of her hotel, she gave the number of the berth at the estuary docks where Phil's ship was moored. That was where she had agreed to have breakfast with Phil Harlow, and she had to force herself every inch of the way, not just because she did not want to see him again,

119

but also because she did not want to go aboard another ship.

The cab-driver eyed her with candid interest when she paid him off and turned to head for the gangplank of the nearby ship. He probably did not get very many fares that wanted to go down here to the waterfront.

Phil was up there on the deck watching. Several men were near him, but when he turned and saw her coming up, the crewmen drifted away. Seamen could be discreet, but as a rule they weren't. Phil Harlow was not a man other men took very many liberties with.

He did not go over to greet her. When she reached the deck and put forth a hand to grip the railing, he stood fifty feet distant coldly staring at her. Then he jerked his head without a word and led the way aft to a large cabin where a table had been set for two. Breakfast aboard a ship was Ruth's idea of simple torture, but she accepted the chair Phil pointed to and, when he proceeded to fill two cups with black coffee, she accepted one of those, too.

He finally looked over and said, "Okay, let's have it. What's your proposition?"

"If you will leave Jack alone, I'll go back to Virginia and not see him again."

Phil continued to stare a moment longer, then he slowly smiled. "That's all? What in the hell makes you think I care whether you run out on Ewell or not?"

"That's the whole point of your anger, isn't it, Phil? You think we've been lovers."

"Sure, I think that. You could never convince me you haven't been. But a little sacrifice on your part doesn't make my feelings any better. As for Jack Ewell, I don't have to hurt him through you. I've already got him half crushed and he doesn't even know it yet. If he'd kept his mind on business and not so much on trying to make a fool out of me through you, he'd still have some bargaining power." Phil glanced up as a burly man wearing a white jacket came in, looking uncomfortable, to serve their breakfast. This burly man looked as though he would be much more at ease in a sleeveless skivvy-shirt and perhaps with a cigarette drooping from his lips. He was the ship's cook. He served them and got out of there as fast as he could. Phil ignored this intrusion but he kept silent until the burly man was gone, for which Ruth was grateful. She was on edge every second she was in this room with Phil, but she had also forgotten, or had *almost* forgotten, that she was aboard a seagoing ship. She drank her coffee and was hardly aware of the gently moving deck underfoot.

"Go ahead and pull out," said Phil. "That's fine with me. But it's not going to stop my campaign at all. Whether you're here or not, take my word for it, I'm going to smear you from one end of San Francisco to the other end. Let Jack Ewell live with *that*. Whether you're here or not doesn't mean a damned thing to me, Ruth. Maybe it'll make Ewell a little unhappier to know you've been unable to bear up under the truth, but for my part, I don't care. I stopped caring several days ago."

She did not having anything more to offer. In fact, she had thought Phil might like the idea of her leaving. After all, *she* was the one he wanted to ruin, out of hatred. His feeling towards Jack, at least up until she'd been seen holding hands with Jack in the parking-lot, hadn't been prompted by hatred. At least she didn't think so, and Phil hadn't sounded resentful when he'd told her about his plan to gain control of Jack's company, last week.

But now she felt disarmed. She had made her offer and he had sneered at it. She could only do one more thing. "What must I do, Phil, to make you leave him alone?"

He was eating when she said that, and went right on eating. He didn't even look at her for a while. Eventually, reaching for his coffee, his black eyes came up, as hard and dry as obsidian rock. "I wouldn't leave him alone for a million dollars. Get that through your skull, Ruth. I wouldn't slack off on what I've got planned for Ewell no matter what kind of an offer you came up with. Listen to me, between the pair of you, you wanted to make a fool out of me. Well, that was your choice. Only it didn't work, and now it's my turn." He smiled. "You talked to your father. Well, what was the purpose of that, aside from trying to make him disbelieve me— to get some money from him to offer me? Forget it. I want you on your knees and I want Ewell verging on bankruptcy. I won't settle for anything less."

She sat gazing across at him, marvelling at the depth of his irrationality. She did not say that there was no money to be offered, she simply sat and looked at him and marvelled. Under that unique stare he went back to his breakfast. Only when she pushed back the chair and stood up, did he raise his head again.

"Phil, I don't suppose there's very much I can do to prevent you from hurting me. . . ."

He rose. "There's *nothing* you can do. Nothing at all."

She went on. "But Jack is something else," she said, and turned towards the bulkhead door.

He made a reedy laugh, flung down his napkin and followed her out on to the sun-swept deck. "He's something else, all right. You'll find out what he is when the crunch comes. He'll forget all about you. After all, you can't be cheap with a man and expect him to respect you."

She saw red for just a moment, and in that second almost turned and swung on him, but she was moving, and by the time she slowed and faltered, the mood was past, so she kept on walking until she saw the gangplank. There were some seamen working nearby, they looked up admiringly as she went past, but she did not see them at all. As she reached the gangplank railing and laid a hand upon it, Phil spoke from behind her.

"It might help if you took an early flight back to Virginia. At least you wouldn't have to face a lot of people who'll hear about you in the next few days."

She turned and said, "How could I ever have thought you were a decent, wholesome human being, Phil? You're a liar and worse." She flung around and went down the gangplank as though she had been trotting up and down them all her life. She didn't even remember her dread.

There were not many taxi cabs near the docks because people who worked down there either owned their own cars or were knowledgeable about public transportation facilities. That meant she had to walk nearly a half-mile before she even found a telephone kiosk, and during that entire hike she saw men watching her. She put in a call for a cab, then waited until it arrived, ignored a wolf-whistle just before the hack arrived, and gave the hack-driver look for look as she gave him her hotel's address. She settled back and thought about what she had tried, what she had failed at, and, where she probably should have felt humiliated, she instead felt cold, calculating anger.

She *had* cheapened herself, but not in the way Phil had suggested. She had tried reasoning and pleading, and had discovered that Phil was beyond either appeal. She thought now, on the ride back to her hotel, that Phil was actually being downright illogical in an unbalanced way. His wrath and resentment had consumed his common sense.

By the time she got back to her studio-apartment she had decided that Phil could only be counteracted in one way, by fighting him exactly as he meant to fight her.

She changed from street clothes into a loose robe, then saw with surprise that it was almost high noon. She couldn't have told from the normal way—stomach rumbles—because lunch was farthest from her thoughts.

She returned to the sitting-room after changing and arrived there just as someone knocked on her front door. She asked who it was, and the answer came mutedly and calmly.

"Jack."

She decided the robe was passable and went to let him in. She smiled, but it was an effort, and when he stepped in and looked down at her, his expression was as calm, as serene as always, but she knew he was curious. After all, she hadn't even broken their date with a telephone call, just that note at the desk.

She took him over to the sofa near the studio-windows and excused her appearance on the grounds that she'd just got home. He nodded, agreeable to this, sat and crossed his long legs, then looked at her with a slightly different expression and said, "I don't suppose you'd care to tell me why we didn't meet at breakfast this morning."

She shook her head. She did not know, yet, what she was going to do, but she *did* know that whatever it was, since it was going to be based on active resistance to Phil, Jack would try to talk her out of it. At least she felt that he would.

Instead of allowing him to keep to this topic she asked a question designed to divert him, and it worked. "What happened at the conference last night?"

He blew out a quiet breath, turned and gazed thoughtfully out the windows, over all those chimney pots and rooftops, and said, "He hurt me a little, but nowhere nearly as much as he'd planned. I had to re-negotiate with the people who are buying me out. They weren't afraid, but this was a golden opportunity to act like they were, and to project an impression that because my company had some trouble, they couldn't pay as much as they'd originally offered. So—to make a long story short, I dropped my price."

"Did they accept?" she asked, "Or do they try and force you down again today or tomorrow?"

He shook his head. "We signed the papers, had them notarised by their attorney, and next week they take over my company and I get paid off. He turned to face her again, and smiled. "Okay, I've unburdened myself to you, so how about some reciprocity?"

She said, "I can't, Jack."

He did not insist. "Okay, but it has to do with Phil, hasn't it?"

"Yes."

He shifted position on the couch, looked gravely at her for a moment, then spoke calmly—and surprised her with his statement. "I got a telephone call just before I came up to see you. It was from a seaman who saw you today. He needed fifty dollars, and I promised to mail it to him in exchange for something. He was aboard Phil's ship at the dock today when you and Phil stood by the gangplank. He heard what you and Phil said to éach other. That's what he sold me for fifty dollars. Ruth, the rest of it's not too hard to guess."

She remembered those seamen, now, but at the time she'd faced Phil at the gangplank she hadn't been conscious of them. She reddened under his quiet stare. "I've never in my life run across such a—devious—bunch of people as are in the shipping business out here," she said, exasperatedly.

He laughed, and that made it easier for her to see herself as he must have viewed her; as a well-meaning but somewhat inept manipulator. She smiled a little, but shrank from telling him the offer she had made.

He did not press for a detailed explanation, which saved her, but he wanted to know whatever had made her think an appeal to Phil Harlow would succeed, and that put her perilously close to having to confess. She skirted the issue by saying, "Just a thought. I've known him for a long while."

"That is exactly the point, sweetheart, you have *never* known him."

She overlooked the lover's name. "Somehow, Jack, he has to be stopped. He is going to ruin you. He told me he had already succeeded, and that you didn't even realise it yet."

Ewell snorted. "He's clever, and he's ruthless, but he's one hell of a long way from being intelligent, and that makes all the difference. He'd like to think he's ruined me, but after last night he's out of the picture. From here on he is shadow-boxing. I don't own the company any longer, but the men who do own it now aren't nearly as tolerant as I've been. They only pretend to be uncomfortable. The first bad move Phil makes and he'll think the sky fell on him. Those men aren't exactly racketeers, but they know all the nice little ways of cracking skulls. Anyway, Phil is out of it. He's done his worst, it cost me a little, and that's the end of it."

Of course that *wasn't* the end of it but Ruth had to sit there knowing what else Phil was going to do—ruin her, and his, reputation. But if she told him she would also have to explain that she'd offered to leave him in exchange for Phil's retraction, and she simply could not bring herself to do that.

She had, she thought, got herself into a real mess by going down there to have breakfast aboard the ship with Phil. It began to dawn on her that any time anyone got involved with Phil Harlow, they had to sink into a kind of quagmire of fraud, deceit and deviousness. The more they had to do with him, the deeper they were certain to sink. She wished now she hadn't gone down there, but she had; she knew what Phil was going to do, and she had to fight back. Worse, she had to fight back alone because Jack never would agree to allow her to get involved.

SIXTEEN

AN EVENING OUT

HE TOLD her he would be back in three hours to take her for a drive up the coast, and to dinner. He didn't ask if that were agreeable with her, and when she rose he smiled and said, "There is just one stipulation—no Phil Harlow this evening," and when she opened her mouth to protest, he raised a hand. "I don't care—no Phil Harlow." He went across to the door and opened it, stood a moment in the opening as though to give her a chance to speak, and when she forced a weak smile and made a little gesture of resignation, he said, "That's much better. Just remember one thing : he's out of our lives from tonight onward."

After the door closed Ruth grimaced in private. Phil was *not* out of their lives. Very shortly now Jack Ewell was going to start hearing whispered rumours, whispered scraps of gossip spread by Phil, and then he would realise just how incorrect this assumption of his was.

But she had had enough of Phil Harlow for one day. She went to bathe and make a very leisurely preparation for her dinner-date. She even took a short nap after putting out the clothes she meant to wear, and when she awakened an hour and a half later, she felt much calmer, much more poised and confident. The reason, of course, was because she had Jack to rely upon.

128

She sat before the dressing-table mirror looking at herself and being very forthright in her private thoughts : what, exactly, had Jack Ewell begun to mean to her? She had told her father that he was handsome, and that was true, but a woman could think a man was handsome—a lot of men were handsome—without necessarily feeling anything else towards them.

She had also her private opinion of Jack : he was a compassionate, highly intelligent, perspicacious man with a depth of great calmness that never seemed to desert him. She was quite certain that she had never before known anyone like him. But that did not imply affection either. Women could know and respect a lot of men without falling in love with any of them.

There was something else; she couldn't define it but she knew it was there, deep down in him. He did not judge people, not even the ones like Phil Harlow he had no use for. It was a characteristic she thought was uniquely his. She also thought she understood how he had developed that trait. She wished other people, including herself, could develop it. She had rarely hated in her nearly twenty-two years, but there had been an occasion or two, and always afterwards she had felt slightly degraded.

Maybe the fact that Jack's parents had deserted him had developed his unwillingness to hate people and to judge them. Maybe, she told herself, being abandoned had been a good thing for him.

Maybe it had made him a better person than he would have been if he'd come to manhood under normal circumstances. Phil, she knew, from his stories of his family back east and his babyhood, had enjoyed a very secure and typical boyhood.

She stopped dawdling after a while, when she saw what time it was, and finished getting ready for their date. And she just barely made it; Jack arrived while she was still giving herself the finishing touches.

He handed her a small box and leaned to kiss her cheek as he did so, then, at her reaction of uneasiness, he laughed. "Don't worry, I'm not going to embarrass you."

That wasn't what had caused her to show slight dismay. She instinctively knew how he felt towards her, and the little box was exactly the proper size and shape for an engagement ring. She wasn't even altogether reassured when he laughed and acted so casual, but she unwrapped the little box, opened it—and smiled when she saw the little golden anchor upon its velvet cloth. Her initials had been elaborately engraved across the top of the anchor, and across the bottom of the thing was the name *Santa Maria*.

She removed the anchor and pinned it on her dress, up high, then she smiled up into his face, leaned and kissed him. "I love it, Jack, it's adorable."

He stood stock-still after the kiss. Finally, he said, "A reminder is all. You two are a lot alike."

She excused herself to get her coat, and when she came back he was standing there gazing moodily out over the rooftops towards the sea. He turned, looked her up and down, and gave his head a hard shake. "Beautiful. Trim as a corvette and beautiful. Have I told you that before?"

She took the tactful way out. "That I looked like a corvette? No, I don't think so." She went over to the door and waited.

He crossed over, opened the door, and looked wryly

130

at her. "You're quite a fencer, Miss Severns. Do you always side-step so deftly?"

"Only when I have to—*Captain* Ewell."

On the ride downstairs she made certain the little golden anchor was showing, and he stood beside her looking at the back of the closed door, his thoughts a long way off. When they started across the lobby, which was gaily lit and unusually full this evening, she saw men's eyes lift. It was a kind of tribute handsome women did not have to enjoy, but most certainly had to expect.

Outside, the evening was still faintly bright with day's ending, one of the blessings of spring and summer. In wintertime it was not unusual for San Francisco to be steeped in darkness by four o'clock in the afternoon.

His car was around in the parking area. He smiled and said he'd had it washed this afternoon, in anticipation of their date. As they were driving out into the twin-beamed brilliance of lighted traffic, he said something that broke his own earlier promise. He mentioned Phil Harlow.

"Got a telephone call this afternoon, an hour or so after I left you. From Phil Harlow. He had just been told that despite his best efforts . . . or should I have said despite his *worst* efforts . . . I had managed to complete the sale of my shipping company last night. He was pretty darned angry."

Ruth drew up tight inside herself. "What else did he say?"

Jack drove a while, merging with the traffic, before answering. "A lot of hot air; I think he'd been drinking. He had one advantage—he was out of reach."

She understood what he meant by that, and turned to look out a window where lighted shop windows were

131

adding to the brightness of the evening. "He's unbeliev-able," she murmured. "I can't have very good judge-ment to ever have thought he was anything else."

He reached to pat her hand. "You'll have company. You're not the only one who thought he might have been better than he was. Anyway, my point in even bringing him up was to let you know that he told me about your offer."

She felt no more dismay than she should have, because she was not surprised; Phil's objective was to use any-thing he could to harm her, and that, of course, included taunting Jack with her offer to leave the West Coast and never see Jack again.

She didn't speak; there wasn't anything to say, or, if there was, she couldn't think of it. She kept looking out the window as the car moved steadily through the soft gloaming towards the motorway.

As Phil turned on to the ramp leading up to the elevated throughway, he said, "Even if Phil had accepted your offer it never would have worked. Virginia's only an overnight flight from San Francisco." He slowed to make sure it was clear to merge, then shot ahead. "I don't give up that easily. You ought to know that much about me by now."

She finally found words. "The idea was to make him leave you alone long enough for you to complete your sale."

He said, "I understand. But the sale didn't mean all that much to me."

She looked at him. "All that money didn't mean that much?"

He grinned. "Hell, no. Money's never meant that much to me, and that is probably why I don't own ten ships and a Cadillac with a telephone in it, like Gino Bruno and some of the other hot-shots."

He got into the high-speed lane and the car lunged ahead. Dusk was settling in fast now, coming down from the northward hills with giant steps. It was still possible to discern city rooftops for another ten or fifteen minutes before their speed carried them well away from the city and into the less cluttered environs. Traffic was light, this time of evening, except for the gigantic trucks that moved over two-thirds of all freight in California. They were never much of a problem anyway because they stayed in the lanes that were meant for them, leaving plenty of room for faster-moving pleasure vehicles.

Finally, there was the ocean on the left, an oily expanse that seemed willing to simply lie out there reflecting every subtle change in light and darkness, hardly seeming to pitch and roll, as Ruth looked at it.

When she was quiet for a long time, Jack took the hint and switched the topic. "Tomorrow you've got to come across the Bay with me," he said, shooting her a look. "There's a part of San Francisco you haven't seen."

She was positive that there were probably a dozen parts she hadn't seen. She smiled as she agreed to go, and only when she saw that look of his closer did it suddenly dawn on her that she had just done a very foolish thing. She had agreed to go with him, and she should have known he meant crossing the bay on the *Santa Maria*.

There was no graceful way to retract, but she sat and desperately rummaged for such a way until, up ahead on their left, she saw a cluster of lights upon a high headland overlooking the sea, and when he slowed to

leave the motorway by the nearest ramp, it became
obvious to her that this was their destination.

She was correct. The place was one of those shoreside
complexes that had rooms, bar, restaurant, all under
one sprawling roof. There were even some shops,
although when he escorted her from the parking area
the shops were closed and lights in their windows were
as near as anyone could get to buying novelties or attire.

As they entered the elegant lounge he leaned down
and said, "A better-class meeting-place than that place
where we met and danced."

He took her to the bar after being told there would
be a slight delay before a table was ready, and when
their drinks arrived he explained a fact of commercial
life to her. "They make several hundred per cent more
profit on their bar-room than they make on their dining-
room. Invariably, they steer people in here for a few
drinks first."

The highball she had was called a *cucaracha*, which
was Mexican for Cockroach, and it tasted faintly of
chocolate. She hadn't asked for it, but it was pleasant.
She said she doubted that it would have much of a jolt,
and Jack looked from her to the glass, then rolled his
eyes. She took her cue from that, even though he said
nothing, and when the barman came to solicit re-orders,
she declined.

Moments later they were called to a table in the
dining-room, and she had to smile. Jack understood the
smile, and winked. "Telepathy," he murmured in her
ear. "As soon as they see people aren't going to re-order,
the barman sends out a telepathic signal and the *maitre
d'* slithers up. Sneaky lot out here, but much more
circumspect than the people at the other dive."

She was sure of that. The dining-room was full, and the people looked more like the kind of people she had seen in the hotel dining-room. The men were successful-looking, well-dressed, well-groomed, and older-looking. The same with the women. She saw several men nod to Jack, and saw him smile back. She also felt the steady glance of some of the women upon her when Jack held her chair.

The waiter who came to take their order winked at Jack. He winked back. Ruth thought it wasn't exactly the kind of greeting to be expected under the circumstances, but as soon as the waiter departed Jack leaned and explained.

"He used to sail with me on the *Santa Maria*. When he got married his wife didn't like being alone two and three months at a time." Jack shrugged and straightened back up off the table. "Women are like that, you know."

She laughed at him. "No, I don't know that women are like that, but if they are, what's wrong with it? A woman marries a man to have a family to look after. She doesn't need to get married at all if she's content to live alone."

He scowled at her. "Is that how you feel?"

She almost answered, then understood where this kind of a conversation could take her, and raised her eyes to look past him while she sought a different topic—and got the shock of her life: over by the door, in company with Gino Bruno and one other burly man, Phil Harlow was standing perfectly still. He had seen her, had recognised Jack even though Ewell's back was to him, and his lip lifted slowly in a coarse and malevolent sneer.

She dropped her eyes to the table-top, took in a shaky

breath and said, "Jack, maybe we ought to go. Maybe we could come here another time."

He looked at her, stared, then slowly hitched around in his chair and looked backwards. He and Phil looked directly into one another's eyes. Gino Bruno, obviously suddenly uncomfortable, nodded jerkily at Jack, and plucked at Phil's sleeve.

Jack heaved a sigh and faced forward again. "Lousy luck," he told her softly. "Spoil our whole evening."

SEVENTEEN

THE COLOUR OF VIOLENCE

WHEN Phil and his pair of companions entered the bar-room and were out of Ruth's sight she felt better, but only temporarily because she knew they would shortly re-emerge, when a table was ready for them. She looked at Jack, and suddenly recalled that remark he had made about it being advantageous for Phil that when he had telephoned Jack earlier, he had been out of reach. She could almost feel all the little aspects of certain violence falling into place, and even when Jack smiled at her she was not very relieved.

"He may mind his own business, Ruth, and you can bet money on it that if Gino has anything to do with it, there won't be anything. Gino is a manipulator, not a strong-arm lad."

She managed to smile back, but with a sinking sensation in her stomach because over his shoulder she saw Phil and the other two come back from the bar-room. They'd only been in there long enough for one drink, but Phil's colour was high; she was sure he'd had something to drink before arriving.

She deliberately looked in the opposite direction as a waiter led the three men across the room, and when she saw Jack's head turn, she still refused to meet those black, contemptuous eyes.

Their meal arrived and the waiter who brought it, the same husky, greying man who had winked at Jack earlier, looked amiably at Ruth and said, "No better prime rib served anywhere on the West Coast, ma'am," as he set her plate down with a flourish. She smiled at the man and gradually looked back towards Jack. Phil and his friends were somewhere over behind her, and it was a large room, so, presumably, they were a long way off. Not long enough, she told herself, but perhaps it would seem that they were.

Jack gravely looked across at her. "We make the best of it, eh? The food is generally excellent up here. Afterwards, we'll cruise up the coast and watch the moon come up over the peaks. It's something worth seeing when the moon is nearly full."

She concentrated on his words to the exclusion of whatever Phil might be saying scornfully behind her somewhere. She tried to remember whether the moon was nearly full or not, and failed dismally.

The greying waiter was right, her meal was superb. She was cheered by this. Jack nodded when she commented. "This place has been catalogued as one of the best eating places in the entire country. It should be, they charge like the devil, but the reason is that they never use anything but the very best. The meat is said to be choice number one supreme." He grinned. "I would think any *one* of those designations would get the idea across."

He was purposefully, and gradually, working all her tenseness out. It was uncanny how he could do that. This afternoon at her apartment he had also done it, and by the time he had left, she hadn't felt very cheerful, but at least she had felt much better. Now, it worked the same way. Of course the fact that she could not see Phil helped, and as the time passed she was able to think of other things. She ultimately remembered who was behind her only because, inherently, she realised they would be discussing her—and Jack too—over at that far table.

She made up her mind not to let this awkwardness spoil either their meal or their evening together, and rather aggressively concentrated on eating, and afterwards praising the food.

People came and went. The establishment was every bit as popular as Jack had implied that it was. Once, for a short while, there was music in the bar-room where evidently someone had put money into the canned-music machine.

Another time, when a large, gay party of men and women came in, a kind of spontaneous cheerfulness permeated both dining-room and bar-room. Finally, near the end of the meal, Jack winked and said, "A lot of anxiety for nothing," meaning that now, they were finished eating and ready to leave and nothing untoward had happened. She agreed with him, rose and picked up her coat and purse. She was tempted to look back but she didn't. Jack waited until she came around to his side of the table, and to the hovering waiter he passed two crisp bills, and another wink; then he took her elbow and started quietly out.

She actually relaxed by the time they got back out into the night. Evidently Phil had too much sense to make a scene, or otherwise, perhaps his two companions had prevented him from making the effort.

Jack turned and led her down the covered ramada out front of the restaurant, towards the distant exposure that showed the sea and the distant white strand of empy beach where noisy breakers came rolling inland to shatter against the cliff below. By day, it was a spectacular sight, but by night it had a strange, haunting kind of soft and enduring beauty that was totally different. While he held her arm, looking outwards, he said, "Life and death—daylight and dark." Then he turned and smiled. "Is that morbid?"

She might have thought so another time, but tonight with the dark-running ocean far below and far out, like some endless-flowing tangible Eternity, she thought his words appropriate. "Poetic," she said, and turned as a slam of feet approached from farther back along the wooden-floored walkway.

She knew even before she could distinguish the hulking silhouette who was coming. Evidently Jack's intuition was just as attuned because as he started to turn he moved her slightly to one side, slightly to the rear.

"Not much privacy out here," said a thick, slurry voice she recognised as belonging to Phil.

Farther back a gross, very thick and squatty man made a whining complaint. "Phil, for Chriz' sake come on—forget that, will you?"

Harlow did not look back nor act as though he had heard the fat man. He was concentrating his entire attention upon Jack Ewell, fifteen feet ahead, with his lanky build shielding Ruth Severns. Phil gave his head a hard shake and spat out more words tinged with biting scorn.

"You damned fool, Ewell, she's going to make the same kind of an ass out of you she did with me—

her, and her sweet Virginia accent and honeysuckle beauty."

The fat man and another silhouette loomed up behind Phil. The taller, thicker man said nothing, but the gross man whined again. "Damn it, leave it be, Phil, we got business. Who'n hell cares about that other stuff anyway? Come along, will you?"

Jack spoke, finally. "That's good advice you're getting, Phil, you'd better take it."

Phil said, "Ewell, you bastard," and inched ahead a yard.

Ruth thought her heart had stopped. Jack remained as still as stone, then he moved so suddenly, in such a blur of shadows and darkness she did not realise what he was doing until she saw Phil raise a clenched fist, saw Jack block that strike and twist sideways so he slammed a short blasting right hand into Phil's middle, and when Phil convulsed, saw Jack shove him off and fire a second, higher blow that nearly broke Phil's neck as his head snapped on his shoulders. Then Phil buckled at the knees and the other man, silent up until now, ripped out a curse and jumped ahead. He had hardly got moving when he stumbled and fell. From behind him, where Ruth hadn't seen the other shadow, she now caught sight of a greying, dark head, and a waiter's jacket. The waiter who had once sailed with Jack had moved in, eased a foot forward as the other man jumped for Jack, and tripped the stranger in a simple schoolboy's take-down. The fallen man twisted as he hit the floor and the waiter leaned down, grinning like a death's head.

"Stay down there, friend, if you're wise, because if you get up I'm going to break half your ribs."

The downed man twisted, but Gino Bruno shook his head at him. "Stay," spat Bruno. "You got to act like a horse's rear too; it was Phil's been drinking, not you. Now I had enough."

Jack had his right fist at his side. From behind, Ruth saw him flexing the knuckles. She also saw the colour of violence, finally, when the fat man named Gino toed Phil over on to his back. It was claret-colour. It was over Phil's face and down upon the white of his rumpled shirt-front.

Jack and the gross man looked long at one another. The fat man fished out a cigar and bit down hard upon it without making any attempt to strike a light. He swore softly, and helplessly, as he surveyed the wreckage. "It wasn't my doing," he told Jack. "I told 'em to lay off it. They both been drinking, but Phil's worst. Did you have to hit him that hard? He's all bloody."

Jack's hunched shoulders loosened as he answered. "No, I didn't have to hit him that hard, Gino. I wanted to. He's had this coming for a long time. And maybe worse. So have you, for sitting in with him while he tried hard to bust me. But tonight you're lucky. Tonight I only half-kill men whose names start with H. Another night it'll be your turn; the night I half-kill the ones whose names begin with G."

Jack looked on as the greying waiter growled at the man he had tripped. "Get up on your feet! Mister, you got a choice: you want some more action, come on out back with me. Otherwise, fade, and do it fast!"

The burly man was cooled-out and sensible. He shot Gino a look and said, "I'll wait in the car." He edged past the waiter and stalked off without another word. The waiter's teeth shone. He winked, Jack winked back, then the waiter headed back towards one of the many doors leading into the building where laughter and sounds of eating came mutedly out into the dark of the ramada.

Ruth moved from behind Jack and looked downward. He's hurt," she murmured, and Jack looked down too, ignoring the fat man for the time being.

"He'll be all right. It's just a few loose teeth and a smashed lip."

The fat man agreed. "He'll be fine by tomorrow, Miss. He's asked for it." The fat man was disgusted. "He's a fool in a lot of ways."

Ruth looked at the obese, porcine face and detested Gino Bruno with a healthy hatred. "And you, of course, didn't have anything to do with what he's been trying to do to Captain Ewell!"

Bruno stared stoically and said nothing. He shifted the unlit cigar from one side of his mouth to the other, looked venomous, but was far too prudent a man to flash back at Ruth, with Jack standing there looking at him, waiting for an excuse.

She knelt beside Phil, leaned and removed the hand-handkerchief from his jacket and placed it gently against his battered lips. Gino Bruno flung away the cigar and leaned. "Give me a hand," he said to Jack, and grabbed for Phil. Between them they got him upright, and Jack helped Gino get an arm around Phil's shoulders, then Gino said, "Ruin my shirt and coat, this louse, and by gawd that's going to cost him another couple hundred." Gino started away with his dead-weight. For all his obesity and shapelessness, obviously Gino Bruno was a physically powerful man. He carried Phil, who was a head taller and almost as thick, as though Phil hadn't been half his weight or size.

Jack leaned on a railing watching until the sulky man in the expensive sedan got out to help put the unconscious man in the back, then Jack raised his right fist in the soft moonlight and gazed as it as he worked the fingers. "Got a jaw like cast iron," he muttered.

The knuckles were bruised and bleeding. Ruth saw that and dug for a handkerchief in her purse which she handed him. He looked. The handkerchief was no more than four inches square and had a lace border. He laughed and handed it back, then lifted his left hand to her shoulder and a little roughly pulled her to him.

"I'm sorry. That's the last thing I want you to have to see."

She could have told him that it was also the last thing she had *wanted* to see, but she didn't. She said, "Can you drive, or shall I drive from here on?"

He still smiled. "You drive. But I've still got that sight to show you on up the coast a few miles."

When they were moving again, she felt better. For a few moments back there, while she'd been kneeling beside Phil, she'd felt faint. But now, as she slid under the steering-wheel of his car and waited until he had got in on the other side, she felt much better, almost completely normal. She punched the starter, wheeled clear of the parking area and headed the car towards the motorway. At her side, Jack was working his bruised hand. "Don't want it to get too stiff," he explained.

She swung hard left on to the motorway, corrected the car, then, as they headed northward again without any traffic around, she said, "You have a powerful right, Jack," and they both laughed.

EIGHTEEN

A SECRET PLACE

THERE was a three-quarter moon, but it rode a troubled sky tonight, bunched-up clouds moving southward, out to sea, obliterated it from time to time, plunging the world into a kind of opaque gloom, a sort of pale kind of moist brightness. It was an eerie night, and probably because it was a week-night there was little traffic and even fewer parked cars along the parking areas that were interspersed along the beach access.

Normally, surfers, young people of all kinds, built bonfires on the beaches at night and partied. Tonight as they drove northward, Ruth saw only an occasional parked car and no beach-fires. When she commented, Jack said, "Come back Saturday night."

There was no wind, the night was hushed and brooding, its seaside opaqueness broken only when the moon came from behind clouds and brightened the earth, turning all that flat expanse of steely water to tarnished silver. It was a night to match Ruth's feelings, partly troubled, partly bright and promising. She looked at Jack, saw his smile, and smiled back. They said nothing.

The land had a gentle roll to it, north of San Francisco, there were broken little jutting places where rocky bases and sodded tops thrust outward into the sea.

Sometimes those places had storm-twisted trees growing out upon them, and sometimes there was only hardy grass and underbrush to hold the soil. Northward, the land pitched more, and rose to greater heights, with a promise that farther ahead there would be less gentleness to the land.

It was different along the seashore than it was inland, on the drive up to his house on top of the headland. Along the beach highway one was never unaware of the power of the sea, on the left, because it was audibly close. Inland, upon his secluded headland, the sea was below and distant, something to admire without a sense of close involvement.

For Ruth, who instinctively felt that the sea was never going to be completely out of her life, there was a stirring sensation of kinship with it as she drove beside it up the seashore highway. The tides that rushed, in frothy force, against unyielding stone bulwarks in the moonlight, had a beauty that touched her spirit and her soul.

When they finally came to a turn-off and Jack told her to take it, down off the raised freeway, she could see the stair-stepped moonlight out across a mile of ocean-top and admire it for its loneliness and for its isolation. The sea, at night beneath a ragged moon, was a distinct and separate world, an alien environment that enticed with a strange allure.

The road she drove over continued on down towards a tilted projection that jutted into the surf. Out there, with a shaft of free moonlight silhouetting them, stood several gnarled trees, not very tall, but thick and sturdy with the kind of obvious strength any upright growth would have to possess to live here where, in wintertime, salt spray whipped to sixty and seventy miles an hour screamed inland out of the heart of ocean storms.

They stopped where two large white boulders barred further progress. He climbed out without a word and she did the same. In front of the car he held out his left hand and led her down to the slight lift, the slightly tilted incline where those trees were.

It was silent down there although she could feel how winter's fury lashed this spot just from looking at the stunted trees. Even in its serenity on this night, the attitude of the trees seemed frozen in an expression of tortured resistance to wind, so the place was storm-haunted.

Jack took her to the largest old tree which was nearest the twenty-foot cliff-drop to a sliver of white beach. At first she saw nothing, but he lifted her hand and she felt the cold, rough surface and stepped into tree-shadow to see.

A heavy steel or iron ring was embedded in the ironwood trunk of the mighty tree, facing the sea, and below it, almost engulfed by circular tree-growth, was a visible segment of a matching chain, thick and massive, but old now beyond reckoning, covered with scales of rust and peeling iron.

She stepped back and looked towards the ocean almost as though expecting to see the vessel that had been secured to this place.

Jack said, almost apologetically, "It's nothing to bring a girl all the way out here for, is it? It was discovered about fifty years ago. A friend of mine showed it to me one time when we were driving north to see about a refrigerated fish contract."

She asked the obvious question. "Who put it there?"

"No one knows. Some scientists from the University at Berkeley examined the chain and said it was probably made in England. Drake sailed these waters, you know, and so did a number of other Englishmen, including a man named Vancouver, but the mystery is—why would anyone go to all the trouble of emplacing that ring and running the risk of running aground in the shallows at this spot? Even in those days, a couple hundred and more years ago, ships had good anchors, and San Francisco had a very good bay. Why did—whoever he was—tie up at this place, like he was furtively keeping out of sight, and why didn't he anchor, instead of trusting to the tree?" Jack turned, surveyed the surf, and gestured. "There was no second tree to keep him from drifting into the shallows and going aground."

Ruth said, on the spur of the moment, "He used his anchor to keep from drifting. Used the tree to keep his ship from drifting southward, and his anchor to hold it against the tide, northward."

Jack looked at her. "Very good," he said, and laughed. "That's probably what he did. Now tell me *why* he used this place?"

She knew nothing of the history of the West Coast but knew something of the history of her own coast, so she transposed a little of the latter knowledge to fit the exigencies of the former. With a look up and down the coast, which was marked with additional little jutting headlands which would limit visibility from any great distance, she said, "He was a pirate. His ship sprung a leak. He didn't dare go down to San Francisco bay but he had to make immediate repairs, so he tied up right here."

Jack's steady regard showed admiration, even in the

148

indifferent moonlight. "You know something odd—you are more than likely correct. That's the dominant theory. Even my local history book confirms that pirates roamed off this coast." He continued to study her. "By any chance have you been boning up on California history?"

She couldn't keep from showing her sense of triumph as she answered him. "I've never had any occasion to read a book on California history. But every coastline from New England to British Columbia has had pirates, hasn't it? California shouldn't be any exception." She laughed at his sober expression of respect and stepped back closer to finger the massive ring. It was cold to the touch, and flaking rust came off at her touch. She turned, still clinging to the ring, and looked out at the secretive sea where the long-gone ship had probably ridden out its tethering.

Jack said, "There is another theory. They tied up here because it was fairly secluded, and they embedded the ring to mark the place as well as to tie up when they returned. Only they never came back, and somewhere between this tree and the hills behind us is buried a chest of gold doubloons." He laughed, made an expansive gesture, and said, "Help yourself. You see those little mounds back nearer to where we left the car? That's where subscribers to the buried-treasure theory have come out with shovels and dug."

She still clung to the old ring as she said, "Has anyone ever found anything?"

He shrugged. "If they have they kept quiet about it. I've never heard of anything being dug up." He moved closed to the tree, and her. "It's a riddle that has always fascinated me, but it probably seems like an odd place to bring a girl on a date."

She kept watching the dappled sea without raising her eyes to his face. "It's a delightful place, Jack. Barring the veranda back there where we encountered Phil, I've never gone anywhere with you that hasn't been delightful. You've got a knack. . . ." She turned slowly, away from the sea. The quiet turmoil in her heart made it very clear that she could no longer avoid looking squarely at something that had been maturing slowly ever since that first night when they had danced together. She was in love with him.

When he stood like stone looking down, she smiled sweetly upwards. She understood his gravity; *he* knew what he wanted exactly as *she* also knew, but he had inhibitions, and he had strong reasons for his inhibitions. She was a woman; how did a man ever know that a woman, after the first passion, would not live with hidden regrets until they overwhelmed her—then run away and drop from sight?

She could have forced him; she could feel the masculine needs roil the atmosphere where they stood. He was a virile, strong man with all the hungers all such men always had; but she didn't want him that way, with a ring through his nose, tributary to something she controlled.

She let go of the iron ring and stepped away from the tree where moonlight brightened some gravelly soil, and down below the surging sea ran with force against slippery black rock, and moonlight paled the bluish froth.

He moved out there with her and lay a hand lightly upon her shoulder, turning her almost without effort. "You know what it is," he told her. "Maybe you haven't felt it as long as I have, but it goes back to the night we danced. To the first time I ever saw you. It was as though an invisible thread ran from you to me. I've been in love with you, Ruth, since then." He dropped his arm. "It tied me in knots that someone like you would believe in someone like Phil Harlow." He rubbed his swollen right hand gently with his left palm. "I was happiest tonight when he forced the issue and made you see him truly."

She had seen him truly before tonight, but she didn't mention that. She stepped up, raised her hands to lean, and tipped her head. When he kissed her, his hands moved to her waist and swayed her inward. It started out as a gentle embrace but within seconds she felt the strength of his hands and the steel of his upper arms, and she responded with a sudden fire of her own, but only momentarily, and immediately afterwards she pushed until his grip loosened.

She lay limply against him, her back to the speckled sea, eyes tightly closed and with the uneven strong cadence of his heart in her ears.

"Phil never really existed," she murmured. "Not the Phil Harlow I believed in."

He understood. "Then you'll have no regrets."

That was true. She would have no regrets about Phil, but she had almost done something to Jack Ewell she would have regretted as long as she lived.

She clung to him, and gradually opened her eyes to twist barely enough to see the running of the tide. "You know what he's going to say about me, Jack. It won't reflect very well upon you."

"He won't say anything, sweetheart. Not after tonight. Harlow may not be rational where you are concerned, but he's rational enough where business is concerned.

One rumour by him and he'll think the world fell on him. I'll get that idea across. Gino can help." His grip tightened protectively. "Anyway, the people who might believe Harlow wouldn't know you on sight, so forget it."

She was comforted but not entirely reassured, although she kept this to herself as she pushed back and looked upwards. "We'd better get back," she said, and waited to be kissed again.

The second time it was easier for them both. Whatever he felt was under control, and all that she felt was a strong relaxation of inhibitions and resistance, but she only showed it by melting in a yielding way against him.

They stood a moment, afterwards, beside the ancient tree, then turned and went slowly back to the car. Her thoughts were tempered with a different kind of sweetness than she had ever felt before. Although years back when she'd first imagined herself in love with Phil Harlow, there had been something similar; not as deep nor as wholly total as this sensation was, but similar.

At the car they stood a moment hand-in-hand, then she voluntarily turned towards him and slid both arms around his waist, while above them the lopsided old coasting moon slid behind one of those fat clouds that was drifting from back beyond the distant sweep of far-away mountains out across their little thrusting headland towards the yonder sea, allowing that obscure milky paleness to dull out everything down below.

NINETEEN

A SURPRISE FOR RUTH

MORNING was the advent of another environment, the unsteady moon was gone and with it the billowy clouds of that other ethos. Ruth awakened slowly, as though coming down from a vast height where serenity as deeply enduring as only peace could possibly be, had cushioned her in layers of lassitude.

She knew the sun was shining because beyond her bedroom door there was a golden brightness coming past the studio-windows into the sitting-room. Its reflections ran along the little connecting hallway and died just over the threshold. She turned up on to her back and lay a delicious long moment looking at the stippled ceiling.

The echo of all the soft things they had told each other last night lingered in her drowsy consciousness. He had asked her to marry him and she had kissed him instead of answering, and later, when they had turned the car back towards the city, he told her of the honeymoon he'd had in mind—a flight to Hawaii, a month of beach-loafing and laughing, then a slow cruise homeward on one of the majestic sea liners. He had laughed about that, looking self-conscious. "Dreams," he'd said. "Didn't you know men have those dreams too?"

She remembered countering with: "How did you know women had them?"

His answer had been a joke. "You know I read all kinds of books and magazines."

She hadn't accepted him, but they had both understood that this was only a formality, because physically and emotionally, in every way that really mattered, she had. The words would come, some day. A woman, somehow, knew that once the words came, part of the bright magic got lost. Women wanted that bright magic to last as long as it possibly could.

She rolled over, looked at the sunshine, sat up and pushed back her hair. Then she jumped out of bed and went to shower. She very seldom felt hungry in the morning, but now she did, and the reason she'd finally jumped out of bed was because *he* would be down there waiting, looking at his wrist and speculating about whether to telephone her or not.

It was late, there would be no way to alibi that fact, although if anyone would understand why she was late it would have to be him. Finally, as she was leaving the shower, the telephone did ring, but when she went to answer it, the caller was Gino Bruno, not Jack Ewell. Bruno had tried to locate Jack in his suite, and, failing, had taken the liberty of seeing if, by any chance, Jack might be with her.

She didn't like that although Bruno kept his voice absolutely toneless, without even a hint of implication, as he explained his call. "I got to pass a message along to Ewell this morning. It's about that call he give me last night after midnight. Maybe you could see him soon and tell him."

She agreed, but cautiously. "I could, but if you really want him—"

"Naw, Miss, you can do it easier, I suppose. Just tell

154

him Gino Bruno called and said he'd take care of it personal. You got that? Bruno will take care of it personal."

Ruth did not repeat it but she was sure she'd remember it verbatim, and as she put the telephone down, she smiled just a little : grammar somehow failed to convey the real meaning of threats as well as did poor grammar, and she had no doubt at all that Gino Bruno's comment had something to do with a threat.

She finished dressing and went downstairs half-expecting to find no familiar face in the dining-room. She got the surprise of her life. Jack and a second man were eating at a table over near some french windows. They were conversing easily as they breakfasted and although that other man's back was to her when she stepped into the dining-room archway, she knew him on sight.

Her father.

Jack saw her. He'd been watching for her. He smiled and started to rise. So did the older man, but as he turned she saw the impish little smile. She knew that smile from every Easter-egg hunt, every birthday and Christmas morning since she could remember. Whenever her father had a surprise, he used this particular impish smile. She went over and kissed his cheek as he took one of her hands and squeezed it, then she turned and Jack was silently laughing at her expression of surprise. In defence, he said, "Don't blame me, it was his secret. I didn't even know who he was when he came to the table a little while ago."

They all sat down and a smiling waitress hovered for Ruth's order. Afterwards, she said, "Dad, why didn't you let me know you were coming?"

"More fun this way," he replied. "Anyway, it was

155

one of those sudden notions of mine. I'd never seen the West Coast and this was a good time of year to do it." He studied her from twinkling eyes. "Do you always get up so late?"

She blushed, and the waitress arriving with her coffee and toast, ahead of her regular meal, saved her from having to answer. Afterwards, Jack took over, explaining about the ring in the old tree up the coast, and also mentioning the buried-treasure theory. Her father was interested; at least he listened politely, but she also thought she recognised that steady, shrewd look on his face : he was measuring Jack Ewell by a man's standards. It didn't worry her very much; she was sure she knew Jack and that whatever her father decided would have to be about the same as what she already knew.

Of course, if she'd thought on it, there was some reason for her judgement to be open to question : she had also thought Phil Harlow had been wonderful, and she had thought she had known him, too.

When her main course arrived her father and Jack had an excuse to resume eating, but her father, as she remembered very well, seldom ate much, although he could be expected to drink two cups of creamed coffee every morning. So he nodded to the waitress when she hovered with the coffee-pot, and afterwards he seemed to be considering something, as though wishing to speak. That reminded her of Bruno's call. She told Jack what the gross man had said.

Jack nodded without commenting, but when she kept looking at him, he finally made a little gesture as though none of this were important, and said, "I had a little talk with him last night after we got back to the hotel. Nothing much. Just suggested that if he wanted to stay healthy, and if he wanted his friend to stay healthy, he had better make certain his friend did not sling any dirt." Jack looked apologetically at Ruth's father. "Nothing very serious," he murmured, by way of explanation, and went back to eating. Ruth saw her father's sceptical gaze rest upon Jack's purplish and swollen right hand. Her father was no novice at life, he would guess how Jack had got that hand.

She said, "It was Phil," to her father, and he did not act at all surprised.

"Of course. Now that we've got him up here, out in the open, that's why I flew out yesterday. In fact, I tried to locate him last night when neither of you were in."

Jack raised his head. "No need, Mister Severns. Phil's out of it."

Her father seemed perfectly willing to believe that. "All right. Just as long as you are sure of that, Captain. I've an aversion to men maligning women, particularly when the woman happens to be my daughter."

Jack smiled. "Strange that we should feel the same way, and we never met before this morning."

Her father laughed. "Stranger, Captain, that it should be so easy to sit here this morning and have breakfast as though we were old friends."

Jack's smile brightened. "How would you care to go across the bay on my ship this morning, Mister Severns?"

Ruth knew that her father was no sailor. She could not recall off-hand, from among all the tales he'd told her of his boyhood, whether he'd ever been on a sea-going ship, but she was sure that if he had, it couldn't have been more than once, or perhaps twice, so he wouldn't be much of a seaman.

He surprised her with an easy acceptance. "I'd enjoy

that very much, Captain. I think the view of San Francisco from the bay ought to be about the best way to see the city."

Jack's eyes danced with amusement, but he did not look at Ruth when he answered her father. "You are absolutely correct, that *is* the best way to see the city. The trouble is that not everyone can be convinced."

Her father was a shrewd man. He understood Jack's implication without any noticeable delay, and looked at Ruth. She smiled weakly. "Absolutely, Dad, that's the only way to see San Francisco."

The men laughed.

She was not as fearful of crossing the bay on the *Santa Maria* as she had sounded. Lately, her association with the sea had blunted her dread and fear of it. Of course she had not been away from a dock while aboard yet, but she had at least overcome the initial fear that had arisen from total ignorance.

Jack looked at his wrist, then dropped his napkin on top of the table to indicate that he had finished breakfast. That was her cue, and she knew it was. She smiled, patted her father's arm, and said she'd be back as soon as she'd got her coat and purse. On the way out of the dining-room she didn't think about the forthcoming trip as much as she thought of her relationship with Jack Ewell.

It wasn't that she couldn't tell her father. After all, she was very close to being twenty-two years of age. In a girl that was full womanhood; she would only be responsible to herself.

What caused the dilemma was that she had only known about her feeling for Jack the night before. At least she had only openly manifested it the night before, and because she was a woman, and, woman-like, was still not entirely willing to admit how deeply she felt, even to herself, she could not bring herself to want to confess anything to her father.

Standing briefly before the dressing-table mirror upstairs, holding her purse and coat, she looked at herself, wondering about her father's reaction. She wouldn't blame him if he greeted her confession with scepticism. This time he probably would, if that was how he felt, because he had masked his feelings before in order to save her feelings, even though he had not liked Phil. This time, when she knew how men could be, finally, her father probably wouldn't try to spare her. Once was enough.

She left the apartment and rode back down, thinking that she would not be able to put them both off for long, and also wondering why she would want to put them off. She loved Jack Ewell. It was that basic and that simple. She hadn't agreed to marry him, but if he gave her a ring she would accept it and melt in his arms.

When she reached the lobby she got another surprise. Over by the front doors her father and Jack were talking together, and although her father was smoking one of his long cigars, the kind she had known him to smoke ever since she'd been a child, Jack was also smoking one, and she had never before seen him smoke. In fact, she had assumed that he did not use tobacco.

She walked towards them wondering if Jack was doing that just to humour her father, and while she did not smoke and therefore knew little about the habit, as she watched she could see that Jack was enjoying that cheroot with the élan of a man who was most certainly not smoking his first one.

She said nothing as the men turned, then held the door for her to precede them out into the mid-morning warmth. As they flanked her heading for the parking area, Jack caught her eye and slowly winked. She was tempted to say something. Instead she slowly winked back.

There was a slight, gusty wind coming inland from the sea. It swept gulls inland with it. As they were driving out of the parking area Ruth suddenly thought of that wind, of its effect upon a seagoing vessel out in the bay. Her heart sank steadily, until her father smiled and patted her knee as he said, "Beautiful day. I had some idea they only had smog out here."

Jack answered. "That's down south of here, down in Los Angeles. Up here we have much cleaner air."

She knew he was being facetious, and yet he was also telling at least *some* truth. San Francisco had its eye-stinging, onion-scented smog too, but thanks to sea breezes like the one blowing this morning, the air was as likely to be salt-scented and clean as it was to be smoggy.

TWENTY

THE CAPTAIN'S LADY

JACK'S arrival alongside his ship was a signal to the men aboard. A blast from a steam whistle made Ruth jump. Obviously, he had called ahead because no sooner had he escorted his passengers up the gangplank than Ruth detected an increase to the pulse of motors. On deck, she felt that throbbing even more noticeably, and although she did not see the casting-off, very gradually the ship began to drift astern. It was such a gentle, slow movement she hardly noticed. Her father smiled and led her to a railing. Jack looked a little anxiously at her, then excused himself. It was like being abandoned on the brink. She saw him hasten towards a ladder, a metal stairway, and go flinging up to it towards the bridge. Her father kept hold of her arm and with her nearest hand she clutched the cold steel railing.

The *Santa Maria* made a flushing sound, a noise of furious beating and that rearward motion ceased. Very gradually the ship's raised bow yawed clear of the dock, swinging ever so slowly as the engines held her steady. It was an experienced manoeuvre, Ruth saw that without loosening her grip on the railing. Whoever the helmsman was, and whoever was manning those below-decks engines, were perfectly co-ordinated in this casting-off process.

The wind came and went. As the ship gave way and turned towards the middle of the estuary heading southward on a complete turn, the wind whipped across Ruth's face from changing directions and at her side, where her father was standing, obviously enjoying himself, she saw how his hair was tangled by that breeze.

They cleared the wharf, found the channel, and beat their way down the same waterway she had seen other ships beat their way upwards towards moorings. There was that steady pulsing underfoot, and the ship responded slightly to the tide and the drift of current, but it was responding like a large trained animal who knew exactly what was expected of it.

Ruth's father patted her hand, clenched round the railing, and asked if she'd like to go aft with him and watch the wake. Only dimly conscious of what a 'wake' might be, she declined, and when he walked away, jaunty in his rolling gait, she was glad to be left alone with her tight-wound fear. She *knew* there was no danger. She also knew that as sympathetic as her father and Jack would be, they could not also avoid feeling just a little hint of disappointment, if they knew how terrified she was.

The thing to do, of course, was to face down the fear, to overcome it without any help. She forced herself to turn and look down. It seemed an incredible distance down to where an oily sea hissed alongside the steel hull. She waited until that view had lost most of its terror, then turned deliberately and looked aft where a wide, curling white wake widened as it fell rearward from the ship, its waves running in diminishing size towards the docks on one side and towards the distant opposite coast on the other side.

Finally, she took the major step by releasing her grip on the railing and turning to walk for'ard down the narrow port-side decking, in the direction of the scooped bow. A seaman with curly dark hair and a swarthy look loomed up, smiled as he passed, and continued towards the stern. She remembered two things about him : one, he had a tiny gold ear-ring through one pierced ear, and two, he was barefoot. For some reason he reminded her of where she and Jack had been the night before—up where a pirate ship had probably tied up.

She was passing the ladder—the stairway—where Jack had disappeared, when someone came clanging down the steel steps making her stop and wait. It was Jack. When he turned and saw her heading for'ard, he smiled broadly and offered her a very welcome broad hand—the left one.

It was unbelievably easier to walk on out to the bow with someone holding her hand than it had been to go half that distance alone. In fact, by the time they got up where the breeze was stiffest, she was wondering if it wouldn't actually be possible to enjoy this weird sensation of moving over water while personally standing still.

They came to the breakwater, swung slightly to port to keep the centre of their channel as they headed out into the raw sea, and Ruth thought she felt the ship shudder as though from an unseen blow. Without realising it, her fingers dug into Jack's hand. He looked at her, looked at the sea, then watched some landmark without moving until he was satisfied with their new course, and finally he took her over where a large wooden box had been placed next to an upright tube that seemed to come from the lowest depths of the ship, and eased her down upon the box.

It was a great relief. She did not want to act like this, especially with him, with someone to whom the rolling of a ship was something pleasant, and to whom the stiff little breeze meant freedom and freshness. She smiled at him and concentrated on watching him to the exclusion of the vast desert of rippling grey-blue that was all around him, below and far out.

She couldn't have deluded him; not only had he demonstrated an ability to read moods from her expressions, he had also the seaman's inherent awareness of fear in non-seamen.

Her father came strolling ahead. He had his sea-legs. With a compliment to Jack on the condition of the ship, he strolled on past. Jack watched, then looked down at her. "It takes time," he said. "I've heard of people being born with the knack of it, but I can tell you I've been sea-sick a hundred times."

She was surprised, and for a moment or two she thought he was simply saying that to make her feel less ashamed. He wasn't.

"A couple of years ago we were wallowing in a pitching sea off Manila," he said, grinning in recollection. "I had no warning, and as a matter of fact I've been on worse seas almost every summer of my life. The urge came over me and I barely made it out of the wheelhouse." He raised his head as an incoming ship blasted on her horn. Instantly, someone on the bridge of the *Santa Maria* let loose with an answering blast. He pointed to the incoming ship. "Recognise the name?"

She twisted half-around, but finally had to stand up to see. The incoming ship looked enough like the *Santa Maria* to be her twin. She saw the name: *Pinta.*

She had thought the *Pinta* was to be dry-docked over

in Honolulu for a week. He agreed that she was, but he also informed her that for a bonus, paid by him, over and above what his insurance carrier had to pay, the repairmen had agreed to work round the clock. The *Pinta* had been made seaworthy in less than two days.

His explanation was simple. "To keep the shipper happy," he said, shrugging off the additional cost. "In the long run it'll make him less anxious to cancel out. The new owners will like that."

The new owners, she remembered, had already put up the purchase price for his company. This fresh expense, then, was out of his pocket. She understood him doing that, but she did not say anything. They stood side-by-side near the railing watching the *Pinta* coast past at less than half-speed. On her bridge a man who looked doll-size held up a bright blue reflector. Jack smiled but that was all. When Ruth looked enquiringly upwards he said, "It's a sort of private code. Blue reflectors mean right-on, or all's well."

By the time his other ship was past Ruth had left the packing crate, had gone over to the railing with Jack, and had quite forgot to cling to the railing. Even when her father came over and said, "Your colouring is a lot better, Ruthie," she didn't reach for support.

Her father left them. Evidently he was having quite an adventure. Jack smilingly told her that he had already been down to the engine-room and into the forward hold. "Might make a first officer out of him, or perhaps sell him a ship."

She smiled. "Only if the ship could navigate over the hunt country back home. His first love is the land." She thought of something. "Jack, will you come home with me?"

He blinked. "Are you going back?"

She hadn't meant it as he took it, as though she were going back to Virginia right away, perhaps going back with her father. She lay a hand upon his arm.

"Someday. Not soon, but someday."

His anxiety vanished. "Sure. If you'd like, right after I'm out of the shipping business and we are married." He gave her a crooked little grin. "We *will* be married, won't we?"

"What's the alternative?" she asked, teasing him.

His answer came right back. "A life of sin."

She turned quickly to hide the blush, and far up the estuary the *Pinta* let loose another blast on her horn, for no special reason that Ruth could see. Jack leaned, looked, then explained. "To let the dockmaster know," he said, and, taking her hand, went towards the for'ard deck where the spray and breeze stung, but in a pleasant way.

"You haven't said you'd marry me," he reminded her. "Is it Phil by any chance?"

She snapped her head around at him. "Phil! Of course not. How could you even think such a thing?"

He turned placating at once. "I don't understand women very well, sweetheart. But there has to be a reason, doesn't there?"

There was a reason, but it wouldn't sound very sensible if she told him, so she put up a hand to hold back her hair, looked around to be sure they were alone, then raised up quickly and kissed him squarely on the lips. "I'll marry you," she said, and the wind whipped her words away the moment she'd uttered them, but he had heard, so he opened his arms and held her.

She could feel the toss of the ship and if she closed

166

her eyes it seemed more acute, so she kept them open.
He released her, finally, when a gangling blond man
came for'ard, his eyes fixed impassively on Jack when
he said, "A call came for you a few minutes ago,
Captain. The skipper of the *Pinta* is asking . . . if he
saw a woman aboard when we passed a while ago."

Jack laughed but the blond man kept his face wooden.
"Call him back and tell him I said that no wonder he
got rammed over at Honolulu, he doesn't keep his eye
on course."

The blond man departed without ever lowering his
head. After he was gone Ruth asked about him, and
Jack shrugged. "He's been married four times. Every
time they've run amok after he's been at sea for a month
or two. I think after the last time he turned into a
misogynist. As a matter of fact if a man's going to follow
the sea, maybe that's the best attitude to take." He
winked. "*If* a man can take it."

Her father materialised from the starboard side of the
ship to point to the Golden Gate Bridge which lay dead
ahead.

For Ruth, it was the most bizarre view she had ever
had of the famous span. She was *under* it.

The water was frothy with tiny white-caps where the
wind was brisking up in the bay. It reminded her of
something Jack had once said about the days of sailing
ships. She wondered, now, how they ever managed to
stop those old-time vessels when they had all canvas
hoisted, before they reached one of the nearby shores
and went aground. She asked, and Jack had an easy
answer.

"Shed canvas. Dropped all sails about where the
bridge is, and if the pilot or the skipper knew his

business, the momentum would just about carry them to dock."

She saw the forbidding Alcatraz rock, which had at one time been America's foremost maximum-security prison, and which subsequently had gone through a series of unhappy sequences, each one leaving it looking more rundown and desolate. Gulls came out from there to circle the ship, heads cocked, bright eyes searching for some sign of food. Later, most of them returned to the island, but a few optimistic birds coasted gently in the *Santa Maria*'s wake; occasionally a ship's screws chopped up surfacing fish. Scavenging gulls did not overlook any opportunity to pick up a free meal.

Ruth finally lost most of her fear. It may have been because she and Jack were together, but more probably it was because it is impossible to stay terrified for ever. When he slid an arm around her waist and suggested that he take her on a guided tour of his vessel, she was perfectly agreeable, but if he had made that suggestion an hour earlier she never would have had the courage to accompany him.

They passed completely beneath the bridge. She saw cars up there no larger than match-boxes, and for the first time she was conscious of the freedom that went with being on a moving, sea-going ship.

TWENTY-ONE

TO SEA AND BACK

THEY tied up at a small dock across the bay and Ruth could distinctly see rolling green hills in the middle distance; the countryside across the bay still had some vestiges of rural life, although down along the waterfront and for some distance rearward commerce and industry filled every foot of ground.

Jack was gone while a great mechanical boom swung cargo over the side in a great net. Ruth and her father, having never seen this loading process before, stood and watched. Her father did not think the net was very efficient. He said it looked to him like an old fishing net no longer usable in the sea. Ruth had no such judgement to make. She simply told him that if there were a better way she was sure someone would have come up with it.

Stevedores on the dock and shipboard seamen exchanged cordial insults all throughout the loading process, and sometimes they were racy enough to make Ruth pretend that she could not make out the words. Her father suggested that they lay aft but she smiled and shook her head. She was a big girl now.

Jack returned without his jacket and with the sleeves

169

of his blue workshirt rolled up. He told them the cook would let them know when lunch was ready and they would eat it in his cabin. She remembered the last time she had eaten aboard a ship and blocked that out by looking at Jack, whose bronzed arms and throat and face seemed to match perfectly with the reflection of sunlight off shipboard copper and brass.

Her father mentioned the cargo net and Jack turned good-naturedly to watch it swing up and over the side with its load of different-sized wooden crates. "If they used pallets," he explained, "it not only would take more time to stack the crates, there would also have to be some kind of protective netting around the outside. Dockside labour is damned expensive. With the net they can toss the boxes in and regardless of size, when the net lifts off, everything is secure." Jack did not say there was a better way but he smiled at her father as though to imply that he agreed about the net. Then he took her hand and held it as he twisted to point along the deck towards a cabin below the bridge. "That's my hole-in-the-wall. If you want to go wash or rest, help yourself." He dropped her hand as he faced forward again, and the swarthy seaman with the little ear-ring appeared, smiling disarmingly, and looking shiny with perspiration. Jack was wanted on the telephone.

When they were alone again Ruth's father, gazing in the direction Jack and the swarthy seaman had gone, leaned and said, "How old is he?"

Ruth teased him. "The sailor with the ear-ring? I'd guess perhaps twenty-five."

Her father straightened up and turned. "You know perfectly well who I mean : Jack Ewell."

She said, "In his thirties. Why?"

"He looks and acts so young, sometimes. I doesn't seem possible he can own a ship."

"A shipping *company*," corrected Ruth. "An office and *two* ships."

Her father's eyes twinkled. "Excuse me. *Two* ships." He assumed a casual stance at the railing. "When are you going to marry him?"

She did not look at her father. "I suppose whenever we can get the time. Do you object?"

"Not at all. *This* time, not at all," her father replied, calmly, and fished forth one of his long cheroots and lit it despite a stiff little wind that came to annoy him. "The last sea-captain we had in the family was back during the Civil War, when my grandfather skippered a blockade runner for the Confederacy." He puffed, cocked his cigar at a raking angle, and stood thoughtfully quiet for a moment. "Fathers foot the bill when their daughters get married. That's the custom, you know."

She knew. She also knew it was almost a lost custom, but she said nothing because she knew her father: he hadn't reminded her of that for nothing.

"I'll go home tomorrow," he went on, finally. "Someone has to be there to get the house ready. You send along the list of people you want invited and leave everything else to me. All right?"

She hesitated; she had no reason to believe Jack would want one of those elaborate Virginia weddings. For all she knew he'd want something private in some little local chapel. On the other hand, she knew how much her father wanted to do this for her; she owed him this much and more. It was a prickly position to be put in. She was about to make some vague, uncompromising

171

answer when that horn on the bridge let loose with a blast that startled them both, and afterwards her father, cigar at an angle, stepped out where he could see down below, his interest in what was going on giving Ruth a breather.

She excused herself and went down where Jack's cabin was. There was not much chance that he'd be there, not while they were taking on cargo, but whether he was or not, being in the cabin would save her from having to answer her father.

Jack wasn't there. His cabin had a tiny bathroom with a shower, and the wall-bunk was convertible into a large table. Otherwise, the cabin was immaculate and orderly, with charts on top of a sideboard held flat by bright-headed pins. There were books, an inordinate number of them, in racks that completely encircled the walls at head-height, and when she read some of the titles she had to smile. Only about one out of every five or six books was on navigation, shipping, subjects pertinent to his business; all the other books were on academic subjects ranging from basic history to lofty philosophy.

The cabin had three windows, one, the largest, looking towards the bow, one each on the port and starboard bulkheads. There was filtered sunlight inside that made the cabin seem actually very comfortable although it was not a very large place, and everything had been compacted and designed to minimise waste space.

There was a box of fat cigars on top of the shelf directly below the forward window, but that did not surprise her. There were several framed pictures of ships, and one or two of groups of laughing seamen.

The cabin reminded her very much of its inhabitant. It was clean and trim and sensibly ordered. When she went to wash and to afterwards stand near the forward window looking ahead, beyond the bow where gulls dipped and wheeled by the dozen over a series of old warehouses that lined the dock, she thought of him standing in this same place thinking of all the private things his kind of a man would reflect upon.

His world, beyond that window, was as large as he chose to expand it. He had never said he'd gone to Europe, and in fact she thought that his ship was probably not large enough to haul cargo that far, profitably, but there was a lot of world out across the Pacific, and she was sure he had seen it all, had experienced a lot of things he could tell her about on stormy nights.

She smiled. In exchange, she could tell him practically nothing; a woman who had grown up in Old Dominion Virginia with tradition and comfort around her, wasn't really fitted for the outside world. Phil had told her that, and he had been right. But such a girl, when she became a woman, did not have to remain narrowly insular.

The door opened. Ruth turned and met the friendly stare of a man whose battered face and greying hair indicated that he, too, had seen a lot of the world. He said, "Cook, ma'am. Just thought I'd come by and set up the trestle-table."

She watched the large, overweight man lower a sideboard that had looked like part of the bulkhead, support it with a pair of hinged uprights, then turn and smile as he said, "I hope you like lobster, ma'am. That's what we'll be having."

She liked lobster very much and told him so. At the door, the battered man studied her a moment, still smiling, then he said, "Not many folks visit the galley when they go aboard coasters. That father of yours sure gets around." He chuckled and moved out of sight upon the yonder deck.

Ruth had a sudden thought: was her father making himself an annoyance? The cook hadn't acted like it, but there was no way to tell, really, because a man like the cook would smile anyway. Or would he? She reflected on his battered face and decided that perhaps, after all, the cook would not pretend.

She went to the doorway opening and looked back up where she had left her father. She had a notion about suggesting that he stay on deck, but he was nowhere in sight and she had no intention of going all over the ship looking for him—after all, this was a man's world and a woman popping her head in and out could have some embarrassing consequences.

But she did return to the deck and went for'ard to see if the hatch had been closed. It had, the dockers and their crane were gone, and even as she decided that everything had been completed, she felt the ship grind gently upon dockside rubber fender as it dropped astern a degree at a time. She knew from having been through this before, that they were going to swing their bow slowly, and when they had adequate headway, they would begin the slow turn away from the dock. She smiled at herself for being such an old hand.

Someone let go with another blast from that horn. She gave a little start, then wondered if people ever got accustomed to having that confounded thing cut loose when no one was expecting it. The answer, of course, was that after a while people on board knew when the horn would sound—coming to a mooring, casting off from one, saluting a passing vessel, signalling arrival, in general making known any change in routine.

She saw her father coming across the deck below, towards the steel ladder, heading up where she was. A moment later she heard a small deck-bell ring behind her and turned to see the smiling cook, only now he had on a starched white jacket and had even combed his grizzled hair. She smiled back and headed for the cabin where lunch had been put out.

Her father arrived in a moment, looking not particularly hungry but definitely intrigued by this experience he was having. She joined him at the doorway, and after he had passed through first, because she hesitated and looked all around, he said, "Jack's down with his first officer going over manifests to be sure they got everything they're supposed to haul. Did you know this cargo is to be delivered in the Philippines?"

She hadn't thought much about the cargo. "Is he coming up?"

Her father, standing up by the trestle-table surveying their meal, bobbed his head up and down. "Yes. Allow ten minutes."

She wasn't hungry anyway, so she told her father to go ahead and eat, if he wished to, that she'd wait on the deck for their host, then she went slowly back to that vantage place at the overhead railing where she could see the deck below, which was empty now, and farther off up where the bow dipped and rose as the ship broached a running tide as it came about, where she could see the distant, smoggy skyline of the city across the bay.

It only occurred to her when Jack finally arrived, and she turned to watch him come up the ladder two steps at a time, that somewhere back on the crossing, she had lost her fear.

Of course, if a rough sea came up she would probably find that fear again in a hurry, but right now, leaning on the railing smiling as Jack approached, she was hardly aware of being aboard the ship. She had adjusted to the vibration, to the lift and fall, even to the yawing the vessel achieved until it was right with the current again.

She wasn't holding to the railing when Jack came over, smiling, and leaned down to kiss her cheek. "Got your sea-legs, I see," he told her. "Next you'll want to take over the helm."

She laughed. "Next I'll want to go ashore and stay there. But you're partially right, I'm nowhere nearly as nervous as I was."

"In that case," he said, reaching for her hand, "suppose we go get some lunch. I'm ready to eat deck-plates, paint and all."

She moved ahead with him, but just short of the cabin she hung back and said, "Jack, my father wants us to have a Virginia wedding."

Jack considered this with a quizzical expression, then nodded. "Suits me. Whatever a Virginia wedding is, it suits me. What is it?"

"A house full of people you don't know, punch in a silver bowl, music and dancing, much kissing and hand-shaking. Not much privacy, I'm afraid."

He laughed. "Sounds wonderful. When do we do it?"

That, of course, was what he was concerned about, so she started forward again as she said, "Any time that you think we should."

He halted her roughly. "Tomorrow?" At her look he laughed. "Okay, two weeks. But this evening, after we get back over to the dock, suppose you and I stay aboard the *Santa Maria* and discuss all this?"

176

She cast a sidelong look upwards and did not answer as she moved up to the doorway. If they stayed on the *Santa Maria* on a moonlit night, they wouldn't do a lot of talking, she was sure of that.

TWENTY-TWO

THE NIGHT AHEAD

IT TOOK longer, for some reason, to get back across the bay than it had taken to go over and pick up their cargo. At least it seemed to take longer to Ruth, because after lunch, when Jack went off somewhere alone and her father went aft to sit in the breezy sunlight in one of the deck-chairs, leaving her to wander along the port-side railing watching the Golden Gate Bridge loom up, there was less sunlight and brightness than there had been.

She hadn't looked at her watch, not when they had originally cast off, and not when they had left the wharf over where they had picked up cargo. She didn't look at it now, although the idea crossed her mind, because a huge, white excursion ship came majestically under the bridge heading inland with the stiff breeze. She braced, and sure enough, someone cut loose on their horn. Within a moment the great white dowager let loose with an even louder answering blast. Ruth smiled. It reminded her of two little boys.

She saw people lining the railing of the excursion ship. The *Santa Maria* yielded in the roadstead keeping plenty of water between the pair of ships, otherwise the *Santa Maria* held to a general return course.

178

Ruth finally decided that it wasn't the lateness of the day that made San Francisco seem gloomier, it was the polluted air that stood over the city like a great, grey pall. It cut out much of the sun's rays. She turned when someone settling against the railing beside her captured her attention. It was Jack, with an apology. "I don't mean to be for ever running off somewhere, and abandoning you, but if it isn't the phone it's something else. Sometimes I feel more like a baby-sitter than a ship's captain." He jerked his head and asked if she'd noticed the size of that excursion ship. She had, so he told her it was three times the draught of the *Santa Maria*, and he then had to explain what 'draught' meant.

She hadn't seen her father since lunch and asked if Jack knew where he was. She mentioned the possibility of his being a nuisance around the working crewmen and Jack wagged his head.

"No trouble at all. The crewmen aren't that hard-pressed. Oh, they act busy when I show up, but otherwise they have plenty of time to be helpful. Your father has learned more, I'll say that for him, than anyone I've ever had on board before. He's not afraid to ask questions."

"Annoying ones, I'm afraid," she said.

Jack laughed. "He's not the annoying type."

"He likes you, Jack."

"That's good, because I like him. He's promised to teach me to jump horses over obstacles in the Virginia fox hunts." As he said this Jack's eyes narrowed with humour and his lips curved. "I didn't dare tell him—but just the sight of a horse scares me stiff. I can put up with dogs, but anything bigger than that turns me off."

She wanted to say something reassuring. The reason she didn't was because it suddenly struck her that everyone, out of their normal environment, finds something to be fearful of. With him it was horses, with her it was ships.

They started their wide-running course to head around the breakwater into the calmer sea of the estuary, and several pleasure craft got out of their way. Three functionally ugly, low-riding fishing boats came chugging up, and Ruth said she hoped everyone was keeping a wary eye on everyone else.

Everyone must have been, because the *Santa Maria*, much larger than any of the smaller vessels, got all the leeway she needed to make it up into the calmer water.

Ruth noticed the change in current at once. She turned to gaze back at the choppy sea of the open bay. In a way, she had felt most exhilarated out there in the open sea.

Jack guessed her thoughts and said, "We'll finish taking on cargo tomorrow morning. Now that you're seaworthy, and if we don't have to be in Virginia for the wedding for a couple of weeks, how would you like to go out to Hawaii with me and, if we have time, on over to Manila?"

"Could we do it?" she asked, a trifle breathlessly. "We'd have a lot of ground to cover to get to Virginia on time, wouldn't we?"

He was not worried. "We can make the run by sea, then catch an aeroplane at Manila and fly back; we could be in Virginia in time for dinner the same day we had breakfast in Manila."

She looked at him, feeling thrilled at this prospect of a genuine adventure; it probably meant just another routine sailing to him, but to her it promised to be the adventure of her life. She smiled and nodded.

"All right. But let's see my father off at the airport tomorrow first. Okay?"

He said, "Okay. Now I've got to get back to the bridge." He bent, kissed her squarely on the mouth, and turned quickly to hasten away.

She could see the dock ahead. The estuary was a busy place with many small vessels riding at anchor or tied at wharf-side. In a way she regretted coming back here because it mean the *Santa Maria* would have to be warped to the dock again, a prisoner against her will.

Ships were made to sail free upon the unfenced water; regardless of how man's constricting capabilities had halved and quartered, then re-halved and re-quartered the land until everyone was allotted just so much ground to live upon and to move upon, the sea remained an untamed vastness, and the ships that rode upon it were the last really free things.

Ruth was surprised at her own thoughts, but they were rational, even after only one little bay-crossing, because even the blind had to feel the full power of freedom that only came upon the sea.

Her father strolled a bit sadly down to stand with her while the *Santa Maria* eased with extreme and careful slowness into her dock-side berth, and was made fast with bow and stern lines, her motors allowed to die while a wrist-thick cable was plugged into a dock-side electrical outlet to complete her dependency upon the land-side world.

Her father said, "I felt twenty years old today," and smiled.

She saw shadows forming behind the tall buildings

and could tell by the sound that the city was beginning to unwind after a long day, and for some inexplicable reason, she felt sad too.

Jack came, finally, wearing his jacket again and looking presentable, to escort them down the gangplank to the car.

Her father said how much he had enjoyed himself and she saw Jack smiling to himself about that. Her father paused on the dock to look back, and shake his head. "A man could get attached to the *Santa Maria*," he said.

Jack's answed was softly said. "She's an honest vessel, Mister Severns. No matter who owns her, if they treat her just halfway fairly, she'll work for them like a mule."

At the car, it dawned upon Ruth for the first time that selling his ships might not be like just selling a business, to Jack. If he felt affection for them, it might be more like parting from old friends. She thought of that all the way back to the hotel, where they let her father out, and as they were heading back towards the dock again, she said, "Jack, all that loafing you want to do after you sell out : are you sure you *can* do it?"

He looked at her. "Why not?"

"You'll miss the ships and the sea."

He considered that for a while. "The sea will be out there where I can see it. As for the ships—maybe I'll miss them—but they never were pleasure-craft, you know. I've never worked so blasted hard in my life as I have since I've owned my own craft." He threaded through some dingy streets taking a short-cut back to the docks. "The *boats* I'll always remember, but the *shipping business* I'll never want to recall. Anyway, maybe some day we'll buy one of those cabin cruisers and do a little coasting, just for the hell of it." He looked at her. "You'd be first officer."

They left the car about where they had left it before, and this time as they strolled towards the gangplank there was a peaceful dusk settling out over the oily water. Lights shone from the bow and stern of the *Santa Maria* even though it was tied up, and at the bridge there was more light.

He led her to the gangplank, kissed her then handed her on ahead, and this time she navigated that vibrating long ramp with all the assurance of an old hand at boardings ships. Even when they got topside and she could look out over the nearest rooftops, a sensation that had troubled her that morning, she still felt confident. In fact, when he took her by the arm and strolled aft where the deck-chairs were, she felt the lift and gentle fall without being more than passably aware of it.

She saw the empty after deck and asked where the crewmen were. He laughed. "Scattered all up and down the waterfront. This used to be the notorious Barbary Coast. It's tamed down a lot, but you can still buy anything you want, and crewmen don't very often stay aboard when they can go ashore. Not even in San Francisco where they've been in all the dives a hundred times."

He took her to the railing, slid an arm around her waist and wondered aloud if her father felt abandoned. She did not think so as she leaned sideways against him, and smiled softly ahead into the lowering night.

"He had a full day," she said, which was true. "We'll pick him up in the morning and take him to the airport." She turned and nestled close. "We'll meet him again in two weeks."

He held her close. "Honolulu, the Midways, even Bora Bora if you'd like, then Manila." He gave her a squeeze. "For three days we'll have a full moon."

She cocked her head. She had thought the moon was already full. It wasn't, not quite, so he was correct, which pleased her even though it made her wrong. She didn't mind. Being wrong about something like a full moon when a woman was in love wasn't critical. She nestled close again.

"I don't want to take you from the sea, Jack. You are so natural a board a ship, it doesn't seem right to put you ashore."

He did not argue. "Remember, we can still go to sea. Let's wait a year or two and then decide, but I can tell you one thing: I'll never go to sea again the way I have in the past, for months at a time."

"Before—you had no one special to come back to, did you?"

He knew what she was thinking, when she made that statement into a question, so he teased her. "Not here in San Francisco, but in Seattle and Vancouver and Portland and Honolulu and—"

She swung without aiming and he ducked just in time, then they parted laughing and she led the way for'ard, past the oblong opening to his cabin and even beyond that railing where she had stood while watching the loading, and moved out across the tipped-up deck towards the bow. From there she could see city lights ahead and on her left, multi-coloured and sometimes flickering. There were a million people out there, and she was standing on the deck of a ship, alone among them.

He was not there when she turned, but he emerged

within a moment from his for'ard cabin. She thought he had gone after a cigar, but as he approached she heard the music gaining strength. He had turned on a stereo set and had left the cabin door open.

She smiled when he opened his arms, fitted into them perfectly, and for as long as they danced in the pewter moonlight, she was perfectly content to be where she was without talk, without any kind of feeling except that gentle, warm one that surfeited her.

The music lasted longer than they danced. It evidently was a tape, one of those half-hour or hour-long tapes. Jack stopped dancing near the far side of the deck where the music was least audible, and where moonlight flickered over sluggish water, and slid his hands down her to the waist, then tugged.

She raised both hands to his head, ran bent fingers through his hair, and responded to his kiss with her sweet and willing fire. She was not aware of anything, the sea, the ship, the movement one caused in the other, the soft moonlight or starshine, the sound of water against the dock and the ship, she wasn't even conscious of the distant, and closer, sounds of San Francisco.

She only thought of *him*, and of a week like this, each night in a different harbour, under a different-tinted moon, and finally, back to Virginia to make it all binding for as long as she lived.

When he lifted his lips and said, "I didn't know it was really like this," she slid both hands down to his shoulders and pulled him down. Without her speaking, they kissed again, but when they broke apart that time, it was because she pushed clear, twisted in his grip and looked away, out over the estuary. Too much of this, and she knew what the result would be. All the resolve in the world could not avoid corroding, and if someone didn't actually have all that much resolve in the first place. . . .

He turned her back, held her hand, and gently pulled. She heard the music again, but for a while she hadn't heard anything at all. When they came to the companionway leading back towards his cabin, he released her hand.

"It gets chilly out here after a while," he said. "I've got a sweater that'll fit you."

She cocked her head at him. "But of course I really should go into the cabin and help you look for it."

He gave a little self-conscious laugh. "That would help, of course, but if you'd prefer to stay out here. . . ."

She moved close, turned him with both hands, pushed him to the bulkhead, then shoved him on over the steel threshold, following him into the cabin. The music sounded a little too loud, so he went over to mute it, then he turned as she closed the door, and opened his arms again. She went forward, as before, willing and trusting.

Angel in Abbey Road

Angel in Abbey Road

JUNE MORTIMER

"Can't you see, Miss, she's sick. You can't turn her away!"

Fearfully, still unable to speak, Emmeline stared at him. "Don't worry, it's nothing catching!" How could anyone so young sound so bitter? They were children! And something was very wrong!

Miss Emmeline Rodgers closed the wrought-iron gate behind her, not even noticing its squeak, and walked wearily up the short garden path to her front door. She did not notice either that the stone slabs of that path were cracked and uneven, they had been that way for so long, nor that moss was growing on them and might make them dangerous in wet weather.

She did notice, with a sigh, that weeds had sprung up again in her flower bed and that the lawn was looking frightfully ragged. It was such a little patch of lawn, almost pocket-handkerchief sized, but more than she could cope with these days.

She could deal with those weeds, however, they must come out. No question of that! The weeds had encroached everywhere else but she would not allow them to do so here, in this tiny strip of garden edging her path; that she would keep clear for the sake of her crocuses in winter, her petunias in summer, for the look of her house ... for the sake of her pride ... but not now ... she was tired now. They could wait until the morning. She would deal with them tomorrow ...

She paused on the step of the plain old-fashioned villa that was her home and searched in her bag for her elusive key. It was a good, capacious leather bag, old, but well kept, polished and cared for like her neat little shoes.

She opened the door and let herself into the house, savouring the welcome peace of it. Every piece of furniture, even the rugs and ornaments, were dear to her and seemed glad to have her back.

And there was Grimalkin ... witches' cat! What a silly name to have given her, how Bertha had scoffed at it! But she was a witches' cat, sinuous and black, with yellow eyes, and she had appeared so mysteriously one night some years ago, promptly making herself at home. Despite enquiries Miss Rodgers had never been able to find out to whom she had belonged and had been glad when no one claimed her ... She advanced now, with an exaggerated saunter to meet her mistress, purring and winding herself ecstatically round Miss Rodgers' legs, knowing that at last there would be food, a fire, a lap. Once certain she had captured the attention she required, she ran through the open door of the parlour to cast a reproachful look at the empty grate, clearly expressing her disapproval.

Emmeline smiled.

'All right! All right! In a moment!' There seemed nothing queer about talking aloud in an empty house if one spoke to a cat; it saved one from the ignominy of talking to oneself.

Emmeline drew off her gloves, noting a worn fingertip which she would be well advised to darn before it became a hole. She lay them on top of her bag on the little table in the hall, next to the brass vase of honesty which had been there for over a year. How well it lasted! She loved to see the light catch the pearly discs. She took off her hat, finding space for that, too, putting the hat-pin beside it, anxious that it should not be lost, glanced into the mirror, patting into place a wisp of grey hair, smoothing the knot into which it was drawn at the back of her neck. Then, without taking off her coat, went down the short, dark passage to the kitchen, passing the seldom used study, a tiny room, lined with books, many of which she

had never even opened for they had belonged to dear
Papa; past the dining-room which was left in aloof dignity,
used even less than the study, though she regularly
polished the heavy silver candlesticks which stood, one
at either end of the velvet cloth covering the table.

It was silly, she supposed, to struggle so to keep this
house going when so little of it was used now: just the
front parlour, which was her living-room and cluttered
with all the things she liked most to have around her,
this kitchen and her big front bedroom upstairs. Silly?
Yet she clung to it desperately. Here she had lived most
of her life, all her life, in fact, since the First World War
when her brother had been killed and they had moved
away from the larger home of her childhood, with its
associations that only brought grief. How long ago it all
was! A dream world, almost beyond memory, yet
strangely, at times now, the picture of that childhood
seemed more vivid than the years in between.

She could see Ernest quite clearly as a boy ... and
Mamma ... dear Mamma in her wide-brimmed hats and
sweeping skirts! Papa, too—such a fine-looking man with
upright bearing and his military moustache! That was
how she liked to remember him, not as the frail person
he became in his latter years, plagued by bronchitis. The
Mamma of her childhood scarcely seemed to be the same
woman as the querulous tyrant she became after her
husband's death: a demanding old lady with a wandering
mind and feeble body who for years had succeeded despite
that frailty, or perhaps because of it, in ruling Emmeline's
life with a rod of iron, such had been her daughter's
sense of duty. There had been love and pity, too, though
at times, Emmeline remembered with shame, she had
rebelled in her heart.

Looking back now, it seemed as if most of her life had
been taken up by caring for other people. She felt there

must be more to life than this, but always Mamma had insisted that she was not strong enough to work, even had there been need for it, which there was not. It was only during the dark war years of the nineteen forties that she had been allowed to take a voluntary post, then she had found that she was able to work and to enjoy it. But when the war was over her parents' health deteriorated rapidly and she had been forced to set aside her plans of continuing along the road to independence. They were dependent upon her now, took all her time, until it was too late.

When the shock of her mother's death had passed and Emmeline had realized she was free at last, she found she no longer wanted to make a new life; she herself was now too old. She no longer felt the pull of the outside world which had beckoned so often when she was a prisoner of duty. But her little world was at last her own; her house, her garden, her books; at last she had time to enjoy them. She could eat when and what she pleased, go out or stay in as she pleased, potter in her garden, lovingly polish her furniture or neglect everything for a book—just as she pleased.

Was there any wonder she did not want to give it up!

But times grew steadily harder. The investments lost in the war had not seemed to matter so much then, there was still enough left for her modest needs. Money, however, lost its value in a way that could never have been foreseen. Each year its purchasing power grew less. It was hard now, almost impossible, to keep going on her pension and the little income that was left. Yet she did not want to give up her home! As her hold on it became more precarious so it became more and more precious to her. She made one small economy after another and each saving in succession was swallowed up in the mountainous spiral of prices. She was faced for the first time in her life with serious financial difficulties at a time when she surely deserved to enjoy a little comfort, to be free at least from anxiety.

The problem became more and more pressing, loomed larger and larger in her thoughts so that eventually, although she considered it distasteful and most unladylike to discuss matters concerning money, she found herself confiding in her one friend, Bertha.

Bertha was so much more a woman of the world, having worked for many years in the library. Indeed it was only through Emmeline's regular visits to the library that her friendship with Bertha had come into existence at all. Now Bertha had retired and another, younger, lady presided over her desk, and they were just two old ladies living within walking distance of each other, their contact restricted to occasional afternoon visits and gossip over cups of tea.

Bertha's situation was not quite the same as Emmeline's for she had a small, very small, circle of acquaintances and a married nephew living in the same town, while Emmeline's only relative was a distant cousin, a middle-aged lady living in the North, also unmarried, but holding a responsible position of some sort in the business world. But Bertha also lived alone and was also, it transpired, finding that life grew steadily harder. Her tentative solution to the problem, however, was most alarming—that they might join forces and live together!

Emmeline was secretly most distressed. This was an answer she did *not* want to hear. To sell up her home and go to live with Bertha; surely things would never come to that? For Bertha to come and live with her? Equally distasteful! Bertha was all right in her way, but an afternoon with her was quite long enough. It was such an ungracious thought, but after an hour or two with Bertha she was always glad to return here to the blessed peace and solitude of her own home. The prospect of having her here permanently was so frightening that it made Emmeline wish she had never spoken of her difficulties. She drew to her comfortingly, the obstacles that stood in the way, not the least of which was Bertha's adored pekinese Chang Foo who would never be able to live on amicable terms with Grimalkin; for the first time Emmeline felt some affection towards the spoilt little dog! Then there was the reassuring knowledge that Bertha was as reluctant to make the move as Emmeline was to give up her home. Each lady would prefer to remain where she was.

But the seed of an idea had been planted in Emmeline's mind and slowly it took root. If Bertha could occupy that spare room, why not someone else? Someone who would be out all day and make few demands? A business woman who would only want a clean, quiet room to come home to ... Was this the solution? ... To take in a paying guest? A lodger? ...

Poor Mamma would surely turn in her grave! But then Mamma had never needed to concern herself with financial problems; when Papa had passed away she had willingly let all those matters be dealt with by Emmeline.

Yes, a lodger it would have to be! The more she thought about it, the more impressed she became by the idea, and there was added urgency now. Not only did she need the money—she needed someone in that spare room to keep Bertha out!

So she set about putting the plan into action. She cleaned and tidied the room with extra care, emptying the drawers of the dressing chest and taking out the one or two things that hung in the wardrobe. And as she worked she drew mental pictures of the woman who would occupy the room.

A teacher, perhaps, with a pile of books to be marked

each evening ... a librarian or even a shop assistant—from a very genteel shop of course!

She sighed. She just did not know! She would have to wait and see! She had done her part, surely the Lord would send her someone nice! She had a simple and implicit faith, which enabled her to accept for the best whatever the Lord saw fit to send into her life. Perhaps because of this simple philosophy she had never become embittered by what many might have considered to be an empty and wasted life.

Her task completed, she surveyed the room, seeing it suddenly through a stranger's eyes—a cold room, rather shabby. Since she had no intention of providing meals she realized she could not expect to get a great deal for it.

It was time to stop dreaming and face reality. There was no point in further delay; she wrote out the advertisement and handed it in. Paid for it with precious shillings from her purse hoping that before long they would be replaced.

Only then did she mention the matter to Bertha and she had not been pleased ... had been full of dire predictions, filling Emmeline with a vague sense of unease.

It had not been a pleasant afternoon and she was glad it was over. She put on the kettle before taking off her coat; then, with Grimalkin running ahead of her she went back to set light to the fire. She nursed the little flame, delicately feeding it chips of wood and finally she carefully poised the coal; then she went back to the kitchen where the kettle was beginning to boil. She made the tea and set it aside to draw while she laid the tray. It would not have occurred to her to omit the dainty cloth or to slice the bread any thicker although it might have meant that she could spread the butter just a little thicker, too; but all was prepared to dainty perfection while Grimalkin managed to lap up a saucer of milk without seeming to cease her purr, then sat fastidiously cleaning herself.

There! Everything was ready!

She carried along the tray and prepared to settle down for a cosy evening in front of the fire, pitiful little fire that it was, but cheerful and warm enough if she sat close. She drew the heavy velvet curtains, shutting out the night. A chilly late October mist had come down, drawing haloes round all the street lamps. She was glad to be safe inside. Grimalkin sat on the mat jealously guarding the fire, watching with one lazy yellow eye—the other being closed in sleep—for Emmeline to be done with her tea and ready to accept her on her lap.

The clock ticked loudly, whirred, struck, then marched steadily on towards the next half-hour. A piece of coal slipped, suggesting a good spot for another lump, but Emmeline leant forward and propped it back up again. The mist muted all noises from outside so that the creakings of the old house were more distinct; the faint, flickering flame of the fire and the turning of the page of the book quite clearly heard, but they were friendly little sounds. The evening wore on.

Grimalkin heard the footsteps before the squeaking of the gate caused Emmeline to look up. A visitor at this hour? Whoever could it be? She gave no thought to the advertisement because it couldn't possibly be anyone in connection with that yet. But someone was coming. She heard approaching steps on the path, then the sudden pealing of the bell, which caused Grimalkin to spring from her lap and stare in the direction of the front door with huge yellow eyes.

Somewhat nervously, Emmeline went into the hall.

She called: 'Who's there?' but her voice was very faint and no one answered.

She wished she had one of those modern front doors

with a panel of glass let in so she could see, however dimly, who was standing there. The narrow windows on either side of the door had stained glass so were no help and anyway she would feel a fool peering through them.

Perhaps whoever it was would go away. But that would be silly, too. The bell pealed again, more insistently. Emmeline crossed the square of Turkey carpet, switched on the light and reluctantly unbolted the door.

Her heart was beating very fast but when she opened the door it almost stopped!

A young man was standing there ... the kind you saw sometimes about the town and avoided! A thickset young man, looming out of the mist, looking considerably taller than he really was to Emmeline's five foot two. A tough looking young man with thick dark hair curling to the collar of his leather jacket—only it wasn't leather, of course, but plastic—even she could see that. He didn't have on a proper shirt either; the jacket wasn't closed and she could see his shirt; it was one of those knitted things that fastened with a lacing in the front and none too tightly at that, so one could glimpse the manly chest beneath. He was the kind of young man you heard about, who went round tackling old ladies ... the sort of young man who was as likely to climb through your window as to ring on your doorbell ... nor was he alone ... she vaguely saw a second figure behind him.

Nervously she moistened her lips. 'What do you want?' It came in little more than a whisper.

'I come about the room.'

'The ... room?'

'The one that's advertised to let. This is 54 Abbey Road, isn't it? It says so on the gate. You've got a room to let ... "Large back room, comfortable" ...' he quoted.

'I'm sorry!' Her mind flew round like a bird in a cage,

looking for a way out, a way to get rid of him. 'It's already let.'

'Can't be, can it?' His dark eyes intent on her face narrowed slightly, his mouth was a determined line. 'The paper hasn't come out yet. The typesetter spotted it, gave me the address.'

'I ... I'm sorry ... perhaps I didn't make it clear...' What exactly had she written? She struggled to remember. 'I meant it for a lady, you see, a single lady, one out at business all day.'

'Like her?' He gestured to his companion with a jerk of his head, still not releasing Emmeline from the compelling grip of his eyes. 'She's quiet enough. She won't give you no trouble.'

Emmeline's gaze moved slowly to the young girl who stood, almost hiding behind the man, slim, frail looking, her hands pushed deep in the pockets of one of those coats with the wooden buttons. The hood had fallen back and her hair hung in long, stringy tails over her shoulders. Her eyes looked enormous beneath the thin, plucked line of her brows.

'I'm sorry.' Emmeline took a step back. She need only close the door. They would have to go away. If they didn't she would call the police—or could have done if only she had a telephone! She felt helpless, vulnerable as, to her dread, the man also made a slight movement.

She saw him put his foot in the doorway! Her eyes travelled down the tightly trousered leg to the shoe, with its fancy gold buckle at one side. She was afraid!

Her eyes were riveted in fearful fascination to that foot, her mind vaguely groping to take in his words.

'We won't make no trouble, honest. You won't hardly know she's here. We've got to find somewhere.'

Then, for the first time, the girl spoke, in a flat hopeless voice, the words bitten off short as if she was struggling to keep back the tears.

'It's no good, Harry. Come on!'

Emmeline looked up slowly, saw the thin white hand on his coat sleeve, persuading him away.

And a voice inside her, too, was begging, 'Go! Go!'

'Please. I can pay you. I've got the money.' But his foot was inching back off the step ... a little further ... a few more seconds and she would be able to get the door closed.

There was a look of desperation on his face, but the girl had already turned towards the gate, her shoulders slumped.

Then, before Emmeline had time to register hope, relief, it was more than the girl's shoulders that had slumped. She gave a little sigh and just crumpled up, there on the path, and, in an instant, he was on his knees beside her, saying her name over and over, 'Greta! Greta!' as if he, too, was not far from crying.

She couldn't just leave them there, could she? She couldn't shut the door now? What was she to do? She didn't need to decide, didn't even know exactly how it had happened, but there he was, in her parlour, putting the limp girl down on the sofa, kneeling beside her, chafing her hands, looking anxiously into her face. The light from the lamp fell softly on to it—such a young face. Why, she was little more than a child! Pale, deathly pale; shadows smudging under her eyes, freckles standing out across her nose like oversized grains of pollen.

Emmeline, standing in the doorway, heard herself saying: 'I'll get some water.'

Her hand was trembling so that she could hardly hold the glass under the tap. She went back along the passage. The door still stood open, letting in the cold and mist. She saw, but her mind did not register, the case still standing on the step.

The girl's eyes were fluttering open as Emmeline went back into her secure little room—secure no longer because of the presence of these two strangers. He was murmuring something, soft words of entreaty. He turned to Emmeline and took the glass from her, held it to the girl's lips, his hand no more steady than hers had been.

She sipped a little, then gently pushed his hand away. Her large grey eyes, still slightly dazed, turned to Emmeline.

'I'm sorry.' And, as she whispered the words, those eyes filled with tears.

She made as if to get up but the man's hand detained her. He got to his feet, set the glass down carefully, where there was a little mat on the table, then he turned those intense dark eyes again to Emmeline. The light was stronger on his face now, showing he, too, was much younger than she had thought, little more than a boy.

But, man or boy, he was desperate.

'Can't you see, Miss, she's sick. You can't turn her away!'

Fearfully, still unable to speak, Emmeline stared at him.

'Oh, don't worry, it's nothing catching!' How could anyone so young sound so bitter? 'But she's got to have somewhere to go—somewhere decent, respectable!' He said the word as if it hurt him.

They were children! And something was very wrong! What had happened? What was she getting involved in? Her mind flitted through the possibilities.

She hardly recognized her own voice as she heard herself addressing the girl, ignoring him: 'Have you run away?'

The girl dropped her eyes, Emmeline saw a tear slide down her face, to be knuckled away by a childish hand, but it was the boy who did the talking.

'Run away? She's been slung out!' There was an ugly twist to his mouth.

The girl made a movement, touched him, his hand moved instinctively down and his fingers latched over hers.

'Look, Miss, there's nothing wrong, see. There's not going to be any trouble or anything. Your advert. don't come out until tomorrow ... Nobody else is going to be after that room tonight ... She won't mess it up. Just one night, please.'

His other hand had gone to his pocket, he was pulling out money, crisp pound notes, holding them out to her and, when she did not take them, putting them down on the table. She did not know what to do. Part of her mind was still numb with fear, part of it filled with pity.

Grimalkin, who had sat all this time with a startled look, staring at the intruders, got up now and walked towards them. She sniffed at the girl who, as if by instinct, put out a hand and scratched the cat's head, then she crossed to the boy, rubbing herself against his legs, purring. She didn't seem to mind them!

'Only for tonight!' Emmeline still seemed to be listening to herself speak, heard her own words with horror.

The boy bent down suddenly to stroke the cat as if to hide from her the trembling of his mouth. He no more than mumbled: 'Bless you.'

Then he was fetching the case, shutting the door and Emmeline realized fully what she had done.

'You haven't even seen the room!'

'It'll be all right.'

They were all in the hallway. She saw his hand reach out again to catch the girl's, saw the almost desperate way their hands clung together.

Grimalkin, having given their mounting figures one

quick look, returned to the dwindling fire.

Slowly, reluctantly, Emmeline led the way up the stairs, opened the door of the spare room.

He gave no more than a quick glance over her shoulder as she switched on the light.

'It's a nice room. A very nice room. You'll be all right here, love.'

The girl looked about her, nodded.

But this was not to be all. He had only put down the case when he turned again to Emmeline and dropped the next bombshell. He was in complete control of himself again, the voice once more was hard.

'Are you going to let me stay with her?'

Emmeline was shocked. 'No!' Her fear returned in full force. To add strength to her refusal she challenged him: 'You're not even married, are you?'

He shook his head slightly. 'Not yet.'

'It's out of the question!'

She felt she had no strength for another battle of wills, felt she could face no more, but the battle did not come.

'O.K.' He gave in.

Now it was the girl's turn.

'What'll you do, Harry?' She, too, was afraid, anyone could hear that.

'I can go to Sally.'

'You can't. You know what she said.'

He shrugged. 'So? I can go home. What's the difference?'

It was as if Emmeline was no longer there, as if they were the only two people in the room.

'We'll work it out. Tonight's fixed up, let's leave it at that.'

The girl sat slowly down on the three-quarter bed, a look of dull hopelessness spreading over her face.

The boy frowned, then seemed to remember that they were not alone.

'It's good of you, very good.' But he made no move.

'All right.'

Emmeline did not know what to do next, she backed out of the room, went slowly downstairs. She could hear the faint murmur of their voices.

If only it was not too late to change her mind! She stood gazing into the fire.

Then footsteps came quickly down the stairs, she heard the street door close. He had gone! The relief of it! She was still overwrought, but it was the boy she was afraid of; surely from the girl she had nothing to fear? She went into the hall, crossed to the door, was about to push home the bolt, when she heard the girl's voice from the staircase behind her.

'Don't lock the door!' Not a command but a plea.

'He's gone, hasn't he?'

'Only to get us something to eat ... please!'

'But I told you ...'

'He won't stay long, truly!' The voice still tense, on the edge of fear.

They retreated slowly, the girl back up the stairs, Emmeline to her parlour, where she sat rigid on her chair, hands clasped tightly on her lap waiting, listening. She could hear no sound but the ticking of the clock, the drip of the kitchen tap—she could not have turned it off properly. There was no movement upstairs. What was the girl doing?

His footsteps were quick and light, she heard them this time before the gate gave its tell-tale squeak ... his approach along the path, the door opening, closing ... then his step on the stairs. She stayed riveted to her chair, but the girl had come to the head of the staircase to meet him. Emmeline could not help hearing her greeting and his reply.

'You were quick!'

'Not their busy time! I thought I told you to get your hair dry—you haven't even started!' There was a strange tenderness mingled with his brusque scolding. 'Here, give me the towel, I'll rub it for you. What d'you want to do, catch pneumonia or something?'

The girl's voice was quieter, Emmeline could hear but a murmur, they had gone into the room but had not closed the door.

She sat stiff in her chair. It was like a dream ... a nightmare ... There she had been but a few hours before thinking of some gentle lady—most definitely a lady!— whom she would make welcome in her home. How far it was from this reality! The house suddenly seemed alien because of those two upstairs! Why had she ever had the idea of letting a room? Tears gathered in her eyes, but she must not give way ... Tomorrow it would be over ... There was only this one night to get through and her clock was ticking away busily, an old friend doing its best to hurry the time along.

The last coal fell, extinguishing the faint glow in a flurry of grey ash. Grimalkin opened her eyes and looked hopefully across at her.

'No,' she said in little more than a whisper, 'I'm not making the fire up any more tonight.'

But she was cold. All the warmth and cosiness seemed to have left the room when the door had stood open letting the cold night air flood in.

She sat on, like a statue. When was he going? He must go!

At last she could bear it no longer. After all it *was* her house! It took all her courage to get across the room and up the stairs. She wondered how she was going to get him out. She could threaten him with the police, but suppose he had noticed there was no telephone? ... They were clever, these people, she had heard they were clever!

The door stood open. They were sitting on the bed, side by side. There was a piece of newspaper spread on his lap and the distinctive smell that met her nostrils told her they were finishing a parcel of chips.

What could she say?

He saw her, rose, screwing the paper up in his fist. The girl stood up, too, wiping her fingers on a handkerchief.

'O.K. Miss. I'm on my way.'

Was it to be so easy? She felt weak with relief.

'Thanks again. Good night.' He walked past her, down the stairs, the girl following him. If only they were both going!

They stopped by the door, she supposed he was about to embrace the girl yet could not look away, but he only said something softly, smiling down at her, then pressed her nose gently with one finger and turned away.

He had gone!

She wanted to run down and bolt the door, but could not bring herself to pass the girl who stood for a moment like a drooping flower, her head bent, then turned and herself slid the bolt home before coming slowly back up the stairs.

Emmeline waited. The girl drew level. She was small, not more than an inch or two taller than Emmeline herself. A child. Only a child.

'Thank you for letting me stay.'

'Only for tonight.' She must stress it.

The girl nodded. 'Good night.' She went into the room, closed the door.

Emmeline went back downstairs. She raked the fire. She picked up the half empty glass of water, set it back down again, took up, instead, the two crisp notes that lay on the table, smoothed them, stood looking at them in her hand, undecided. She could not take them and put them in her purse—not for one night. After a moment she put them on the mantelshelf, weighted down by a china ornament. She would keep some and give the rest back to the girl in the morning.

She completed her usual evening tasks and went upstairs to bed, but she could not sleep. The whole house seemed restive, listening.

Her thoughts strayed ever and again to the girl lying in the next room. Was she sleepless, too? Was she listening to the night sounds of the house? How foolish to have let her stay! Suppose the girl had eloped! Suppose an irate father came pounding on the door! Suppose she, Emmeline Rodgers was held to blame! But she hadn't run away ... she had ... what was it the boy had said? ... She had been slung out ... Why?

A sudden dreadful thought struck her. Why hadn't she thought of it before? It was obvious wasn't it?

At that very moment she heard a muffled sob. She lay there, every nerve tense, but the sobbing did not cease. It grew in intensity. There in that room, alone in the dark, her head no doubt under the blankets or the pillow, that child was crying as if her heart would break.

Another ugly thought reared itself in Emmeline's mind. If what she feared was true, just how desperate was that child? Just how afraid? Would she ...? Oh, no. It was too horrible! But one read of such dreadful things ... it only needed sleeping pills or a box of aspirin ... Should such a terrible thing happen how would she ever forgive herself? How could she go on living in this house?

Emmeline got out of bed and pulled on her dressing-gown. She stood on the dark landing, praying silently that the girl would stop crying, go to sleep; but the racking sobs kept on.

At last, lifting a timid hand, Emmeline tapped on the door.

The crying ceased abruptly. The air felt charged, as if she could sense the girl holding her breath.

'Are you all right?' What a ridiculous thing to have said! 'What is the matter?'

Silence. Then: 'I'm sorry!' in a choked voice from the other side of the door.

Another breathless silence. But Emmeline couldn't go away now, softly she opened the door, glad that there were no keys in the inside locks.

'I didn't mean to wake you.'

She could only faintly see the figure huddled on the bed.

'I hadn't gone to sleep. My dear, you mustn't cry like that. You'll make yourself ill.'

Again, 'I'm sorry,' then, 'I couldn't help it. I don't know what to do.'

The words came tumbling out.

It was no good standing here like this in the dark, she crossed the room and switched on the bedside lamp. The girl hid her face, but not before Emmeline saw that it was dreadfully swollen and disfigured with weeping, the skin all blotchy, the eyes and nose red. She put out a sympathetic hand and the girl seemed to cringe from her.

'Is it very dreadful trouble? ... Are you going to have a baby?'

Was this really her voice? She, who never interfered in other people's affairs?

'Yes,' Greta nodded, almost gnawing at her hands, the knuckles were all red and sore.

'I don't know what we're going to do.'

'Surely ...' She began to piece it together. 'Wouldn't

your parents help you?'

The girl sat suddenly upright, staring at her through strands of tangled hair.

'Help?' she said. 'They chucked me out! ... I'd been scared to tell them,' she gulped, and, as Emmeline smiled kindly and encouragingly, her lined face registering concern, went on, 'I told Harry first, once I knew for sure—he didn't seem to mind ... he made me feel much better. We wanted to get married anyway ... he said we'd just have to tell my people and set the date ... I was frightened ... I knew they'd be angry, but I never dreamed ...' She broke off, fighting for control. 'We went straight home then and Harry told them. I never thought it would be like that ... I didn't think my Dad even knew the words what he called me and Harry ... and my Ma in the background saying over and over, like she couldn't think of nothing else "What will people say? What will the neighbours think?" ... Then my Dad tells us to get out ... He says since Harry's made me a street woman, that's where he'd better take me—on the street! ... I don't know how Harry kept his temper. He just says "Shut up!" through his teeth, then he wouldn't say another word but I could see he was white with rage.'

Emmeline was horrified. 'You poor child!' She sat on the edge of the bed and stroked the girl's arm, as she might have stroked Grimalkin. It was the only way she knew of giving comfort.

After a minute Greta went on: 'Could've been worse I s'pose. I mean if Harry hadn't stuck by me or something ... He's ever so sweet.'

It seemed to Emmeline a strange way to describe that tough looking young man, but she said nothing, just kept her hand comfortingly on the girl's arm.

'He took me upstairs to pack some things. I was so upset I couldn't think what I was doing ... and my Dad followed us, standing there by the door, swearing at me all the time ... it was horrible. I couldn't seem to do nothing. I just took things out of drawers and put them back, not getting anywhere. Harry packed some stuff in the end, just anything and anyhow and his hands was shaking. ... I only lasted out till we got to the road, then I got sick.' Her face twisted for a moment into a grotesque travesty of a smile. 'He took me to the old horse trough and made me sit on the edge of it and wash me face.'

'Then you came here?'

'Oh, no. That was yesterday, see. Harry took me home to his place. He said it was going to be all right, that it wouldn't make any difference to them, not one more, 'cos there's six of them anyway ... but it did ... it did.' She looked as if she would cry again and covered her face with her hands.

'Surely they didn't turn you away, too?'

The girl brushed desperately at her long strands of tangled hair which seemed to be getting in her mouth as well as her eyes. She twisted it almost savagely back from her face and rummaged under the pillow for her sodden handkerchief.

'... Not exactly. His Ma was getting the supper when we walked in ... Harry just says 'Lay another place, Ma, I've brought Greta home" and she looked up a bit surprised, but she said "All right" ... then she saw the case ... and it all come out. She said "Harry how could you?" then she started to cry, not like she was angry nor nothing, but like everything was too much for her and she couldn't take any more. She went on about "how was they going to manage" and "where was they going to put me?" and then about all the years of struggle and how, just when he starts to bring a bit into the house, he has to bring another mouth, too, only it wouldn't be just one, it'd be two ... and how were they going to manage

... that came into it all the time, like my Ma keeping on about the neighbours ... Harry didn't argue with her or anything, he just says "You mean we ain't got room for Greta, Ma? Where there's no room for Greta, there's no room for me," sort of gentle like. Then we was out in the night again. He told me it'd probably be better anyway, to be on our own straight away, that we'd find a little place. We went to a café and got a paper and some food—only the food was a waste, 'cos we couldn't neither of us eat nothing, and we looked for a room to let. But the first one we went after was already taken and when we went to see about the second one Harry just took one look at the street and he said he wasn't having me live there. Anyway, it was so late we went to his sister—the one what's married. She was ever so kind, really. They've got such a tiny place, two little rooms and a kitchen—and they've got a baby—but she let me stay. "Just one night" she says.'

Emmeline took the girl's hand between hers, anything to stop her making those knuckles more sore. It was as cold as ice.

'He says it'll work out, but I don't see how. I asked Sally, after he'd gone, if she didn't know how I could get rid of it—the baby, I mean. She didn't like that. She said if I wanted to hurt Harry cruel, that'd be the way to do it ... but it would be the answer, wouldn't it? 'Cos I don't know what we're going to do ... how we'll manage ... only I don't want to hurt him.'

'Of course you mustn't do such a thing, or even think about it! He's going to marry you, isn't he?' This, to Emmeline's old-fashioned mind was the first consideration.

''Course!' Again that funny grimace that might have been a smile.

'You're old enough?'

'I've turned eighteen!' An almost defiant toss of the

head. 'And Harry's as near twenty as makes no difference. That's no problem. It's how we're going to live.' She crumpled again. 'I can go on at the shop, but not for ever, and Harry don't get a lot yet, 'cos he's still learning. He's doing printing; it'd be silly for him to look for something with more money, now, and waste all the years he's done. Once he's finished he'll get a good job and we have to think of the future ... They gave him time off this morning to look for a place for us to live, but he still couldn't find anything that we could afford ... we've got to eat, and there'll be things we'll have to buy ... All the places that's cheap are so crummy and he said he wouldn't be happy to leave me there on my own. I didn't reckon it'd matter 'cos I'd be out all day, but he says what about the nights when he's got to go to the Tech? ... Then one of the chaps at work setting up the adverts saw yours and we come round here. Harry was real pleased, he said it seemed such a nice place.'

Emmeline dropped her eyes as the girl went on: 'Oh, I quite understand you want someone older, some dear quiet old lady like yourself to keep you company ... it was good of you to let me stay the night. I couldn't ask Harry to take me back to Sally; but, lying here in the dark, thinking that was only two nights taken care of, and of all the nights ahead—and then, later on, there'll be three of us, I just couldn't help crying, though he said I mustn't. I know he's worried sick.'

Emmeline was wrung with pity.

'I'm sure you'll find something. You can stay on for a week, if you like, while you look.'

She was angry with herself for having said it, although the radiant joy that spread on that disfigured little face made the few words—and the long week that they involved—worthwhile.

Downstairs the clock chimed mellow approval.

'Now you must get some sleep. I'm going to fetch you some warm milk and an aspirin.'

'You're ever so kind, really you are.'

The appalling realization of what she had done should have kept Emmeline awake for the rest of the night. She fully expected it to do so, but, within minutes of slipping between the sheets once more, she was as peacefully asleep as the girl in the next room.

The long argument with herself started next morning, as soon as she got up and put on the kettle. She would take the child a cup of tea ... she would do it every morning for a whole week now. She could not go back on her word ... But she would have to tell whoever came to see the room that it would only be available in a week's time. What if the girl should make a mess of it, so that no one else would want to take it? She would have to make sure that did not happen. Once the room was safely let to someone else she would feel safer, the dreadful week stretching ahead would not seem so long.

She felt tired this morning. She was not used to emotional upsets. She did not want to be involved in other people's troubles.

She heard the girl in the bathroom, met her on the landing, handed her the steaming cup.

Greta looked much better this morning, still pale but almost pretty. Her hair was pretty, too. It must have looked so stringy before because it was wet, now it was soft, shining, a pale goldy brown. Things might not be too bad. She was quite neatly dressed—the skirt far too short, of course, but that was the fashion these days—she wore a plain sweater. With that little girl face and that long straight hair, she looked something like Alice in Wonderland.

She went into the room and set down the cup.

Emmeline looked beyond her, through the open door. Why, the room was quite tidy! The bed made and everything in its place!

Her relief was short-lived.

There came a brief ring at the door, and, before she had time to wonder who it might be, the girl had flown down the stairs and was pulling back the bolt on the door.

The boy stood outside on the step and, as the girl let him in, the morning turned quite grey and all Emmeline's kindly intentions shrivelled.

She slipped into her room; she heard them talking; heard them come upstairs ... more conversation ... the girl's voice low and urgent, his interjecting only an occasional word. She would be telling him about last night! It was too late to change her mind.

Wearily Emmeline went downstairs, into the parlour to draw the curtains. The room looked comfortingly the same. If only it was all a dream! She glanced towards the door that opened on to the landing. It was not a dream! There could be no mistaking his big, dark figure in the doorway. They were both there, standing in silhouette, sharing that single cup of tea, passing it from the one to the other until it was finished. Then she heard him say, quite distinctly: 'I'll ask her.'

She turned quickly away, not wanting him to know she had been watching, bent to straighten a cushion. She heard him come down the stairs, knew from the prickling of her spine that he stood behind her.

'Miss?'

She turned slowly, reluctantly.

'Thank you for being so good to Greta ... for letting her stay on.'

'Only till the end of the week!' She managed to hide her fear of him.

'I'll look very hard. I'll find somewhere by then.'

'Very well.' As she made to turn away again he asked: 'Could you lend me a knife?'

'A knife?' She stared at him, scarcely comprehending. What would he want with a knife?

Her bewilderment showed, for he went on: 'You see, I'm such a fool, I brought some bread for our breakfast and some butter, but I didn't bring a knife.' A grin spread across his face, transforming it.

'I'll get you one.'

He followed her into the kitchen, which was still dim in the early morning light. She was terribly conscious of him, his presence seemed to fill the whole room.

Grimalkin stalked out of the shadows, came to greet him as a friend—silly animal! He stooped and scratched the cat's head.

'Hello, Kitty.'

Emmeline opened a drawer and took out two knives, one for the bread, one for the butter.

'What's her name?'

'Grimalkin.' She opened a cupboard, took down two plates.

'The witches' cat?' he sounded surprised, amused—so even modern children still heard fairy tales!

He reached out a strong muscular hand to take the things she held towards him, meeting her eyes with those dark, compelling orbs of his.

'Some witch!' He added a quick wink to that broad audacious grin and was gone, leaving her breathless.

She moved about the kitchen, performing the habitual tasks unthinkingly. She felt cold, longed for the comfort of her warm cardigan—but it was upstairs in her room—and they were up there! How ridiculous to feel an interloper, here in her own house, she chided herself. How silly to shiver when warmth was in reach. Yet she was still reluctant to go. Now this would never do, she told herself, sternly. Afraid to move around in her own house, indeed!

She mounted the stairs, but softly; went to her room. She could see the jersey there across the back of the chair ... she could hear the young people talking...

'What are you going to do with yourself?'

'Go back to work.'

'Sure you feel up to it?'

''Course, idiot!' Then, less sure of herself: 'Harry, does it show?'

'No.'

'I feel it does.'

'Well, it doesn't. Listen, it's not going to show till I've got that ring safely on your finger, see, you little goose!'

What words were these? No 'sweetheart' or 'dearest' ... she called him an idiot, had called him stupid the night before, he called her a little goose, yet the derogatory words were used in such a way as to convey a wealth of affection. It was hard to understand. She tried to imagine such a scene in her time, what young people in her day and age might have said to each other in such a situation, but failed hopelessly.

'What'll I tell them?'

'Nothing ... Sally phoned yesterday to say you were sick, you don't need to add to that.'

'But ...'

'It was only one day, Greta.'

'Only one day?' she sounded amazed. 'It seems—months.'

'I know.'

There was silence. Emmeline had pulled on her cardigan, already it was warming her. She would slip quietly back to the kitchen. She didn't mean to glance through the half-open door, her eyes strayed there of their own volition. The two inside didn't notice, they were locked as one in a close embrace. Emmeline felt her colour rise as she quickly averted her eyes and tiptoed down the stairs.

The girl came into the kitchen a few minutes later.

'Thank you so much.'

She washed the knives and plates, dried them, laid them on the table.

'I'm going to work now. I won't be back till about seven.'

In the hallway the boy was waiting, holding her coat.

They went out into the chilly morning. The door closed behind them, their footsteps rang on the path, the gate squeaked open, closed.

Silence flooded the house. Emmeline breathed a sigh of relief.

When she went to tidy the room she found that her ministrations were unnecessary. All was neat and tidy, everything in its place. The room might never have been disturbed, save for a faint fragrance lingering on the air— not the sweet smell of lavender which was Emmeline's favourite perfume, it was something more subtle, but sweet, yes, hauntingly sweet.

And that was all...

Had she gone, perhaps? Really gone, after all?

Emmeline tiptoed across the room as though there was someone there to see her spying and opened the cupboard door. There were a couple of garments hanging inside. Dresses? Surely not! They looked more like shirts, gaudily patterned shirts ... on the floor collapsed a pair of those long suede boots that girls wore today ... Greta would be coming back!

As the day wore on, Emmeline began to feel more relaxed. She went out to do her little bit of shopping, passing the time of day, courteously, with the people she met who were known to her. It began to seem like any other day.

... Still like any other day when, in the late afternoon, after her customary doze, Bertha arrived.

They had tea together. Emmeline was hesitant to tell of her adventures. Bertha set down her cup. Emmeline noticed the stain of lipstick on it with distaste, thought how ugly it looked, so—obscene—the lips printed there on the fluted china rim. There had been no stains on the girl's cup, that morning, she found herself thinking ... She had already curbed a desire to tell Bertha about that white smear of powder alongside her nose ... it was silly to let such little things irritate her, but they did! ... and those biscuit crumbs spilling down her frilly front as Bertha ate up the last biscuit ... But then Bertha was not fastidious as she was herself, she was a rather puffy sort of woman, puffy face, puffy hands, puffy ankles ... and she had not forgotten the advertisement. What was this she was saying...?

'You must be very careful who you take. Make sure you ask for references and, whatever you do, don't reduce the rent ... you're asking little enough as it is. Make quite sure...'

'It isn't that easy.' Emmeline halted her.

'Oh, you'll find ...' Bertha looked up sharply. 'Don't tell me someone's been already!'

Emmeline nodded and, little by little, the story was told. Bertha listened in growing amazement, her eyes popping behind her glasses, her mouth hanging slightly open.

'But you should never have let them in!' She closed it with a snap.

'What else could I do? The girl fainted, I tell you. Could I just leave her there lying on the path and shut the door?'

Bertha gave a sniff.

'I should have done!' Nodding her head so decisively

that her double chin wobbled. 'That's an old trick! You shouldn't have been taken in by it! Why, they probably planned it all beforehand. Just like the gypsies! I remember once, when I was a girl, and Mamma...'

'Yes,' Emmeline interposed quietly. 'You've told me.' How well she knew the tale of the gypsies!

'Well, it's exactly the same sort of thing. You'll have to get rid of her. Let the room to someone else so she has to go!'

'That's what I intend to do.'

'Better make sure she doesn't let *him* in in the middle of the night! And keep a watch on your silver!'

Oh, dear, Bertha wasn't very comforting.

Night was approaching and with it came a thin drizzle of rain. Emmeline was busy in the kitchen when she heard the bell. Were they back already, or would it be— could it possibly be—her deliverer? The quiet gentlewoman to whom she had intended to let the room?

It was a woman! A large woman, not stout—buxom —that was the word! A buxom young woman—or was she so young?—with excessively black hair and long eye lashes to match. A big red mouth which was laughing heartily as she put a hand on Emmeline's arm, a hand with brightly coloured nails, nicotine stained fingers and a brilliantly flashing ring.

'My dear, I nearly slipped on your path! You nearly had me here in a plaster cast!' Again that laugh, echoing through the silent house. 'It's the room, dear, I've come about the room.'

It was the laugh that did it, the laugh, the loud voice, the over-friendly approach. Emmeline shrank from it. She couldn't bear it, couldn't live with it! In her mind's eye Greta's quiet figure appeared, a silent little ghost, soft-footed.

'I'm sorry,' she said, 'the room's been taken.'

'Oh.' The woman's face was wiped clean of her smile and suddenly looked older, harder. 'That was quick, wasn't it? Well, then,' she tossed her head setting the large gilt loops of earrings jangling, 'that's that, isn't it? Good night, then.' And, turning on the step: 'You want to do something about that path, you know. I could have had a nasty fall.'

And she was gone, leaving blessed silence behind her. It was as if the house shuddered. But she'd gone! It hadn't been so difficult! The right one would come!

It was the young couple who came next although he didn't stay long. Ten minutes maybe, a quarter of an hour, and she heard him go again and the girl moving quietly about in the room, then silence.

Silence ... broken by yet another peal of the bell. Oh dear, she wasn't used to all this activity. Grimalkin sprang from her lap again in disgust and began to clean herself as if she was saying that she washed her hands of the whole affair.

Once more Emmeline opened the door, to discover a man this time. A lean man in late middle age, with a seamed face shaded by a wide brimmed hat. In his hand he held a newspaper.

' 'Evening, ma'am,' he began. 'About this advert...'

A man! Oh, no! That would never do!

'I'm sorry,' she said, flustered. 'I ... that is, I intend to let the room to a lady, I live alone you see ...' Oh, dear, she should never have admitted that, what a muddler she was! 'A lady...'

'It doesn't say so,' he pointed out, a trifle belligerently it seemed to her. 'You should have said so...'

'I ... oh, dear, I thought I had ...'

She saw his eyes go past her, lift to the staircase and herself turned slightly. Greta was there, looking straight at him, her young face set and hard. Of course, in her agitation she had forgotten, she was not alone!

'... And, anyway you're too late, I'm afraid. The room is already taken.'

'Oh, well, that's different.' He was turning away. 'Good night, Ma'am.' He was going. Going and she wasn't alone ... but when she turned from bolting the door the figure had gone from the stairs, melted away like a wraith and all was silent save for the ticking clock. One could almost forget Greta was there ...

When she put on the kettle for her last cup of tea she remembered. Remembered the girl sitting cold and lonely in her room while she at least had the faint warmth of her little fire and Grimalkin for company, although sulking, she had refused to return to Emmeline's lap. After a moment's hesitation she poured another cup and carried it carefully upstairs. The girl looked up, startled. She was sitting on the bed, hunched over a book, looking lost in an enormous sweater that must surely be his. Her face lit with pleasure, the grey eyes beautiful, the hand that took the cup as cold as ice.

Such a sweet girl, Emmeline thought, to have got herself in tow with such a dreadful boy.

... And she hadn't seen the last of him, of course. He was there early the next morning, but Emmeline kept out of his way, nor did they come and ask her for anything, although no doubt, they ate their bread and butter as before. Later in the day, when she was dusting, Emmeline found a long, sharp knife lying on the dressing table, a vicious-looking knife.

Only one other caller came about the room. She arrived during the afternoon, and as soon as Emmeline saw her, her hopes rose. Here, at last, was the sort of person she had in mind! A neat, even smart, middle-aged woman, well spoken, with a slightly authoritative voice.

She was a widow and worked as a doctor's receptionist; all this Emmeline learnt in a few minutes, while she, in her turn, explained that the room would only be available in a few days' time.

'Your present lodger is leaving you?' The woman, Mrs James sounded slightly suspicious.

'Yes, she's getting married.' It was true, wasn't it and Emmeline did not want her to think that there was anything wrong with the room.

However, when they went to view it, Mrs James did not seem very impressed by what she saw.

'It's very cold.' She sounded disappointed. 'Not quite what I expected.' Her eye seemed to find, unerringly, the worn patches in the carpet, to spot at once the mottled corner where the backing had worn off the mirror. She crossed the room and laid a hand experimentally on the dressing table, as if she expected to find it rickety—which, fortunately it was not! Her gaze rested on the bed, scanned the wallpaper; one hand thoughtfully fingered the texture of the curtains.

'You did mention breakfast?'

Emmeline had not.

'Tea,' she faltered, 'morning tea ... and toast,' she added lamely, trying not to sound too desperately persuasive.

'Mmmmm ... there is no power point?'

'I'm afraid not.'

'I have my own kettle and toaster, you see, and of course this room would need a heater.' She stood for a moment, deep in thought. 'I wonder ...'

'Available from next week, you said?' she was already going towards the stairs. 'I'll let you know ... I'll probably take it,' she added condescendingly.

And that was all. No one else came.

'She'll be back, I'm sure,' Bertha comforted. It was all

the comfort she did give, in every other respect she was filled with foreboding.

There was worse to come, of that she was quite sure. Without actually putting it into words, she blamed Emmeline that the room was not empty, ready for Mrs James' immediate occupation.

And it seemed her dire forecasts were to come true ...

All was quiet in the next room, and Emmeline herself was dozing off that night when she heard the whistle. A distinctive whistle that immediately alerted all her senses. Seconds later it came again, from somewhere just outside, clear, like a signal. She lay rigid, listening, then heard a movement from the room next door, heard the door open cautiously, a rustle, a creak on the stairs. Emmeline's heart began to beat painfully in fear. She longed to ignore what she had heard, to go to sleep and forget about it, but such a thing was impossible. She had to do something. Reluctantly she got out of bed, put on her gown and her soft slippers, moving as stealthily as the girl must have done. She opened her door no more than a crack and peered out.

It was dark below, but a faint glimmer showed her Greta at the door. She could hear the bolt being carefully drawn, then moonlight flooded in and from out of the shadows she saw his figure.

She wouldn't have it! Not in her house! But how was she to stop it, she a frail old woman, he a powerful, stalwart young man? Emmeline trembled.

Despite her age, there was nothing wrong with Emmeline's hearing, the girl's sibilant whisper carried up to her.

'Harry, whatever d'you want?'

His voice was pitched low. The old lady crept on to the landing, leaned forward, listening.

'I didn't mean to get you up—didn't think you'd have gone to bed yet.' She could not hear every word, but pieced the conversation together.

'I wouldn't have disturbed you, but I know how worried you are ... look, there's a chap at Tech. who reckons he knows where we can get a place. I'll go round there tomorrow. I thought maybe you'd sleep easier if you knew.'

'I will. I can't help worrying, Harry.'

'Well, don't, see? I told you it's going to work out.' Then he added something else, so low that she couldn't catch it as he took the girl in his arms, moonlight shone white on the hands that crept round his neck.

This was the moment! Now he would be coming in! Emmeline braced herself. But, no! Long minutes later Greta slipped from his arms, came in alone ... she was bolting the door, coming towards the stairs ... Emmeline drew back into her own room, weak with relief. She reached the window and held back the curtain in time to see him going down the road, a dark shadow, passing the street light, hands in pockets.

Below, her little clock struck ten.

The week passed without disaster. The weekend came. Saturday morning.

Emmeline had not long returned with her shopping. Half a pound of butter, a small packet of tea, a chop, a small portion of mincemeat and fish for Grimalkin. She was unpacking the basket, talking in her usual fashion to the cat, when the bell rang.

She hadn't thought of him coming in the daytime, started with dismay to see him there alone.

'She's not here,' she said, defensively.

He did look very like one of Bertha's gypsies, she thought, with that dark hair and those eyes ... and a sack resting at his feet.

'I know. She's at the shop.' He pushed the sack with

his foot. 'I brought you a bit of wood, thought it might be handy for the fire.'

'Oh! ... Thank you!' She didn't know what else to say.

'Shall I put it round the back for you?'

'Yes.'

It would mean letting him into the house and she was alone!

He swung the sack on to his shoulder ... so effortlessly ... a big sack!

She swallowed, nervously, then led the way, desperately conscious of him at her heels.

'Where d'you keep it, then?'

'Out here, there's a little lean-to shed.' With trembling hands she took down the key and opened the door. The shed was dark and rather dirty—full of spiders—another of those places that needed to be cleaned up properly if only one had the strength or inclination.

He was tipping out the wood.

'What a lot of it!'

He gave her a quick grin. 'They practically give it away down the lumber yard.' Which wasn't strictly true.

'It'll be a big help! ... How much do ...?'

'To you? Nothing!'

'I'm very grateful.' What more could she say?

'Don't you think I might be the one that's grateful?' and he went on quickly, not looking at her, 'I had an old aunt, great aunt I s'pose, she's passed on now, God rest her, that used to find coal pretty expensive. I mean, living on a pension and all that; I guess it's even worse now ... I'll just stack it up for you.'

'... Most kind ...' she was edging away as he began the task, she escaped indoors and turned the key, feeling safer. He'd gone into the shed, she waited, standing back from the window, watching ... such a dark little shed! He emerged at last with an axe in his hand, the blade gleaming, freshly sharpened. She tried not to hear Bertha's voice inside her head 'You'll be murdered in your bed, if you're not careful!' A shiver ran over her.

She heard the rhythmic ring of the axe, the thud of the wood. She tried to busy herself. It was a long time before all was still and even later when she heard his knock echoing through the house. Of course, she had shut him in the yard!

Reluctantly she went to the door, conscious that, here at the back, there was no chance of anyone passing, no one to see.

He was holding out the key of the shed. She felt foolish.

'How silly of me! I must have locked the back door ... habit...!'

He was in the kitchen, now.

'Not a bad habit to have, is it? Being on your own. Mind if I wash my hands?'

'Not at all,' she fluttered, opening a drawer to take out a clean towel. He had his back to her. What broad shoulders!

He shook the water from his hands, took the towel from her.

'Thanks.'

'I should be thanking you!'

'Keep you going for a bit.' ... smiling ... He had nice teeth.

She ought ... oh, dear, she wished he would go, but she knew her duty...

'Can I make you a cup of tea, perhaps?'

He glanced at his watch, shook his head.

'I promised to meet Greta, don't want to cut it too fine. Thanks all the same.'

He had gone! She could scarcely believe it. He had gone!

She returned to the kitchen, wonderingly took up the

key that lay on the table then went outside and fitted
it into the lock.

Her eyes took in the stack of wood, all cut and neatly
piled, a few short, heavy pieces set to one side, and
everything swam before her as her eyes flooded with tears
... Silly! Silly!

She just hadn't realized that the week had gone so
quickly after all and was surprised to find Mrs James on
the step one evening. How well cut was her suit! How
dainty her blouse!

'About the room ...' She stepped inside, the door
remained open. Her eyes seemed to take in everything—
the cobweb in that inaccessible corner where, try as she
would, Emmeline couldn't reach it; she seemed to be
looking for dust on the hall table.

'I'm afraid I couldn't find anything ... else ... after all!'
No need, surely to sound so disparaging? 'Perhaps we can
come to some arrangement? I'm sure you could have a
power point put in, in fact I know someone who would
see to it. One other thing ...' Before Emmeline had a
chance to say a word. 'Until we can make some arrangement, I feel it would be quite reasonable to ask you
to see about breakfast, don't you?'

Pleasant. She was pleasant and ladylike, but bossy!
Oh, dear! Emmeline had a picture of herself being bossed
about here in her own home. She hated to admit it, but
she was inclined to let people take advantage of her—
Bertha had told her so over and over again.

Now would be the time to put her foot down. This
time she must handle things right!

Just for a moment her thoughts were distracted. The
young couple had come in almost on the woman's heels.
They slipped in quietly, nodding a greeting. Mrs James
turned and looked at them with unashamed curiosity,

the boy returning her look, his expression wary.

Mrs James was speaking again, sounding distant: '...
hot water, I suppose there's no difficulty over hot water?'

Emmeline caught one despairing look from a pair of
pleading grey eyes.

'I'm sorry, but just at the moment I can't take you.
You see, the young lady will be staying on.' There! She
was always saying something to surprise herself these
days!

'Staying on? But I thought ...' Mrs James sounded
incredulous.

'You said—' resolved Emmeline's quiet voice—'That
you would let me know, not that you would take the
room. I'm afraid—that is, I'm sorry—but it is no longer
available.'

'Well, really!' Now she was annoyed. Suddenly the
room that had seemed so second rate became most
desirable. 'This is most inconvenient!'

But Emmeline remained adamant and the door closed
behind her indignant figure.

The boy and the girl still stood in the shadows on
the stairs, watching and listening in disbelief. Now he
came down.

'I heard you,' he said steadily. 'You really mean it?'

Oh, what a mess she had got herself into!

He was taking her hands in his, looking down at her.
They couldn't be tears in his eyes, could they?

'I've tried. Really I have. I've looked everywhere. Last
week I thought I'd found something. But, when I went
to see, it was so dirty and the woman was smelling of
drink ... I just couldn't let Greta go there, I couldn't!'

'Only for a time,' Emmeline managed to say, feeling
suddenly as moved as he was. 'Only for a time.' ... and in
her heart she felt peace.

She was a nice girl, a nice quiet girl and already the

extra money was proving to be a help.

But it couldn't go on indefinitely, could it? They must see that.

It was almost routine, now, having the girl there, taking her tea when she woke and sometimes of an evening—if he wasn't there. She even got used to him coming in the mornings, knowing he never stayed long. It was all right if she kept out of his way.

He didn't often come of an evening, she was glad about that. But he was there now. They had come in a little while ago and he was still there. She glanced at the clock, it was getting late!

Ah. Thank goodness, he was coming down the stairs now, but not to the door.

She couldn't go on looking at her book, knowing he stood there.

'Miss Rodgers?'

'Yes?'

He came hesitantly into the room.

'There's something I want to ask you...'

He didn't seem to know how to begin. He looked from her to the fire, a bigger, brighter fire now, from the fire to the mantelshelf then back to her.

'You've been awfully good to Greta, I mean, knowing what it's all about and that ... and still treating her nice. I think you ought to know, it's all right now ... you see, we got married today.'

What did one say under the circumstances? Congratulations? They seemed a little out of place ... She murmured something unintelligible.

But he hadn't finished.

'She's had a pretty rotten time, one way and another; it wasn't much of a wedding for a girl, I mean, it's something they look forward to, isn't it?' he was floundering but she didn't see in which direction until it was too late, if only she had she might have been able to cut him short, save herself some embarrassment.

'It's hard on a girl, getting married and having to do without her man ... and we never ... only that once ...' She felt herself beginning to blush at the implication of his clumsy words and looked quickly away, but not before she had noticed his own colour deepen. The younger generation were so brazen, she had heard, it wasn't possible that they still knew how to blush, was it? Especially not a boy.

'You won't send me away, will you?' He blurted out the last words in a low voice, stumbling over them.

She was acutely, painfully embarrassed, wanting more than anything to terminate this interview. That was the reason she shook her head, only vaguely realizing he would take it as acceptance.

But deep in her heart stirred an underlying pity for Greta. Emmeline's thoughts of a wedding were still surrounded by romantic dreams. Even now a girl must look forward to that special day when she would float down the aisle in a cloud of white, her friends and dear ones gathered about her. Fate had denied such a day to the girl upstairs, just as it had denied it to Emmeline ... Only once had she seen in her dreams the face of the man who might have waited for her at the altar, Robert's face ... He had never even said he loved her, but there had been looks, smiles, giving her cause to hope that one day ... but Robert had been Ernest's friend, like Ernest he had gone to war, and like Ernest he had never come back. There had been no one else, no one.

Greta may not have had her white wedding but she had her man ... Above her Emmeline heard the door close.

*   *   *

But she hadn't intended him to stay. She had only meant that one night. Now, a week later she was still wondering how she could explain.

Never, never had she intended to have him in the house like this.

She no longer took Greta the cup of tea in the morning. How could she bring herself to knock on the door at that hour, knowing *he* was there? She got up at her accustomed time but waited in her room nervously until she heard him go to the bathroom and shut the door, then she would pick up her handbag, which contained all her worldly wealth, and scuttle down to the kitchen, there to occupy herself distractedly until she heard the front door close behind them.

At least she had won one little victory and she hugged the knowledge of it to her for comfort. They had asked her for a key and she had refused.

'I'm always here, aren't I?'

At least she knew he could not get into the house on the brief occasions when she left it.

Nor had they argued the point. Just accepted her refusal. For the first time she felt a delightful sense of power, however small. They were afraid of giving her a reason to turn them out! That was it! That was why they were so quiet, so unobtrusive, so tidy.

But she was still uneasy, her thoughts tangled.

She did not want him in the house, yet now, on the evenings when he was not there—and that was frequently —she was anxious. What did he do? Why was that girl left there so often, sitting on her own? She had mentioned the technical college and, no doubt that accounted for the nights when he came in soon after ten but surely it could not be the reason for him staying out so late on other nights? Past midnight, it was. She knew. He had no key. Greta had to wait up to let him in, but Emmeline would not relent. She did not want him there at all, she would tell him so when she summoned enough courage. No key. Instead she would hear that distinctive whistle—he did not ring the bell, no doubt for fear of waking her— but she lay awake just the same. Then Greta would creep down to let him in.

She imagined so many things, each idea more frightening than the last and Bertha did not help.

If only she did not find herself confiding in Bertha, yet she had to discuss her fears with someone and there was no one else. Bertha seemed to take such a macabre delight in the situation. The victory concerning the key she dismissed with scorn.

'If he wants it, he'll get it. They all know how to take impressions. They use soap, you know. I believe it's quite easy.'

But there was no evidence of it was there? If he *did* have a key Greta wouldn't have to get up to let him in at all hours of the night ... or had he contrived to get one and wanted to give her the impression that he had not? She suppressed a thrill of fear.

'I'm telling you,' Bertha warned. 'They're getting you just where they want you. From the moment you let him get his foot in the door...'

Oh, why had she used that expression? Deliberately, perhaps! Emmeline turned cold at the memory of that first night, still she could see that foot planted with deliberation on the threshold, preventing her from closing the door ... now he was living in the house!

Bertha's eyes had taken on an almost fanatical gleam as she leaned forward, speaking in a conspiratorial whisper although there was no one to overhear them.

'I'll keep an eye on things, don't worry! I'll come round every day that you don't come to me, just to make sure you're all right—if I see anything suspicious I'll report it...'

Bertha only meant to be helpful, to make her feel better, but, after that, whenever she appeared, looking anxiously round and whispering, 'Is everything all right?' Emmeline only felt worse, more nervous than ever.

She must tell them to go!

She summoned all her courage. It was no use procrastinating, she must tell them this weekend—this very night before she slept!

But, as darkness fell she grew more timid ... she would have to be stern with herself! After all, what could they do?—No! She must not ask herself questions like that! Bertha had already supplied too many answers, horrible answers! As the corners of the room grew mysterious in the dusk those answers sprang to mind.

By the time the ring came on the bell she had worked herself into quite a state, it was with cold and shaking hands that she opened the door.

To find reprieve!

Greta was alone, she came in smiling, rubbing together hands that were cold for a very different reason.

Emmeline felt a weight lift from her shoulders. Fate had been kind to her. He was the one she had to speak to, not Greta! And he had not come. She could do nothing. It would have to wait until tomorow.

But whoever said 'Tomorrow never comes' was wrong. Emmeline woke with a sense of heaviness, reluctant to meet the day.

She was loath to get up. Then she heard a noise from the next room, someone was moving, very quietly.

There was no escape. With a sigh she began her own day.

She was busy in the kitchen when Greta came in dressed for the street.

'I'm just off,' she said. 'I've left Harry asleep. He was terribly late last night. He's still dead to the world.' A smile touched her lips.

And she went about her business ... Leaving Emmeline alone in the house—with *him*, wondering, ever wondering what he did that kept him out so late.

She did not venture upstairs, too nervous even to go and tidy her room, but found plenty of little jobs below to keep her occupied, trying to shut out the voice of conscience which kept telling her that now would be the time to speak to him, as soon as he was up and about, while there was no chance of meeting Greta's sad and pleading eyes.

It was almost ten before she heard him stir. She should brave him now, but she dreaded doing it. Instead she retreated once more to her kitchen where she rinsed her stockings, the kitchen towel, her duster ... They must be hung on the line though goodness knows if they would dry on such a day. There was no wind, it was still and cold.

She lingered outside, sweeping up some leaves that had fallen from one of the potted plants. Stalling ... stalling.

Back at last into the house, to the welcome warmth of the kitchen, in time to hear the front door close.

She had left it too long! Too late! He had gone. She couldn't tell him now. Relief once more, save for that nagging voice that told her she had delayed on purpose.

The house was quiet, her own, her very own. Yet, almost as if she were not sure of being alone, she crept upstairs, paused outside the door, tapped, which she would never have dared to do had she expected him to be there, and, finally, opened the door on the empty room.

Her breath escaped in a soft sigh.

The room was as usual, neat and tidy ... yet not quite as usual ... no doubt he was not naturally meticulous, his sense of order not equal to the girl's. She straightened the counterpane a little, adjusted the folds of the curtain.

And he stayed ... another week passed.

She came in from her shopping and a brief visit to Bertha one afternoon to see that the Christmas roses were coming up. Poor things amongst all those weeds! Oh, dear, she had still done nothing about the flower beds, it was always tomorrow and tomorrow! She put tasks off more and more, see how bad things were now!

She went straight in and found her old gardening gloves, exchanged her coat for an old jacket, tied on her apron and searched in the dusty shed for her little fork. The pile of wood was growing steadily smaller, taking up less and less space. Soon there would be none left.

She went back to the front garden, bending stiffly down and began to dislodge the weeds—or some of them—others were amazingly stubborn, or broke off. Her hands were stiff and awkward. It was tiring and the cold struck upwards from the ground, but at last her Christmas roses could breathe. Unfortunately, the cleared spaces only made the rest of the bed look worse.

Grimalkin came to see what she was doing, inspected the discarded weeds with disdain and plaintively asked for some milk.

She would have a break for a while ... Ah! She thought she would not be able to straighten her aching back!

It grew colder outside, the house warmer, she neglected to return to the task. The little fork pointed accusing prongs at her from the draining board, but she left it there; she even forgot to clear away the pathetic little pile of weeds, fruit of her labours.

She began to prepare her supper.

She could not ignore her lodgers, her own determination forced on her the necessity of letting them in herself. Now, as she opened the door, he looked at her accusingly, as though somehow she had failed in some task or duty, and his voice sounded rough.

'You been pulling up them plants?'

She remembered too late the wilting weeds left on the path. What business was it of his anyway? she thought with annoyance, as she replied:

'My flowers were getting choked.'

'Well, leave it, it's not a job for an ol ... for a lady like you. It's too darned cold. I'll see to it for you at the weekend.'

He had such an abrupt way of speaking! But he didn't forget.

He started the task halfway through Saturday morning, having once again slept late. In the afternoon they were both at it, the girl's fingers plucking up the tiny weeds that his were too clumsy to deal with. They chattered together all the time, laughing. She watched, screened by the net curtain. What amused them so, these youngsters from a world so far apart from her own?

He looked so very much younger, laughing like that, only a boy. And that's all he was when for a brief time, such as this, he could let the mantle of responsibility slip from his shoulders.

He was bending down to the girl, now, taking her wrists, pulling her to her feet. She was shaking her head. He was insistent, it was obvious he thought she had done enough. She gave in, sinking down on to the step and at once he was scolding again, pulling off his jersey to use as a cushion. Then he worked on, the girl sitting watching him.

Emmeline felt a sharp pain, a stab of sorrow twist in her heart.

Their very closeness seemed to emphasize her own loneliness. She felt a sudden yearning towards them, a longing to do something for them, as they were so willingly doing something for her.

But there was nothing she could do.

Nothing?

She went into the kitchen and made a big pot of tea. She had to get the pot from the very back of the cupboard, it was so seldom used any more. She set the tray, then poured a cup for herself, before carrying the rest outside.

They did not hear her coming. She startled a look on the girl's face that she was never to forget, a look of such touching love and devotion as she watched the boy bent to his task.

Then she saw the little garden. It was transformed! When last had it looked this way, how many years since old Joe Dawkins had come to attend to their tiny plot and left it looking as it did now, a delight to the eye?

She did not know what to say, how to express her gratitude—yet they seemed as delighted with the tea as she was with their labours.

He was always so brusque when she had something to thank him for. He was telling her now that he had taken the moss off the path—it might look pretty but it was dangerous.

She left them sitting there on the step, heedless of the cold.

Greta brought the tray back later, thanking her again, washing up the cups carefully. She, too, turned aside the words of thanks.

'We enjoyed it. It was fun.'

Upstairs she could hear the bath water running. They would be going out soon. Would Greta again return alone and he after midnight, sleeping away half the following morning?

She had to leave them alone in the house then, while

she went to church, but nothing ever appeared to have
been disturbed in her absence. Each Sunday she returned
to an empty house, at some time while she was at the
service they always left, slipping the catch on the door,
locking it behind them. Where they went, what they did,
she did not know, but they stayed away most of the day.

The neatness and order of the garden gave her pleasure,
although Bertha was not impressed.

'Soft soap, you'll see!' she declared, a prophet of gloom.
'Soft soap.'

But Emmeline's eye dwelt on it with much pleasure,
when she returned from the customary visit one afternoon.
With so much pleasure, in fact, that she did not at first
notice the figure huddled on the doorstep. She had closed
the gate—which no longer squeaked and had been treated
to a coat of paint from a forgotten tin that Harry had
unearthed from the little shed when he brought the
second load of wood—and was walking up the path before
she saw her. Greta was getting stiffly to her feet, still
nursing Grimalkin, who had been settled on her lap.
However long had she been sitting there?

'My dear child!'

How pale she was, even to her lips, and the marks of
tears, dried now, smudged her face, emphasizing its childlike simplicity.

'I wasn't well. They sent me home. I couldn't get in.'

'Oh, my dear.' Such overwhelming guilt—made worse
because the child had begun to cry.

Emmeline opened the door and ushered her inside.
The tears fell on Grimalkin's fur as Greta bent her face
over the cat trying to hide her distress.

'Please! ... I'm not upset 'cos I was locked out. I've
lost my job!' She caught nervously at her lip with her
small even teeth. 'I fainted ... and she guessed ... I

suppose she can see ... she said I must leave at the end of the week. It's not fair! I could go on for a good while yet. I've got to go on.'

'Never mind, never mind.' Emmeline's arm was round her. For a moment she felt strong compared with the girl's frailty. 'Don't worry about it now.'

Greta was shivering. It would be her fault if anything happened. The child was frozen, locked out like that because she, Emmeline, wouldn't let her have a key.

'But it's so wrong.' The girl would not be comforted. 'There's Harry working hisself to a shadow ... as if it wasn't enough with him on his feet all day and off to Tech. at night, he has to go and get hisself this job at the steak house. He says it's nothing ... just putting plates of food down in front of people ... but half past six till midnight twice a week! ... and he says it's nothing! ... We thought we was going to manage fine, we're doing all right on what he brings in that way, and you letting us stay here.' Emmeline's heart gave a lurch and she could not meet those swimming grey eyes ... 'He says I must keep what I get to buy things for the baby.' She mentioned it now, without embarrassment. 'Only—if I have to leave ...'

'You mustn't upset yourself. You must just trust.'

Greta looked up at her, still smoothing the cat's fur.

'I should, shouldn't I? We've come such a long way already, just like Harry said. I mean, when I remember how we weren't even married and had nowhere to go ... he kept telling me to trust him, that he'd look after me. And it's been working out. I suppose we'll manage.'

'I'm sure you will.' But Emmeline was still concerned by what had happened, too anxious for the girl's health to think anything of her having to give up her job. 'The main thing now is for you to get warm,' she said. 'Then you'll feel better. Go straight upstairs, have a nice hot bath and get into bed. I'll bring you up something to drink.'

'How sweet you are! You've been so good to us.' A smile chased away those tears, then, to her surprise, Greta bent forward and dropped a kiss on her cheek.

She took off her coat, hat and gloves, suddenly feeling brisk and full of purpose. While Greta had a bath she filled her own hot water bottle and went up to the room. The girl's coat was dropped carelessly over a chair, her shoes discarded on the floor. Emmeline folded the cover and put the bottle between the sheets then went back to the kitchen to make some cocoa, glad that she had enough milk to spare. Carefully she carried the cup upstairs. It looked delicious. There was nothing more comforting than cocoa!

Greta was about to get into bed, except for the thickening of her body she looked just like a child in her flannelette pyjamas. Some colour had come back into her cheeks.

'Now you drink that and try to get some sleep. It'll do you good.'

Greta took it gratefully.

Emmeline went back down to the kitchen. Try as she would, she could not keep her eyes from the spare key that hung from a hook on the wall alongside the heavier key for the lean-to shed. It seemed to condemn her. 'Guilty'!

... And he would be angry when he knew. She feared his anger.

But he wasn't angry when he came in, just worried. He was there soon after five. There had been no need, had he realized it, for him to ring the bell. She had not locked the door. Now she opened it to him fearfully.

'Greta wasn't feeling well, she came home.'

'I know, she phoned me.' There was a line of anxiety between his brows.

'She had a bath and went to bed. I think she's feeling better.' She dared not tell him how Greta had been locked out, he would know soon enough, and then ...

He nodded briefly and went past her up the stairs, two at a time.

She waited, standing in the hall, listening to their voices, expecting to hear his raised in anger. They stayed pitched low and level until he exclaimed: 'I don't give a damn about the job!'

Still nothing about her being locked out ... nothing.

Emmeline went to the kitchen, again her eye was drawn to the hook on the wall, magnetized by the key she had denied them.

Then, at last, he came down, but instead of coming to find her he went out. Perhaps Greta had not mentioned it yet. When she did, then he would be angry ... When she did ... If she did ...

He returned later with some packets, cartons of hot food and coffee. Still he did not come to find her, nor seem to see when she emerged from the shadows to watch him go upstairs.

Time went slowly by. She ate her simple supper with little appetite, began to wash the few dishes, to dry them.

Then she heard him coming ... now he knew!

Hastily she took down the key, hoping that by giving it to him now, she might assuage his anger. She turned to face him as he came into the kitchen, putting the hand that held the key behind her back.

'Miss Rodgers.' He did not seem angry! 'I don't know what to do. I'm supposed to be going out. Greta insists I do, but I don't want to leave her. Do you think she'll be all right?'

'I'm sure she will.' Was this to be all? 'I'll keep an eye on her if you like—she'll probably sleep.'

'It's very kind of you.'

'Not at all.' Trembling, she produced the key from behind her back, held it out to him. 'She won't need to wait up for you.'

'Thanks,' as he took it, nothing more! There wasn't going to be any scene! Hadn't Greta told him? It seemed not.

Perhaps he would never know!

But Emmeline remained tense, prepared for trouble and waited for it to break about her head when she heard their voices raised the next morning.

But still it had nothing to do with Greta having been locked out.

'I'm not having you go back there!'

'And I'm telling you I'm going to see the week out.'

'Now listen to me...'

'Oh, Harry, can't you see ...' then her voice broke on a sob and all that could be heard was his murmured comforting.

Greta got her way, she went back to work. They left not long after, with their arms about each other.

... And no one said any more about the key ... nor had Greta come to any harm.

Bertha seemed to treat this latest development as a triumph for her judgment. Emmeline was becoming reticent on the subject but, little by little, the details were drawn from her and Bertha wove them into fantastic patterns, unravelling to Emmeline's wondering ears, an amazing tale of cunning and deception.

'It's just the next step, don't you see? It was all put on, a way of getting the key *from your very hands*.'

'But that's ridiculous, he didn't ask for it.'

'There was no need, was there? You played right into their hands, but if you hadn't given it, then you can be sure he would have asked ... or demanded.' Bertha waved the objection aside. 'Clever, yes, but not ridiculous. I tell you they work it all out, step by step ... You're beginning to get fond of her, aren't you ... oh, yes you are.' She would brook no interruption. 'That's part of it, too. She's to soften you up, allay your suspicions, until you're putty in their hands. Look how neatly she dropped that hint about his working in a steak house, you believed that didn't **you?**'

'Why shouldn't it be true?'

'You see! I'm telling you ... be careful!'

'But what harm can they do?'

'Harm? They're just waiting! Do you suppose your old family silver has no value? Nor that Waterford glass you'd rather starve than part with?'

'They don't even know I've got it.'

'Don't they? How long do you suppose it will be before they find out now? You're being watched I tell you. You're too regular in your habits.'

'I can't believe ...'

'You're too gullible, that's your trouble. Look how she got into the house in the first place ... how *he* got in!'

'Yes,' Emmeline agreed, reluctantly. 'I didn't intend that. I only meant for their wedding night.'

'Wedding night!' Bertha gave a snort of mingled amusement and disgust. 'Wedding night, indeed, with her in that condition—little hussy that she is! You're a fool, Emmeline, a soft-hearted fool. But you'll see. Whether your stuff disappears little by little, or whether, one night you suddenly wake up to find ...' Behind her glasses her eyes grew wide with excitement.

'Please!'

'I'm only telling you to be careful. It's so easy to meet with an accident, a fall, perhaps.' A fine spray flew from her lips as she spoke. 'I think I should stay, one evening, until they come in, get a good look at him in case I'm

ever called upon to give a description, after all who else
has seen them?'

It was horrible. In the daylight she could make herself
mock at Bertha's dire predictions, but now, at night...

What else had she said?

'I'm sure while you sit here, so trusting by your fire,
they're up there making their plans.'

Surely not!

But what were they doing up there, so quiet in their
room? The blood ran hot to her face. Of course, there
was that, but so early? Suppose Bertha was right, that
even now they were plotting, laying careful plans? It was
all too dreadful to think about. Yet, with so little else
to occupy her mind she could not seem to stop her
thoughts straying in that direction.

Should she meet with an accident who would ever
suspect? Perhaps the girl had told him how she had been
locked out and he had said nothing, planning vengeance?

Would it not be better to know? She was helpless, yet,
if they were planning something, at least she might be
prepared. If those dreadful suspicions had some foundation she could at least run away.

It was her very fear that sent her creeping up the stairs.
Like a shadow she moved; like a ghost halted outside the
door, ashamed of herself yet driven by fear.

And what was this? She was just in time to hear him
say: 'All right, if you're so much more clever than me,
let's hear your ideas.'

Dear God! Bertha had been right! She could believe
it of him—she had feared him right from the start, but
that girl, with her sweet face! Was it just a façade? Was
she as much to be feared as he was?

Tense, she stood, scarcely daring to breathe as the girl
began, slowly thoughtfully: 'All right. How's this? I spy
with my little eye, something beginning with "B".'

Emmeline felt an hysterical giggle rise in her throat, but somehow held herself in check, one hand clinging to the wall for support.

'Bed!' Triumphant!

And the girl's scorn. 'Trust you! No, my friend.'

His voice, slightly aggrieved. 'Basket, then. Your basket there.'

'No!' In slowly mounting glee.

'Buckle?'

Disappointed. 'Which one?'

'On my left shoe.'

'No, the other one.'

'Well, you're not so darned clever, are you?' And he was laughing.

Children! Tears stung Emmeline's eyes. They were nothing but children and all she did was mistrust them! She had a sudden mental picture of herself, a dimpled little girl in a gingham dress, neat and tidy, waiting with orders to stay that way, for Mamma and the carriage. And Ernest, in his stiff collar and long stockings, waiting with her, helping to pass the time ... I spy ...

She felt a deep loneliness, a longing to make reparation for her foolish suspicions, of which those two were not even aware. She tapped on the door, wishing, as soon as she had done so, that instead she had crept away back down the stairs.

'Yes?' The springs of the bed creaked, slightly, then he was opening the door, that look on his face defensive, not defiant as she had always imagined it to be.

'You wanted something?'

She wanted to ask them to come down and join her, just for a few moments, anything to blunt the edge of her loneliness, but she saw that he had his coat on, that thick pseudo-leather jacket.

'I ... but you're just going out.'

'No!' Surprised, then realizing that she was judging from his attire, 'Oh, my coat? No, I was cold.'

'It is cold. I was wondering if you'd both like to come down for a cup of tea. I'm just going to make one ... The fire's still quite bright.'

Pleasure chased the surprise from his face.

'Thanks, we'll be right down.'

She made the big pot. Perhaps it would be as well not to put it so far back in the cupboard. She set the tray, hesitating over her most delicate cups, thinking of his big hands, then using them all the same ... the heavy chased silver sugar bowl ... a little plate ... oh dear, only five small biscuits left, her favourite kind with the sugar sprinkled on the top. They looked so few on the little plate, perhaps she should not put them there at all ... yet it was nice to have a biscuit with one's tea; she left them; the jug of milk ... now the kettle was boiling. She poured the water over the leaves, inhaling the delicious aroma as she did so.

Carefully she set the pot on its stand and lifted the laden tray.

They had come down already, she could hear them as she neared the parlour door.

'D'you like kids, Greta?'

Wasn't she doing enough eavesdropping? But would it be the right thing to butt in now, if they were going to speak of their child? She rested the corner of the tray on the edge of the table.

'I dunno, really. I haven't had all that much to do with them, not little ones that is.'

'I like 'em. Maybe that's why I like you, you're not much more than a kid yourself.'

'Oh, Harry, you do love me, don't you? Truly love me?'

'Nooo!' He drew the word out on a low chuckle. 'I only married you because I got fed up with the way my

Ma was doing my shirts!'

'Oh, you beast!' But softly!

She would never understand them. Emmeline took the full weight of the tray and pushed open the door.

Greta had taken the chair on the opposite side of the fireplace and he was sitting on the rug at her feet, his head against her knees, her hand held to his cheek. His eyes were on the fire not knowing how her gaze was fixed in adoration on top of his head. He got to his feet as soon as Emmeline entered taking the burden from her, placing it carefully on the table where once he had placed the glass of water.

Emmeline thanked him, then began the task of pouring out.

Was it too strong?

No, they liked it that way.

He handed the girl's cup and saw Emmeline seated with hers before once again taking his place on the floor.

No, he preferred to sit there.

They were too poor to have any chairs at his house, Greta explained, gravely, while her eyes danced, and he'd never got used to them.

He grinned.

Emmeline was bewildered. Did they spend all their time being rude to each other, she wondered?

They each took a biscuit.

She had thought it would be hard to find anything to say but somehow the conversation flowed easily enough, Grimalkin providing the topic by shamelessly begging crumbs.

She got up to refill their cups. Suddenly she was enjoying the chance to play hostess. She offered the remaining biscuits, they both refused, though she saw the boy's eyes on the plate, the look of temptation. Why, she thought, in amazement, he's hungry! No one had ever been hungry under her roof before. She had to be careful, very careful, could afford no luxuries, but she never went hungry. What was a biscuit to offer a hungry boy? She recalled her brother's healthy appetite, his greed for fruit cake, the plates of bread and jam he had demolished, the piles of toast! Toast, of course! The very thing! But how to mention it? How to suggest that one's guest might be hungry?

Was an excuse necessary when the coals were glowing so redly?

Tentatively she made the suggestion, saw their faces light up at the idea.

How delightful it was to give such pleasure! He went with her to the kitchen and she completely forgot to be afraid of him.

He cut the slices of bread with quick, capable hands, thick slices, one after the other, diminishing the loaf, but her dish of butter he refused, assuring her that they had plenty of their own, which, he said, no doubt to save her feelings, needed to be used up. He ran up the stairs, two at a time, to fetch it, whistling softly.

When he came back she put the long toasting fork into his hands and watched him set about the job in the old-fashioned way while Greta teased him for appearing to be so helpful when all he really wanted was an excuse to sit even closer to the fire. She even found herself joining in their laughter as he admitted the truth of this.

But join the feast, she would not, having too much respect for her digestion at this time of night.

They gave the lie to their story that the butter needed to be used up for they spread it sparingly. She remembered the slices of her youth, with the butter soaking through and dripping in golden pools on to the plate. There had been no thoughts of waste in those far off days!

And they had been hungry! The pile disappeared

rapidly. Though the operation stole most of the glow from the fire it didn't matter somehow, there was a warmer glow in her heart.

She was to sleep that night with a serenity she had not known in a long time and from then on the situation became so much easier.

She let her fears and suspicions come tumbling down like a house of cards. No more would she listen to Bertha's ugly suppositions. If there were any truth in them she would have to take the consequences, but no more would she live under that terrible cloud of doubt and fear; anything would be better than that.

She could not completely conquer her nervousness of him, but she refused to dwell on it any longer. To counteract her fears she let her growing affection for Greta flourish. Little by little she drew closer to the girl and found ever increasing pleasure in her company. Now instead of Greta spending her evenings alone in her room, Emmeline would invite her down to share the fire. It seemed so selfish to leave her sitting there in the cold, smothered in that great jersey of his, with the sleeves rolled back and back. Goodness knows why she wore it, surely she had jerseys enough of her own, but perhaps it gave her some mysterious added warmth and comfort when he was not there.

They were quite content and at ease to sit and read, although gradually conversation came more easily to them and occasionally Greta would confide in her. She had been able to tell Emmeline of her infinite relief when she found another job at the receiving depot of a dry cleaning firm.

'Harry wasn't keen on me taking it,' she told her. 'But it's too soon for me to stay home all day; what would I do with myself? Besides I can sit down most of the time and I must go on working a bit longer, for my maternity grant as well as the pay.'

Emmeline did not understand all these new financial arrangements but did not admit her ignorance.

'I've told him I'll give it up in the new year...'

They sat on either side of the fireplace, Grimalkin on Emmeline's lap. Greta's hands were busy with one of the tiny garments she was making, her needles clicking busily over the white wool.

In due course she invited admiration of the little jackets and tiny bootees. It was easy to praise her work, the knitting was smooth and even, the finish neat.

Emmeline began to look forward to enjoying her company in the evenings.

There were advantages, too, she found, in having a man about the house.

Although she could now afford to call in a plumber about that leaky tap it was no longer necessary to do so; Harry fixed it himself, taking no more than ten minutes over the job.

The shed remained stocked with wood so that the house no longer felt so cold and the garden remained tidy, although nothing much was growing now, the earth was bound in the grip of winter.

It was not the cold alone that made her reluctant to go out to visit Bertha, although she tried hard to ignore or to turn aside her continued frightening innuendoes. If trouble lay ahead, if indeed, she was being duped, then she would not think about it. How could she go on looking for evil when they did so much to make her life easier?

When the weather was really bad Harry would bring in fuel for her before he left and they would offer to do her shopping to save her the necessity of having to go out.

... 'Trying to alter your ways, to accustom people to not seeing you about each day ...' Bertha would mutter, annoyed to have her suggestion ignored.

Then there was the matter of the washing...

Her personal things Emmeline dealt with herself but for some time now, she had been sending the large household articles, sheets, table cloths, towels, and so on to the laundry. She could ill afford it but they had become too much for her.

Greta saw her making up the parcel one day.

'Why don't you let us take them down to the laundrette for you?' she asked. 'It would be no extra trouble.'

Emmeline had often wondered how they coped with their washing, now she knew ... another of these strange, new fangled ideas!

'We're taking some stuff down tonight. Harry carries it so you don't need to worry about me!' She turned Emmeline's half hearted protests aside. 'Really, there's nothing to it.'

In truth Emmeline was a bit doubtful as to just what a laundrette was, although she had heard of them; Greta enlightened her:

'There's all these washing machines, see. You just put the stuff in and wait for it. It's easy! I usually read a book while I wait and Harry goes over his notes or something till it's all done.'

Did 'All done' include ironing? Emmeline doubted it, but the things were returned to her all smooth and ready for use.

... And they made light of it, as if it were indeed, all done by magic!

Even those few pennies saved made a difference. How nice not to be parsimonious for once! How nice to spend that little bit on chocolate without thinking twice! Emmeline yielded to the impulse feeling a delightful sense of recklessness as she did so.

Now she could enjoy the pleasure of generosity, too. Share her little treat—and not with Bertha whose lips always twitched in a way that suggested your gesture was being scorned.

She kept the slab intact until that evening, knowing that she would have Greta's company, for by now she knew on which nights Harry worked, on which he was home and on which he went to the Technical college.

Now she broke the slab in half insisting that Greta took her share: 'For all your kindness.'

She, in her turn, set aside half her portion, keeping it for her young husband. 'I'm sure he'll enjoy it,' she explained. 'Especially since he's given up smoking.'

Little things, tiny things that added pleasure to Emmeline's day.

Little glimpses, too, of another way of life. How things had changed since her younger days, more even than she had realized. Take the matter of the scissors, for example!

When she had heard him say, 'I'll go and ask her!' she had almost expected that the subject of the room was going to be raised again, for it lay between them still, untouched, unspoken of though she was aware of their continued uncertainty, their fear. She saw it in his eyes each time he paid her the rent, he was still expecting her to tell them to go. Well, there was no harm in their staying a little longer, she would not insist on their going yet...

But it wasn't about the room.

His request was most unexpected. 'Could you lend us some scissors? Just for a little while? We've only got a silly little pair that's no use to anybody.'

So she found some that met with his approval and gave them to him, only later gathering for what purpose they were needed.

The argument that ensued was mystifying.

Their voices floated down to her.

'Yours doesn't need doing.'

'Yes, it does. Just half an inch, else it gets split.'

'It looks all right to me.'

'Well, I won't touch yours, if you won't do mine ... and mine first, I won't have you backing out!'

'O.K.'

'Hang on, I'm just going to wet it. Make the job easier.'

'You'll get cold.'

'No I won't ... just the ends, you can't do it otherwise, it's too slippery.'

There was the splash of water followed by: 'Come on!' on a note of impatience.

Silence. Minutes ticking by; concentrated effort of some kind!

'There! I hope I haven't made a mess of it.'

'You've hardly touched it!'

'It's enough.'

'All right, your turn. Want to take your shirt off?' She presumed he did. 'Lord, I don't know where to begin!' Laughter, then: 'Stand still, you fool! ... Oh, Harry, what if I make an awful mess of it?'

'You've got to look at it! Not me! Just tidy it up, that's all.'

She knew now what they were doing and could almost picture them: Greta intent, serious, the tip of her tongue caught between her teeth in concentration, he, trying to keep still and yet at the same time watch what she was doing.

She recalled her father's regular visits to the barber, how he maintained his neat, military appearance, even towards the end ... Her mother too was always concerned with her appearance even when nothing else mattered and all her looks had gone. How she had raged at Emmeline's clumsiness, when she had acted as coiffure once those regular visits to the hairdresser had become a thing of the past—not so much due to the fact that there was little money to spare for such vanities, for

Emmeline would gladly have made sacrifices to keep her
mother happy—but the old lady had no longer been fit
to go out.

Whatever would her parents have thought of the way
these two children were chopping at each other with her
dressmaking scissors and making a joke of it! How times
had changed!

'I seem to have taken an awful lot off and it don't make
much difference! I like the way it is, anyway!' Greta
seemed satisfied, at last, with her labours. 'How's that?'

'Fine!'

'Don't I get paid?'

'Sure. Come here.' There was a long silence.

Then came the sound of the things being gathered up,
followed by:

'Hey, I've just remembered something!'

'What?'

'Haircuts have gone up in price. Come back woman.'

To be young! To be young like that! But would she
want to be young in today's troubled world?

Although things had improved for Emmeline, she
realized they were not going too easily for the young
people. They laughed a lot and seemed so happy together,
but Greta looked increasingly pale and tired, more than
once she caught Harry watching her anxiously, even as
she herself was doing.

He had without doubt lost weight and in the end it was
he who succumbed. He got drenched one night going to
evening classes; this alone might not have laid him low,
but he developed a bad cold and the following two nights
was working till past midnight. It proved to be too much
for him.

When Emmeline saw him on the Saturday he looked
drawn and dark eyed, on the Sunday he kept to his bed.

Greta went out towards midday, presumably to get food for them. Her face was troubled, he was her strength and she needed him to lean on. By night he had started to cough, a harsh, cruel cough that tore at his chest.

Stubborn as he was he went back to work on Monday morning but, before the day was over had returned. Emmeline was out at the time but as soon as she let herself into the house his cough told her that he was there.

That evening Greta came down to the kitchen to her for a short while and spoke of her anxiety. He had a raging temperature, of that she was sure, but would not hear of her calling the doctor. Throughout the night Emmeline could hear him coughing and three times Greta got up to fetch him water.

She was pale and drawn when she set off for work the next morning, her forehead creased in worry.

Emmeline was left in the house, listening to him coughing, coughing. It upset and disturbed her, try as she did to ignore him.

Should she do something? Was there anything she could do? She knew she was still a bit afraid of him, still had little to say to him when Greta was not there.

She should have been glad of the distraction when Bertha came, but her customary: 'Is everything all right?' set Emmeline's nerves further on edge.

'Quite all right,' she replied, irritably.

Then the coughing came again and Bertha clutched at her arm, raising one hand in a listening attitude as if to attract her attention to something she had not heard before. Not heard before? She had been listening to it all night!

'Is that—*him*?' she asked, pitching her voice to a thrilling whisper.

Emmeline nodded.

'So, he's in the house, is he?' As if that should make a tremendous difference to all they did or said.

Emmeline made some tea, hoping to divert the other's thoughts, but Bertha was now listening attentively.

'It's T.B.' she avowed, decidedly. 'I remember so well a poor young cousin of mine—not a *first* cousin, you understand—' as if T.B. were too dreadful a disgrace to be closely associated with her family, '—she just *faded* away. Of course we were terribly worried, afterwards, dear Mamma was so afraid we might have been—' She paused to give the following word its full dramatic effect '—*contaminated*, you know. Not that she lived in the house with us, you understand, but she had visited us once—before anybody *knew*—and one can never be too careful! ... I expect you still haven't insisted that they go? ... Well, I suppose that's your funeral.' Was it imagination, or did she use the final word with relish?

How glad Emmeline was to see her leave!

She was debating whether or not to make some fresh tea and take it upstairs when she heard the front door open and Greta come in. For one dreadful moment she thought the girl, too, had become ill and went to meet her, but Greta was already hurrying up the stairs as best she could, poor child, there was no disguising her pregnancy now.

She had brought him something hot but met with such ingratitude that Emmeline burnt with fury against him. She did not think of the hopeless despair behind his anger, that, forced into inactivity, he had time to lie and brood on the responsibilities, the problems, the future held.

'For pity's sake, what did you want to come dashing home for? I told you I'd be all right. D'you want to kill yourself.'

'I didn't run.' Yet she was breathless.

'I should hope not!'

And when she left again, within a few minutes...

'Don't go hurrying. Be late for once. It won't make any difference.'

Emmeline felt ashamed. It had been so unnecessary for Greta to come all that way. She could have done something. Should have done. What was there to be afraid of in a boy who was sick? Tomorrow she would tell the girl there was no need for her to come.

She would make a pot of soup, that was simple enough! There was more she could do, surely?

Listening to that tearing cough she had thought of the many times she had lain in that very room where the boy was now and had listened to her father in the front room that was now hers, tormented night after night by bronchitis. She had known how to bring him a measure of relief, should she not try it now for Harry?

Somewhere in the cupboard was that old spirit burner, the last dregs of a bottle of Friars Balsam that had been gathering dust since her father's last illness. She searched and found them, tipping the bottle to the light. Yes, there was still some left. She poured a little into the tin basin, added some water, filled the lamp, put a box of matches in her pocket and made her way carefully upstairs. Putting some of her load on the floor she took a deep breath to give her courage and tapped on the door.

'Harry?' Had she ever called him by his name before? She could not remember doing so.

'Yes?'

She opened the door and transported her paraphernalia to the dressing table where she set it up out of the draught.

'It's an old-fashioned idea, but I'm sure this will help you.'

She had dared no more than glance at him. He lay on the tumbled bed, his colour unnaturally high, his eyes heavy, yet fever bright, watching her. She applied the match and waited for the little flame to spread in a circle of blue, releasing the healing fumes which gradually filled the room, evoking for her sad nostalgia for days gone by.

Dear Papa! A lump came to her throat and she peered attentively at the lamp, pretending to adjust it as she struggled to regain her composure. No use now to burden herself anew with the old grief, there were things to do, this boy to be cared for.

'Can I get you anything?'

He shook his head, but still his eyes followed her every movement, she found it as impossible as ever to guess what he was thinking.

It took courage to approach the bed, to straighten the sheets and turn the pillow, to lay on the table the book he had tried to read, even given up pretence of reading. He was so hot!

However did they sleep, those two on that one bed? She suddenly realized it was an indelicate thought and turned away to hide the pink creeping over her face. She went to fetch him a glass of water, a cool cloth to wipe his face.

'Thanks.'

The coughing subsided considerably and when she returned later to see if there was anything further she could do she found him sleeping.

How easy she found it to slip back into her old role and how grateful Greta was for her help.

'His mother wanted him to go back there for a few days.' It was the only reference she had made to either of their families since that first night. 'But he wouldn't ... said he only wanted to sleep and he'd get more peace here for that—which is probably true.' She told Emmeline. 'He wouldn't go back anyway, he's too proud to take help from anyone—except you!' She added, with a smile that left the old woman glowing, 'He says why should he need anyone when he's got a wife!' She smiled, but it was a smile close to tears, she had been very worried.

It was a pleasure for Emmeline to give what help she could. It was, after all, little enough, and this time she was able to watch the speedy success of her ministrations. Whereas nursing her father had been a losing battle and in spite of all her care she had watched him continue to slip further and further backwards, before long Harry's strength had reasserted itself.

Within a day or so he was up again, sitting in their room poring over some books and papers and by the end of the week had declared himself fit to return to work. Nothing they could say would dissuade him.

'You stubborn cuss!' Greta declared, stamping her foot.

But he looked down at her with that special smile telling her, 'When someone's unhappy, it steals all their strength, see, but I'm happy, girl, very happy. O.K.?' and there was nothing more she could say.

The weather was on his side, having arranged a mild spell which he declared was especially for his benefit, and, although he had lost still more weight and was troubled by the cough, which persisted in a much milder form for several weeks, he was soon driving himself as hard as ever.

The very day he went back to work, the letter came. Looking at the familiar writing Emmeline realized just how long it had been since she had last heard from Jean.

The letter was full of apologies for the fact, full of Jean's many activities. She scanned the contents quickly before sitting down to re-read it more thoroughly.

'... and so, dear aunt, it seems unavoidable that I must delay my visit to you a little longer...'

How much disappointment that one short sentence would once have brought, now it did not seem to matter so much. Was Jean's annual visit—she seldom came more than once a year and each year had a reason for the visit having to be shorter than the one before—just a duty, she wondered. Was she a nuisance, a responsibility Jean could well do without? Her heart grew sad at the thought.

Yet, if Jean should come now, where could she put her?

At last she would have a legitimate reason for telling them to go—but would it be worthwhile for the few nights Jean would stay.

At least the delay made it unnecessary for her to make that decision yet. She read on:

'You mentioned taking a paying guest. Have you given the matter further thought? Do you in fact think such a step needful? Perhaps you would be glad of some company, but is there not some friend...'

Some friend? The carping presence of Bertha in place of the delightful—yes, she admitted she found it delightful—presence of Greta? But Greta was going to have a baby, she must not loose sight of that fact.

How could she explain all that had happened to Jean, and what would Jean's reaction be? Not a sympathetic one, she feared. No, it would be better not to burden Jean with the long tale now. She would just mention that she had someone living in the house and go into details when Jean's visit was more imminent, perhaps she would not refer to it at all.

'... I would dearly have loved to see you before Christmas, but fear this will now be impossible, though I hope to be with you for a day or two at least, during the New Year.'

She refolded the letter with a sigh.

At least, now, there would be no need to make those preparations, to put on the show of well-being she always contrived for Jean—the full larder, the roaring fires, the achievement of which took many weeks of careful living before and after.

No need for the pretence.

She was already feeling relief instead of disappointment, yet only a short while ago the receipt of such a letter would have made her feel so lonely, so unhappy!

Now she had other things to think about ... not since she had been a little girl and had inadvertantly discovered a wax doll hidden away in a cupboard had she felt such a thrill over a secreted parcel. For at last her surprise was ready. Several times since its completion she had unwrapped the carefully crocheted bed jacket, telling herself she was merely checking to see that the ribbons were a perfect match, but in fact, delighted to hold the pretty garment, to anticipate Greta's pleasure on receiving it. Her second gift, the baby blanket, was almost completed too—not before time! Christmas was fast approaching. Should she use blue or pink ribbon to decorate the blanket, she debated? Or was white safer? No, she fancied a touch of colour! But which should it be? Both! She decided with something approaching a grin. She would put on bows of both colours and pin a paper question mark to them, that would be just the right touch!

Her gift to Jean would have to be sent through the post now. She saw about it that very day, packing the box of dainty Swiss handkerchiefs with her usual care.

There were but few other preparations she had to make for Christmas. Her mailing list for cards had diminished to only a few names; she bought a large bottle of Bertha's favourite toilet water but little else extra. The postman was not overburdened when he came to her door, except on the day he brought the parcel. This was indeed an event! Emmeline was puzzled until she saw the writing. Jean! And what a wonderful gift the wrapping disclosed! In amazement she lifted out the soft mohair knee rug, admired its glowing colours! How beautiful! How light! How warm! It was the most magnificent gift she had received in years. Did Jean perhaps realize how much her visits meant to the old lady? Had her conscience troubled her?

It was bitterly cold on Christmas Eve so she was not tempted to linger long looking in the brightly lit shop windows, but hurried home with her meagre purchases.

In the friendly warmth of her kitchen she set about her annual task, making mince pies in case someone should call. The vicar and his wife usually paid her a brief visit at this time of year, then, of course she always took some to Bertha, and she would like to invite her lodgers to come down one evening when they had no plans of their own, and have something to offer them that would make it a special occasion.

One thing she could still do was make pastry, although the fingers that prepared the dough were stiff now.

Once in those far distant days of childhood Christmas had meant so many plans and preparations, the house had been all abustle with them. But since her youth—since Ernest's death—Christmas had been a much more solemn occasion, a religious festival, and observed as such, without the additional excitement of entertainment or parties. Perhaps it might have retained some of its gaiety had they still lived within distance of her young friends, but once they had moved away, her shy disposition, her sheltered existence, had robbed her of the opportunity to make a new circle of friends; from 'the quiet little Miss Rodgers' she had emerged into the 'retiring, middle-aged Miss Rodgers' and was now 'the elderly Miss Rodgers' without having more than briefly touched the lives of those outside her tiny family unit.

She put the pies into the oven and before long the sweet rich scent of them baking had pervaded the kitchen and stolen into the house.

How nice it would have been to have made a big fruit cake and decorate it with frosting, she thought! But who would eat it?

All too soon her simple preparations were complete, she tidied the kitchen and ate her lonely supper by the fire, glad of Grimalkin's company.

Greta came in, alone again, looked around the door to say 'Hello' and went upstairs before Emmeline could see with what she was encumbered, but a little while later she came back down, looking slightly distracted.

'I don't s'pose you've got a flower pot, have you?' she asked hopefully.

Emmeline looked surprised. 'I must have somewhere. There used to be quite a few in the shed, but whether or not they've all got broken I couldn't say.'

'Can I look?'

'Of course, but it's dark.'

'I'll get a torch. You see ... it didn't seem much like Christmas, so I got us a tree—just a tiny bit of a one—but I never thought of anything to stand it up in. Shall I show you?' she added all in a rush.

'I'd love to see it.'

Greta came back with her coat on once more and a torch in one hand, the tree, no more than the tip of a branch, in the other.

'It's a pretty little one isn't it?' she looked at it in critical admiration. 'I thought we ought to have a tree— it being our first Christmas ... I think Harry knows I feel worse about my people right now, it kind of hurts more when we go to his place, so we decided we'd be better on our own for most of the day, but I've got to make it like Christmas, somehow.' A shadow had fallen over her face.

'Of course. It's a lovely tree—such a pretty shape. A perfect miniature.' Emmeline replied kindly. 'Let's see what we can find for you.'

They went to fetch the key of the shed door. Greta wouldn't let Emmeline go out into the cold with her, even to hold the torch. After pulling a face and admitting that she did not like spiders she took Grimalkin for company. The cat, who had been showing considerable interest in the tree until one of the needles had pricked her nose, was now further affronted to be picked up without ceremony, and tucked beneath the girl's arm. However the shed was full of interesting shadows and the search proved all too short for the animal's liking. Greta soon found a suitable pot, in fact she took the first one that presented itself and with a shudder wiped off the cobwebs adhering to it. Grimalkin was now disappointed to be lifted up again just when she was about to investigate a most interesting scent. But more entertainment of an unusual sort came her way as Greta searched around the yard for stones with which to wedge the little tree firmly into the pot and the cat pounced enthusiastically on the elusive flickering beam of light from the torch, quite forgetting her dignity. At last they had gathered sufficient and the tree was standing upright, a small, proud emblem of the blessed season.

Greta came back inside and took from her pocket two strands of tinsel which she twined around it and then stood back to admire the effect.

Emmeline could recall only too clearly the trees that had stood in the corner of that other lounge, reaching almost to the ceiling and glistening with decorations.

'You know,' she said. 'Somewhere I've a box with a whole lot of decorations that we used to use every year. It must still be there in the lumber room. I wonder if we could find it. Shall we try?'

'Oh, how lovely! Yes, please!' How readily the girl's face lit up!

The lumber room was cold and musty. It must formerly have been a dressing-room, tucked between the two bedrooms, and was now seldom opened. There was a wardrobe stuffed with moth eaten, long outmoded clothes of no use and little value, which should have been thrown away long ago. Walking sticks and piles of old books and journals littered the floor; a chair had the horsehair stuffing showing through the seat and in one corner stood the abandoned doll's house that Emmeline had never been able to bring herself to part with. Greta discovered it with delight and had to be coaxed away if they were ever to find that elusive box. There were hat boxes—were they ever used these days?—a trunk full of papers, two worn, leather cases and boxes and cartons of all sizes. Whatever did they all contain? Emmeline had long forgotten. They found the one they sought at last, unearthed it and carried it down to examine the treasures it held.

They searched through the box with careful fingers, finding the smallest most dainty of the decorations. What memories came flooding back! What Christmases those had been, when life was full of hope and promise! How many years had passed since these pretty trinkets had last been exposed to the light! The little baubles and figures were unlike anything to be found in the shops today and Greta exclaimed over them many times in delight, each seeming to please her more than the one before. She found it hard to decide which ones to use, for the little tree would not hold many. She no longer intended to keep the tree in their own room, she wanted to display it where Emmeline could enjoy it too. Could she not put it in the hall?

They cleared the vase of honesty and all the other knick-knacks from the hall table so that there would be nothing to detract from the beauty of the tree. They disguised the humble flower pot with coloured paper, winding about it the original strands of tinsel, then one by one hung the decorations, standing back to admire the addition of each, until the tree was complete in all its splendour.

As she worked Greta confided in Emmeline that she had a present hidden away for Harry although they had agreed not to buy presents this year.

'He's going to be angry with me—' The fact did not seem to worry her—'But I've got him some new shoes. Heaven knows he needs them, his have been fixed twice and they're nearly through again, but he won't get himself any.'

Shoes? Emmeline recalled her father's, always neatly polished, made to measure. No one would have thought of buying them for him—'same make as before, they're bound to fit'!

At length the tree was laden to their satisfaction and Emmeline suggested that, to make the evening complete, they might listen to the carol service together.

'That would make it just perfect!'

They sat by the fire, enjoying the old, familiar, well-loved words, joining softly in the singing, the wavering old voice and the fresh young one mingling with the trained ones coming from the radio.

When the service was over and the last strains of music had died away Emmeline thought, as the girl was doing, of the boy who had yet two hours of work ahead of him. She felt that he, too, should have a share in some of the glow that surrounded them and suggested reviving an old custom.

Greta was charmed by her idea.

Before putting out the light they drew back first the heavy curtains, then the net ones and set a burning candle on a small table in front of the window to watch for him and to welcome him home.

Then they went up to bed, lingering on the landing to give a last satisfied look at the tiny tree, barely visible in the faint light.

Christmas had come after all to that house in Abbey Road.

Early the following morning Emmeline crept down to lay her tissue-wrapped box on the table next to the tree, only to find to her surprise, that a small parcel already lay there, neatly wrapped and addressed to her. She could hardly believe her eyes. Her shaking hands fumbled with the paper and found inside a pair of gloves, so like her old worn ones that she knew they must have been purchased with great care. She had to blink away her tears.

The house was quiet, still ... it could have been empty, but she knew she was no longer alone, here under her roof was someone who cared enough to have a thought for her on this special day. She felt a glow of happiness spread outwards from her heart through her whole body.

Before she left for church she wrote a short note and pushed it beneath their door. 'My dears, Thank you for your lovely gift. Please feel free to make yourself some tea, this morning ... with seasonal greetings...'

The church was crowded; had she not been early she might have had difficulty in getting her usual seat.

After the service the faces of her few acquaintances were lost in the crowd of strangers, but Emmeline no longer felt unwanted or alone, instead she had a sense of importance—this year she had someone to hurry home to! Foolish thought! What did she, an old woman, mean to them? But it was nice to know that someone would be there, that she need not let herself into an empty house this Christmas morning. A little girl walking proudly, pushing a new dolls pram smiled at her; she passed a boy riding a shining bicycle. Then suddenly she thought 'Suppose they have already gone out!'—forgetting for the moment that Greta had mentioned they would be spending the day on their own—and hastened her steps.

She need not have worried.

They were in the kitchen. One glance showed her that the parcel had gone from beneath the tree, then Greta came into the passage, almost running to meet her, and threw her arms about the old lady.

'Dear Miss Rodgers! Oh, thank you—they're so lovely!' She was almost incoherent in her delight.

Somewhat startled, Emmeline submitted to her kiss, returned it, kissing the girl's soft cheek.

'We've only just made tea, it's still hot. You will have some won't you?' Then she broke off with a laugh. 'Listen to me, inviting you into your own kitchen!'

'I'd love a cup.' Emmeline's wrinkled face creased with happiness.

'. . . And look!' Greta took a step back, spreading her skirt like a little girl displaying a new party dress, showing off the softly gathered deep blue dress that disguised her figure. 'Isn't it pretty?' she asked, shyly. 'Harry didn't keep his word either! He said he didn't want me having nothing but his sister's stuff!'

'It's lovely.'

'You should have seen his face this morning,' Greta dropped her voice, approaching a whisper. 'I just put the shoes where the others had been, and he'd slipped his feet into them without even looking before he noticed!' Her face shone with happiness, then she put her hand on Emmeline's arm.

'Do come now, or the tea will be cold.'

Harry was there in the kitchen. His eyes met Emmeline's, sharing with her, through a quick grin and a slow wondering shake of his head, his amusement at Greta's bubbling excitement. The gesture did more than he could ever have realized to draw Emmeline into their magic circle.

He poured the tea for her and they sat around the table, all together. Then Greta glanced across at her husband as if looking for a cue, his eyes bade her do the talking and she began, a little hesitantly.

'Miss Rodgers, are you going out today?'

'No, my dear.'

'We wondered ... your friend?'

'She has her family. I usually spend a very quiet Christmas, what more would you expect at my age?' she shrank from sounding in need of sympathy. 'I usually visit my friend—or she me—on Boxing Day.'

Greta didn't look sympathetic, she looked pleased. 'Then won't you join us? We're only going to have a sort of indoor picnic, but we'd love you to share it.'

Emmeline felt so tempted, but had they asked her just from kindness, hoping for a refusal? It didn't look like it, Greta's face showed only happiness and excitement; Emmeline turned to Harry, he grinned at her but his look warned 'Don't you dare disappoint her!'

'I ... I think it sounds delightful!'

'Oh, good!' Greta clasped her hands with sheer joy. 'We've just got a cold chicken and things and a pudding in a tin, but it's going to be fun.'

'We could warm the chicken up, if you like, and roast some potatoes,' Emmeline suggested, tentatively.

The girl glanced across at the boy for his approval before nodding happy agreement.

In no time the kitchen was a bustle. Here was their feast laid out on the table, the chicken, a tin of mixed vegetables, bread, the pudding; and Emmeline was adding her contributions. They set the pudding on to boil, Greta and Emmeline made stuffing and a sauce for the pudding, pouring in some drops of precious brandy, while they set Harry to peeling potatoes.

Her best idea, Emmeline thought, was the suggestion that they turn the picnic into a party, using the dining-room and setting the table in style. She took out one of her fine damask cloths, the carefully wrapped silver—there should have been nuts, raisins, candied fruit and wine! In a moment of foolishness she took out some of her beautiful glasses, even if they had to remain empty, they added grace to the table.

Greta was enchanted. She fetched Harry from the kitchen to admire. Emmeline took up a silver dish to hold the mince pies and slipped away.

'Isn't it lovely? Did you ever see anything so grand?' Greta was exclaiming in delight.

'It's perfect.'

Then. 'Oh, Harry, I don't think there's anybody what loves someone like I do you!'

'You're wrong, you know.'

'Wrong?' Emmeline could hear she felt hurt at his disbelief.

'There's the way I feel about you ... I'm not much good at saying that sort of thing, not like the fellows in the books you've always got your head stuck in, but, if I look after you, see, if I give you my kid and I take care of the two of you, that's my way of saying it ... and don't you forget that, never.'

When Greta came back to the kitchen her cheeks were flushed and her eyes were shining like two stars.

Emmeline carried through some things she wanted to add to the table, the cruet and the sugar bowl. She stopped just inside the dining-room door. Harry was holding one of the glasses to the light, examining it critically.

'It's good stuff, huh?'

'Yes,' she replied, feeling a slight sense of unease. 'It's very old.'

'It's beautiful.' He said it as a stated fact; was it imagination or did he sound calculating, as he set the glass back on the table?

They made a merry party. When last, Emmeline wondered, had a meal been eaten in that room with such relish, when had the walls echoed with such laughter? The deficiencies of the feast were more than made up for by the conviviality of the company. She could not remember when last she had enjoyed herself so much.

When their feast was over Harry built up the fire in the parlour, insisting that she sat by it. Her hands lay idle on the soft mohair rug that covered her knees, while the youngsters washed up and tidied the kitchen, working slowly and carefully, aware of the value of the things that they handled, leaving them on the table for her to pack away into their proper places in her own good time.

She dreamed and dozed by the fire until they joined her later, Greta taking the chair that was fast becoming her own, he, as usual, sitting on the floor at her feet. Then they encouraged her to dream out loud, drawing from her tales of Christmases long ago, reminiscences of days gone by, which they seemed to find so fascinating.

She was tired, but oh so happily tired, when at last they rose to go, solicitous of her comfort, now that they were going to leave her alone. Her day had been long enough, she was glad, now, to rest, to share with Grimalkin the chicken sandwiches—sliced so thinly that they could only have been made by Greta—which they left by her side.

Bertha did her best to spoil it all next day but her unkind and disparaging remarks could not dispell that feeling of well-being. Emmeline dismissed as old woman's prating the insinuation that she had only been included in Greta's and Harry's plans to suit their own ends, even though, as always, there was a hint of possibility behind Bertha's suggestions. Things could have been planned so that they got the use of her kitchen to warm their food—although the suggestion that they did so had come from Emmeline herself—they might have suspected that she would add something to the meal, but Emmeline refused to believe it.

'So you made quite a party of it,' Bertha went on, with something close to a sneer. 'I thought they'd find out where you kept the silver eventually.'

'Good stuff, huh?' ... Emmeline hastily pushed the mental picture from her mind, she would let nothing spoil that perfect day.

Bertha's day had not been so perfect, she grumbled about various things, chiefly the thoughtlessness and selfishness of the young members of the family. Emmeline nodded, pretending sympathy, keeping from her lips the smile that was in her heart as she thought: 'My children aren't a bit like that!'

Her children? What a strange thought to have had!

The new year brought new pleasure and a new phase of life.

Greta had given up going to work and during that very first morning she came to Emmeline pleading to be allowed to help her in the house.

'I've tidied every single thing I can lay my hands on and look how early it still is!' she said.

Emmeline was busy cleaning the silver and soon Greta was sitting at the table opposite her, polishing away with grateful satisfaction.

The mornings settled into a happy routine, Greta eager to give help, and Emmeline glad to accept it. How careful the girl was with the dusting, lifting each precious object with gentle hands. She sang softly sometimes as she worked—how many songs she seemed to know!

They even went shopping together occasionally, the girl adjusting her own slowing pace to the even slower step of the old lady, her bright eyes spotting more readily the things Emmeline sought on the shelves.

But never did she intrude too far, never disturbed Emmeline's quiet afternoons or came into the parlour uninvited.

It was altogether a delightful relationship.

Added pleasure came the day Greta returned from one of her own shopping expeditions and revealed her plans to make the little garments—jackets and gowns—that her baby would need. See, she had a pattern and this material, she displayed them excitedly. How she was longing to begin! Harry had promised to fetch his sister's machine for her as soon as possible.

Emmeline now triumphantly told her that she had a treadle machine, seldom used any more except for such mundane tasks as making pillow cases from worn sheets, but still in good working order. There was no need to delay if Greta was really eager to set about the task.

Oh, the joy of laying out the patterns! Of cutting the material, of seeing each tiny garment take shape! The grey head and the fair bent over the task together, discussing seams and tucks. It kept them busy for days.

Both tired easily, both needed rest. More and more often they sat before the fire together, sewing hems, embroidering tiny sprays of flowers.

The girl's face lost its gaunt, almost hunted look, took on the ethereal glow of approaching motherhood.

Life had a sweet and even pattern, if only it could have gone on this way for ever . . .

It was, of course, Bertha who made her face reality.

'When are they going, don't you care what's happening?

Do you think that baby will never be born? No doubt that's what *she* hoped at the beginning ... that it was just a dream that would never come about. But it'll be born, you'll have to accept the fact. Have you thought what it will mean? How will you cope with a baby on your doorstep? You surely don't imagine they'll be able to keep it unnoticed in their room? They'll be taking over the house. Do you think they'll be able to go out for their meals then? They'll take over your kitchen, you'll have to be asking when *you* may use it! There'll be strings of wet washing drying in front of your fire. And what sleep will you get, you're not looking well now, how will it be when the child cries all night—and it will!'

It was true that Emmeline was not looking well, she had been feeling very tired for the last two days, now Bertha's voice seemed to beat on her brain. She wished she had not come!

'You must get them out now, before it's too late! You mentioned that you were not feeling well, then I shall say I must be there to look after you. I shall come at once, insist on moving into that room. I can let this house for a time then there can be no arguments, they will have to accept it. You have put up with them far too long—far too long! If you are too foolish, too soft-hearted to do something about it, in the name of our friendship I shall *have* to do something!'

Emmeline protested weakly, her head was aching.

'It's all very well to live in fancy dreams, *they* may keep quiet, but they won't be able to keep a baby quiet, I'm telling you. Imagine the shambles it will make of your house!'

What was the matter with her? Emmeline seemed unable to collect her defences.

'But ... Chang Foo ...' she began, falling back on the old excuse.

'I don't know why we make such an issue of that. Grimalkin can go out in the day time, cats do, you know! And at night Chang will be in my room. They may even get used to each other. Think ...' her voice was soothing now, 'of the peace of having the place to yourself again, no one coming and going at odd hours...'

'But I don't...'

'We must see about it.'

What else had Bertha said? What had she arranged? It all seemed so confused ... The walk home so far ... The sight of the gate so welcome.

The house was quiet ... quiet ... only Grimalkin to welcome her.

She remembered vaguely that Greta had gone to visit her sister-in-law, had said she would only be back with Harry. That had been this morning, or was it after lunch? She felt so strange, so muddled.

She would sit down for a while, then she would feel better.

There was a letter in the box, she took it out. Jean's writing. Would she be coming now, at last? Oh, dear there would be the room to prepare! But she couldn't prepare the room, could she, there were people in it—the children. Her children ... Her children? ... Oh, she was a foolish muddled old woman ... they weren't her children ... But Bertha wanted the room ... she couldn't have it if Jean came...

She tore open the letter, her hands shook as she took out the single sheet.

'I shall be coming to see you soon ...' She scanned the next few lines, Jean still didn't say when ... but what was this ...? 'Very concerned thoughts of you ... making enquiries about a home.' Home? Whose home? Oh, an old age home!

'... Surely it would be better to let the house altogether,

perhaps not as it stands, but unfurnished, you could always keep anything you especially value ...' But I value it all, it's my home!

Grimalkin rubbed against her ankles, hurt at being ignored. It was Grimalkin's home, too, no one even thought of that, no one!

Emmeline began to tremble violently, unable to stop. Things began to dance about strangely before her eyes, then to her horror the stairs began to fall towards her; with a roar the walls came crashing down, burying her, burying her in a deep dark hole.

Emmeline came to herself lying in her own room, but with the queer sensation that her bed was floating. Her fingers plucked nervously at the soft rug that covered her; she tried to lift her hand but the effort required to move it was too great; it was all she could do to open her eyes, the lids persistently wanted to close while she tried desperately to keep them open to reassure herself that she was indeed safe.

There was a faint light burning and her gaze moved slowly from one familiar object to another, the tapestry covered chair, the silver framed photographs on her dressing table, her brushes, the curtains only partially drawn disclosing the star-filled night.

Her eyelids drooped, opened again...

Someone was standing there in the shadows; a man looking down into the street, waiting and watching by the window.

Ernest! Ernest had come home! She strove to cry his name gladly though no more than a half formed whisper came but the man heard the slight sound and looked across to where she lay. Then she saw that it wasn't Ernest at all. The set of the broad shoulders, the dark, unruly hair, the face which became distinguishable as he moved

into the light, were all familiar but did not belong to
Ernest, yet she couldn't remember exactly who the man
was. He reached her bedside his face full of anxiety and
concern and gently took her wrist, a finger resting on her
pulse. She breathed a deep sigh and let her eyes close.
His hand was young, warm and strong, so strong that
she seemed to feel the strength flowing from it into her
very life stream. She no longer tried to remember what
had happened, she just lay still on her bed, relaxed,
comforted.

When she opened her eyes again the face before her
had changed, aged. Of course, this was the doctor! He was
talking quietly but it was an effort to listen to what he said,
too much for her to try and answer him. Then
suddenly the word 'hospital' penetrated her brain, starting
a jangle of fear that tore through her whole body and
focusing her confused thoughts on that one point of
memory. They were trying to make her go! They were
trying to steal her home from her and with the remaining
remnant of her strength she must resist!

Desperately she struggled to sit up.

'No! No! I won't go away ...' her cries of entreaty
were no more than a hoarse whisper.

Firm hands pressed her back against the pillows, a
soothing voice reassured her. Someone lifted her arm; she
caught a whiff of a pungent familiar odour, felt a sharp
jab, then peace and darkness closed over her.

Oblivion ...

All was still when she awoke. The room was in complete darkness. On the air lingered that remembered scent.
Antiseptic? Spirits? It was a smell associated with illness, hospitals. She still could not think clearly, but vaguely
she knew that someone was trying to steal her home ...
someone ... who?

Now they had tricked her! They had been waiting up

there and pushed the stairs down on her, then, while she lay unconscious, they had come and stolen everything away. Now she was in hospital and she would never see her home again. She gave a faint moan of despair.

There was a sudden movement at the foot of the bed. A shadow sprang upon it, a shadow motivated by a low droning. No, a purr! It was Grimalkin, kneading the blanket at the foot of the bed as she always did before she settled down to sleep!

Grimalkin! How had she got in? They would never allow a cat in hospital! If only there was somewhere to hide her.

Too late! Another shadow moved, someone lifted the cat from the bed saying in a whisper: 'Keep off there, you stupid animal, you'll wake her.'

It could not be a nurse's voice, it was a man's. A man in the room? Where was she? The question formed itself into a word, a word so faint it was hardly intelligible.

'Where?'

'Do you want anything?' The man's voice came again, familiar, reassuring. Would he help her?

'I don't want to go,' she pleaded in desperation. 'Where have they taken me?'

'It's all right. Nobody took you anywhere.'

He moved quietly, then soft light flooded the room from a shaded lamp. She saw with joy that she still lay in her own room. The young man stood beside her, smiling, Grimalkin tucked under his arm staring with narrow slitted eyes, indignant at not being allowed on the bed.

'See?'

She nodded, imperceptibly.

'Don't put off the light,' she begged, afraid that, with darkness, all that was familiar and safe would disappear.

'As you like...'

She relaxed. Her breathing steadied, shallow but even.

He recrossed the room and drew aside the curtain, watching for the day as does one for whom the night is too long; the cat was still under his arm. Presently he sat down on the chair with Grimalkin on his lap, idly caressing her fur. He must have been there all the time. She still couldn't remember who he was, she only knew that while he was there she felt safe. He wouldn't let anyone steal her home. She slept.

Gradually out of the confusion of light and darkness, voices and faces, fragments became clear, and the fragments fitted together, formed a pattern. There was a nurse who washed her with gentle competent hands, who made the bed; Greta, looking down at her anxiously, smiling in return to the faint smile Emmeline managed to give her; holding a glass to her lips, though it was not Greta's arm that was around her shoulders, lifting her, supporting her. It was a strong arm—the man's ... She murmured her thanks; the doctor, examining her, talking softly to someone outside the door afterwards.

How often the doctor came she did not know, she only knew it would be the doctor who would send her to the hospital and she must make him understand.

The next time he came she summoned all her strength to implore:

'Don't send me away! I must stay! If I go they will steal ...'

Ah! She was making some impression! His face was alert at once, attentive, although his hand on her arm bade her not to get excited.

'Steal? Who will steal?' His voice remained calm, but curious.

'I ... I can't remember ... They want to steal my house and send me away to a home ...' she sensed that it sounded ridiculous. 'Are the children here?'

'Children?' he still sounded puzzled.

'Greta?'

He smiled, the anxiety lifting from his brow.

'Oh, yes. They've done wonders for you.'

'That's all right, then.' Her voice was fading. 'They won't let anything happen.'

Later, through veils of sleep, she heard someone calling her name in an urgent whisper.

'Emmeline! Emmeline!'

She struggled upwards, through layers of unconsciousness. Woke.

It was Bertha. Emmeline stared for a moment at the face bent over the bed, close to her own. Bertha was trying desperately to hold her attention, to tell her something, but she did not want to be bothered and closed her eyes yet again, turning away her face, feigning sleep until the pretence became reality.

But she was not to be left in peace. Who was this now? Was she dreaming or was Jean really sitting beside her bed? Why hadn't Jean come before when she was alone and lonely? She had no need for her now, she only wanted to rest, to sleep.

Time passed.

Eventually her mind cleared, sorted dreams from reality, accepted the pattern of her days. Other visitors called; the vicar's wife who brought her a vase of delicate snowdrops which gave her infinite pleasure, and left some magazines which she still felt too tired to read although Greta, sitting by the window that afternoon, paged through them when she thought Emmeline was asleep.

... And Bertha came again, tense and anxious, hardly able to contain herself while she enquired how Emmeline was feeling and then bursting out:

'My dear, what are we to do? It happened just as I feared. When I heard you were found at the foot of the stairs I was terrified, but the doctor won't listen! He laughed at me and said those villains were looking after you marvellously—Of course they would! To cover up what had happened! They bungled things, didn't they? Your fall wasn't fatal! The doctor doesn't even think you fell down the stairs at all. No one will believe me! But can't you ... *won't* you remember? ...'

Emmeline felt cold and sick at the frightening words.

'Please!' she whispered, with a gesture of repulsion.

'You must try, it's terribly important!' Bertha insisted, and Emmeline turned grateful eyes to the door which opened to admit the nurse.

'I'm sorry,' she announced with a cheerful smile, 'but I must see to the patient now.' Then she noticed Emmeline's expression, her distress.

'Has she been bothering you?' she inquired when, reluctantly, Bertha had departed.

'No-o ...' Emmeline's reply was doubtful.

Days passed, Bertha did not come again.

She grew stronger and before long was able to sit up in bed, then was helped across to her chair where she could look down from her window to the street below and watch the outside world. Grimalkin on her lap was an unaccustomed weight.

She could remember now how she had returned home that afternoon ... she had been to visit Bertha who had been insisting on coming to live with her in order to force the children out of the house ... and the letter from Jean had been waiting, urging her to move to an old-age home.

That was it.

No one had been hiding, waiting to push the stairs on her. That was all a fantasy of her sick mind, just as Bertha's story that she had been pushed down the stairs was a fantasy ... part of Bertha's insistence that she turn the children out.

She looked down at the street which was growing obscure in the late afternoon drizzle. Harry would be coming home soon. When he came he would help her back into bed. She would be glad to go. She was tired now. Faint sounds from downstairs told her that Greta was busy preparing the evening meal.

Her thoughts drifted.

Why should Bertha insist that the children leave and weave such a fabric of lies all directed against them? She didn't want them to go. Whatever would she have done without them?

But of course, she was forgetting the baby! That was the reason! If only there was to be no baby! If only things could go on as they were! But the baby was the cause of it all, wasn't it? It was on account of the baby that they had come in the first place.

She could see Harry coming down the street, walking quickly through the increasing rain, head down, hands in pockets. She saw him turn at the gate...

Later she heard him coming up the stairs, smiled her greeting and answered his enquiries about her health and how she had passed her day, but instead of helping her back to bed as had become his custom, he sat on the foot of it, facing her, and she sensed the anxiety about him, saw it in his expression now that the fading light from the window fell on his face.

'You're really feeling better?'

'Much better,' she assured him.

'That's good, because there's something I've got to talk to you about, but I don't want to worry you if you don't feel up to it.'

Worry her? She didn't want to worry about anything, but already her heartbeats had quickened in alarm. She tried not to show any trace of fear as she asked: 'Talk to me? What about?' A tell-tale tremor crept into her voice.

He looked at her steadily, trying to decide how best to express himself. One consideration overruled all others and it came out in his first words.

'It's Greta,' he began. 'You know her time's getting pretty close...?'

Emmeline felt a cold shiver run over her.

'... It's not that she minds looking after you ... What little we've been able to do we've done gladly ... but she can't keep this up.'

Here it was! All along their leaving had been hanging over her and now they were going. For how long had she avoided the subject of their still being here because ... No! In her agitation she was getting muddled again! It was she who had been going to tell them to leave, they who had been the ones in fear of being told to go! Now the situation was completely reversed ... Was there no way she could persuade them to stay? A tear of sheer weakness dropped on to her gnarled hands and she lifted pleading eyes to his face but he was no longer looking at her. With blurred vision she saw him staring down at his hands, clasped tightly between his knees, he was frowning.

'It's the stairs, you see. I can't stop thinking about them stairs. I worry about her all day till I can hardly do my work.'

He glanced up suddenly, saw her expression and his tone softened.

'It's not my place to interfere, I know that. I've taken too much on myself already, but there isn't really anyone I can ask ... see? I haven't wanted you to be worried about nothing ... Your niece did come, but we were too anxious about getting you well then to really talk about anything else!'

'So Jean was here!' she exclaimed.

'Yeah, only for a day ... I sent for her ... See what I mean about taking things into my own hands? You were reading a letter when you took ill, I had a look at it, that's how I got her address. You had mentioned her to Greta a couple of times...'

'I see.'

'She's been very worried about you, she's phoned the doctor several times to see how you're getting on, but apparently she's a very busy person. She couldn't stay long, but she's coming back as soon as she can. She wanted you to go into a nursing home...'

Emmeline began to tremble, she hadn't diverted him for very long.

'... But the doc says you get so upset when there's any mention of moving you ... and we're managing O.K.'

'I don't know how I shall ever thank you.'

'Worked both ways, didn't it?' He cut her short. 'We was glad to have a chance to pay back a bit of your kindness ... only it's like this ...' He took a deep breath. 'The doc was talking to me earlier on, he's very pleased with you and sees no reason why you shouldn't be practically your old self again before long except that you'll have to take things a bit easy. He said he was going to talk to you when you felt better and suggest you move your bedroom downstairs ... to save you going up and down ... That set me thinking, if you was to agree to it ... might you do it now?'

'Now?'

He swallowed, amazed at his own temerity.

'You see, if you was to make the dining-room into your bedroom and shift that stuff up here—it's not like you use it much, is it?—then you'd have everything on one level, wouldn't you? You could sit in your parlour for a change of scene during the day ... and when you felt stronger and maybe wanted to do things a bit for yourself, the kitchen's there right on hand ... and there's that little cloakroom under the stairs ...' He tailed off and looked away from her again, embarrassed by the revelation of how he had already arranged things in his mind.

Slowly she accustomed herself to the idea.

'You mean you won't be going? You won't leave me?'

'Bless you, we'll stay just as long as you'll put up with us! But if you did think of moving round ... I wondered if you'd do it now and save Greta them stairs?'

'It's a wonderful suggestion.' Already she was accepting it, but with acceptance came the realization of all the difficulties involved. Her forehead creased in perplexity. She shrank from the thought of the upheaval involved. 'But however would I manage it?'

'All you've got to do is say you agree to it. I'll fix everything up for you. You won't need to worry about nothing, I promise.'

Already she could see a weight was lifting from his mind.

'Of course I agree. Even if the doctor hadn't suggested it for my sake, it would help Greta.'

'Fine!' Then a shadow crossed his face again. 'While we're at it, there's other things we should settle.'

'Other ...?' Her hand stopped its mechanical smoothing of Grimalkin's fur.

'I ... We've had to do things as we saw best ... till you're well anyway ...'

'Yes?' She waited for him to go on.

'Well, Greta's been using the kitchen to get things ready for you and that ... and we couldn't go out and leave you here on your own ...' He paused. 'We've been using the kitchen ourselves ... it seemed the best thing to do ... I'm paying the electricity, hoping that makes things square with you for the meantime.'

She smiled and saw his face clear.

'Of course it's all right!'

She thought then of other things ... how Greta had tempted her appetite with steamed sole and tender portions of chicken and of their straitened circumstances.

'But how have you managed? My food and ... I just haven't given anything a thought.'

'Don't worry about that now. Remember we haven't been paying you any rent the last couple of weeks either. It pans out pretty even, but I kept a note of things so you can see we haven't cheated you.'

'Cheated me? Oh, my dear!'

He grinned, getting up.

'O.K. Business session over! You want to get back to bed now?'

For him the matter appeared to be settled and he only mentioned it once again in the next few days when he asked if she had any objection to the move taking place on a Sunday.

'You see, I can get help all right,' he explained. 'My brother and my brother-in-law will give me a hand—I reckon it'll take the three of us—but one works on a Saturday morning and the other wouldn't give up his football on any account ... We could try it at night I suppose...'

'I don't mind about a Sunday,' she assured him. 'Arrange things to suit yourself.'

By now she was very pleased with his suggestion for, since he spoke of it, she noticed what she had been too self-engrossed to register before—that, although always cheerful, Greta looked very tired and drawn and her movements had become slow and clumsy with fatigue.

'How selfish I have been!' she thought, and from then on made as few demands on the girl as possible and was always relieved to hear Harry come home in the evening and to know that he would take over.

When Saturday came Greta spent most of the day sitting with Emmeline, keeping her company. Once she heard Harry talking to someone downstairs and wondered if his brother had come and they were making preparations. They did not volunteer any information and she did not ask questions.

As she settled down to sleep that night she wondered if she should let them have this room, which was bigger than the one they occupied, but the thought slipped from her mind as drowsiness overtook her.

During the week she had continued to gain strength and now she felt ready to venture downstairs once more —excited, even, by the prospect.

How long had she been confined to her room? She had lost count of the days.

When the time came the children were not prepared to allow her to tackle the hazard of the stairs. Harry lifted her as effortlessly as if she were a child and carried her down. She felt shy and awkward as he held her against his broad chest. It was thus he must have carried her, unconscious, to her room the day she had been taken ill.

But her embarrassment was forgotten as they descended the stairs. Everywhere was so familiar yet looked so strange. She caught a glimpse of the vase of honesty still there on the table, the little brass bell, shaped like a Dutch girl with spread skirts, standing beside it. Here, welcoming her, was her beloved parlour. He set her gently down in her chair before the bright fire. It was all just the same!

She gave a sigh of contentment then turned to the young couple who stood watching her with obvious pleasure.

'Thank you, my dears, thank you.'

Then Grimalkin came sedately through the door, causing a welcome distraction just as her eyes were flooding with more of those ridiculous tears. The cat stared at the trio, disdainful of their emotion, then seated herself on the hearth rug and began to wash herself, obviously of the opinion that it was high time things returned to normal!

'I'd best be making a start.' The boy stated simply, reminding them all that this was more than just a symbol of returning health for Emmeline.

Greta smiled at him as he left the room then turned again to the old lady, easing a cushion into a more comfortable position at her back and pulling the magazines that lay on the small table to within easy reach.

'Would you like to be left on your own to enjoy it all, or would you prefer me to stay and keep you company for a while?'

'Oh, do stay and talk to me, dear,' Emmeline replied. 'There's such a lovely fire to share.'

'All right.' The girl sank into the chair opposite. 'I expect the room is glad to be in use again, don't you?' Then she smiled at her own fanciful nonsense although Emmeline felt inclined to agree with her.

'I'm sure it is.'

'You've got such pretty things.' Greta went on. 'I've quite fallen in love with that little china shepherdess...'

'She was one of a pair,' Emmeline told her. 'But a housemaid that we once employed, broke the shepherd, dusting it. She was very upset about it I remember, but it couldn't be helped.'

'The little shepherdess must have been upset, too,' the girl remarked looking up at the dainty porcelain figure.

Emmeline smiled to herself.

'That's just what I thought when it happened.'

Greta's small, pale face grew serious. 'You needn't worry,

Harry'll be ever so careful moving your stuff.'

'I'm sure he will.'

Already they could hear him in the next room, it sounded as if he was putting the chairs out of the way. Emmeline would have liked to ask him to change the carpet over, too, the one in the dining-room was very dark and might make her room look dismal, but she did not like to, he had enough to do. However was he going to manage? She pictured her solid, heavy furniture and was assailed by doubts. Rigidly she disciplined her thoughts. Her worrying and wondering what was going on would not help matters, she must just accept the change and be grateful that it was being made for her.

The peace of the room was suddenly shattered by the roar of a powerful motorbike turning the corner of the street. Greta glanced at the clock, then towards the window, as the machine gave a final throaty roar and stopped outside.

'That must be Reg,' she said, getting slowly to her feet. 'I'll go and let him in.'

Harry was before her; as Greta went through the door he was already letting his brother into the house.

Emmeline felt a flutter of nervousness as she heard strange men's voices directly outside her door.

'Cor, Harry! You never let on you lived in a place like this! Regular museum, i'n't it, Max?'

A grunt from the other man coincided with Greta's 'Hello!' while Harry shushed them. 'She'll hear you!'

'For goodness sake don't tell me you have to talk in whispers or go around on tip-toe!' The lowered tone was somehow as penetrating as his boisterous greeting.

'She's been sick, remember.'

'Well, let's get on with it, we haven't got all day. Show us what you want done, boy,' the other man cut in.

'You keep out of the way, girl,' Harry spoke again,

more kindly, 'there's nothing you can do, leastways, not yet.'

Greta came back into the room, her shy smile more nervous. Emmeline smiled back at her, equally tremulous.

'Harry's worked out the best order to do things.' Was she comforting herself or Emmeline? 'They'll manage all right.'

'There is a way to get the top off the table,' Emmeline recalled, anxious to be of help.

'Yes, I know. It's got brackets and screws underneath,' Greta replied. 'He undid them yesterday.' Then she took a deep breath to steady herself, picked up a magazine and began to flip through the pages, not really seeing them.

Emmeline did the same but, like the girl, she had no thoughts for the book in her hand, they were all concentrated on what was happening in the rest of the house; no magazine articles could distract her attention from the heavy steps on the stairs, the unfamiliar tread overhead, the deep voices. Instead she found herself trying to distinguish sounds; some—the ring of a hammer on metal as the bed was dismantled and the slump of a carpet being moved, rolled (Good! They were going to change that, too)—were easy, but others proved far more difficult. Once their attention was sharply drawn as someone exclaimed, 'For God's sake, Harry, you'll break your back!' and Greta started up, then sank back into her chair, biting her lip, her hand unwittingly crumpling the magazine, her knuckles white. Her wide grey eyes met Emmeline's, they listened to slow heavy steps on the stairs, then at last coming down the passage and they could breathe more easily.

It seemed an age before the door opened, admitting Harry. Greta was on her feet at once. The day was cold and the women had been glad of the fire but he stood there with his sleeves rolled back from his strong young arms, his shirt unfastened. They could see the sheen of sweat on his chest and face and, at his neck and temples, strands of black hair clung in damp tendrils. Dealing with the solid, old-fashioned furniture was a formidable task.

'How's it going?'

'Fine up till now, but we've struck a snag. I thought we'd be able to make a clean swop,' he turned to Emmeline ruefully. 'Now I'm not so sure. We're having trouble with the sideboard. We took all the stuff out of it yesterday, but I guess I was a bit too optimistic. Even if we can get it up the stairs I doubt we'll be able to make the turn at the top.'

'Then please don't try.'

He was disappointed. 'We had quite a game with the wardrobe, but I reckoned somebody got it up there so we must be able to get it down ... but nobody ever did try to get that sideboard upstairs...'

'It can easily stay,' Emmeline assured him.

'I wanted to have things just the same.'

Emmeline quickly summoned a mental picture of her room.

'You could leave the chest of drawers up there. I can put the table cloths from the sideboard into it and use the sideboard drawers for storing the things from the chest. That would do very nicely.'

'You're sure?' He still sounded uncertain.

'Of course.'

Greta's eyes on him were full of anxiety, not caring for the fate of the chest of drawers but only about him.

'Give it a break, Harry,' she begged. 'Let me make you all some tea.'

'That's a good idea.' He grinned across at her, reassuring. 'C'mon I'll give you a hand.'

'I'll bring you some, too,' she promised, as they left

Emmeline quite alone, for Grimalkin slipped out in their wake to discover just what had been going on.

The door did not catch properly and came open again standing ajar, but she was not in a draught and she did not bother to get up and close it. She leaned back in her chair, eyes closed. She heard them tell the other two about the tea and their reply that they would take the chairs up and then come to the kitchen.

Minutes later the men came back down the stairs and re-entered the dining-room. They must have been standing just inside the door, only a few steps away for Emmeline clearly heard the rasp of a match being struck then caught a whiff of tobacco smoke.

'Well, were getting on.'

'Yeah. Though why Harry puts hisself to such trouble I can't understand. He should've got the old girl taken to a horspital if there wasn't no one to look after her.'

'That might have meant the house being shut up, then he'd have had to get out, wouldn't he? Where would they go? It was the lesser of two evils I suppose.'

Emmeline wished she hadn't overheard. The children had made it seem as if looking after her was a pleasure, had it after all been just a necessity? She started to rise to close the door before she heard any more but the man's next words stopped her.

'Funny thing is ... they don't seem to mind. Harry says she's a nice old bird and they've got proper fond of her.'

'Huh! He's a fool! When I think of the noose he's tied round his neck, I fair shudder,' the other man replied. 'I tell you if I'd got a girl in trouble when I was the age my young brother is she wouldn't have seen me for dust—not now, neither, come to that!' He gave a short, mirthless laugh.

'Come off it, Reg, he wouldn't walk out on her and you

know it. Real nuts about her, he is, you can see it a mile off ... even now, with all the mess she's got him into!'

'You're right there ... beats me how he ever persuaded her, though—no honest! ... Proper good little girl she was ... Wasn't allowed to go here or there ... had to be home by such and such a time ... and Harry put up with it! I can remember one night he took her to a disco and they missed the last bus ... had to walk back so he didn't get her home till near one o'clock. Her old man was so mad he wouldn't let Harry near her for a whole month. Blimey! I can see me putting up with that—I don't think! I'd've soon found another girl! But Harry, he put up with all her old man's nonsense—just to keep her! Funny though,' he began to chuckle, 'there was something he forgot to tell them not to do, wasn't there? Forgot to forbid them the one thing that really mattered!'

Emmeline gasped at the coarseness of his joke.

The other man was laughing.

'Think it would have made any difference?'

'Gawd knows! But I could have told Harry to pick a girl what knew a thing or two if he was going to play that game. Look where it got him! I don't even understand what he sees in her. Mind you, they say those quiet little things can be hot stuff—wouldn't know meself.'

'Well she ain't such a little thing now, is she? Big as a house, poor kid ... Come on, let's go and see what they've done about the tea.'

'I could do with it.'

Their footsteps receded, their voices grew faint.

Emmeline sat still in the chair, her head resting against the high back, her eyes closed. It was only with difficulty that she opened them later when Greta returned, bringing her tea. She felt shaken and upset, not only by the upheaval of the move but also by the fact that the love between the young people, which she regarded as a precious thing, had been so besmirched by the words she had overheard.

Greta was as considerate as ever.

'You look tired,' she said sympathetically. 'This has all been too much for you. But don't worry, they've nearly finished, not much longer.'

It was, however, a long time before the job was finally pronounced complete. Even after the two men had left—without meeting Emmeline, for which she was glad as she had no desire to have a face to attach to the voice she had heard, and, in addition, she was shy of strangers—Harry had called on Greta to help him with the finishing touches. Emmeline was not permitted to see the result until everything had been done.

Then, at long last, she was summoned. With slow steps she went with them, her hand on Harry's arm, and stopped in the doorway of the room that had formerly been her dining-room.

Dining-room? Surely this had never been the dining-room!

Alone she took two wondering steps forward, hardly able to believe what she saw, then turned in amazement to where they stood behind her, he with his arm around his young wife's waist—or where her waist had been—grinning his delight, yet trying to hide the pride and pleasure that shone from his dark eyes.

'O.K.?'

'I ... I just can't believe it! It's incredible!'

However had they transformed the dark and dignified room into such a perfect replica of her bedroom? The positioning of the furniture was the same, the place of the chest of drawers being taken by the sideboard, they had brought down the carpet and changed the curtains over, but that could not have made such a difference, surely?

Suddenly she realized what it was! The room had been re-papered! That was what made such a difference! The paper wasn't exactly the same as in her bedroom but it was very similar in design with a delicate trelliswork of flowers in pink, blue and lilac against an ivory background—the very tones that once the paper upstairs had been, though now those colours had faded to muted shades of their former beauty.

'Oh, my dears. I don't know what to say!'

And she started to cry, but no one could call her a silly old woman for that!

'So long as you think it's all right.' His voice was taking on that edge of brusqueness again, his arm slipping from the girl as he turned away. 'I'll bring those drawers down, then you can swop the stuff around and arrange it as you like. I'll take them up again when you've finished!'

Later, when she had had her supper and got into bed, she lay listening to their faint chatter from the kitchen as they washed up and, looking about her, was deeply grateful. Such care, such thoughtfulness did not spring from necessity, even necessity motivated by the fear of being turned out!

'Harry says she's a nice old bird! They've got proper fond of her!'

The remembered words brought a smile to Emmeline's lips. What would Mamma think to know her daughter was happy at being called 'a nice old bird'!

They came in to say Good night and to see that she was comfortable, lingering awhile as they often did, sensing that she was glad of some company.

Who, she thought, could have two nicer children?

'Greta, my dear,' she said. 'Please look in the top drawer, the left one ... that's right. There's a carved wooden box, can you see it?'

The light shone on the girl's bent head, giving her hair a silken sheen.

'This it?'

'That's right. Will you give it to me?'

She took the box, opening with the ease of familiarity the concealed catch, her fingers searching amongst the old-fashioned treasures inside.

'There's something here I want you to have...'

She found the ring, a half hoop of sapphires that had been her mother's and which she had never been able to bring herself to wear, and picked it out. The girl only wore her plain gold wedding band and Emmeline expected the gift to give her pleasure, but, as she held it out, Greta seemed to shrink back.

'Oh, no!'

She turned to the boy, intending to appeal to him to make his wife accept the gift and, startled, encountered the hard expression on his face. They were both stock still, as if in horror, then he moved towards her, taking the ring, not ungently, from her and replacing it in the box, closed it with a snap.

'We don't want nothing from you.' An edge of anger sharpened his voice.

'Don't misunderstand me.' Had she wounded their pride? 'I want Greta to have it. It's not payment for all you've done.'

He shook his head.

'No.' He was taking the box from her hands, putting it back in the drawer. She caught a glimpse of his face reflected in the mirror, stubborn, his mouth set in that firm line of determination.

'I've made you angry.' She spoke with regret.

'I know people.' He answered her. 'I don't want nobody saying we got what we could out of you. Besides ... anything we may have done for you we've done because we wanted to, see?'

'And I only wanted Greta to have it to remember me by.'

'Remember you?' His voice softened, incredulity wiping out the anger. 'Whatever makes you think we'd need something to remember you by? You don't imagine we'd ever forget you, or what you've done for us?'

He put his hands on the footboard of the bed, leaning on them, looking down at her.

'You know we was in a right fix that night we came here first. When you opened the door I got the funniest feeling that things were going to be all right. Know what I thought to myself?—The light was behind you, see, and it gave you a sort of halo, like you see in pictures—and I says to myself, "Strewth, we've found an angel ... an angel right here in Abbey Road!" ... I wasn't so far wrong, was I?'

The following day Bertha came. Emmeline opened the door to her herself and was greeted by her friend with exaggerated relief.

'At last!' she breathed, catching hold of both Emmeline's hands. 'I'm so relieved to find you downstairs again. I'm certain if that girl had answered the door I would never have got in.'

'Oh, really!' Emmeline tried to keep the exasperation from her voice.

'It's true!' She looked furtively round. 'Whenever I've called lately you've been asleep—so *she* said! No matter what time of day! I told her it was funny for a person to do *so* much sleeping. "She needs the rest!" she replied, calm as you like. I had my doubts whether you'd ever get better ... Under the circumstances ...' she added, darkly.

Had Greta seen that Bertha's visits were upsetting and

deliberately kept her out, Emmeline wondered.

'I'll soon be my old self again,' she pronounced. 'The doctor's very pleased with me.'

'That man!' Bertha sniffed in disgust.

'He did suggest, however, that I move my bedroom to the ground floor, it was an excellent idea, it's so nice to be able to get around. Would you like to see it before we sit down?'

'Downstairs? You've moved downstairs?'

'Yes. It's so convenient I wonder I didn't think of it before.'

Bertha peered over her friend's shoulder as Emmeline opened the door, the first thing that caught her eye was the sideboard.

'Ah!' she breathed. 'I'm glad you kept that where you can see it.'

'It fits in quite well, don't you think?'

'This was the doctor's suggestion you say?' Bertha gave her a peculiar look as she examined the room. 'And you've let *them* take over upstairs?'

Emmeline turned away, ignoring the question and led the way to the parlour. Grimalkin looked up as they entered and yawned as if expressing contempt of the visitor. Bertha's eyes darted round eagerly as though expecting to find things missing.

'What I want to know is what has happened to the dining-room furniture,' she demanded. 'Did *they* sell it for you ... and what sort of price did they tell you they got?'

'Sell it ...?' Now that, she thought, might have been a sensible idea. 'No, it wasn't sold. They took it upstairs—changed the rooms around.'

'You say you don't go upstairs any more?' Triumph was spreading over the other woman's face.

'No, I don't.'

'Then how do you know...?'

'Know?' She didn't follow.

'That it's upstairs.'

'I heard them take it there.'

'And *saw* them? Have you seen it there?' Bertha persisted, with growing excitement.

'No ...' Emmeline admitted. But, really, this was quite ridiculous. Couldn't Bertha see that she was being ridiculous?

'If you thought it was there and they had sold it, they could keep all the money, couldn't they?'

'That's nonsense! I was here when they moved it.'

'Did you watch?' Sharply.

'No.'

'Then where were you?'

'Here.'

In a moment she would stop being amused and become annoyed.

'So you didn't actually see what went on?'

'Well, I wasn't going to stand and watch! There was a nice fire and Greta and I sat...'

'So she stayed with you? Made sure you didn't go to see what was happening?' Bertha cut in. 'How could you tell what was going where? Does moving one piece of furniture sound so different from another?'

Poor Bertha! One should feel sorry for her. To think her innuendoes had once made Emmeline feel afraid.

'I'm quite sure it's all safely there.'

'And I'm equally determined to find out!'

'Then go ahead.'

'I will!'

Bertha rose, a quivering mass of indignation, but not more than a couple of minutes had elapsed before she returned, her indignation turned to fury.

'*Now* will you believe me?'

Emmeline's heart gave a painful skip.

'You mean it's not there?'

'*Not there?* That's what I'd like to know!'

'Whatever do you mean?'

'Well, I'd scarcely got my foot on the stairs when she appeared, positively barring the way! "What d'you want up here?" she asks, cold as you like. How could I say, "I want to see what you've done with Emmeline's furniture," and put her on her guard? They're too clever by half ... even got your doctor standing up for them! ... We have to catch them at it ...' (Emmeline stifled her desire to ask 'at what?'!) '... so I said I was going to fet a copy of the church magazine that you had left upstairs, but she wouldn't let me past, oh no! "It's not upstairs," she says, "I know where she left it, I'll get it for you." But would she move? Oh, dear me, no! Stood right where she was until I came back down. I'd like to know just what they're up to—taken over the whole of the upper floor by now, no doubt—just like they have your kitchen —Oh, yes, (she would not let Emmeline interrupt) I'm not blind to what's been going on there! But what's happened to your dining-room suite, that's what I want to know.'

Bertha had grown red in the face and seemed to be actually swelling with self-righteous indignation. Emmeline was quite anxious about her, but not anxious about the suggestions she was making—had she ever let such ideas upset her? She wondered why, for clearly they were nonsensical.

At that moment the door opened and Greta came in. She had a thin booklet in her hand which she put down on the table beside Emmeline.

'There's your magazine,' she said, while giving Bertha such a look of cold hatred that it surprised Emmeline who was so used to the girl's expression being gentle and kind. Bertha glared back at her making no effort to disguise the venom of her feelings.

Emmeline woke in the night and lay listening; she was accustomed to waking occasionally during the long dark hours but she sensed that tonight something unusual had awakened her.

There was not a sound, nothing stirred, yet she felt certain something was amiss, then she noticed the long strip of light showing faintly beneath her door. Harry would not have come in so late! She got slowly from her bed, sitting for a moment on the edge of it as she had been advised by the doctor. Grimalkin's eyes gleamed at her from the depths of the chair across the room, two luminous points of fire. Emmeline reached for her warm gown and pushed her feet into her slippers, then crossed the room and opened the door.

The hall light shone brightly as did the one on the upstairs landing. She glanced at the front door and saw that the bolt was drawn, then moved towards the stairs. From here she could see that the door of the children's room stood open; a light was burning there, too. Just then Greta appeared, she was fully dressed, even to her navy coat which strained across her figure despite the fact that she had moved the buttons; her face was white and drawn. Emmeline knew immediately.

'My dear!' She began to mount the stairs towards the girl who replied at once:

'Don't come up. I'll come down to you.'

'Is it?' There was no need to complete the question, Greta nodded as she slowly descended the stairs.

'The baby's coming. Harry's gone to phone for a taxi. I hope he won't be long.' Her voice started to rise and was pulled quickly back under control.

'Come and sit down.' Emmeline put an arm around the

girl and drew her towards the parlour. 'Are you cold?'
She could feel her shivering.

'No.' In a tight voice, the shiver was fear then.

Emmeline led her to the chair. The fire had gone out
save for one tiny spark like a lone red window in a deserted
grey street, but some warmth still lingered in the room.

'Can I get you anything?'

Again, 'No,' The girl twisted her face into a semblance
of a smile as she sat on the edge of the chair, her hands
gripped tightly together. After a moment she got up again
and moved restlessly across the room, unable to keep still.
She was by the window when a spasm of pain caught
her and she closed her eyes tightly, the hand that had
been raised to draw back the curtain clenched over the
cloth.

Emmeline, helpless, watched with mingled fear and
compassion. She joined the girl looking out into the dark
empty street then, putting a hand on her arm, said kindly:
'Come and sit down again. He'll be back soon.'

The girl nodded and allowed herself to be drawn once
more towards the chair. Emmeline sat with her, her ears
too straining for the sound of footsteps.

Ten minutes dragged by. The clock struck, emphasizing
the fact.

'I wonder why he's so long.' The girl's voice was sharp
and strained.

Emmeline, thinking of the phone box on the corner,
was wondering too. Her eyes turned yet again from the
clock to the girl's face. She knew so little. How quickly
did first babies come? What if...?

They hears his steps simultaneously, ringing on the
pavement. He was running.

Two pairs of eyes turned to him in relief as he came
through the doorway. He expressed no surprise at seeing
Emmeline up and keeping Greta company, only poured

out in breathless explanation that the darned phones never worked when you needed them most and that it was lucky he had checked where the next nearest one was. By now he had joined Greta, putting his arm across her shoulders, his blunt fingers stroking her hair as he sat on the arm of her chair.

'All right, love?'

She nodded, unable to speak, but she put up a hand to hold his tightly and after a minute seemed to relax.

'The taxi will be here soon.' Only then he acknowledged Emmeline's presence. 'I'm sorry we woke you.'

'It's nothing.'

Greta was leaning her head against his shoulder now, her eyes closed. She said: 'My case, Harry.'

'I'll get it.'

'I put it on the bed.'

He fetched the case, putting it down by the door, then, returning to the parlour, he glanced across at Greta before going to the window. Almost at once, he turned back to the room, letting the curtain fall into place.

'It's here.'

The car had drawn to a stop by the gate noiselessly but now they heard the driver slam the door. Greta got to her feet and her husband's arm was round her.

'You'll be all right girl.'

She nodded, said a husky good-bye to Emmeline and they kissed.

'Good luck, my dear.'

Harry turned back to tell her to get to bed—'It's still some time till morning.'

Emmeline stood at the window. She saw him help Greta into the car and then they were gone and the night seemed strangely empty.

Get back to bed? Emmeline did not feel she could sleep. Nor could she follow the girl in her mind, so ignorant was she of such matters. In her young days a midwife would have come to the house, setting every one abustle, and in due time the prospective father would cease his pacing to wait anxiously outside a door from which came a thin wailing, then the birth of a son or daughter would have been announced. But the procedure at a maternity home was completely unknown to her.

She went to the kitchen and put a small pan of milk on the stove. While she waited for it to warm, she felt Grimalkin rub against her legs bewildered by this nocturnal activity. She gave the cat some milk then carried her own glass back to her room, but the first fringes of dawn were creeping round the curtains before sleep claimed her.

She slept for an hour or two and woke wondering what had happened to Greta and how soon she would know. The door bell rang as she was getting up. Harry must have forgotten his key, but when Emmeline opened the door she discovered instead the trim figure of the district nurse.

'Surprised to see me?' she began.

'I am rather,' Emmeline admitted, ushering her in. The nurse only called twice a week now to check how her patient was getting on.

'Your nice young man phoned me,' came the laughing reply. 'What do you think of that?'

'Harry?' Emmeline was surprised.

'Yes, he was rather anxious about you being on your own and asked if I could pop in to see you.'

'He went with Greta ... the baby...'

'Yes, I know.'

'Then you will have heard?' Emmeline asked, eagerly.

'Not yet,' the nurse shook her head.

'Not yet? But they left hours ago!'

'First babies don't arrive all that quickly.' She spoke from experience. 'You'll hear soon enough, I expect. They must think a lot of you to remember you at a time like that, don't you think?'

'Yes,' Emmeline felt a warm glow of pleasure.

'Now, how are things with you?'

The nurse checked up on Emmeline's health, helped to make her bed and chatted for a few moments with her before leaving, then Emmeline pottered about her kitchen, making everything tidy and at last sat down to rest. She must obey instructions and go slowly—it would never do for her to become ill again now! How kind everyone was, she thought. The nurse had told her that for the next few days her midday meal would be brought to her. Emmeline remembered there was such an organization during the war—'Meals on Wheels' wasn't it?—but she had had no idea the scheme was still in operation.

All morning her thoughts returned to Greta, impatient for news. She had a long wait before Harry finally came, looking so unlike Emmeline's imagined picture of a jubilant young father that at first she feared something had gone wrong, but his face split into a grin when he saw her.

'A girl,' he answered the question in her eyes.

'Oh, how lovely!' She felt a thrill of happy excitement. 'And they're both well?'

'Fine.' Some emotion pulled at his mouth that she didn't understand. Had he hoped for a son? ... But a little daughter! How delightful!

'Is she a pretty baby?'

He grinned again.

'She looks like a funny little screwed up pink monkey,' then, with his eyes still crinkled, 'but don't you dare tell Greta I said so—she reckons she's pretty ... she's got cute little hands ...' Then he turned abruptly away. 'Did you start the fire?'

'I only raked the grate and relit it on top of the clinkers I'm afraid!'

'I should hope so. I'll fix it for you.' He straight away set about the task as if feeling the need to busy himself.

Emmeline failed to understand him. She wanted to know more about the baby—its weight and when it had arrived—she supposed men didn't concern themselves with such things.

'Would you like some tea?' She hid her disappointment.

'I would, but don't you worry, I'll get it. I'll put the kettle on while I'm getting the coal.'

'The district nurse called.' She needed to talk, yet strangely it seemed the subject of the baby was to be avoided though she couldn't understand why.

'That's good.'

'It was kind of you to phone her.'

He merely nodded acknowledgement then picked up the coal bucket. He baffled her, truly he did! But she left him alone. He brought in a fresh bucket of coal and shortly after returned with a tray of tea. Emmeline poured for the two of them, it was hot and strong.

He took the cup from her, still strangely withdrawn and sat down on the chair opposite hers—the chair that Greta usually took.

'Have you had anything to eat?'

He shook his head. 'I'm not hungry.' Then sank once more into his reverie. When he had finished his tea he put the cup down beside him on the floor and at last began to talk, quietly, almost to himself, not looking at Emmeline, but into the fire.

'Have you ever seen a miracle? ... I just did, it leaves you kinda shaken up ... I guess you never saw a baby born, did you?' Still he did not look at her, nor, though he paused, wait for her response. 'I can't honestly say I wanted to. But she was scared and she wanted me to stay with her. They said I might. It was the least I could do, I don't like her being frightened ... I guess it did help her a bit—I hope so.'

'She must be glad it's over,' Emmeline spoke softly.

'So'm I, believe me,' he flashed her a look from those dark eyes. 'Funny, afterwards, she forgot how much it hurt, she was so happy ... and thrilled about the baby ...' he shook his head slowly in wonder. 'Life's funny altogether, isn't it?'

Looking at him sitting there, staring broodingly at the fire, with his workworn hands clasped loosely between his knees, his eyes shadowed from lack of sleep and his unshaven jaw giving him an almost piratical air, Emmeline remembered how once she had been so afraid of him and was inclined to agree with his remark. It was strange that now she was completely alone in the house with him, she found she had ceased to be afraid of him altogether. Between them at that moment stretched an intangible bond of companionship. He felt the need to talk and she was quite prepared to listen.

'She's such a kid to have to go through all that. I couldn't have not stayed with her, I couldn't let her down, never.'

'You're very close, aren't you?'

He nodded, smiling. 'You know I had my eye on her when she was still at school, not that she noticed me. She was dead keen on another chap what was too good-looking by half. Proper fancied himself, he did and she was walking on air when he asked her out. It didn't last long, mind you, he just dropped her. No reason, nothing ... and I knew darned well when she agreed to come out with me it was just to spite him, pretending she didn't care. It was a couple of months before he even looked at her again, then he decided to make a come-back—only, luckily for me, she woke up. She suddenly found that it was better to love someone that loved you back than someone who only loved himself ... He wouldn't have been any good for her anyway ...' He fell silent, again, staring into the heart of the flames, and Emmeline kept very still, not wanting to disturb his thoughts.

Eventually he went on:

'Her family didn't reckon I was good enough for her, neither, and I suppose now they feel justified ... it might have turned out very different. Not that I'm sorry.

'We knew we'd got a long wait ahead, but we didn't see any future without each other and I never meant to wrong her ... only, that day ... I don't know ... it goes like that sometimes ... one thing on top of another ... First the foreman gave me hell for not doing something he knew darned well he never told me to do but he had to find someone to take the blame ... I got home and the old man had it in for me more than usual ... then my old lady's iron bust, just when she had a stack of stuff to do and it was me she asked to fix it ... silly little things really, yet put all together ... By the time I got the iron working I knew I was going to be late to Tech. and that would be more trouble so I decided not to go at all. I only wanted one thing to put me on balance again and that was to see Greta so I thought I'd go round to her place instead. Then I remembered she'd promised to baby-sit for some people she knew. They'd never have approved of my going there, but I didn't even care. I just wanted to see her for a bit; talk to her; hold her, maybe ... you never know the way things are going to turn out ... so today she bore my child.'

Emmeline didn't know what to say. He solved her problem by suddenly asking a question.

'D'you suppose I ought to tell them ... her parents, I mean? ... That the baby's come?'

'You know the answer to that, don't you, or you wouldn't have asked,' she replied wisely.

He met her eyes with a long steady look.

'I suppose so. Greta won't do it. But I couldn't bring myself to talk to them, I'll have to write. I don't want them to have any place in our life, or in the baby's either ... but I suppose...'

'You should give them the chance to make it up and now is surely the best time?'

Yeah ...' He didn't seem very happy at the prospect and Emmeline changed the subject.

'Your family were excited, I expect?' she ventured.

He grinned.

'I guess they will be ... my little sister especially, she was hoping Sally would have a girl but she got a son... My Ma too, it's her first granddaughter.'

'Then you've not told them, yet?' She was surprised.

'Not yet. I should have gone round there first, but I just wanted to come home.'

Home! Here to her house? Was that how he felt about it? Home!

'I should be getting myself cleaned up and off to work, not sitting here, talking a lot of nonsense.'

He picked up their cups and got to his feet, then turned back to her, grinning.

'Greta'll murder me! I nearly forgot the one thing she said I was to be sure and ask you ... We want to name the baby Emma—for you—would you mind?'

The afternoon following the baby's birth there came a ring at the door, then Emmeline heard a key in the lock and a voice calling to her:

'May I come in?'

She had, by this time, risen from her chair and saw that the visitor was her next door neighbour, whose name she did not even know although they always greeted one another when they met and occasionally exchanged a word about the weather. She was a tall, thin woman with a kindly, angular face and greying hair.

'I feel so ashamed not coming before, Miss Rodgers,' she began, 'with you having been ill and all—but then, one hardly wants to entertain strangers when one is not well, does one?—and we are practically strangers, aren't we, in spite of being neighbours for several years?'

'Hardly strangers!' Emmeline protested, mildly. 'Won't you come in?' she was wondering how the woman had come by a key.

'We were so sorry to hear of your illness,' her neighbour said, following her into the parlour. 'I've kept asking after you.'

'I'm much better now. Please sit down.'

'Thank you ... I'm very glad to hear it.' The woman seated herself as she continued: 'But Mr Stokes is still worried about you, you know.'

So this was Harry's doing! It would appear he had become better acquainted with her neighbour in this short time than Emmeline had in all these years.

'... We didn't realize that you had anyone living here with you. We'd seen them come and go occasionally, of course, and wondered. It's funny how one speculates about neighbours, isn't it?'

Emmeline never did, but said nothing, only smiled.

'Even though we hadn't seen you around for some time it didn't occur to me that you might be ill until he came to tell us ...' she chatted on amicably, quite at home. 'How young they get married these days! Or is it our getting older that makes them seem so? She still looks no more than a child...'

'They are young.' Emmeline agreed, it was all the encouragement her neighbour needed to continue her discourse.

'He told me he was worried because her time was getting close and—with you being ill—she was virtually alone in the house. He wanted her to come and see me, to get acquainted—we'd never got any further than nodding a greeting, you know, just like you and I!—and then she would have someone to turn to if necessary, but she'd never been.

'Apparently she said that she couldn't leave you, but he reckoned it was really because she was too shy, otherwise she could have slipped away when the nurse was here. Anyway, he'd made her promise to come to me if things started happening but he thought it would be better if he had a word with me, himself. He says he's out at night quite a bit, working—he didn't say what he does ...' she paused, expectantly, but Emmeline did not fill in the information, it was for Harry to tell them what he did if he chose, so the woman went on: 'He wrote down some telephone numbers, where I could reach him at different times, and asked if I'd mind, because he didn't like to think of her having to go down to the phone herself then ... As if I'd mind! ... He said if he could tell her I was happy to do it then she wouldn't feel she was causing me any trouble if she had to come ... They've got different ways of looking at things apparently ... she didn't want to feel she'd be a nuisance while he reckoned that at times you have to ask other people's help—just as he'd expect anyone to ask his if they needed it.'

She paused in her lengthy dissertation, long enough for Emmeline to murmur, 'Quite so,' before gathering herself to continue.

'Well, she didn't need me after all did she, he popped in last night to tell us the baby had come ... Bless it!' Her face softened, 'So that's all right. But he said he had another favour to ask, and no "if's" about it this time! Even though you're so much better—and we're all glad about *that*!—he doesn't like you being left on your own, especially at night. He says he gets in very late at the weekends, so he wondered if I would look in to see that you were all right.'

'That's very kind of you.' Emmeline could sense the genuine benevolence of this woman despite her garrulity.

'He left me his wife's key so I could just ring and let myself in. That way I wouldn't disturb you and you'd know it was me, in case you're scared of opening the door at night—and if you are I can't blame you— but I thought it would be better if I called first during the day, that's why I came round now. You're on your own all day, too.'

To say she was used to it sounded ungracious and, in fact, she wasn't quite so used to it any more, she was becoming accustomed to Greta being there and already she missed her.

'But I'm practically well now,' she replied quietly. 'And the nurse calls in each day to see that I'm all right.'

'Well, that's nice, but if there's anything I can do ... shopping perhaps?'

'You're very kind. Harry's been doing my shopping for me ... but if I should forget to ask him for something I need ... thank you very much.'

'It's a pleasure, I'm sure. No trouble at all.'

'It's very kind of you, Mrs ...' Oh dear, she still didn't know her name!

'Arnold,' her neighbour supplied, rising. 'Well, remember, don't be afraid to ask. I'm sure Mr Stokes won't mind bringing me a message before he goes out should you need me and I'll look in those couple of nights to see that everything's all right ... No, don't get up. I can let myself out. Good-bye for now, then.'

It was strange living alone in the house with Harry, almost as if she had a son, Emmeline decided in the following few days. A son could not have been more thoughtful. He was always ready to lend a hand often anticipating things she might need done. He did not like her having to be on her own so much and always came home to get his evening meal; although he was by no means an expert cook he managed to prepare several simple dishes even offering to do the same for her. The suggestion secretly amused Emmeline, but she declined politely, assuring him that there was little involved in preparing her light evening meal and she felt quite able to do it.

On one occasion she found him in the kitchen ironing and asked in amazement what on earth he thought he was doing.

'I'm not new to this game,' he told her. 'I'm one of six kids, in a family that size you soon learn where to put a crease in your own jeans.'

He set the iron down on its stand and, picking up the garment, folded it with the side seams together, proving his point.

'Greta's lucky to have such a capable husband.'

He grinned as he picked up the iron again and continued his task.

'I can be pretty helpless when she's around!' He squinted critically at the crease he had made in the denim trousers, seemed satisfied, put them over the back of a chair and picked up a shirt; but he stopped with the iron poised over the collar and looked at Emmeline who was still watching him.

'What's going to happen when Greta gets home? We seem to have moved in here, but you don't need much looking after any more, there's not much she'll need to do for you ... but I don't know how we'll manage if she can't go on using the kitchen sometimes, though we can go back to eating out.'

'Taking a tiny baby with you in all weathers?' ... or would he be prepared to leave the child unattended?

'We may not have any choice ... unless you're prepared to let our present arrangement stand for a while? We'd try not to get in your way.'

She hadn't really given the matter much thought, assuming things would go on from the point they had reached. She could not imagine herself suddenly forbidding Greta the use of the kitchen, any more than she could imagine herself expecting them to exist entirely in the one room as they had before her illness, now that the baby had arrived.

'I'm sure Greta and I can work things out between us ...'

She was eager for the girl's return, every day she waited for news when Harry came back from visiting the maternity home; she read and re-read the note he brought in reply to her letter of congratulation. She received so few letters and always read them two or three times. Each day she read over the latest letter from Jean with its anxious queries about the state of her health, and then Greta's letter which was already becoming tattered at the folds. She smiled over the ecstatic description of Baby Emma and longed to see this remarkable child for herself. In her second letter Greta mentioned a brief and almost furtive visit she had received from her mother and tears came to Emmeline's eyes as she read how painful that visit had been, for Greta's mother had come without her husband's knowledge and had made it clear that she did not intend to come again.

On Saturday, as Emmeline watched from her window, a car drew up outside, with a baby carriage roped to its roof. Harry and another young man got out, untied it and lifted it down. The other man made some remark which started them laughing then they stood for a few minutes leaning on the gate, talking. Finally the young man drove away and, as Harry pushed the pram down the path, the sudden realization of what a difference the baby might make to the household flooded over her.

This was reality.

She went into the entrance hall. The pram stood on the rug and Harry was contemplating it with his hands on his hips. He smiled a greeting.

'It's quite a nice one, isn't it? Needs a bit of cleaning up.'

'It's very nice.' The words belied her true opinion, to her it looked dusty and worn but she did not want to disappoint him.

'I'll take it through the back and see what I can do, if you don't mind.'

He took the pram down the passage, through the kitchen and outside, where he worked for more than an hour. When he had finished he could not resist coming to call her to admire the result.

No wonder he was pleased! He had scrubbed every inch, inside and out, with a nail brush; the rims of the wheels and the handle had been rubbed until they shone.

'Looks better, huh?'

'It looks very nice indeed,' she spoke now with more enthusiasm.

He gave a final rub then took it inside, Emmeline following.

'Where are you going to keep it?'

'Upstairs.'

She thought of those stairs—and Greta. It would be tiring to take it up and down all the time.

'It could stand in the study. It wouldn't be in the way there.'

'It would be much easier for her. Emma'll be sleeping in it at first, she's too small for a cot—even if we had one —she'd get herself lost in it, but the top lifts off, see?'

He demonstrated, turning two wing nuts and, to Emmeline's amazement, lifting the body of the pram clear of the chassis. 'It wouldn't be so heavy to carry.'

So the pram went into the study.

Emmeline closed the door of the little room when Bertha came to visit her and made no reference to what it contained.

'Now's our chance,' Bertha declared, excitedly.

'For what?' Emmeline answered her coldly.

'Why, to see what's going on!'

'No!' Emmeline was appalled.

Bertha was set on going upstairs to discover if all was in order, but also, Emmeline was convinced, to poke and pry. She would make the most of her opportunity, of that Emmeline was sure, she would investigate the box room, no doubt, and make scathing comments about the rubbish hoarded there ... and was she merely keen on making sure the dining-room suite was intact or did she really want to get into the children's room—to peer into drawers and cupboards...?

'No,' Emmeline repeated more firmly. 'I've satisfied myself that everything is in order ...' And if it wasn't? If this unsubstantiated statement were later to be proved wrong? Too bad! She remained firm and would not allow Bertha to go up.

The following morning, however, she did so herself. What possible harm could there be if she mounted the stairs slowly, pausing frequently to rest? But the reason for her investigation was a very different one from Bertha's. Greta was coming home and, Emmeline, unused to the idea that a man could keep house successfully, did not want her to come home to chaos and disorder.

She stood on the landing panting for breath, her heart racing; opposite her was the closed door of the room she had formerly occupied. She would sit there for a few moments. Suddenly she found herself wondering what she would do if she found the room empty.

She turned the knob and pushed open the door. The room had a strange ghostly quality, the furniture was at the same time both familiar and strange in this setting. It was like meeting an old friend unexpectedly in an unusual place and finding that, though years had passed, she had not aged at all.

Emmeline sank down on to one of the chairs. Everywhere was so still and eerie. Then she realized what was different. Downstairs she had always been able to hear the ticking of the clock from the parlour, now that sound was missing ... And the chest of drawers looked strange in place of the sideboard—more strange than the sideboard had looked at first with her bedroom furniture because it kept its old familiar place. The room lacked its dignity with this more cheerful wallpaper. She noted a bright patch, unfaded, where her wardrobe had been.

Gradually her heart steadied, she felt less exhausted.

After a few more minutes rest she got up and moved down the passage, hesitating before opening the door of the children's room. Why! He had kept it quite tidy! It was true that he always left the kitchen in order but she had not expected the same order to prevail here. Not perfect order, but nothing a girl could complain of! There was nothing Emmeline need really do. Her eyes travelled round—dust there was, certainly, a less dusty square showing where a book may have lain for a day or two on the dressing table and then been removed ... but she decided to touch nothing and so not draw attention to the fact that she had been here.

She completed her tour. The bathroom, too, was tidy, clean, although a shirt hung from a plastic hanger on the towel rail over the bath.

She opened the door of the box room. It had been untouched since she and Greta had put away the Christmas decorations, oh, so long ago.

Slowly she retraced her steps. Feeling faintly giddy, halfway down the stairs she stopped and lowered herself on to one of the treads. Really, she was getting as bad as Harry, sitting on the floor! She thought of how happy he had been that morning, whistling softly to himself as he came into the kitchen.

'You're glad she's coming home?' she had remarked, and he had nodded agreement. 'I don't like living on my own.'

On his own, she suspected, meant anything that did not include Greta.

Shakily she got to her feet once more and continued down the stairs starting guiltily as, when she reached the bottom, the doorbell rang.

Guilty at going upstairs in her own house? But her guilt was due to the fact that she had been disobeying doctor's orders, not because she had been prying.

Mrs Arnold stood on the threshold, a covered plate held in her hand.

'Good morning,' she called, in her friendly fashion. 'This is the great day, isn't it? Not home yet, are they?'

'Oh, no,' Emmeline replied. 'She won't be coming till tonight. Harry's going to fetch her after work.'

'I see. I've brought them a cake, nothing very special, I'm afraid.' She held the plate towards Emmeline.

'How kind of you.' She quelled the stab of disappointment and jealousy, Mrs Arnold could not possibly have known that Emmeline intended making a cake that afternoon, her first attempt at baking since her illness.

'You can take a peep.'

Emmeline dutifully lifted the napkin. The cake was iced in pink and white with the words Welcome Home

Baby Emma spelt out across the top.

'How pretty!' Emmeline's admiration was genuine, she could never have achieved anything like that.

Mrs Arnold was obviously pleased.

'Is there anything I can do for you? Some shopping, perhaps,' she asked.

'I would appreciate that.' Emmeline led the way through to the kitchen where she set the cake down carefully. 'If it's not too much trouble.'

At least she could carry out her second plan and prepare a chicken casserole; for this very reason she had hoped her neighbour would call during the morning as she had not wanted to spoil the surprise by asking Harry to buy the chicken.

'Those little cupcakes you brought me were delicious,' she went on, taking a piece of paper from a drawer and writing out her short list. 'You're really spoiling me! Everyone has been so kind ... There,' she looked up with a smile, 'I think that's all I shall need.'

For the umpteenth time Emmeline looked out of the window. It was growing late. How different things would have been, she found herself thinking, if she had turned Harry and Greta irrevocably away that first night or insisted that they go when that other lady, Mrs James, had wanted the room. What would have become of them? She would have had no idea, nor cared. Not even have known of the existence of the baby. Instead here she was waiting apprehensively.

'They're here!' she whispered to Grimalkin, at last and rose to her feet but the cat only closed her eyes in disdain although her ears had turned back, listening to the approaching footsteps.

Emmeline was halfway across the room when she stopped—Would they want her? Would they prefer to be alone to gloat over their child? For a moment she stood, undecided. But it would be a cold welcome, a voice inside her argued. Surely everyone was allowed to become excited over a new baby? She continued towards the door.

They were standing close together on the Turkey rug, dim figures, the shawl-wrapped bundle Greta held to her breast startling white against the two dark coats. Harry was saying: 'A man's lucky when he can hold all that's precious to him in the whole world in his two arms.'

Then the shaft of light fell across them from the opened parlour door calling their attention to Emmeline and Greta came towards her, a joyous smile lighting her face.

'How are you? Have you been behaving yourself?'

Emmeline put a hand on the girl's arm and, with a murmured greeting, drew her into the light. With one tender hand Greta pulled the soft blanket away from the baby's face so that Emmeline could see the sleeping child. She was entranced. Never in her long years had she seen such a young baby before. She gazed at the perfection of the tiny face, the skin so translucent and pearly, the eyes tightly closed, fanning the long lashes across her cheek, the mouth a rosebud. Clutching a fold of the blanket was one tiny hand, Greta gently lifted it, uncurling the fingers against one of hers, mutely inviting admiration of the tiny pink nails.

'She's like her father, isn't she?' Greta spoke with a smile in her voice and now Emmeline could see the resemblance, incongruous, but there. Behind her Harry began to laugh softly.

'What's so funny?' The girl half turned towards him, the affection in her voice belying her pretended indignation. 'You know she's like you ... and you're proud of it!'

'Yes, but you don't know what I told Miss Rodgers about her!' He grinned and winked at Emmeline over Greta's head.

'Then tell me!'

'Not on your life!'

'Oh, you beast!' Despite the fact that she still held the child carefully, Greta drew back a small foot and aimed a kick at him, a mere gesture for she barely touched his shin.

He looked down at her in mock despair, his eyes still teasing.

'Behave yourself, woman. You'll set a bad example to the child.'

'Heavens!' she retorted. 'Am I going to have that thrown at me now?'

Emmeline looked from the one to the other. With Greta's absence preceeded by her own illness she had almost forgotten this was how they spoke to each other. Now the girl turned back to her.

'Has he been as impossible as this the whole time I've been away?' And Harry's dark eyes on her were laughing.

'My behaviour has been exemplary, hasn't it?'

Emmeline felt bewildered but the baby saved her from being drawn into the argument by momentarily opening eyes that were incredibly dark then closing them again and yawning hugely. She diverted everyone's attention.

'My daughter's bored by your conversation,' Harry said, more softly now. 'Here, give her to me.'

Fascinated, Emmeline watched as he took the child with hands that were clumsily gentle, but not, she guessed, completely unused to the task.

Greta, relieved of the weight, stretched her arms then put one around Emmeline.

'Are you really much better?'

'Very much.'

Emmeline felt deeply happy and contented, all her family was safe under her roof once more.

Minutes later Greta took the baby upstairs to attend

to her and Harry went with them. By the time he came back down Emmeline was laying the table in the kitchen.

'I've prepared supper for you tonight,' she told him, a note of pride creeping into her voice. 'To welcome Greta home.'

'That was good of you, but where's your place? Aren't you going to help us eat it?'

'I'm sure on this occasion you want to be alone.'

He shook his head and began to set another place. 'Don't you worry. We've got all ...' he amended what he had been going to say, '... all the time in the world.'

Pale spring sunshine greeted Emmeline when she opened her curtains the next morning. Earlier she had heard Harry come downstairs, now the front door had closed behind him and he had gone for the day. As she turned from the window a light tap sounded on the door.

'Come in,' she called.

Greta entered wearing her dressing-gown and looking slim and childlike once again.

''Morning. I'm going to see if there's more tea in the pot, shall I bring you some?'

'If there's enough, my dear, thank you.'

The girl returned carrying two cups.

'There was plenty, I only had to add some water, Harry always makes it too strong.'

They sat side by side on the bed, enjoying their tea in companionable silence. Emmeline, aware of how peaceful and contented she felt, looked fondly at the girl who smiled back at her.

'I feel so relieved now Emma's safely here,' she said. 'I ought to be worrying about her, about her future and everything, but I'm not one scrap worried. I used to worry dreadfully, once,' she confessed and for an instant a shadow of her old haunted look crossed her face. 'I felt afraid, just like there was a great dark pit yawning at our feet ... waiting to swallow us up. Harry never scoffed at me when I told him, but he said you could walk right round the deepest hole if you went careful and didn't look down. He said I'd only got to hold his hand and he'd never let me fall ... but sometimes, especially when he was very late getting back, I'd start wondering what I'd do if he didn't come ... if something happened to him,' she shuddered suddenly and screwed her eyes tight, to cut short the memory. 'It's somehow different, now. I know we're going to be all right.'

'Of course you are. And she's a lovely baby.'

'Isn't she?' Greta's face softened once more. 'And good, too. She only woke once in the night. I hope she didn't disturb you...?'

'I didn't hear a thing.'

'She does only make a squeak, and she soon went back to sleep after I fed her. It was very funny really,' Greta gave a little giggle. 'I must tell you—Harry put her down for me and guess what he said to her? "Now shut up there's a good girl, your mother and I want to get some sleep" just as if she could understand him! I told him not to be such a fool, you can't expect a baby of that age to do what she's told, so he says, well, his kids is going to have to behave themselves so she'd best get used to the idea right from the start—then, 'cos she'd gone to sleep before he even got the light off, he says "See what I mean", proper pleased with himself! He really adores her!'

The advent of the baby disrupted the household even less than Emmeline had expected. She was a good and contented child and Greta soon managed to establish a routine which left her time to help keep the household running smoothly. Emma became a source of great delight

as well as wonder to the elderly lady. Before long she had
summoned sufficient courage to hold the child on her lap,
an action which was viewed with disapproval by Grimalkin
who otherwise ignored the intruder, treating everything
connected with her with the disdain she considered fitting.

This disdain was echoed in Bertha's expression. She
screwed up her face in contempt whenever the baby was
mentioned.

Then came the letter from Jean announcing that she
was at last able to get away for a few days and would
be coming immediately to see that the improvement in her
aunt's health of which she wrote was indeed genuine.

She had no intention of causing anyone any extra work
she said, she had already made a reservation at a convenient hotel.

Emmeline awaited her arrival with mixed feelings.

She came, loaded with gifts; two books, a tin of biscuits,
eau de cologne, a bedjacket and some flowers. Emmeline
was overwhelmed and did not know what to say.

Jean expressed great delight at seeing her aunt so much
better and viewed the transfer of her bedroom to the
lower floor with approval. They spent a pleasant afternoon chatting and, before she left, Jean had a few words
with Greta adding that she would return in the evening
to discuss certain matters with Harry. This, Greta told her
regretfully, would not be possible as he would be out.

'Another time then,' and the meeting was deferred.

Next morning Jean called again, staying only a short
while for fear that her aunt would become tired and
promising to return in the afternoon.

It was late afternoon before she came and Bertha was
with her; this Emmeline took to be an accidental occur-
rence thinking that perhaps they met on the step or in the

street. Bertha would have recognized Jean since she knew she was coming. She had shown considerable interest in the visit, even enquiring where Jean would be staying.

Anyway, here they were together and Emmeline made them welcome, then went to brew some tea, assuring them that she was quite capable of managing alone. Really, if she let people have their way she would still be treated as an invalid!

Her visitors appeared to be getting on quite well, she thought. She could hear them chatting as she came back bearing the tray, though they ceased abruptly as she entered the room and Jean sprang to her feet.

'Let me take that, aunt. It's much too heavy for you. Why ever didn't you call me?'

Emmeline relinquished her load willingly but refused Jean's offer to pour out. They talked for a while of small inconsequential matters, then reference was again made to Emmeline's recovery and she remarked that if the mild weather continued and the doctor approved she was contemplating taking a little walk soon.

'Just to the corner of the street at first, then perhaps around the block.'

'We must not rush things, but I hope it will be possible while I am still here,' Jean replied, all solicitude. 'For you must not consider venturing out on your own.'

'I shall ask the doctor next time he comes,' Emmeline promised. 'But don't distress yourself on my account. I know that Greta would not let me go out by myself.'

Jean shot a quick look at Bertha who pursed her lips, lifted her eyebrows slightly and gave an almost imperceptible nod.

Jean leant forward and, speaking more softly than she had before, enquired, 'Where is the girl at the moment? I've not seen her this afternoon.'

Emmeline glanced at the clock by which Greta's life

was governed at present. 'I expect she's upstairs. She's usually busy with the baby at this time.'

She looked across again at Bertha who gave her a small malicious smile.

'Aunt, dear,' Jean went on, hitching herself to the edge of her chair so that she was even closer to Emmeline and could be sure of being heard without raising her voice, 'why didn't you tell me what's been happening? ... or write to me about it? You mustn't be afraid.'

'Afraid? I don't understand.'

'Nor did I,' Jean went on slowly. 'It seems so long ago that you first mentioned the possibility of taking in a lodger then, when you wrote no more about it, I presumed you had changed your mind. You can imagine how amazed I was when I received the letter telling me of your illness and realized that you had in fact already taken someone into your house. Of course I was too concerned about you to give the matter much further thought but it came as a great shock to me when I arrived here, not only to see how ill you looked, but to find that young couple living in your home. The letter, you see, was signed H. Stokes, it never occurred to me that it had been written by a man. Quite frankly I was appalled although the doctor assured me you were being very well cared for and he considered it a most satisfactory arrangement. I felt that you should be moved to a hospital or nursing home and told him so, but he disagreed. He said that he had made the suggestion himself but that you became so upset at the mention of it that he feared insistence would be seriously detrimental to your recovery. Unless the situation deteriorated he thought it was better for you to remain in familiar surroundings and that the young woman seemed quite capable and was glad to care for you. I felt forced to give in but I was far from happy about the whole arrangement. I couldn't understand why you had taken in a young couple at all when you had intended letting the room to a single lady. Over and over again I wondered why you had never mentioned them and came to the conclusion that it must have been because you knew I would not approve...'

'And would you have done?'

'Most certainly not! I should have thought you had taken leave of your senses! But then ...' she smiled sorrowfully, 'you were always so kind-hearted, dear aunt,'—she made it sound like 'dear, foolish aunt'—'You took them off the street. They were destitute, weren't they?'

'Destitute?' Emmeline searched her memory. 'I don't know about that. Desperate, certainly.'

'And once you let them in...'

'I saw that they were quiet, considerate and well behaved,' Emmeline continued firmly. 'So there was no reason why they shouldn't stay.'

She looked across at Bertha again and saw something in her gloating expression that made her feel so nervous that she gripped the arms of her chair tightly, wondering what Bertha had been saying while she had been out of the room, soon after they had arrived.

'That's not quite true, is it?' Jean still spoke calmly, her voice coaxing. 'You were afraid of him, weren't you?'

Once more Emmeline looked at Bertha who was smiling now in open triumph.

'Yes,' she admitted, slowly, 'I was at first. But not now, not now!' As she spoke she thought she heard a movement in the passage and glanced quickly towards the door, it would never do for Greta to overhear any of this! 'I don't think we need talk about it.'

'Don't worry,' Jean soothed, 'No one can hurt you now, but you should have told me what was going on.'

'I ... at first I didn't want to worry you, then I realized

there was no need, that my fear was all imagination.'

'But you hadn't wanted a young couple here, had you? It's a single room. Why didn't you tell them to go?' Jean was persistent.

'They had nowhere else to go.'

'They could have found somewhere if they'd had to.'

'Finding somewhere respectable wasn't easy.'

'Or somewhere so cheap? I don't imagine respectability came into it much. Quite frankly I would hardly say he looked respectable, would you? That's what gave me such a shock. I think they would have had to look a long way to find someone else prepared to let a couple share a single room—for a single rent!'

'But how could I charge them more? It *was* only a single room.' Emmeline was growing indignant.

'Are you charging them more now?' Emmeline's lack of reply gave the answer. 'It's not just the room now, is it? She uses your kitchen as her own.'

'We've agreed about that. He pays my electricity bill.'

Jean chose to ignore this, and continued with determination: 'Sole use of the bathroom, too, now, with you using the little cloakroom downstairs; and the pram standing in your study!' So Jean had noticed that! 'Probably the run of the whole upper storey into the bargain!'

Bertha could no longer contain herself.

'Run of the whole house, I'd say,' she cut in. 'I called here when you were in bed, Emmeline, and I use my eyes ... She came through from the kitchen where he was sitting taking his ease—reading the paper and as at home as if he owned the place!'

Emmeline broke in heatedly. 'There was no one else to look after me when I was ill. They waited on me hand and foot! As for using the kitchen they've brought their own crockery, their own things...!'

'What happened when you were ill is a separate matter,' Jean quelled Bertha with a look. 'The part I don't care for is the insiduous way they wormed themselves in here, little by little. It was far too subtle for my liking.'

'How can you possibly know?'

'You can't deny it.' Jean sat back and folded her hands on her lap. 'I would never have suspected what was going on had your friend Miss Matherson not come to see me at the hotel after lunch. What she told me sounded incredible but now you have as good as confirmed it.'

'No, it's not true! Bertha you're prejudiced! Just because you want the room for yourself!'

'I? Why should I want it? I've a perfectly good home of my own.'

'What hold have they over you, aunt? You mustn't be afraid.' Jean was calm but dogged.

'There's nothing, I tell you.'

'Oh, they've been so clever.' Venom tainted Bertha's words. 'She *was* afraid at first—I think she still is—but if she's not it's because they've won her over. He's got her hypnotized like a fox with a rabbit.'

Somewhere a door closed. Emmeline fidgeted in agitation. Greta must not hear this! Was it the front door that had closed? She could not tell with Bertha's voice raised like this.

'He's got all a gypsy's cunning! I tried to warn the doctor but they had deceived him too and after that they wouldn't let me inside. Not once did I see Emmeline again until she was downstairs and able to let me in herself. Over and over I called and always that girl said she was asleep! I'd threaten to wait but she'd say it was impossible. I was at my wit's end!'

'Yesterday ...' Jean thought of it now. 'I told her I wanted to speak to her husband and she said he would not be home...!'

'Nor was he!' Emmeline broke in despairingly. 'He had to go to night school, I could have told you that.' Now she was fighting, her back against a wall filled with determination.

'Night school, indeed!' Bertha scoffed as if she thought robbing a bank was more likely.

'It is suspicious, very suspicious,' Jean spoke musingly. 'Why should they keep such a watch over you, it isn't natural.'

'They might be fond of me,' Emmeline's voice broke as the words were forced from her.

'I'm fond of you, dear aunt. That's why I'm so concerned about all this.' Jean leaned forward again and took her hand.

'I warned you they were subtle,' Bertha insisted. 'At first I feared violence but now, when people have got to know them, they dare not arouse suspicions, but he's clever. In case she's not fond enough of the girl for their purpose they've used the baby. They've made her besotted with the child. How lucky they were it was a girl! A masterly move that—to call it Emma!—a very clever move.'

'What do you mean, clever?' Emmeline demanded.

'Yes, what are you getting at?' Jean queried, still calm.

'Emmeline's been very ill,' Bertha explained. 'Who knows what the doctor told them? Perhaps another attack will be fatal, but before then they will have thought of a way ... I fear, if anything happens, you, her only relative, will find they've persuaded her to leave everything to the child—her namesake!' Bertha spat out the last word with contempt. 'And naming them as trustees! It will be too late for you to do anything about it.'

'It's possible,' Jean nodded slowly.

'No, no! It's preposterous!' Emmeline could not help herself, she began to cry.

'Oh, aunt, dear, don't upset yourself.' Jean was on her knees beside her now, patting her hand. 'I don't want you to upset yourself. There's nothing to be afraid of. No one can hurt you ... and they have no idea yet that anyone has realized ...' she stopped, considering it wiser to pursue the subject no further at this juncture. 'We've tired and upset you. You must rest now. We'll talk about it tomorrow. Of course you're grateful for all the girl has done for you,' she soothed, 'and the baby's very sweet, but you must realize they can't stay indefinitely. I'll come tomorrow, alone, and we'll talk, make a plan.'

'Yes, yes,' Emmeline dabbed her eyes with a handkerchief.

'You're all right, now?' Jean was on her feet once more, giving Bertha a meaningful look. 'It's late, I think we should be going.' She turned back anxiously to Emmeline. 'Did the doctor give you something to help you sleep? You need a good night's rest. Don't worry or mention anything.'

'I'm quite all right. It was silly of me to get upset. Of course, we'll talk about it tomorrow.'

'That's right.' Jean sounded relieved, she did not know of the tremendous effort it took for Emmeline to pull herself together, that she was desperately anxious to get them out of the house, telling herself that once they had gone she would lock the door and never allow either of them in again.

Good! Jean was shepherding Bertha out of the room. Bertha who was winking with excitement behind her pebble glasses.

'Don't worry to come to the door, dear.'

There! They had gone!

Emmeline sank down in her chair, weak and drained.

What horrible ideas! How could anyone have such horrible ideas? It was Bertha who had put them into

Jean's head. But they were untrue. Emmeline was sure there was no grain of truth in them. Why, they would not even take the ring she had wanted to give Greta! If only she had thought to tell them that! But everything had been sprung on her, she'd had no time to collect her thoughts. Of course Jean might not have liked her offering the ring if she was so concerned about what happened to her aunt's property...

She *would* leave it to little Emma, that would show them! And it would be Jean herself who had given her the idea.

The door opened suddenly. No knock. She feared they had come back.

But it was Harry. Something must be wrong, he always knocked first. Emmeline gave one look at his face and gasped, forgetting her own worries. Was Greta ... or the baby?

She had never seen him look like this before, so white and strained; deep lines drawn from his nose to either side of his mouth and that mouth a hard, ugly line.

'I heard what she said!' His voice was held in tight as if he was afraid of losing control of it.

Emmeline let her breath out in a gasp.

'I'm not in the habit of listening at doors,' he went on, 'but I just come in and I was bringing you the paper, I heard what they was saying so I stayed and listened to the rest.'

'Oh, no!'

'You needn't worry,' his voice remained clipped and bitter. 'We'll be out of here in the morning.'

'You don't understand...'

'I understand well enough. I won't have no one get ideas like that about me. I wouldn't stay under this roof not a minute longer if it weren't for Greta and the kid and that I can't take them out on the street at this time of night.'

'No, no!' Emmeline began to sob, as she struggled to get out the words, 'It's not at all the way you imagine. I ...' She became aware that Greta was banging on the other side of the door and that he had one hand against it holding it closed; now the girl succeeded in forcing it open and he spun round on her angrily.

'I told you to keep out of this!'

'I won't! It concerns me, too.' Tears were raining down Greta's cheeks. 'I don't believe Miss Rodgers had anything to do with it! I don't ...'

'What you think don't count!' he cut in harshly. 'Anyway, who's she going to believe, me wot come in off the street or her fine cousin—who's scared for her property—and her goddamned friend who's been sneaking round after me this last couple of months and more, trying to make trouble?'

'Stop it! Stop it!' Greta turned terrified eyes away from him for a moment to look at Emmeline, who seemed to have shrunk in her chair, her shoulders shaking with helpless sobs, her hands gripped together trembling on her lap. 'What d'you want to upset her for? I'm sure she didn't mean any of it.'

'I've told you I'll not stay where there's talk like that about me. Now get upstairs and pack your stuff.'

He put his hand on her shoulder to give her a push towards the door and, as Emmeline stared in horror, Greta swung back her hand to hit him. With one quick movement he had caught it in his fist, holding it so tightly that his knuckles showed white and the fury in his voice was ice.

'Don't you hit me, my girl! Don't you never hit me when you mean it!'

She stared up at him, torn between tears and defiance and Emmeline watched, quaking, helpless. How often hadn't she seen Greta aim a slap at Harry and he had avoided it, laughing in her face, but never before had she seen him look at the girl without love in his eyes nor heard him address her in that tone. Slowly both hands released their hold and hung slackly at his side but he never took his eyes from Greta's face and for a moment she stood still, glaring at him, then she turned away, crossed to Emmeline and dropped to her knees beside her, taking her hands, smoothing them.

'Don't cry, oh please, dear Miss Rodgers, please don't cry.' Though the tears were still wet on her own face.

From the room above, baby Emma, neglected just as she was about to have her evening feed, let out a thin persistent wail. Harry still stood by the door and his voice, when he spoke, was still clipped and harsh:

'See to your child.'

'It won't hurt her to wait a minute,' Greta was too worried about what effect all this upset would have on Emmeline to leave her. She pulled out her own clean white handkerchief, dabbing at Emmeline's tears, while she, in turn, said brokenly: 'It was none of their business. I tried to stop them. I was so afraid you would hear.'

'It's all right. It's all right.'

The baby's wailing increased in intensity; Harry turned on his heel and without a further word, left them. A corner of Emmeline's mind registered that he went upstairs, that the child's crying ceased, but the rest of it was concerned with her desperate effort to make Greta understand, to prevent their leaving.

'I don't know where they got such ideas. Bertha was behind it all I suppose, she was always complaining to me about your being here. I admit I didn't want you at first and she knew that, but afterwards ... I didn't want you to go.'

'You've been wonderfully good to us.'

'Bertha took such a twisted view of everything, and

she must have told Jean.'

'But you don't believe them, do you?'

'No, of course I don't.'

'Then it doesn't matter.'

'But it does!' Emmeline struggled to think and talk rationally. 'I was quite content here on my own but I was lonely. I didn't realize how lonely ... Then, gradually, you became my family and made up to me for all the things I'd missed ... that I hadn't even known I'd missed ...' more tears began to fall and again Greta calmed her. 'I don't want you to go ... if I was alone now I'd know that I was lonely. I want you to stay. I've grown so fond of you and little Emma. More than anything in the world I want to watch little Emma grow. I've been so looking forward to that.' She took a deep breath that was half sigh, half sob. 'I never had a child of my own.'

'It's all right.' Greta still crouched beside her.

'They were wicked things Bertha said and Jean was wicked to agree with her.'

'But perhaps she didn't understand.'

'How could she? ... I know I've been a nuisance—a worry—to her. She's always done her duty by me, but that's all I've been to her, a duty. I never had a share in her life. You two gave me a share in your life that became very precious to me ... you're not old or lonely so you wouldn't understand ... you have a husband and a child of your own so even when you are old you won't really understand ...'

'But you've got a special place in our lives, in our hearts, too, surely you know that?'

'I only know one thing—that I've been the cause of your first quarrel!'

'Our first quarrel?' In her heart Greta knew this was their first serious disagreement but for Emmeline's sake she made light of it. 'Don't you believe it! We've quarrelled plenty of times ... it's worth it, you know, just to make up!' then, looking seriously into Emmeline's face, she added, 'but don't you think it might be better if we was to look for another place now, we haven't tried for ages and having a baby might give us some priority, at least on the council lists.'

'No!' Emmeline gripped her hand convulsively. 'I don't want you to go.'

'You could get in someone older, quieter, like you intended to—we'd still come to see you.'

'It wouldn't be the same,' Emmeline replied piteously. 'Not the same at all.'

'Well,' Greta patted her hand and got to her feet. 'I'll go and calm Harry down and try to talk some sense into him and I must go and feed that poor child.' But still she lingered. 'Is there anything I can get for you, first?'

'No, dear. See to the baby. I'm all right now.'

'Sure?'

'Quite sure.'

'All right then.' The girl bent and dropped a kiss on the grey head before she went out.

Emmeline sat gazing into the fire, feeling as if she had weathered a severe storm and was surprised at finding herself still alive. Gradually the little sounds of the house soothed her, the steady ticking of the clock, the faintest murmur of voices from upstairs. Grimalkin reappeared from under the china cabinet where she had fled when Harry had come into the room breathing fire and brimstone; she crossed the room cautiously, her ears flattened, then sprang on to Emmeline's lap. Emmeline stroked her automatically and soon the cat's purr added its soothing note to the returning harmony.

Some time later the door opened again, this time after a hesitant knock and once more Harry stood there.

'Greta says I should be ashamed of myself,' he volunteered from the doorway, 'I've come to apologize.'

Emmeline managed a wan smile. She felt very tired.

'Come and sit over here,' she invited.

He came and sat awkwardly on the chair opposite, not looking at her.

'God, I could do with a cigarette!' he remarked unexpectedly.

'Why don't you go and get some?'

He shook his head. 'And have to go through giving it up again? 'Sides Greta don't like it—she reckoned every time I lit one I was knocking a nail in my coffin, silly kid.'

That was better, thank heaven, Emmeline thought in relief, it was the way he usually spoke of her.

But there was something strange in this little scene, in the way he was avoiding the issue, it reminded her of something. Something that had happened before in this very room. Suddenly she remembered, her thoughts flying back over the years.

Long, long ago a small boy had kicked a ball over their fence, breaking a window, and had run away. He had returned later, no doubt on orders from his mother, to confess and apologize. She had been sitting here with her father when he had been shown in. Just as Harry had, the child had stood inside the door stammering the words: 'I broke your window, sir, I'm sorry.' Her father had scowled at him and, again like Harry, the boy, his apology made, had changed the subject. 'You've got lovely flowers in your garden, sir. Dahlias aren't they?' Amused, her father had softened.

The picture faded and her eyes focused once more on the young man sitting opposite her, a young man with a great deal of worry and responsibility on his shoulders and only his pride and determination to help him bear them.

'I didn't believe those ugly things they said, Harry,'

she told him. It had to be discussed, sorted out.

'It was Bertha's doing, and, when Jean stops to think, she will see how preposterous the whole notion was. Bertha is jealous and she has become a bit queer I'm afraid. You see, she was my only friend. She didn't like me to have anyone else. I wasn't very happy about it when you first came here and Bertha got queer ideas right from the start, but I got used to you, fond of you both, while she just kept building on her queer fancies. I suppose I should have written to Jean and explained at the beginning, but I thought it easier to tell than to write—only she didn't come. So, of course, when she did, she got a surprise and Bertha was able to plant her seeds of doubt on fertile ground. What happened today was so unexpected that I couldn't think straight.'

His dark eyes searched her face for the truth but he said nothing.

'I'll not answer the door to her again. I'll not see her any more.'

'You mustn't do that!' he interrupted quickly, but without anger.

'Why not?'

'Because she's your only relative, for one thing and because it'll look as if what she said was true.'

'But it's not! You know it and I know it.'

'And who else?'

'You know what she wants to do?' Emmeline's shoulders sagged.

He nodded. 'Turn me out.'

'And send me to a home.'

'She can't, not if you don't want to go.' He spoke so calmly that he gave Emmeline courage.

'You really don't think so?'

'Not while the doctor reckons you're well enough to stay.'

'You mean she can't make me do anything?'

'No one can make you do anything you don't want to ... not her ... not me,' he added softly.

'I didn't want to go to hospital ...' she recalled.

'And nobody made you...'

'Only because you and Greta were here.'

'You're better now, you don't need us any more,' he stated simply, without emotion.

'I need Greta, surely you realize that? Not to look after me but for company. Can't you see that?'

He bit his lip, considering.

'You don't imagine anyone else would believe that nonsense, do you? Mrs Arnold? Or the doctor?'

He shrugged. 'Where does it stop? Your Miss Matheson is out to make trouble. She already told the doctor she was convinced I had pushed you down the stairs. He didn't believe her—but that sort of thing is hard to take. I wondered what she had been saying to you. The nurse agreed that she seemed to be upsetting you, so I told Greta not to let her in while you were sick, I guess that didn't help her feelings towards me. Now she's succeeded in getting someone to listen to her.'

'But you say Jean can't force me to turn you out?'

'Not unless she can prove anything against me—and that'll be difficult since there's nothing to prove. But *you* can turn me out, just like you could've any time, if you'd only put your foot down.'

'But I didn't want to! ... Only at first, and rather half heartedly even then. You mustn't go, Harry,' she leant towards him in a gesture of appeal, 'you can't take Greta and the baby away from me. No doubt you could find somewhere more convenient, but I don't want you to go ... It's very cramped for you, even with Greta using the kitchen, I know that, and you've nowhere of your own to sit, which seems so silly when all those rooms are standing empty...'

He kept a stubborn silence, his face averted, his mouth hard and his eyes narrowed as if in pain.

'I've been thinking for some time of making the upper storey into a little flat, since I won't be using it any more.'

'That sounds like an excellent idea. It would certainly bring you in more than you're getting now. Only this time be careful you get the right tenants.'

'I meant for you and Greta.'

'I can't afford it. You fix it up nice, you'll get someone.'

Tears filled her eyes again. 'But I didn't mean for anyone else, I meant for you and Greta and the baby.'

'We manage.'

'Harry, what do I have to do to get you to stay?'

He had no time to answer her. Greta came in with the child in her arms. She looked anxiously from the one to the other.

'Emma's come to say good night.' She would not word the question she longed to ask, but her eyes asked it of her husband, as he got to his feet and for a moment stood looking down at his child already on the blissful borders of sleep.

'Good night, poppet.' Greta smiled up at him anxiously and he smiled back, before she turned to Emmeline, saying on the child's behalf:

'Good night, Miss Rodgers.'

Emmeline put up her old veined hand and tenderly touched the child's tiny fingers, but she could not reply, the tears that filled her eyes were choking her throat.

'Put her down, love, then come back here.'

'I was going to get your supper. Aren't you hungry?'

'We can eat later.'

'All right.'

He watched her go, while Emmeline tried unsuccessfully to wipe away her tears without being noticed. He crossed to the window, giving her time to compose herself.

'You know Emma isn't going to stay like that. Babies grow quickly, they make more noise, they become children.'

Emmeline nodded. 'That was what I was looking forward to. I hoped for a family of my own, once, long ago—I suppose every woman does—eventually I accepted it was just another dream that would never come true, and then ... I want to see her grow, can't you understand that?'

'We won't stop at one child.' He drove his point home.

'Of course not, only children are lonely, but ... please?'

He turned from the window. From his expression she expected a final refusal, instead he said, quietly, 'All right I give in.'

'Oh, thank you!' She clasped her hands in rapture.

'For Heaven's sake, get this straight, it's we who are in your debt. Remember that.'

'I meant what I said, Harry about making the changes to the house.' She had to get everything quite clear. 'It wouldn't be too difficult, would it? I won't ever use the dining-room furniture again, it seems silly to keep it. I don't know why I didn't think of that before. I should have sold it. To think of all your trouble getting it upstairs!'

He grinned, reluctantly.

'You mean you want me to get it down again?'

'Would you?'

His grin broadened. 'I guess so, if you want me to.'

'And the other little room is only full of rubbish. I've been meaning to sort it out for ages but it seemed such a task. If someone were to help me ... Once the rooms are empty they would only need redecorating, wouldn't they? ... And we could have a little kitchenette put in ...'

'We?'

'You would help me?' she asked it hesitantly. How used she had become to seeking his help. It was instinctive now.

He sighed, but more in amusement than annoyance.

'If you want me to help you I suppose I'll do it.'

'You did my room so beautifully.'

He sat down once more on the chair opposite her, ready to listen to her plans.

'There isn't any great hurry, after all, is there? You could take your time. I know Greta told me that by the end of the year you'd have finished studying and would be in a position to find a proper home ... now, if I had a nice little flat to offer you by then...'

He gave her a look that could only be described as amused exasperation.

'You know, you're a real crafty woman!'

'Am I?' she asked a little breathlessly, growing happier and more confident by the minute.

Greta's light step approached and she stood in the doorway trying to gauge from their expressions what had been happening.

'Come here.' She went and Harry pulled her down on to his lap.

'You'd better be in on this. You know I'd been making some plans about brightening up the yard and making a little place for Miss Rodgers to sit outside when summer comes, but it seems I'm not the only one who's been making plans ... You're going to have to be a consultant interior decorator, how d'you fancy that?'

Greta eyed him mystified.

'What d'you mean?'

'Well, we're thinking of turning the upstairs into a flat ... and we'd better do a good job of it, 'cos you and I might decide to take it when it's done, see?'

Delight radiated from her smiling lips and eyes.

'D'you mean it?' and as he nodded she kissed him.

'Hang on, girl, there's a place for everything! This is a business discussion.' But he kissed her back. 'We've got to get everything clear because . . .'

'Because of Jean coming tomorrow.' Emmeline still anticipated this event with trepidation.

'That's right.'

'Couldn't we just . . .?'

'We'll get it all straight right away, see?' His expression was serious again. 'You tell her I'll be here tomorrow night and anything she's got to say about me I want to hear, that's all. Greta'll stick by you, to back you up, won't you, love?'

'Of course.'

'She can talk straight about how she feels and I'll talk straight back. Don't worry, I'll keep my temper—she can make things as secure legally as she likes, she's got nothing to fear from me and nor have you.'

'And if she doesn't like it . . .' Emmeline began.

'She's your family,' he reminded her.

'Not as much as you are, or little Emma . . . I'd like to know I've done something to make her future secure . . .'

Harry took her meaning and his wariness returned.

'You put a roof over her head, isn't that enough? If you do anything else—and you know what I'm talking about—you'd make of me exactly what they're saying I am and she wouldn't thank you for it. You wouldn't want to do that, would you?'

Emmeline met his dark, penetrating gaze and as she murmured, 'No,' they both knew she had given a promise.

'Then let's hear just what you've got in mind and decide how best we can go about it.'

Outside the shadows had fallen and covered all that was left of the day in a blanket of darkness but inside the little old-fashioned room the three gathered about the fireplace were drawn even closer, warm and secure together in the golden globe of light that spilled from the softly shaded lamp.

THE END

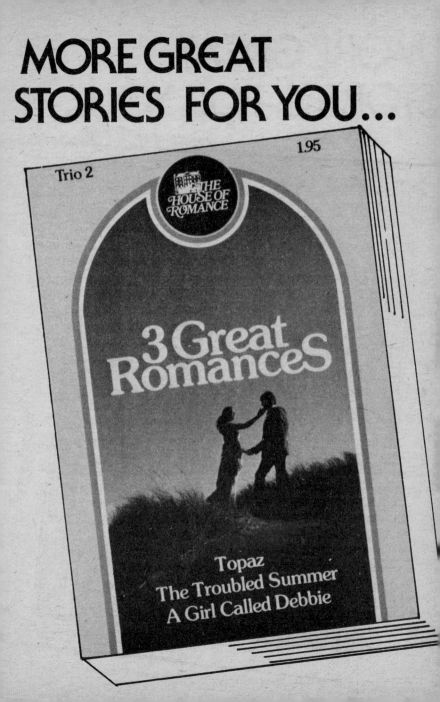

MORE GREAT STORIES FOR YOU...

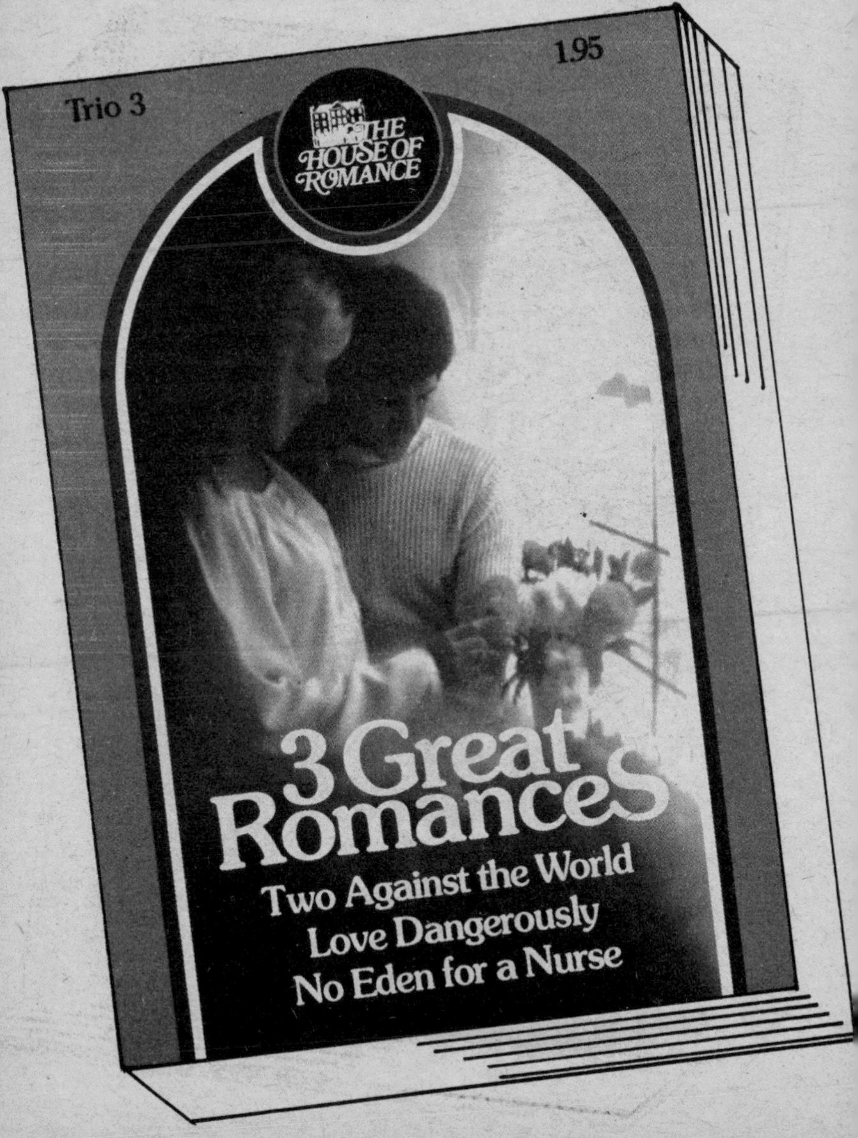

MORE GREAT STORIES FOR YOU...

THE HOUSE OF ROMANCE

Readers' Service,
Suite 27k,
300 East 40th., St.,
New York, N.Y. 10016

Canadian Address,
Suite 2626,
2 Bloor Street East,
Toronto, Canada.

Please send me the House of Romance Trio Volumes
I have indicated.

- [ ] **Trio 1 @ 1.95** per volume
  Cupids and Coronets by Charles Stuart
  Loves Treasure Trove by Julia Davis
  The Heart's Own Sweet Music by Georgina Ferrand nd
- [ ] **Trio 2 @ 1.95** per volume
  Topaz by Francis Hart
  The Troubled Summer by Janet Roscoe
  A Girl Called Debbie by Elizabeth Brennan
- [ ] **Trio 3 @ 1.95** per volume
  Two Against the World by Harriet Smith
  Love Dangerously by Peggy Loosemore Jones
  No Eden for a Nurse by Marjorie Harte
- [ ] **Trio 4 @ 1.95** per volume
  Nurse in Danger by Edna Murray
  Man from the Vineyards by Marjorie Stockholm
  Stranger in the Shadows by Angela Gordon
- [ ] **Trio 5 @ 1.95** per volume
  Love Has a Hard Heart by Kathleen Bartlett
  Springtime of Joy by Georgina Ferrand
  Run Away from Love by Grace Richmond
- [ ] **Trio 6 @ 1.95** per volume
  The Crystal Cage by Juliet Gray
  Tomorrow's Promise by Iris Weigh
  The Inconvenient Marriage by Winnifred Mantle
- [ ] **Trio 7 @ 1.95** per volume
  Tessa Jane by Joan Warde
  Victim of Love by Joan Marsh
  Love is a New World by Helen Sharp
- [ ] **Trio 8 @ 1.95** per volume
  Whispers of Fear by Brenda Castle
  Love Has a Double by Beth Gorman
  Angel in Abbey Road by June Mortimer

Name_____

Address_____

City/Town_____ Zip_____

State_____

I enclose $_____for_____books plus 25c
to help defray postage and handling costs.
(No C.O.D's please)